Only
in the
Movies

Only
in the
Movies

by
Jean Ann Geist

Eli Kenoah Enterprises
Bowling Green, Ohio

Copyright 2011 by Jean Ann Geist

ISBN: 978-0-578-06961-6

Cover watercolor by Sascha Instone

Design and layout by Laura Tolkow

Printed in the United States of America
by Walch Printing, Portland ME

Eli Kenoah Enterprises
P.O. Box 1283
Bowling Green, OH   43402

Dedicated to

Chris

Sascha and Chuck
Jude and Wendy
Eli Abraham and Noah Keenan

*With love and gratitude
for a wonderful life*

And with special thanks to

Mom and Dad

PROLOGUE

april

Large black shapes roiled the water below the precipice where Cassandra Grace Mikhailov Alexander knelt. Early spring storms fed the current carrying logs and other debris down the Maumee River, eventually dumping all into Lake Erie. Torrents of rain would better suit Cassie's mood, but the canopy of stars studding the Northwest Ohio sky only mocked her despair.

It would be so easy, she thought. *Who would really care?*

She imagined her body, limp and lifeless, caught in an eddy, rolling over and over. Or, perhaps, some early-morning fisherman would find her floating along the shore. She prayed for the courage to take that one final step, while fearing a God who would grant such a request.

Shifting her weight, stones boring into her knees, she balanced on the edge of the cliff, leaning her torso into the darkness, willing fate to cast her into blessed oblivion. Night sounds filtered through the constant rumble of the water. Bullfrogs croaked in search of a mate, while buzzing insects heralded the passing of winter.

She settled back onto the safety of the ledge, lowering herself to a sitting position, legs dangling over the edge. Hours might have passed...or only minutes. Time held no purpose for her anymore.

"You'd probably botch it, anyway," she told herself. "You're no good at anything, including this."

She rose to her feet. With one last, longing glance into the black solitude below, she turned and retraced her path back to the parking lot.

"So, what'd you do last night, Cas?" Anita Morales' voice rang altogether too cheerful as it piped through the phone line from her home across town.

Best friends since elementary school, Cassie did not hedge her reply, "Stood for hours on the edge of the Maumee, trying to decide whether or not to take a dive."

Seconds passed with only the ticking of the kitchen clock to break the silence. Cassie had nearly decided she had done the impossible—rendered "The Mouth" speechless—when her friend shot back with studied derision, "What? Nobody there to push you in? You don't have the guts to go it alone, Alexander. You're too responsible."

"What do you mean, too responsible? To whom? For what?"

"To that bag of bones you call mom, for one."

Cassie knew better than to take offense. Anita loved Martha Mikhailov as though she were her own mother and had gained more than a few of her spare pounds on Cassie's mom's chocolate cakes.

"I knew mother would be in good hands, though she'd probably never forgive me for releasing her to your torment for the rest of her days."

"Okay, so how about the Alumni Reunion Committee? What would we do without your organizational skills?"

"That damnable reunion. I can't go and watch Paul with that bimbette hanging all over him, Anita. I just can't face all those gossips who were counting the years 'til we'd end up in divorce court." Though she felt foolish at the admission, Cassie blinked back tears of anticipated humiliation.

"So sit with your back to them and talk to the rest of us—you know, your friends who've stood by you through thick and thin for the past thirty years!" Anita chided.

Cassie's sniffle carried across the phone lines.

"Aw, Cassie, c'mon, don't start sniveling on me now. Tell ya what, you sit tight, and old 'Nita will be over in a shake to make it all better."

"No, Anita, you're right. I've got to pull it together. Losing Paul wasn't the end of the world. Though his timing could've been better."

"Cas, no one is going to believe you embezzled money from O'Shay's! Whoever started that rumor ought to be hung up by his thumbnails. Surely Paul doesn't blame you for the company going into bankruptcy—he was the CEO, for Pete's sake! Besides, I'd love to see how clean *his* hands are in all of this!"

A gulped shudder was the only response Cassie could muster. How could she tell her friend the rumor had turned into allegations when the auditors had found discrepancies within her computer files?

"Aw, jeez, I'm sorry, Cas. Listen, you get spruced up. I'm going to take you to Van Gogh's for lunch. No arguments. Be ready in an hour."

Cassie cradled the receiver against her cheek long after the click on the other end signaled the call had been disconnected. She felt leaden. The effort to shower and dress loomed monumental. "Oh dear Lord, why didn't I just jump when I had the chance," she lamented as she heaved herself off the barstool and toward the master bedroom.

In little more than sixty minutes, Cassie found herself belted into Anita's front seat, half-listening to her friend's continuing monologue.

"You've lived here for, what, a year? Two? I'll never get used to all the twists and turns they insisted on putting in this reclaimed bean field you all call a golf-course community. Why they didn't build the roads at right angles the way God meant them to be is beyond me!" Anita complained as she started to take yet another wrong turn while leaving Cassie's recently constructed gated neighborhood.

Anita drove a battered old Chevette, an oddity among the late-model hybrids and sports cars parked in the driveways leading to expansive faux-Victorian homes.

"This place must keep the local 'Landscaping-R-Us' in business!" Anita jibed as they passed yard after yard showcased in exotic plants and shrubs, all professionally arranged and heavily mulched.

"If you came over to cheer me up, you sure have a strange way of doing it." Cassie added her good-natured grumble to her friend's diatribe.

"I was simply trying to distract you from your troubles by pointing out the opulent neighborhood in which you live."

"Yes, well, not for long. Paul is selling the house out from under me. On the unemployment checks I'll be receiving, I won't even be able to afford to live in the government-subsidized housing over on Fairfax," Cassie interjected.

"Selling the house? How can he do that? Your name's on the deed, too!"

Cassie turned her head away from her friend.

"Cassie, your name *is* on the deed, isn't it?"

"Even though I was in charge of the company's books, Paul always took care of our personal finances. Several years back, when we refinanced for a lower interest rate on our old house, I suggested my name be included on the mortgage. Paul became outraged and said I didn't trust him. He did all of the mortgage arrangements for this house while I was at work. After the episode with the refinancing, I didn't even bother to ask him about it. Now I wonder if, even then, he had been planning to leave me."

"A prelude to kicking you out and running with the profits." Anita swore softly in Spanish.

"That sums it up real good," Cassie sent a rueful glance toward her friend before turning her face back to the window.

"He stopped by last night to pick up a few of his things and then hit me with an, 'Oh, and by the way, Cas-hon, I'm selling the house so you'll have to find another place to live.'

"'Cas-hon!' What a joke! He calls me 'Cas-hon' while evicting me from our home. Do you know what he said to me when he asked for the divorce? That I *bore* him! He spent nearly thirty years trying to mold me into the perfect Stepford wife, and then says I no longer excite him. Look at me—I'm an over-the-hill Barbie doll! Even Ken wouldn't give me a second glance now."

"Can't, Cas, I'm driving. But, I do remember what you look like—medium height, ash-blonde hair, maybe a streak or two of sophisticated silver. Owww! You're not supposed to punch the driver, at least not until we're at a stop sign!" Anita rubbed her arm gingerly as she eased up to an intersection.

Cassie settled back against the dingy gray upholstery of her seat and smoothed the crease in her crisp gabardine slacks.

"I'll bet you ironed your pants before we went out, didn't you?" Anita asked, knowing how her friend would respond.

"Yes, well, we *are* going to Van Gogh's." Cassie tried to hide the defensive tone in her voice.

"That's part of your problem, Alexander. You can't relax. Everything has to be perfect. Look at your hair."

Cassie's hand automatically patted the knot she had twisted into her shoulder-length hair, ensuring the clasp still held her coiffure secure.

"Don't worry," Anita continued, "a strand wouldn't dare get out of place. That's what I mean. It's perfect."

"There's nothing wrong with wanting to look my best. Especially now, with Paul dumping me for a child-bride."

Anita sighed, "No, I guess not," and said no more until they arrived at the restaurant.

CHAPTER ONE

may

The tall, bronze-complexioned man studied the building before him. With a glaring late-spring sun glinting off its tin roof, the red brick school looked much as it had when he graduated from Tecumseh High thirty-two years ago. Though most would say his achievements since marked him a success, Jaimé Alvarez felt the same old insecurities gnawing at his vitals. It wasn't too late to back out, he told himself. He could just write off his ticket to the Alumni Banquet and Dance that night as a donation to his alma mater.

But, *she* might be there. His Porcelain Princess. In spite of all that had happened over the intervening years, she still possessed a small piece of his heart—and he wanted it back.

She was most likely a portly grandmother by now. That would do it—seeing her in a matronly polyester dress and thick wedge-heeled shoes ought to knock those leftover adolescent longings right out of him.

Besides, he had foolishly allowed Melanie Adams to distract him last night at the Roadhouse. Back in the day, Mel had been a cheerleader and wouldn't have given him a second glance. Her attention had fed his flagging ego, and when she suggested he escort her to the alumni reunion, it seemed to be yet another way to prove his success.

Cassie hung back in the shadows watching the couple cross the gymnasium floor. Thirty years melted away as the all-too-familiar stride of the man held her mesmerized.

"Cassie! Cas, did you see who's here with Melanie-the-bitch? I didn't know Jimmy was back in town!" Cassie tried to blend in with the rough brick wall as Anita's hissed whisper rang in her ears.

"Yeah, 'Nita, I saw. So Jaimé's back in town and he's with Melanie, so what?" Cassie attempted a casual stance. Though the majority of their acquaintances, including Anita, had Anglicized Jaimé's name, Cassie used the Hispanic inflection, pronouncing the *J* as a hard *H* and accenting the é as he had taught her that long-ago summer.

Anita continued, barely taking a breath, "He looks great, doesn't he? Sort of like that Jimmy Smits guy on…what was that cop show? *Hill Street Blues*? No…*NYPD Blue*."

Not willing to take the bait, Cassie shrugged, "Guess so. I don't know—it's kind of dark in here. I, ah, need to make a restroom run before the festivities start. I'll catch up with you later." Cassie ducked through the door to the hallway before Anita could say more.

Safe in a bathroom stall, Cassie allowed herself free reign of her emotions. *Jaimé! Oh my Lord, not my Jaimé! With "If you've got it, flaunt it" Melanie Adams* latched on his arm!

Cassie had seen Jaimé Alvarez only once since that summer after her senior year. He had graduated two years before she had— the same year as Paul—and left Northwest Ohio to enlist in the Marines. After a tour of duty in the Mediterranean, Jaimé had returned to his hometown for one last summer fling before using the G.I. Bill to attend college in the east. He had graduated with honors from Harvard Law School, and soon after, moved to Canada to pursue a career in environmental law. The last she had heard, a number of years ago, he had been involved in contentious litigations over the James Bay Hydro-Quebec Project fighting for the Cree and other First Nations' peoples.

But, now Jaimé was back. He was here at Tecumseh High. The butterflies that had hatched in Cassie's stomach fluttered to her throat.

I'm going to be sick, she thought then scolded herself, *This is ridiculous! You're nearly a doddering old woman, not a high school ingénue!*

Cassie rested her forehead against her upturned palms as she mentally lashed out against her first love. She berated him for leaving her without looking back. Berated him for not calling or writing. Berated him for not being there when she needed him most. During their one chance encounter a few years after Cassie's marriage to Paul, Jaimé's demeanor toward her had been cool and impassive. A summer fling was all she had been to him, but the course of her life had been forever altered.

"Cassie, are you in there? Cas, you all right?" Anita's disembodied voice floated over the stall door.

"Yeah, 'Nita, it's me. I'll be out in a minute."

"Hurry up, they're going to recognize the honored classes!" While each class was acknowledged during the program prefacing the alumni banquet, tradition held those celebrating a multiple of a ten-year anniversary stand while individual members present were introduced. As part of the class celebrating its thirtieth reunion, Cassie and Anita had been commandeered to serve on the Alumni Committee, and Anita was anxious to have the program run smoothly.

The largest class to graduate from Tecumseh High boasted fifty-two students prior to the school's consolidation with those of two neighboring small towns in the 1980s. However, dedicated alumni, from Mrs. Agnes McElroy and old Simon Potter, Class of '34, to the youngest graduates from the class of '85, still gathered in their former high school each spring for the annual Alumni Banquet and Dance.

The event was especially well attended this year as the alumni commemorated the 100th anniversary of Tecumseh High's opening. Elderly parents ambled into the auditorium, accompanied through the heavy double-doors and down the sloping aisles by their middle-aged children. Aunts, uncles, nieces and nephews greeted each other as they passed. Though the building still functioned as an elementary school, little had been done to refurbish the once grand old hall. Row after row of red velvet theatre seats, worn threadbare by a century of adolescents' fidgeting and innumerable parents watching those same adolescents perform during class plays, band concerts, and commencements, stood sentinel to the passing years. Ornate marbleized columns divulged their plaster origins, as age chiseled away at their decorative fleur-de-lis which lined the arched ceiling.

The alumni had gathered by classes in the huge old auditorium and were now shuffling into their seats. Since Melanie graduated with Cassie and Anita, she and Jaimé would have their choice of sitting with their class or with his. Cassie searched the crowd for Melanie's white-blonde hair, finding it easily as it contrasted against Jaimé's jet-black razor cut. Dismay filled her as she realized they had chosen to join the members of her class. She swallowed a hard knot that had lodged in her throat then followed Anita down the aisle.

No Anita, not there! Cassie protested silently. Anita had selected seats directly in front and to the left of where Jaimé and Melanie sat, rapt in conversation.

Cassie ran her hand along her tightly coiled French twist, then tugged at the cuff of her powder-blue silk blouse. The stiff collar encircled her long slender neck while small pearl buttons cascaded down the front to the waistband of her straight navy-blue skirt. *Oh why didn't I, just this once, wear something sexy?* she lamented to herself as she eased past the people occupying the aisle seats. She smiled and exchanged pleasantries with her classmates, while studiously avoiding the couple behind her. However, she had no more than sat down, when Melanie said, "Cassie, darling, it's been such a long time. Where *have* you been keeping yourself?"

Cassie took a deep breath and turned to meet Jaimé's eyes. "Melanie, so good to see you again." She hesitated just a heartbeat before continuing, "And, Jaimé, the Canadian hinterlands seem to have agreed with you."

Melanie twined her arm around Jaimé's. "Yes, haven't they?" she cooed, as she stroked his muscular forearm possessively, while batting her lacquered eyelashes at him. "Cassandra…" Jaimé's voice still held the hint of his Caribbean ancestry, adding a lilt to her name as only he could. Cassie felt a catch in her throat along with a rising panic as her semblance of composure threatened to crumble. A hand on Jaimé's shoulder diverted his attention, and he turned to greet an old classmate.

Cassie gratefully shifted her gaze forward, where an aging alumna rapped a gavel against a podium in an attempt to quiet the assemblage. Slowly the hum of voices dropped off, until, with one last tap of the gavel, the woman addressed the crowd.

The program droned on, with each class standing for applause, and the honored classes introducing each alumnus present. As they announced the class two years ahead of hers, Cassie reluctantly turned and scanned the faces until she locked eyes with her former husband. Paul had the courtesy to drop his gaze as Cassie shifted hers to the woman at his side. By far the youngest person in the auditorium, the new Mrs. Paul Alexander exuded a confidence not yet put to trial by the man at her side. Cassie almost felt a twinge of sympathy for the child…almost….

As she returned her attention to the elderly emcee, Cassie caught Jaimé watching her. She affected an air of nonchalance, hoping to stave off any pity he might be feeling for her. She squared her shoulders, as she tried to concentrate on the anecdote being shared by the woman on the stage.

The Alumni Banquet and Dance followed the program, and row by row, they filed into the hallway and down the stairs to the school cafeteria. Tables topped with chipped Masonite had been covered with rolls of white paper. Silk orchid and ivy arrangements served as centerpieces for each, in a futile endeavor to transform the elementary school cafeteria into an island paradise. Jimmy Buffett would have felt at home among the colorful paper parrots and inflated pink flamingos dangling from the ceiling. Chicken wire trunks wrapped with brown crepe paper sprouted plastic palm leaves from their tops. A local Elvis impersonator doubled as the deejay, blaring "Margaritaville" loudly from speakers simultaneously emitting a steady crackle of static.

Cassie accompanied Anita to two tables tagged for their class by large hand-lettered signs. As she watched couples selecting their chairs, she realized for the hundredth time how society was geared toward pairs.

"Tell me again how you talked me into coming tonight?"

"Simple, I said I wouldn't go if you didn't. And you know your ma and I would never let you live it down if I missed the alumni banquet after working on it since last winter!"

Cassie glared at her companion as Paul and his bride settled at a table across the room, while Melanie clung to Jaimé as they entered the gym. She felt the prickle of curious stares from her old classmates, awaiting her reaction to either couple.

"And, remind me one more time of just who my friends are, okay?"

"Well, there's Jules and Arnie for two."

As rotund as her husband was slender, Julie and Arnie Klotzenmeier were the embodiment of Jack Spratt and his wife of nursery rhyme fame. They had married the week after graduation and had increased the earth's population by five children and six grandchildren.

"Hey, Cas, 'Nita, how's it goin'?" Arnie draped an arm across Cassie's shoulders.

"Been better, Arn, I've got to admit."

"Yeah, who'd a thought ol' Paul would turn out to be a cradle-robber! The ink wasn't hardly dry on your divorce papers before he…ouch, sugar, whaddya hit me for?"

"It's okay, Jules. Arnie's only saying what everyone else is thinking!"

"Nah, that's not what I meant, Cas," But Arnie's protest earned him another warning jab from his wife as Jaimé and Melanie approached them.

"Hi, guys, mind if Jimmy and I join your table?" Melanie flashed them her charm-school smile, while clinging to the man at her side.

Cassie wanted to shout, "Yes! I mind!" as Anita waved her hand toward two empty chairs.

"So, Jimmy, what brings you back to the home front?" Arnie asked the question that had been preying on Cassie's equilibrium.

Jaimé Alvarez slid into the chair across from his Porcelain Princess. *Okay*, he told himself, *so she didn't dress in matronly polyester*. Worse yet, the small buttons traveling down the front of her obviously expensive silk blouse took his thoughts in directions they definitely had no business going. *C'mon, Alvarez, you're not twenty anymore, with all your brains between your legs*, he chided himself. He slouched back in his chair, casting a hooded glance at the chic woman Cassandra had become. It took him a moment to realize all but Cassie appeared to be waiting on him to answer Arnie's question.

"Got some business in Cleveland. I'm doing some Lake Erie wetlands consulting between Canada and the states at the regional EPA office, and brought the kids down to visit with their grandparents."

For the first time, Cassie looked directly at him. He must have gotten her attention by his mention of Tina and Ben. Could be a good sign. *Díos, help me!* he invoked, as his muscles tightened involuntarily.

"I didn't know you had children! Did you know that, Cas?" Julie asked in a transparent attempt to bring Cassie into the conversation.

"Oh, yes," Melanie purred, "they're spending the night with

my Tamara. Such delightful children!" As she spoke, she twined her fingers possessively around Jaimé's where they rested on his knee. He fought the urge to return her hand to her own lap as he watched Cassie visibly withdraw from him.

"Tamara," Anita repeated as she returned Melanie's saccharine smile, "How old is your *grand*daughter now, Mel?"

The appearance of a high school student with a tray of tossed salads prevented Melanie from further comment. Jaimé drew his hand from hers when the boy put the plate of iceberg lettuce before him. While the salads were being served, Arnie casually mentioned the closing of the O'Shay Catsup Factory, earning him another elbow in the side from his wife.

"O'Shay's? Thought it looked pretty deserted when I drove by there today," Jaimé commented. "That's bound to hurt the town. How many people did that put in the unemployment line?"

He noticed Cassandra clasp and unclasp her hands in her lap, as though intent on practicing an isometric exercise.

"Cassandra?" Cassie's head jerked up as he said her name. She swallowed hard, and clenched her teeth together before answering him, "Lots of people, and you're looking at the one who was first in line."

"But, didn't the Alexanders own controlling interest in the plant? I thought catsup was where Paul got all of his money."

"The man has catsup in his veins," Anita muttered.

Without contradicting her friend, Cassie directed her response to the man across from her. "You're right, Paul owned the bulk of O'Shay's. His father was CEO until five years ago. When Charlie was killed in an auto accident, Paul took over the company. When the plant failed back in March, I..." She swallowed hard then started over, "I had been the accountant at O'Shay's for twenty-five years. I should have realized what was..."

"Cas, you can't blame yourself for what happened," Anita repeated the litany she had been reciting to her friend for the past two months. "Besides, what did you get out of it? You didn't even get the severance pay the line workers received."

"You know what Paul said, 'Nita, 'bankruptcy laws wouldn't allow family members to benefit.' And, then of course, there's…"

Anita cut Cassie short before she could mention the suspected embezzlement, "You can bet your sweet behind Paul and his little honey made out like bandits. And you get nothing but an eviction notice!"

"'Nita!" Cassie's cheeks flamed as she glared at her friend.

"Okay, okay, time for a change of subject," Anita conceded.

Jaimé wanted to ask more. *What about alimony? Don't they have divorce lawyers in this hick town?* Instead, he scooted back in his folding chair, as another high-school boy cleared away their salad plates.

Melanie immediately insinuated her hand back into his. Jaimé Alvarez studied the woman before him as he unconsciously wrapped his fingers around the hand of the one at his side. He had fallen in love with Cassandra Grace Mikhailov while watching her hopscotch on the playground at St. Jude's elementary, her pigtails flying as she skipped her way from block to block. While he shot baskets in the boys' area, he would surreptitiously steal glances at the girls as they jumped rope double-dutch, not content until he had located her telltale bouncing blonde braids. Looking at Cassie now, she still seemed as tightly strung as her childhood plaits. But he had known the fire that burned beneath her cool exterior.

As he watched her, he wondered if any of the coals they had stoked on long ago summer evenings still smoldered. Or did nearly thirty years being married to a pompous jerk like Paul Alexander douse what few sparks might have otherwise survived?

During the course of the meal, Jaimé noticed Cassandra spent more time moving the food around on her plate than eating it. Conversation followed an innocuous course from the state championship basketball series his senior year to cafeteria food fights to pranks pulled on their teachers. Dessert consisted of a selection of homemade pies. As he devoured his slice of coconut cream, Cassie barely nibbled at her wedge of lattice-topped cherry.

She met his eyes only once, with a defiant look that could

only be interpreted as, "Pity me and you die." If only she knew pity was the last emotion he felt toward her right now. He couldn't wait for the dishes to be cleared, and the music to begin. If there was one thing Cas had loved in high school, it was dancing. And before the last song rasped from those worn-out speakers, he would hold Cassandra Grace Mikhailov Alexander in his arms once again, if only to the crooning of an old love song.

"Okay, kids, it's time to turn back the tide of time!" The Elvis-wannabe disk jockey tried out his best Mississippi twang, "Here we are in our own little tropical paradise so slip on your dancing sandals and let the evenin' begin!"

Cassie felt her toes tapping to the beat of a popular disco tune. "Come on, guys," Anita urged, "Let's hit the dance floor before Alexander here embarrasses us with her chair-dancing." Cassie hadn't realized her toe-tapping had led to swaying in her chair until Anita's teasing drew it to her, and everyone else's, attention.

Cassie saw Paul and the bimbette stroll out onto the floor, their arms wrapped around each other. "Somebody oughtta tell them this isn't a slow dance," Anita snarled as she grabbed Cassie's arm. Cassie allowed herself a masochistic moment as she watched her former husband move in perfect rhythm to the beat of the song. One thing she had to admit about Paul, he could definitely dance. It seemed, throughout their marriage, the dance floor was the only place they were at all in synch with each other.

She positioned herself with her back to the man who had stolen the best years of her life, closed her eyes, and felt the pulse of the music course through her veins. One song followed the next, and still she danced. When Anita tired, Arnie became Cassie's partner.

The deejay's voice transported Cassie back from the world to which she had retreated. "Whoowee, folks, hasn't this been great! But we'd better give those old hearts out there a rest. So, let's slow it down a little with my good buddy Elvis and 'Are You Lonesome Tonight?'"

Arnie held out his arms, and Cassie gratefully slipped into their circle. He held her loosely, so as to not feed the ravenous gossips scattered about the room. Though Arnie led with halting steps, Cassie was able to follow with ease. She averted her eyes as Jaimé glided by with Melanie's head resting dreamily on his shoulder. In the corner of the room, Paul and his child-bride were barely containing their passion for each other, gyrating hip to hip.

"Looks like they forgot the rules about PDA," Arnie said as he awkwardly turned his partner away from her ex-husband.

"Hard to believe he's capable of affection—public or otherwise," Cassie retorted, as she briefly rested her head on her tall, lanky friend's chest. "My apologies, Arn. I get upset when anyone else feels sorry for me, then throw myself a pity party. Well, that's the end of it. It's over and good riddance to him."

Arnie took her chin in his hand and tilted her face up to meet his. "Aw, Cassie, he isn't worth your tears." Her friend's unexpected sympathy threatened to unleash the floodgate Cassie had held in check all evening. With one deft movement, she extricated herself from Arnie's loose grasp and dashed toward the restrooms.

"Cassandra, are you in there? If you don't come out, I'll come in after you!"

"Go away, Jaimé, and leave me alone. You'll just make matters worse."

"If I remember right, there are only three stalls in the little girls' room. That should make it easy to find you."

Cassie groaned, as she buried her head in her hands. She could not face him now, she just couldn't!

"Cassandra, I'm coming in."

Fortunately, the two remaining stalls in the restroom were empty, but Cassie didn't know what sort of scene was unfolding in the hallway outside. She did know if she didn't come out, she would be the talk of the town—as though she weren't already.

"Damn you, Jaimé," she cursed, as she swung open the metal door.

"Princesses shouldn't swear." He was leaning against the pink-tiled wall by the paper towel dispenser, arms crossed over his broad chest.

"Jaimé! You are as brash as ever!" After a quick check in the hallway, Cassie grabbed his hand and pulled him from the restroom.

"Where can we go to talk?" he asked, refusing to release her fingers.

"Nowhere. You don't seem to realize the last thing I need is more trouble. My life has single-handedly fed the gossip mill in this town for months, without adding you to the fodder!" The pleading despair in her eyes was all that kept him from dragging her off to an empty classroom.

"Then at least allow me one dance."

Defeated both by his will and her deepest desires, Cassie relented, "One, that's all...."

"That's not nearly enough, princess, but it'll have to do."

"Jaimé, your porcelain princess shattered into a billion pieces years ago. Not even Humpty Dumpty's men could find them all!"

The Righteous Brothers sang the opening chords to "Unchained Melody" as they walked back into the cafeteria. Cassie was aware of heads turning as she let Jaimé take her hand in his. He pulled her toward him, but she held her body erect, allowing only minimal contact. Jaimé tightened his hold as he steered Cassie away from another couple, and she sucked in her breath as her breasts gently rubbed the front of his jacket. Her body's burgeoning awareness of him put her on high alert.

"Jaimé, this isn't a good idea!"

"You used to like dancing with me. Have I suddenly developed two left feet?"

"You know it isn't your dancing, it's you. High school was a long, long time ago—a lifetime ago. We've changed. You don't know me; I don't know you. I don't *want* to know you."

"Ah, *querida*, you are so wrong," he whispered as he nudged her closer.

Cassie felt the blow to her back before she saw anything. Paul's face menaced above her as he spun her around. His breath smelled of whiskey as he spat, "You hangin' around with that Spic again? You probably kept him on the line the whole time we were married. You always did like dippin' your hands in the Mexican trash."

Jaimé's body went rigid. Cassie could sense his rage in the set of his jaw. His dark eyes flashed his anger. She felt him shudder and take a deep breath before placing his hands on her shoulders and gently nudging her aside. "*Mejicanos* treat their *señoras* with respect—maybe it's time someone taught you a little, Paulo."

Cassie slid in front of Jaimé, wedging herself between the two men. She faced her former husband—disgust replacing the fear normally brought on by his drunken rages.

"You're an ass, Paul. I only just now realized how big of a one you really are. I don't need you. I don't need your money. I don't need your house. Your control of my life is over. I'll see whom I please, when I please. Now, you'd best leave before you make more of a spectacle of yourself than you already have." Cassie took a deep breath, turned her back on the man who had caused her untold pain, and placed her hand in Jaimé's.

"Now where were we before we were so rudely interrupted?" Cassie's entire body blazed with humiliation at the scene Paul had made, but she was determined not to give into knees threatening to buckle at any second.

She allowed Jaimé to pull her close, using his body for support. Her eyes met his. "Tell me everyone's not staring at us, please?"

"Sorry, no can do. But, stick with the Spic, kid, and we'll get through this together."

"Oh, Jaimé, why did you do it? Why did you come back to a place that gave you nothing but grief?"

Jaimé looked away from her and glanced at the faces around the room, settling on a table filled with the cream of local society. His first employer, Herb Tyler, glowered in his direction. Tyler had accused Jaimé of stealing from one of the apartments he had been hired to clean and fired him on the spot.

"I don't know. I guess to prove something to them. Or maybe, to me. No matter how successful I became, no matter how big a case I won, memories of this town brought my head down to size. I guess I wanted what I now know I can never have—the respect of these people."

Cassie caught sight of Julie and Arnie across the room, talking with a small group of loyal friends. "We can't judge the entire town by Paul's actions. There are some good people here…."

"Yeah, all willing to give the 'Mexican boy' a chance—just like your old man."

The bitterness in his voice seeped into her. The song had ended, and they stood facing each other on the dance floor. She could not deny what her father had done. Worse yet, she had allowed herself to be his pawn, thus inflicting the gravest injury to Jaimé.

As the next song began, Melanie sidled up behind him to reclaim her date. Casting a glare at Cassie, she wrapped her arms around Jaimé, giving him no recourse but to dance with her.

When the last note played out, Cassie was nowhere to be found.

CHAPTER TWO

june

"What am I going to do 'Nita?" They sat around the small gray Formica and chrome table in Cassie's mother's tiny kitchen.

"That no good son of a..."

"Mother!"

The withered woman hunched over the table and puffed on the stub of a cigarette.

"I told Leo he was no good. But, you know your dad. He set his stubborn Russian mind on something, and there was no sidetracking him."

"Yes, well, my father had a twisted view of what was good for me." Cassie barely attempted to hide her disdain.

Cassie's mother had grown accustomed to overlooking her daughter's antipathy to her father. "You could always move back into your old room here, baby."

Cassie rolled her eyes at her best friend, then sighed as she told her mother for the umpteenth time, "Mom, we'd end up hating each other. Besides, my allergies can't handle your smoke. If you really wanted me to move home, you'd give up those cancer sticks once and for all."

"Yeah, yeah, I know. I'll quit one of these...." A coughing spasm cut off Cassie's mother's words mid-sentence.

Anita interjected, "You could live with me, but my apartment is so small, I can barely fit my stuff into it."

"I know you both mean well, but I need to find a place of my own. I'm tired of living at someone else's whim." Cassie again scanned the classified pages of the local newspaper spread out before her.

"Until I find another job, I can't afford any of these. And, as long as there's a shadow of an embezzlement scandal hanging over me, no one is willing to take a chance hiring me. Especially for anything having to do with accounting."

She flipped the newspaper shut as the jangle of the telephone startled them all.

"I'll get it," Cassie said reaching for the outmoded aquamarine1970's phone.

"Hi Aunt Nell," Cassie's voice softened as she smiled into the phone. "Of course, I'll stop by the home today. A visit with you always brightens my day! ... Sure, I could pick that up, no problem. Is there anything else you need? ... Yes, Aunt Nell, I'll tell her. I love you, too." Cassie hung up the receiver and nodded toward her mom.

"Aunt Nell sends her love, and wants to know why you haven't been by to see her this week, Mother."

"I been meaning to, but she nags me so about my smoking. Besides, all those old folks in the home give me the willies."

Cassie laughed. Martha Mikhailov still didn't acknowledge the fact that she was a day over sixty. It was getting hard for her to explain her nearly fifty-year-old daughter! Her sister, Nell, was seventy-nine to Martha's seventy-six, and had moved to the Pleasant Valley Convalescent and Rehabilitation Center after a disabling stroke the past fall.

Cassie smoothed her Capri pants and made sure her crisp

cotton blouse was tucked in at the waistband. "I'll catch up with you guys later. I'm going to pick up a few things for Aunt Nell and drop them off at the home." She gave her mom a quick peck on the cheek and winked at her friend, who was helping herself to another of Mrs. Mikhailov's homemade chocolate chip cookies.

Cassie loved her eccentric Aunt Nell. They were as different as day and night, which perhaps explained their mutual affection. Nell Gibson had spent a wild youth, running away from home to join a USO tour, dancing her way across Europe and America as the last of the great swing bands gave way to rock 'n roll. After a stint in Hollywood as a chorus girl in B-grade movies, she returned to St. Louis and eventually joined her sister in Ohio. Cassie's mother had alluded to the scandal that had driven Aunt Nell from Hollywood, but neither woman would tell Cassie more.

Aunt Nell waited at the nursing home door, propped up in her wheelchair. Cassie kissed her forehead warmly, and gave her an impromptu hug.

"Now, what's eating at my Cassie girl," Aunt Nell's words were hesitant and slightly slurred. Cassie leaned away from their embrace to look at her aunt's familiarly-dear face.

"How can you be so perceptive? I came here to visit with you, not to talk about my troubles."

"It's that Paul again, isn't it. What's he done to my girl now?" Aunt Nell had never had children of her own, and she treated Cassie more like a daughter than a niece.

"Let me push you back to your room, then we can talk."

"No, they moved that old busybody, Greta Goebel, in with me. She'll tell the entire home your troubles and embellish them to boot." Cassie knew Aunt Nell and Greta were long-time friends, but following her aunt's instructions, pushed the chair to the empty lounge at the end of the hall.

"So, now tell Aunt Nell your troubles, and I'll do 'Auntie Magic' just like when you were a wee one."

"I am afraid you would have to have an awful big bag of tricks to help me out of this one, Aunt Nell, unless you've been playing the lottery and holding out on us."

"That bad, is it, little one?" Cassie smiled at being called a "little one" at her age.

"Well, you know O'Shay's closed, and I lost my job."

"What I know is that scoundrel you married squandered away his father's company, then tried to blame it on your bookkeeping." Nell Gibson didn't try to hide her contempt for her niece's ex-husband.

"Well, now he's sold our house and given me until the end of the month to move!"

"That...that...that worm! That toad!" Aunt Nell fairly spat the words out, barely slurring the syllables. "And, now, child, you have nowhere to go."

"I could move back in with mother, but her smoking gives me asthmatic fits."

"Living with my sister would give me fits, and I don't have asthma! She offered to take me in when I moved to the home, but I knew she'd drive me batty before the week's end!"

Cassie laughed at her aunt and gave her another spontaneous hug. "You are too much, Aunt Nell. I love being with you so, I don't know why I don't stop by more often!"

"You're here nearly every day, sweetheart. You couldn't treat me better if you were my own." The wistfulness casting a shadow over Aunt Nell's features disappeared as quickly as it came when her gray eyes lit up with a sparkle, "Wait, I have it!"

"You have an apartment for me in your magic bag, Aunt Nell?"

"Not an apartment, a house. My house! It's sitting empty out there on that old farm just waiting for the vandals to wreck it. The tenants I rented it to didn't last two months, and it's hard telling what damage they've done. I'd love nothing more than to have you move into it. It will belong to you in God's good time, anyway."

"The farm?" Cassie had loved her Aunt Nell's home in the country. Before she married Paul, she had passed most of her summers there helping to muck out horse stalls and feed the chickens. Afterward, Paul resented her spending time with her aunt, so she could only sneak out for occasional surreptitious visits.

"It's fallen into a bit of disrepair since Clement died. I couldn't keep up with the maintenance by myself. Probably what landed me in here," Nell sighed, suddenly weary.

Clement Jones had been Cassie's aunt's long-time companion. He had fixed up the tack shed as a room, insulating it against the harsh Ohio winters. He wouldn't scandalize Nell's reputation by moving into her house, but shared meals, and if the neighbors were right, a bit more than that, with her. Over the years, "Uncle" Clem had taught Cassie everything from how to pound a nail to which nail or screw to use to best accomplish each task. Though Leo Mikhailov had dismissed Clement Jones as a worthless freeloader, Cassie had come to love her adopted uncle and had felt a closer affinity to him than to her father. Both men had died within a month of one another and Cassie had rebuked herself numerous times for grieving the loss of her aunt's companion far more deeply than that of her own father.

"The key's in my nightstand drawer," her aunt continued. "Wheel me back to my room, and I'll fetch it for you."

Cassie helped her aunt into her bed and tugged the sheet up to her chin. Kissing her wrinkled brow, Cassie thanked her for yet again coming to her rescue.

"Hmpf," Nell smiled good-naturedly, "and you thought I was too old to do 'Auntie Magic'!"

Cassie grasped the key in her hand and vowed to never again doubt her beloved aunt.

"Your aunt said the place was in a state of disrepair, but I'd call this a disaster!" Anita batted at a cobweb dangling across the archway from the dining room to the living room.

"I'm glad Aunt Nell isn't here to see what those ne'er-do-wells who rented her place have done! There's trash all over!"

"What do you think happened to the wallpaper here?"

"Oh, that's where Aunt Nell's pet raccoon, Bandit, tried to chew through the wall. She always said she intended to repaper the dining room."

Dried animal droppings lay in the corner. "Looks like some of his cousins made themselves at home in here a bit more recently!" Anita wrinkled her nose in disgust. "We'll have to find where they got in and plug up the hole."

Cassie looked about the room in despair. "How will I ever get it cleaned up in time to move by the 30th? That just gives us until next Monday!"

Anita took a long look about her before answering, "We'll do it, honey. Just you wait and see!"

The following Saturday, Cassie unloaded a bucket stocked with cleaning supplies, a mop, and a broom from her mom's old Chrysler LeBaron. Paul had had Cassie's Mazda repossessed the day before. Cassie knew she would have to find a replacement soon—she couldn't afford the gas this tank guzzled! However, right now she had more pressing needs. Anita pulled in behind the Chrysler in her little Chevette, followed by Arnie and Julie in their aging minivan.

"I can't tell you guys how much I appreciate your help!" Cassie called as Julie pulled a vacuum cleaner from the back of the van. Arnie came armed with a toolbox.

"Just show us what needs done!"

Cassie exchanged a knowing look with Anita as she laughed, "You may regret the day you spoke those words, Arnie Klotzenmeier!"

Several hours later, the kitchen and the first floor bedroom were habitable. "I found where the raccoons had been getting in. The window in the basement was knocked out. I hammered a piece of plywood across it for now, but we'll want to get that replaced." Arnie reported, coming up the stairs from the cellar.

"You guys are the best friends this old lady could hope to have!"

"Just who are you calling old, Cassie darlin'?" Arnie drawled.

"If I remember right, my birthday comes before yours, so if you're old, what's that make me?"

"Pretty darn near fifty," his wife replied with a smirk.

"Yeah, but I don't need the Viagra yet, do I sweet thing?" He gave a lecherous arch to his eyebrows and wiggled them at the women.

"I think this is more than I want to know," Anita laughed, as she gathered up a pile of dirty rags. "I'll take these home and wash them for you. Just think, tomorrow evening, this will be home!"

Cassie looked about her with apprehension, "I think I'll do a little more work here tonight. Thanks again for everything!"

Julie and Arnie had to get home to babysit two of their grandchildren, and summer bowling league had begun for Anita, so Cassie sat on the stoop of her new home, waving good-bye to her friends.

"I can't believe we found a dead mouse in the cupboard under the sink," she sighed to herself. "Guess those weren't tea leaves in the back of the drawer by the stove." Again, she marveled at her friends' willingness to help her tackle the job of making her aunt's home livable again.

Arnie and Julie had left their commercial-grade vacuum cleaner, and Cassie set to the task of sweeping the dining room and living room carpets. She would have to have them shampooed before moving too much furniture into the rooms.

Darkness shrouded the farmhouse unnoticed by Cassie, as she continued her chores with a single-minded determination. She refused to think of Paul with his bimbette. Refused to wonder if she was driving the little red Mazda now. Refused to allow herself to give way to either anger or pity…or hurt that Jaimé had not even stopped by to see her before he left town soon after the reunion.

Jaimé was Jaimé—a wanderer. She knew little about his life since high school, only that he had married an Inuit native he had met during a brief stint in Alaska, and that she had died in, of all things in today's world, childbirth. Cassie hadn't known about Jaimé's second child, or even whether the child whose birth resulted in its mother's death had lived. She had heard through the grapevine Jaimé had moved from place to place throughout Canada, helping First Nations fight for one environmental cause after another.

His parents still lived in nearby Bowling Green, where his father had retired from teaching at the University. Cassie had encountered them on a few occasions, but they had exchanged little more than the obligatory pleasantries.

She forced her mind in another direction, planning the layout of her furniture. The elegant, yet austere, furnishings with which Paul had insisted they decorate their home would seem out-of-place in these worn, comfortable rooms. Cassie regretted not purchasing more at her aunt's auction back in November, but she could not have predicted then the dire straits in which she now found herself. She vacuumed the living room, letting her mind drift to the hum of the machine's motor.

"What th'...Holy Toledo, Jaimé! You scared the living daylights out of me!" Cassie clasped both hands over her heart, as she dropped the sweeper handle.

Jaimé Alvarez deftly clicked off the switch to the machine with the toe of his sneaker, his eyes twinkling in merriment.

"You really should lock your door, princess, especially when you're out in the country alone."

Recovering from her shock, Cassie retorted, "I will from now on, but it looks like I've already let the varmints in!"

"By what Arnie said, you've spent the day chasing them out! Have you taken a break yet from..." Jaimé glanced around the still disheveled-looking rooms, "...from this?" He swept his hand in a way that included the entire house.

An inopportune rumble from Cassie's stomach answered his question before she had a chance to reply.

"I thought not." He patted her stomach as though to quiet the rumble. "Never fear, Mighty Mouse is here to save your day!"

"Don't even allude to mice, mighty or otherwise," Cassie

groaned to Jaimé's retreating back. By the time he returned, she had sunk down on the carpet in exhaustion.

"Fried chicken. I smell KFC! You stopped by the Colonel's on your way here! You are my hero, Jaimé Alvarez!"

"I've waited thirty years to hear those words, and all I needed was a bucket of fried chicken? If only I had known then that a batter-dipped thigh was the way to the Ice Princess's heart!"

"The Ice Princess?"

"I, uh, it was just a nickname some of the guys used to call..."

"Me? They called *me* the Ice Princess?"

"You out-classed them, Cas; you carried yourself like an aristocrat. You were always a step ahead of everyone else. They were afraid to ask you out, so they made up stories about how cold you were."

Cassie chewed on a drumstick, before taking a long drink of cola.

"Do you know how many dates I had in high school, Jaimé? Precious few. All because they assumed I was stuck-up! An Ice Princess? How about you, did you think I was made of ice?"

Jaimé wiped his fingers on a paper napkin while eyeing the woman next to him. Her hair was braided into two short plaits that stuck out around her neck, much like those he remembered from their grade school days. Her face was smudged, in spite of her attempt to wipe the grime from it. She wore an oversized white shirt over slim-fitting jeans.

"If I thought that at first, you proved me wrong that summer when I came back from the service. You were anything but cold."

Cassie felt the flame creep up her neck to her cheeks. She turned away from the man at her side before answering, "We had best forget that summer, Jaimé. It was a mistake, an aberration that shouldn't have happened."

"Maybe you've been able to forget what we had, but it's been eating at me. I need to know why, Cassandra. Why did you marry Paul?"

Cassie toyed with telling him the whole sordid story. Perhaps he did have a right to know. After all, it was his baby. But it was so long ago, and she didn't know if she had the courage to face his anger if he found out the truth. So instead, she gathered up the remnants of their dinner and put them back in the paper sack.

"Thank you, Jaimé. I truly was famished. You are a gem to have driven all this way to bring me dinner. I'm sure your children must be waiting for you...."

"Ma's watching over them. I told her I wouldn't be back until late. So, you can't evade me that easily. Out with it, Cas, what happened?"

"Can't you just believe I fell in love with Paul? You're the one who left town without looking back! Big shot eastern lawyer too good for his home town!" Cassie's tone sounded more accusatory than she had intended, but, dammit, she was the one who had had to face the consequences of their summer together. He had skipped out as soon as the autumn winds began to blow.

The pain imbedded behind Cassie's eyes stopped Jaimé cold. Whatever long-hidden secrets rendered her so much hurt would remain so for this evening. It was obvious she was exhausted beyond her limits to endure any further probing.

"Let me drive you home, Cassandra. You're too tired to manage these country roads tonight. I'll bring you back out tomorrow."

Cassie surveyed the house from where she sat. Without a bed, she couldn't spend the night. Even if Arnie had plugged up the raccoon hole, she wasn't brave enough to sleep on the floor. And Jaimé was right—she was too tired to safely drive the ten miles back to town. She nodded her head in defeat.

Jaimé drove an unpretentious late-model sedan. He opened the passenger door for Cassie, then walked around the front of the car and eased onto the driver's seat by her side. Cassie's heart thrummed in spite of her exhaustion. She felt his presence reverberate throughout her as he turned the ignition and pulled around the U-shaped driveway. She closed her eyes and leaned her head against the leather seat. She breathed in his distinctive scent, smiling into the darkness. He turned the radio to the local oldies station, letting the Eagles fill the silence. The hum of the wheels against the pavement lulled Cassie into a drifting sleep.

Jaimé grasped the steering wheel with both hands to keep from caressing the face of his sleeping princess or holding the hand lying loose on her lap. He knew he shouldn't have driven out to her aunt's house, but once Arnie had divulged her whereabouts, Jaimé was powerless to stay away. He should run. Run as far and as fast as he had the last time. But that was the problem. He had run away. And found that there wasn't a place on this continent that was far enough to erase the pain—and the pleasure—this town had inflicted upon him.

He thought about the woman at his side. What sort of life had she led? She had alluded to secrets…secrets that evidently involved him. And what was that bullcrap about a million-and-a-half dollars missing from O'Shay's till? He would bet his life Cassie was no more involved in any wrongdoing concerning that money than he was. Paul Alexander had been a thorn in Jaimé's side for longer than he cared to remember. He had teased and tormented Jaimé into more fights than he could count—usually at times when Jaimé was outnumbered and outflanked. He smiled wryly, remembering he hadn't lost them all. Paul had required surgery on his nose after one such bout. His smile faded when he recalled Cassie's ex-husband had nearly done it again at the school reunion. Jaimé knew he should stay away from Cassie, if for no other reason than it would further aggravate her problems with Paul.

Jaimé nudged Cassie awake when they pulled within the city limits. "You'll need to give me directions to your place, Cassandra."

Cassie stretched before opening her eyes. She wanted the ride to go on and on, but the streetlights and city noise replaced the country solitude.

"Turn right at the Haus of Pizza and head toward the edge of town. We're in the King's Acres subdivision."

"Subdivision? You don't have to have an ID card to get into a subdivision, sweetheart. King's Acres is where all the high mucky-mucks live. Stands to reason Paul Alexander would have a house there!"

"Yeah, well, after tomorrow my King's Acres' ID will be about as much use as my American Express card. My credit's so lousy around here Arnie had to rent the U-Haul to move my stuff out to the farm."

Cassie swiped her identification card through the slot in the metal box standing guard in the middle of the drive, and the automated gates swung open. Quiet anticipation settled over them as Cassie directed Jaimé around the bends and curves surrounding the world-class golf course.

"These houses are something else! It's hard to believe anyone would need that much space to live," Jaimé commented.

"Just big empty shells over a lot of hot air—I've never met any real people the entire time I've been here. Everyone was too busy working to keep up with the neighbor next door or across the fairway.

"Oh drat, what's he doing here?" Heaving a deep sigh of resignation, Cassie leaned her head back against the seat.

The chrome of a monster 4x4 pick-up glinted under the reproduction gaslight illuminating the driveway to a magnificent stone home. The truck dwarfed Jaimé's midsize sedan as he pulled in beside it.

Jaimé leaned over and brushed a stray strand of hair from Cassie's cheek, "Do you want me to come in with you or would it be better if I were out of the picture?"

"You've done enough already—you shouldn't become more involved in my problems."

"That's an evasive answer to a direct question. Do you want me to come in with you?"

The look she gave him was all the answer he needed. "You don't have the strength tonight to face Paul alone. Here, let me help you with that." Jaimé lifted the catch on Cassie's seatbelt, before hurrying around the car to open her door.

Paul slouched against the jamb of the arched doorway under an elaborate portico. "Well, isn't this cozy. Gone slumming again, Cas-hon?" As had become the norm over the years, whiskey slurred his words as he sneered at his former wife.

"What are you doing here, Paul? This is my home for another twenty-four hours. You're trespassing."

"Trespassing, shit. Don't get mouthy with me, or..."

"Or, what, Alexander?" Jaimé stepped forward, "If I remember right, you're good at playing the tough guy with someone who's weaker than you or when you're surrounded by your hoodlum buddies."

"Back off, Jimmy boy. This doesn't concern you."

"As long as I'm the slum you're referring to, I guess it does."

Cassie positioned herself between the two men, hoping to buffer their words from developing into actions.

"Hey, bitch, this is one of my good linen shirts!" Paul pulled on Cassie's shirtfront with his fist, jerking her head back to bring her face close to his. Before Jaimé could react, Cassie slammed both of her palms against her ex-husband's chest, nearly knocking him over the porch rail. Breaking away from his grasp, but still holding her face within inches of his, Cassie spoke in even, clipped tones, "Don't you *ever* lay a hand on me again. Not *ever*, do you understand?" She accentuated each word with a poke to his chest.

"You're choosing to side with the Spic over me? You'll live to regret this, dollface. You can bet money on that." As he heaved himself away from the doorway, Paul bumped Cassie into Jaimé, who steadied her by placing his hands on her shoulders.

"We'll assume that was an accident, Paulo." Jaimé received only a parting glare in return.

Cassie drew Jaimé into the house and closed the door before sinking against his chest for support. She trembled with exhaustion, rage, and latent fear. He wrapped his arms around her, gently rocking her in a calming motion. He rested his cheek against the top of her head, wanting nothing more than to comfort and protect her. She shifted her head so she could look up at him. Her eyes were luminescent with unshed tears, her quivering lips stoking his desire for her.

"Ah, *querida*," he lightly brushed her cheek with his finger, "you need rest. Do you want me to stay the night in case he comes back?"

"Yes…no…who knows what he would do if he returned in the middle of the night and saw your car parked outside. Besides, there's no need for the uppity gossips around here to drag your name through the gutter along with mine."

"There's nothing more people here can say about me they haven't said to my face a long time ago. But, you do need to sleep. And, I'm not sure how much rest you would get with me in the house." He kissed her forehead, tipped her chin up with a touch of his finger, and wiped a stray tear from her face with his other hand.

"Sleep well. I'll see you tomorrow."

Cassie locked the door behind Jaimé then leaned her forehead against the jamb while he backed out of the driveway. She watched as his taillights disappeared into the black night, before pulling away. She latched the deadbolt then braced a chair against the doorknob. She ascended the stairs to the bedroom that, until this spring, she had shared with Paul Alexander. The door was ajar, revealing chaos within. Her clothing lay strewn about everywhere, ripped into pieces. Her lingerie drawer had been dumped, and the contents shredded into remnants of lace and satin. Her jewelry box sat open on her dresser. Cassie crossed the room, knowing what she would find. Paul had helped himself to all of her expensive pieces. Cassie had already planned to return any heirloom Alexander family jewels to her ex-husband, but she had hoped to sell the diamond and emerald pendant, strand of pearls, and various other gifts Paul had given her over the years. She had earned them, dammit, and thought she might garner sufficient money from their sale to finance a good used car.

It wasn't until she sank down onto the side of the bed to survey the extent of the damage that she noticed their wedding picture. The oak frame lay in pieces amidst shards of splintered glass. Paul had ripped the photo in half, and with heavy heart, Cassie retrieved the torn pieces from the floor. A chill ran through her as she deciphered the words "Die Bitch" scrawled across her gown.

She had often enough felt the sting of Paul's temper, but he had everything he wanted now. What possible reason would he have to wish her harm? As understanding of the depth of her ex-husband's psychosis flickered through her, she let the photo drop to the floor as though it had spontaneously caught fire.

Cassie backed slowly toward the door and slipped into the hall, closing it behind her. However, before she could make her way down the stairs, an impulse sent her back into the room to retrieve the desecrated wedding picture. She grabbed a large coffee-table book on the Ohio Canals off the shelves in the hallway, stuffed the photo inside, and carried it down to the living room with her. She scooted the book under the couch, pulled an afghan Aunt Nell had crocheted—and Paul had particularly detested—over her body, and fell exhausted into a deep sleep.

An incessant knocking pulled at Cassie, but no matter how hard she ran she couldn't get to the door. Paul grabbed for her afghan, but she wound it more securely about her body. She felt it twist around her legs then she was falling...falling.... Cassie landed solid on the living room floor, waking her from her unsettling dream. The knocking was, indeed, at her door, followed by Anita's frantic voice calling Cassie's name.

Cassie dragged herself off the carpet and waddled to the door, still tangled in her aunt's blanket. She tugged the chair away from the doorknob and unlocked the deadbolt and chain, only to be greeted by a caravan of her friends ready to move her belongings to the farmhouse.

"Omigosh, what time is it?"

"Time for the city mouse to move to the country," Anita said as she whisked on into the house, followed by Arnie and Julie along with their son and daughter-in-law. Jaimé stood at the back of the entourage. He chucked her chin as he entered the house.

"Time to get up, sleepyhead." His smile was soft and warm,

and Cassie wanted nothing more than to exchange her worn afghan for his strong arms. She closed her eyes and leaned her forehead against his chest only for a second, before summoning all of her strength to face the day ahead.

"Cassie, what happened to the armchairs?" Anita stood by the fireplace where, until yesterday, two matching antique Queen Anne's chairs had sat on either side of a small Persian rug.

"Paul!" Cassie hadn't looked beyond her demolished bedroom last evening to discover the extent of her former husband's vindictiveness.

"I thought he got the house, but you got the contents!"

"Yeah, that's what the court said. They were ugly chairs, anyway, and too fragile to really use."

Anita gave Cassie the look that said, "You aren't going to let him get away with this, are you?" but Cassie cut her short, "Let it go, 'Nita, it doesn't matter. They're just chairs."

They moved from room to room surveying the bits and pieces of furniture Paul had left behind.

"Guess this makes the moving a whole lot easier," Arnie quipped as they entered the nearly empty library.

"My books! He took my books!" Cassie hadn't blanched when they passed the spot once occupied by a nineteenth-century grandfather clock or when the wide-screened TV was missing from the family room. But her books had been her solace and her friends throughout her loveless marriage. She allowed herself only a moment of mourning for her lost treasures before darting from the room.

"Arnie, no! Nothing's up there!" Arnie ascended the oak stairwell before Cassie could stop him.

"Sweet Heaven, Cas, what in the Sam Hill happened?" Arnie stood in the doorway of her ransacked bedroom.

"*El Diáblo!*" Anita cursed as she surveyed the destruction, with Julie and the others at her heels.

Jaimé made his way to the front of the group while Cassie hung back in the hallway. When he returned to her, his eyes had darkened with concern. "I don't think it's a good idea for you to move to your aunt's house, Cassandra. If Paul is capable of this, who knows what he might do next!"

"No! I'm not going to let him intimidate me ever again! My life is my own. Not Paul's…and not yours. With or without your help, I am moving today!"

"Okay, maybe you're right. It's just that…"

"Jaimé, it's sweet of you to worry about me, but I'm a big girl now, not some helpless child. I can take care of myself!" Remembering the wedding photo safely hidden under the couch, Cassie shuddered behind her words of bravado. She had never spoken of the darkest side of her relationship with her former husband with anyone: not her mother, not her best friend, and definitely not with the man facing her now. This house would remain a mausoleum for untold secrets, left to rot in their own decay.

Jaimé tucked his hands on either side of the afghan Cassie still wore wrapped around her shoulders and planted a quick kiss on the tip of her nose. Cassie's normally restrained hair had worked free from her braids and fell in strands around her face. He toyed with one while he said, "Maybe you could tell us what to move first, then jump in the shower…."

For one of the first times in her life, Cassandra Grace Mikhailov Alexander had forgotten about her appearance. Like a deer caught in headlights, her eyes opened wide as she realized how awful she must look. She had on yesterday's rumpled clothing and most likely her mascara had run to her chin.

Anita laughed, "It's alright, Cas, considering what you've been through, you look great!"

Flustered, Cassie felt a blush cover her face, "Yes, well, um…." Not wanting to chance Jaimé's discovering the ugly message scrawled on her wedding picture, but needing to shower and regain her composure, Cassie took a quick peek in the guest bedroom behind her. Fortunately, she and Jaimé had interrupted Paul last evening before he had reached this room. "I think I'll use this furniture for my bedroom at Aunt Nell's. Would you mind moving it first?"

As the crew debated the best way to get the mattress and springs down the stairs, Cassie snuck into her bedroom, where, with luck, she would be able to find a fresh change of clothing.

After a quick shower, Cassie donned an old pair of black stretch capris she found stuck in a bottom dresser drawer and tossed on another of Paul's expensive shirts that he had failed to remember was hanging in a garment bag in the back of her closet. She buckled a wide black leather belt around her waist, and twisted her hair into a French braid. She stepped into the hallway determined not to give Paul Alexander the satisfaction of flinching at his game.

"Wow, you do clean up nicely, Alexander...or should I say Mikhailov?" Arnie whistled as Cassie emerged from the steamy bathroom. Jaimé nearly dropped his end of the antique wrought-iron bedstead as he backed down the stairs. He rather liked the vulnerability of the doe-eyed, afghan-wrapped princess. The woman at the top of the stairwell stood as a barefoot tigress, ready to trample whomever crossed her.

"Nah, I decided to keep Alexander," Cassie rejoined, "I've worn it for a long time and rather like the ring of it. Besides, my former father-in-law's memory deserves to be honored by more than the snake he sired."

"Yeah, Charlie was a good man. He must be rolling over in his grave after what happened to O'Shay's. You were always the apple of the old man's eye. I think he regretted you weren't his daughter. He always said you were too good to be married to his son!" Arnie said as he hefted his end of the bed frame, jostling Jaimé's attention back to the task at hand.

"It's hopeless, 'Nita," Cassie sighed, as she tried to assemble a usable wardrobe from the remnants of Paul's rampage. "I might as well go to the Goodwill store and start over again. Lord knows, with what's in my bank account, I can't even afford to shop at the discount stores!"

Jaimé returned with Arnie, after securing the bedroom furniture in the rented U-Haul truck. "We've got everything up here loaded, Cas. We're ready to start with the living room. You've said you don't want to press charges against Paul, but why don't you make a list of the missing furniture just in case you change your mind. If you have a camera handy, you may want to take some photos of this room, as well."

"The living room?" Cassie felt an instant of panic. "Would you get the books from the shelves from the hallway first? At least Paul left those behind. Um…a camera. I think mine is on a shelf in the guest closet in the foyer."

Cassie flew down the stairs with the ruse of finding her camera, hoping the couch still hid the book with the hapless wedding photo inside. She arrived just as Arnie and his son moved the davenport.

"Oh!" Cassie exclaimed, "There's my book *Photographs of the Ohio Canal Era*! I've been looking for this. Thanks so much for finding it!" Cassie grabbed the book as Arnie bent to pick it up. "I'll just take this and pack it with my things upstairs." Cassie clutched the volume to her chest as she hurried toward the foyer closet.

"What was that all about?" Jaimé asked as he entered the living room carrying a box of books.

"Beats me. Cas was in an all-fired hurry to get that book. Must be something special to her!"

In less than an hour, all of the remaining furniture had been loaded in the truck. Julie and her daughter-in-law had boxed up the contents of the kitchen cupboards. Cassie had given up on sorting her wardrobe and had shoved everything into two suitcases, hiding the book with the torn photo in the bottom of one. "I've wasted a lifetime in this room. The furnishings, or what's left of them, can stay—they're nothing but bad memories to me. Help me look around, 'Nita, to be sure I've gotten all of my personal stuff. I don't want anything left behind that would ever connect me to this place!"

After one last search, they pushed the over-stuffed luggage

into the hallway. Cassie pulled the door closed behind her. Jaimé watched and waited at the top of the stairwell, not wanting to intrude on Cassie's past. Her future was what concerned him now. When she turned her back to the door, he quietly called to her, "Cassandra...."

"I'm ready, Jaimé...I'm ready."

By late afternoon the sum total of Cassie's earthly belongings had been moved to her Aunt Nell's old farmhouse and temporarily arranged for her occupancy. A thrill of anticipation overcame her as she realized she was truly free to begin a new life. "This is it, guys. Cassandra Grace Mikhailov Alexander meets the big wide world! I feel like a kid again. If I'd known how good a mid-life crisis felt, I would've had one a long time ago!"

Jaimé smiled as he wrapped an arm around her waist and pulled her to his side, "I have to admit, princess, the place looks a whole lot more inviting than it did just twenty-four hours ago."

After devouring a hard-earned pizza, they christened the house by sharing a bottle of champagne and a box of exquisite dark chocolate truffles Jaimé had retrieved from a cooler in the trunk of his car.

"A country chalet fit for a queen," Arnie quipped as he bowed graciously to Cassie.

"None of this queen stuff, or princess, either," Cassie said with a pointed look toward Jaimé. "I think I'll get me a goat, a few chickens, and maybe a cow or two and put this farm back into business!"

"Not in that barn, you won't," Arnie inclined his head toward the dilapidated structure at the curve in the drive.

"It's not so bad. It just needs a few boards and a new coat of paint..."

"Oh no, Cas, getting the house up to snuff is one thing, but I'm cutting out of here before you get any ideas about the barn," Arnie gathered up the pizza box and empty champagne bottle and quickstepped backward toward the U-Haul truck.

"That's okay, Arn." Cassie laughed, "Tomorrow is another

day!"

She bid her friends good-bye with hugs of appreciation for all. Only Jaimé remained. As the sun drifted low in the sky they stood arm in arm while muted shades of pink and purple silhouetted the oak and maple trees sheltering the house.

"It's strange, but I feel as though I have come home," Cassie said with a subdued voice.

In response, Jaimé turned her toward him, tilted her chin and brushed her lips ever so softly with his, "Just so long as there's room for me, *querida*, just so long as there's room for me."

She savored his caress momentarily before pulling away. "No, Jaimé…it can't be like this." Her eyes searched the darkening skies before locking with his. "You have your life, your career, your children to care for. I need to learn I can depend on myself before I allow anyone else into my life. I can't afford a relationship now, not with you. Especially not with you!" She pleaded for understanding, "I don't mean to be ungrateful for all you have done—without your help, and the others, I'd be sitting at the curb outside King's Acres surrounded by what was left of my belongings. But, it's too soon for me to give myself over to someone else…to you…."

She rose up on tiptoe and lightly pressed her lips to his cheek, then backed away. She allowed herself one last, longing look at him before hurrying up the walk and through the door, pulling it tight behind her.

Jaimé stood in the gathering dusk staring at the closed door. A flash of anger at Cassie's quick retreat was immediately supplanted by the realization that she was right. He did have obligations he could not ignore. Rather than helping her heal the wounds Paul had inflicted, he could easily exacerbate her pain. Besides, before he could help her, he needed to find out why she had married Paul. He didn't think it was vanity that kept him from believing she had simply fallen in love with Paul as she had said the night before.

Jaimé replayed the accusation Cassandra had hurled at him— that he had left town without looking back after that long ago summer. But he had written letters, long letters, after studying legal cases late into the night! She was the one who hadn't responded. For the time being, however, he would have to let her have her way, and back off. He had been neglecting Tina and Ben, and he was due in Cleveland in the morning....

Alone in the large rambling old farmhouse, Cassie sank to the floor. Bracing her shoulders against the door, she surveyed her surroundings. She waited for the shiver of fear that should naturally overtake her at night in a strange house in the country. Instead, she felt oddly comforted, the walls sheltering her like a timeworn patchwork quilt.

She forced thoughts of Jaimé out of her mind by imagining improvements she would make to the house as soon as she had a steady income. She would repaper the dining room, repaint the battered white wainscoting and chair rail, and eventually replace the hideous red-orange shag carpet that most certainly dated back to her youth. As she designed room after room, she felt her eyelids grow heavy and curled up on the couch into a weary sleep.

She did not awaken when the sound of tires crunched over the gravel of her driveway. Did not hear the vehicle stop in the darkened night beside her barn. Did not see the two men slip between the doors that hung ajar just enough to allow them access to its interior.

CHAPTER THREE

july

Cassie spent the next week methodically scouring each room. She delighted in rediscovering the nooks, crannies, and built-in cupboards that gave her Aunt Nell's home its unique appeal. An open staircase led from the living room to the bedrooms above, and a narrower "servants" stairs angled back down to the kitchen from the north bedroom.   Cedar lined all of the closets, including the one upstairs that Aunt Nell had converted into a half-bath. She ascended the pull-down ladder to peek into the attic—shrouded forms and boxes were stacked around the open area begging to be investigated another day.

She climbed back down the ladder and sat on the bottom step, looking at the rooms surrounding her. So many memories—so many wonderful summer nights spent watching stars move across the dark country sky from the small window beside the built-in Jeffersonian bed Uncle Clem had made just for her. So many mornings waking to the smell of fresh-brewed coffee and the sounds of Aunt Nell and Uncle Clem discussing the day ahead—so far removed from the vitriolic arguments that had so often awoken her at her own home.

Her aunt was always taking in itinerants in need of a bed in exchange for a day's work or students wanting an inexpensive alternative to the pricey apartments in Toledo or Bowling Green. Cassie recalled the summer after her eighth grade, when her family was especially tight for money and her mother had taken a job waitressing in Toledo. Her father didn't trust Cassie to stay at home by herself, so had grudgingly allowed her to spend the entire summer vacation on the farm. Cassie was thrilled and had passed the days helping Aunt Nell in the garden or tagging after Uncle Clem while he worked with old Ginger, his collie, tending the sheep and cattle.

One day in late July, an old pickup broke down in front of the farmhouse. When the man came to the door, Aunt Nell discovered the truck belonged to a migrant family who was on their way to work in the tomato fields at Old Man McAlister's down the road. Rather than have the family stay in the often poorly maintained migrant housing provided by the farmer, Aunt Nell invited the whole group to stay in her upstairs! Cassie soon became fast friends with the daughter, who was just a year older than she, and ended up spending her days caring for their toddler while the rest of the family labored in the fields. Though Cassie worked long hours, she would always remember that as one of the best summers of her life.

Cassie eased the attic ladder back up through the opening from where she had pulled it down, and slipped the trap door covering it back into place.

On the following Saturday, Cassie's mother drove her Aunt Nell out to the farm. While Martha Mikhailov chided her daughter for moving so far from town, Nell Gibson was thrilled to be in her former home again.

Observing her usually impeccably dressed niece in worn, snug-fitting jeans and a scoop-necked tee-shirt with her hair pulled back in a casual pony tail, Aunt Nell smiled. "Cassie, dear, you look wonderful!"

"Thanks, Aunt Nell. This is the best I could do from this new boutique I'm shopping at these days."

"Boutique?" Martha Mikhailov questioned, "I hadn't heard of a new shop in town!"

"Probably not, Mom," Cassie laughed, "it's called the Goodwill store!"

"Cassandra Grace! Your father must be turning over in his grave!" her mother exclaimed. "To think that his Russian princess has stooped to shopping at second-hand stores."

"That's enough, just enough of this princess garbage! Where did my father come up with his Russian princess story, anyway?"

"Who knows? He always claimed he was somehow related to that Russian couple they made that movie about. You know, the one where they all got killed in the end."

"Nicholas and Alexandra? My father claimed to be related to the Romanovs? That's crazy! All of the Romanovs, except maybe Anastasia, were annihilated in the Russian Revolution."

"You know that, and I know that. But your father became obsessed with the idea he was a... What was that name again? A Romanoff? I think that's why he was so set on your marrying Paul."

"Paul? Why Paul? What does he have to do with Nicholas and Alexandra?" Cassie puzzled before a light flickered in her mind, "Oh no, because his name was Alexander? My father sold me out because Paul happened to have the *last* name of Alexander?"

"Well, that and the fact he was the son of the richest man in the county. Your father truly wanted the best for you." Cassie gave a derisive laugh, blocking out the worst of her memories, as her mother continued, "He thought Paul could give you everything you deserved—everything Leo couldn't afford. He worked long hours so you would never have to wear hand-me-down clothes—so you would look like the princess he thought you were."

"I needed a real father more than another cashmere sweater. And without meaning to be unappreciative, if I never hear the word 'princess' again, it will be too soon!" Cassie exclaimed in exasperation.

After her mother and aunt left for town, Cassie wandered aimlessly through the house pondering the new revelations about her father. She had grown up living in a dilapidated apartment building in a subdivision skirting the river near Anita's and Jaimé's homes in the Mexican-American settlement called the Lower Eastside. Her father had never approved of her friendship with 'Nita and flew into a rage the first time Jaimé walked her home. He forbade her to see either of them again.

Throughout her years at Tecumseh High, he insisted Cassie meet her friends at the soda shop or the movie theater downtown, rather than have them know his daughter lived near the Lower Eastside. Against her protests, he paid lavish prices for her clothing, ballet lessons and modeling school. Rather than fight his headstrong determination to mold her into the daughter he had envisioned, Cassie eventually acquiesced to his will and suppressed her own.

Her sole act of defiance had been the summer after her senior year—her summer with Jaimé. While her father refused to allow her to see Jaimé, she had cajoled him into relenting on his ban of her friendship with Anita. So, under the guise of going to the movies or shopping with 'Nita, she would sneak down the trail to the river where Jaimé awaited her. As they couldn't risk being seen together in a public setting, they would spend the evening lying under the stars discussing their dreams.

Cassie stepped out the back door of the farmhouse leading to the deck overlooking the pond and the woods beyond. She sat down on her aunt's old slat-wood glider and gently rocked back and forth as a radiant sunset rippled on the horizon, while a heat from a completely different source sizzled within her.

Long-suppressed memories flowed from her subconscious, replaying one of her last nights with Jaimé. It was on a balmy evening late in August and they lay sharing a blanket nestled in the copse of trees that had become their secret retreat. She could recall the details as though it were yesterday....

"I leave for Boston on Monday," Jaimé whispered, resting his chin on the top of her head.

"What am I going to do without you? You'll be at Harvard with all of those big-city girls, and I'll be here taking night classes at the University. Father's fit to be tied because I took that job at O'Shay's. He doesn't want people to think I can't afford to go away to school. I can't understand why he doesn't see everyone knows I'm a sham, a fake. He's worked so hard to build this image of me I think he believes it's real!"

"Hush, querida, you may not be his princess, but you are mine." Jaimé lowered his lips to cover hers as she arched to meet his embrace. He eased the tail of her sleeveless blouse from the waistband of her khaki shorts and slipped his hand underneath to caress her breast. Her fingers trembled as she worked to unfasten the buttons of her top before he took over. He spread her shirt wide and, at first, she felt shy as the full moon revealed her nakedness. But then he deftly drew his tee-shirt over his head. Instinct overcame her timidity and she pulled his bare chest down to cover hers.

Hungered desires that lay smoldering for months leapt into a full flame fed by the knowledge their summer together was crashing to an end. While the breeze rustled the oak leaves overhead, Jaimé Alvarez swore his undying love to the woman he had coveted since childhood, and she, in turn, pledged her heart to him.

Her memories left Cassie feeling bereft and betrayed as clouds skittered across a nearly full moon—the same moon that had shone on her and Jaimé thirty years ago. Jaimé had broken his vow, and her heart, then—she would not allow history to repeat itself.

Monday found Cassie pouring through the want ads and

completing one job application after another. Two branch banks had advertised for tellers and one small local firm needed an accountant. Though sales held no appeal for her, she also applied at various retail stores throughout the area. As manual dexterity wasn't her forte, she bypassed factory line-work, leaving that as a last resort. She even stopped by the branch library to see about a part-time position as an aide.

Cassie had not been awarded alimony due to O'Shay's bankruptcy; however, she had received a meager settlement that, even though she lived a Spartan existence, was being slowly whittled away. With what little remained, she purchased a used Ford Festiva with 80,000 miles on its odometer and a large dent in the fender. *At least,* Cassie thought, *at 35 miles-per-gallon, I might be able to afford the gas to drive it back and forth to work. Assuming, that is, I find a job.*

On her way to the title office, she passed Craig Herman, the toadie Paul had hired as her assistant the final years at O'Shay's. She caught a glimpse of him in his perennially starched white shirt and bow tie as he turned his freshly waxed black Lincoln Continental onto Palmer Avenue. *You might have guessed, the "Craigster" ends up with the Lincoln and good old Cas gets the beater with the bad paint job. Life is just not fair!*

Cassie thought about Craig on her way home. He was like an annoying mosquito, always buzzing around making a nuisance of himself while she was trying to work on the financial reports at O'Shay's. As he knew next to nothing about digital spreadsheets or computers in general, she found it hard to take him seriously and failed to find anything productive he had accomplished during his years with the company. But Paul thrived on the Craigster's lapdog adulation and enjoyed watching him jump through hoops whenever Paul tossed him a bone—or a bonus.

The phone was ringing when Cassie walked through the door, and she grabbed it as the answering machine clicked on. "Cas, it's Paul. Call me when you get in. It's important."

She let the message play out. *Oh drat, what now?* Cassie

thought as she took a deep breath before punching the number Paul had given her into the phone.

"Hey, babe, how's life in the country?" Cassie's stomach turned at the sound of her former husband's voice.

"I'm sure you didn't call to discuss the pleasantries of the day, Paul. You said this was important, so make it short."

"If that's the way you want it, Cas-hon. All I wanted to do was to give you a heads up that the sheriff was asking a few questions about the missin' money and was just a tad bit ticked-off you had moved out of town without giving him a forwarding address. He mentioned something about if you couldn't stay put he just might have a place where he'd be able to find you when he wanted you—lovely bars on the windows, too." Paul paused a moment for effect, "Oh, he talked to Craig, too. Seems the Craigster was able to remember some information that was of interest to Billy Joe."

Cassie's heart sunk as she slid onto a kitchen chair. The county sheriff, Billy Joe Crenshaw, had been a drinking buddy of Paul's since high school. She could only imagine the direction of their conversation earlier that day. She took a deep breath before answering with a false sense of calm into the mouthpiece. "Thank you, Paul, for the information. I am sure you and Billy Joe had a great time reminiscing about all sorts of things. I'll definitely give his office a call to update my change of address." She clicked the phone offline before Paul could respond any further.

Cassie sat unmoving, the phone still cradled in her hand. She dismissed Billy Joe's threat to lock her up. At least she didn't think she could be incarcerated for inadvertently forgetting to report her move. She hadn't left the county, after all. She was far more concerned with whatever story Craig had purportedly "remembered."

What could have happened to a million-and-a-half dollars? Cassie racked her brain for the thousandth time since the auditors discovered the loss. She had reviewed the files on her secured computer, and figures that had added up one day were completely awry the next. *It had to be a series of small errors or, perhaps, a minute miscalculation that had snowballed over time.* But she prided herself on her mathematical acuity and didn't believe she could have possibly made that type of mistake without catching it long before it reached such cataclysmic proportions. No one had access to those files but Cassie. The auditors had confiscated her computer, preventing her from further scrutinizing the files. Cassie was convinced the answer lay within those files, and given access to the computer and enough time, she could discern what had happened to the money.

The ring of the telephone startled Cassie, and she picked it up, prepared to tell Paul just exactly where he could stick his information. Instead, Anita greeted her with "Hey, Alexander, whaddarya doin' next Saturday morning?"

"I had planned to do some more repairs here, 'Nita, unless you have a better suggestion."

"Well, as a matter of fact, I have in my chubby little hand a flyer for a workshop you and I are going to attend."

"A workshop? This had better be good!"

"We need this if we are going to get your place in shape. It's called 'Barns Again!' and it's put on by the state to help people like you save ramshackle old barns like your aunt's."

"As much as I would love to, I don't have any money to spare to fix the barn, so the workshop would be a waste of time. Besides, I've got bigger problems to contend with," and Cassie proceeded to tell Anita about Paul's phone call.

As the week wore on, Cassie heard nothing more from her ex-husband or from his crony, the sheriff. Unfortunately, she didn't receive any responses from her job applications either.

Saturday morning found Cassie sitting beside Anita on a hard folding chair listening to a presentation on the various styles of barns found in Northwest Ohio. Though interested in what the man in bib overalls at the podium had to say, Cassie still felt the workshop, as she had predicted, was a waste of their time. She stifled a yawn as the next speaker was introduced.

'Nita jabbed Cassie in the ribs, "Wow, that dude is hot! Get a load of those blue eyes. Check out his ring finger—is he married?"

The man walking to the podium was of medium-height with an unruly shock of sandy blonde hair dangling over his forehead. As Anita had observed, his eyes were as blue as the sky on a clear summer day. They sparked with enthusiasm as he began talking about the economics of saving old barns rather than letting them cave in on themselves and building much less durable pole buildings. The speaker headed a small company that not only shored up and restored century-old barns, but also salvaged parts from barns that could not be saved. His Power Point presentation included photos of various barns he had resurrected from a slow death.

Against her better sense, Cassie found herself listening to the man with a growing excitement. Half of the charm of her aunt's farm lay in the rustic barn. But the west attached corncrib had already collapsed and half the boards on the back lean-to had rotted out or were missing altogether. She wondered if the barn could possibly be saved.

As the blue-eyed barn guru left the podium, the bib-overalled man announced a fifteen-minute break before the final speaker. Anita jumped up and nudged Cassie toward the sandy-haired man. He was listening intently to an elderly couple describe their farm, but momentarily diverted his attention to Anita and Cassie with an appreciative nod. Cassie glanced down at the unadorned ring finger on his left hand—not even a telltale white band. A sidelong glance at Anita confirmed her friend had observed this, as well.

As the older couple began another round of questioning, the speaker tactfully suggested they might want to help themselves to refreshments before the program reconvened. He then turned his charm on Cassie and Anita with dimpled smile. "You ladies are half the age and twice as pretty as most of the folks at these workshops. What brings you here on a beautiful Saturday morning?"

"Flattery, Mr...." Cassie searched her memory for the name that was given when the man had been introduced.

"Windmiller. Sam Windmiller," he supplied. His twinkling blue eyes focused on Anita as he continued, "But my friends call me Windy."

"As I was saying, flattery, Mr. Windmiller, will get you…"

"…A thank you," Anita interjected. "I'm Anita Morales and my ungrateful friend here is…"

"…Cassandra Alexander." Cassie extended her right hand to Sam Windmiller. "And my friends call me Cassie. 'Nita's right. At my age, I shouldn't be so hasty to reject a compliment."

As Cassie began describing her barn, she noticed Sam Windmiller's gaze stray repeatedly to her friend. Before they parted, Windy asked Cassie to write her name and telephone number on the back of one of his business cards.

"I have a small job out your direction next week. If you'll be around, I'll give you a call and stop by to give you an assessment of what it would take to fix up your barn."

Mr. Bib Overalls brought the room to attention. With a quick thank you to Sam Windmiller, Cassie and Anita hurried back to their seats.

"You *are* going to call me the minute you hear from him, aren't you?" Anita asked as she drove her Chevette back toward the farm.

"*Him?*" Cassie teased her longtime friend. "This from the woman who idolized John Travolta in his disco days and wore out all three *Indiana Jones* videos because she thought Harrison Ford was the hottest thing since the Beatles invaded New York, but wouldn't give a flesh and blood date the time of day?"

"C'mon, I'm not that bad!"

"Not that bad? When's the last time you dated anyone for longer than a month?"

"Well," Anita thought a minute, "Tom. Tom Crystal."

"Tom Crystal? You went out with him, what, two dates?"

"Yeah, but they were a month apart." Anita shot back as though to prove her point.

"The fact is, 'Nita, you've set your standards so high St. Peter himself couldn't meet them. You think a mere mortal like Sam

Windmiller will stand a chance against the hunks of the Silver Screen?"

"Not that it will matter anyway. What would a guy like Windy see in a pudgy *Chicana* like me? It's all your mother's fault, you know." Anita sighed.

Cassie angled her head toward her friend, smiling at her uncharacteristic display of insecurity. "Ah, you're right. Other than a beautiful heart-shaped face, smooth skin the color of a cafe latté, a voluptuous figure, and a wonderfully warm personality, I have no clue what a man would see in you!"

"Thanks, Cas, I was fishing for that. You were a little slow on the draw, though!"

Cassie heard the phone ringing as she unlocked the side door to the house. "Drat, where did I leave that thing," she complained as Anita grabbed the telephone from the counter and handed it to Cassie.

"Hello…Yes…Oh, Mr. Windmiller…Okay, Windy…" Cassie exchanged a glance with her friend, "This afternoon? Well, sure, if you have the time…2:00? Great! See you then."

"Two o'clock? Today?" Anita's face lit up with anticipation. Cassie had only had time to give the barn a cursory inspection, so after a hurried lunch, she and Anita walked back to the dilapidated structure.

"Do you think there's any hope for it?" Cassie asked, casting a skeptical eye about the interior. They climbed the two-by-fours nailed into one of the support braces forming a ladder to the haymow.

"Look at this cool antique bushel basket!"

"What's this old desk doing over here? Oh, jees, it's keeping someone from falling down that hole! Why would there be a square cut into the floor?" Cassie wondered aloud.

"To drop a bale of hay down to the stall underneath," came Sam Windmiller's voice from below.

Both Cassie and Anita peeked over the edge of the haymow to see Windy standing on the barn floor. "Don't come down, I'll come up."

In an instant he had joined the women exploring the mow. "This is a great old Lake Erie Shore barn," he commented looking around. "Check out those beams. See the grooves? The different levels of depth in the cuts show that they were hand hewn with a felling axe and a broad axe. Those babies are at least a foot square and forty feet in length. Imagine the tree they came from! Probably an oak that grew right around here."

"The roof's in great shape," he continued. "That's the most important thing. Someone's taken the time to re-shingle it in the past ten or fifteen years. The structure doesn't sag. Foundation could use a little shoring up. Oops, there's a crossbeam over yonder that needs replaced, but I have one we salvaged from an old barn in Paulding County that was falling down. Nosiree, I don't see why we couldn't get to work on this beauty in the next week or so."

"I can think of one really big reason." Cassie interjected. "Though I'm thrilled that you can save Aunt Nell's barn, we don't have any cash to put into it right now."

"Your aunt owns this place? Do you know if it's paid off? If you're serious about saving the barn you need to act reasonably quickly, or the corncrib and back lean-to will take the whole structure down with them. They'll twist it off the foundation, and once it's no longer square, it'll just be a matter of years." The touch of sadness in Windy's voice made it sound as though he would be losing an old friend. "Maybe, if your aunt's as keen on saving this barn as you are, she would consider taking out a home equity loan to cover the costs. I can give you a good deal on materials, and while not free, the labor would be inexpensive."

They spent the next hour checking all aspects of the barn. Cassie assured her newfound ally she would approach her aunt about the loan. Anita left for home, stars in her eyes, soon after Windy departed.

On Monday morning, Cassie received a call from the director of the branch library in town asking her to come in for an interview that afternoon. When Cassie walked into Evelyn Maples' small office behind the library's circulation desk, she immediately felt at ease. The room exuded a warmth that was reflected in the attractive, dark-haired woman who sat behind an aged wooden desk that was worn to a golden hue through years of use.

After the initial pleasantries, the director scanned Cassie's application. "I have to be honest, the job only pays minimum wage, and I am wondering why someone with your experience would want it?" she asked with candor.

Cassie hesitated only a moment before explaining the circumstances of the bankruptcy at O'Shay's. "I've applied for the few jobs related to finance that have become available, but it's my sense that, until my name is cleared of any embezzlement charges, no employer will take the chance on my being responsible for their books."

Evelyn Maples perched her elbows on her desk and brought her hands together pressing her fingertips against each other. She perused Cassie for a moment before replying, "I admire your honesty. I had, of course, heard about the trouble at O'Shay's and wondered if you were involved in that mess. Maybe others won't take a chance on you, but I would very much like you to work with our books."

Cassie hadn't realized she had been holding her breath until it came out in a whoosh. She barely listened as the librarian explained Cassie's schedule would be flexible, some evenings and Saturdays totaling around thirty hours per week. After over four months without work, Cassie reveled in the fact that someone would hire her for anything but flipping burgers.

She stopped by her mom's for a quick visit to share her news about her job before driving to the home to talk to Aunt Nell about the loan. Cassie had qualms about asking her aunt for the favor, as she knew Nell would give her the gown off her back if she needed it, and she didn't want to take advantage of her aunt's generosity. But repairing the barn would definitely enhance the property, and Windy had convinced them it would be much more cost efficient to fix it now rather than waiting even a year or two.

Cassie needn't have worried. Aunt Nell fairly jumped from her wheelchair with glee when Cassie explained their anticipated project to save the barn. She had already given Cassie power-of-attorney and directed her niece to start the paperwork for the home equity loan that afternoon.

By Friday, Cassie had completed the training for her new job. Though it was basically shelving and back-up staffing at the circulation desk, Cassie enjoyed interacting with the public and keeping the books in order. She borrowed a volume on the Library of Congress cataloging schedule to study over the weekend. She then stopped by the bank to sign the final papers for the loan. Windy had promised to be at the farm early Saturday morning to begin the task of removing the caved-in corncrib.

Cassie sat on the bottom step of the deck watching the sky envelop itself in muted shades of pinks and purples as the sun blazed a slash of gold across the horizon to the west, silhouetting massive grain elevators that stood sentinel beside the railroad tracks nearly a mile away. *Midwestern skyscrapers*, she marveled to herself, as she perused the flat, glaciated landscape.

Less than two hundred years ago, nearly all of Northwest Ohio had been covered in the Great Black Swamp, the remnants of a glacial lake from the last ice age. Though she had grown up in the area, she learned about its geography in an old videotape she had borrowed from the library. It described how farmers had drained the swamp and felled the huge oaks that grew there, eventually turning the impenetrable morass into some of the most fertile—and flattest—farmlands in the nation.

Cassie tried to envision the swampland as it might have been while she munched on fresh vegetables and a low-fat yogurt—not much of a dinner but, with the temperature in the 90's and the humidity even higher, she didn't have a desire to cook for herself.

Her mind wandered back to the present. It had been three weeks since she moved to the country, since the day Jaimé had exited her life for the second time. Much to her surprise and cha-grin, the pain was no less, even though this time his departure had been at her request. She submerged the gnawing ache back into the recesses of her heart, swallowing a spoonful of yogurt over the lump that had formed in her throat.

'Nita kept in contact with Jaimé's parents, who informed her that he had been called back to Canada for some last-minute ne-gotiations with the government, and against the both their wishes and those of his son, had taken Ben and Tina with him.

Cassie refused to give way to the hurt once again threaten-ing to surface. He could have at least stopped to say good-bye. Granted, she had told him she didn't want a relationship, but if he truly cared, wouldn't he have driven out to the farm before leaving for Ottawa? To add salt to her wounds, Melanie had brought her granddaughter into the library and gloated she had spent one of Jaimé's last evenings in town having dinner with him at his par-ents' home.

Cassie tamped down a surge of jealousy as she braced her elbows on her knees and rested her chin in the palms of her hands. She barely noticed as the setting sun reflected its glory on stri-ated clouds floating just above the cornfield, lining their jagged edges with neon orange. A soft brush against her legs startled her out of her melancholy, and she looked down to see a longhaired, butterscotch-colored cat rubbing her ankles.

"Hi, guy, where did you come from?" The feline looked up at Cassie with one good eye. Skin had grown over the other, disguis-ing some long-ago-healed wound. "Boy, fella, you sure have picked up a few burrs." Cassie finger-combed out what she could before the cat let her know he'd had enough with a gentle nip to her hand. He sniffed Cassie's empty raspberry yogurt container then gave her a look that clearly said, "Is this all you have?"

"Just a minute, fella, I know milk-fat isn't supposed to be good for you, but I'll get you a little skimmed. That should be okay." Cassie returned with a small bowl of milk and a saucer of shredded chicken she had scavenged off the top of a cold slice of pizza. The cat lapped the milk, nudged the chicken around on the plate before devouring it, then climbed up on his benefactor's lap. Cassie scratched the fur between his ears and he lifted his head into her hand. With her middle finger, she stroked his leathery nose, causing him to rev up the volume of his purr perceptibly. The sun finally ducked behind the curvature of the earth while Cassie and her new comrade watched in contented companionship.

Cassie woke early Saturday. Throwing caution to the wind, she had risked fleas and other nasty parasitic creatures by allowing her newfound friend to sleep at the foot of her bed. Given his unkempt condition and that her closest neighbors, Mack and Liz, lived on the old McAlister homestead over a half-mile away, she assumed the cat was a stray in search of a good home. "We have something in common there, little fella. I know Aunt Nell wouldn't mind my sharing her house with another stray."

Cassie was already sizing up the job ahead when Windy arrived in a truck hauling a large yellow machine with a scoop shovel mounted on the front and a long jointed metal arm ending in a bucket on the back. A dump truck pulled in after him and a husky-built man emerged from the driver's side carrying a Styrofoam cup of coffee.

"Don Johnston, I'd like you to meet Cassie Alexander." Windy introduced the man as "his good friend and mover of the heavy stuff—and," he added with a twinkle in his blue eyes, "no relation to the *Miami Vice* guy!"

"So, who's this slack-eyed joe that seems to have found a cream-puff to take him in?" Windy asked as he stooped to pet the cat tagging at Cassie's feet.

"Slack-Eyed Joe? That's a much better moniker for a rough and tumble guy like you than Butterscotch," Cassie said as she, too, bent to scratch what had quickly become a favorite place between the cat's ears. "I think the name's a keeper along with you." She scooped the cat up in her arms and nuzzled his face against hers.

Windy and Don set to work dismantling the tangle of siding and rusted tin roofing that had once been the corncrib. Anita arrived mid-morning with two bags of groceries for lunch.

"You're looking awfully dressed up for a Saturday morning," Cassie teased her friend as she helped her unload the food.

"I don't look too obvious, do I? I mean I don't want to look like I'm coming on to him or anything."

Cassie raised her eyebrows as though she couldn't believe what she was hearing, before assuring Anita she was a knock out no man in his right mind could resist. They walked out to the barn together. Windy stood up and leaned against a long board he had just pried loose from the rubble while watching the women approach. He flashed a dimpled grin at Anita confirming all of her primping had been worthwhile, before introducing her to his partner.

Don made several trips to the landfill with the dump truck throughout the afternoon, hauling away debris from the corncrib, while Windy manipulated the backhoe, shoving the remaining detritus into piles before loading it onto the truck.

"We should have both the corncrib and the rear lean-to framed out and ready for the siding next week. Are you sure you want to put up the boards yourself? It will be quite a job for one person." The look of skepticism Windy gave Cassie did nothing to bolster her confidence.

"If you start the first board and show me how it's done, I'm sure I can handle it. You guys are great, but there's so much to do around here I have to stretch out Aunt Nell's money to cover a lot of projects. Besides, you said yourself you're scheduled for a barn razing and salvage job next week. If I decide I absolutely can't do it, I'll let you know."

Windy shook his head as though he still didn't believe she was going to try to install the siding herself, but assured her he would order the boards and have them delivered by the time they finished framing the structures. He then drew Anita aside while Cassie and Don exchanged knowing smiles.

Anita could barely contain her excitement until both trucks pulled out of the driveway. "He asked me for a date. An actual go-ing-to-the-movies type date! It's not until next Saturday, though, so you're going to have to put up with my mood swings all week."

As the week progressed, Anita's temperament proved as volatile as she had promised. One day she was too fat; the next day, her hair was all wrong. She and Cassie poured through Anita's entire wardrobe for just the right outfit—not too informal, not too dressy. In the end, they spent an evening trooping through the mall with 'Nita trying on garments in a half-dozen different stores. She finally settled on a two-piece summer-weight red suit with a scalloped-edged, scoop-necked ivory shell underneath. They both declared it classy, yet casual. A simple wide-linked gold chain necklace and matching earrings completed the ensemble.

True to his word, Windy had the corncrib and back lean-to framed out and was waiting for Cassie when she arrived home from the library Friday afternoon.

"Okay, lesson one, have the right equipment. I took the liberty of buying you a sturdy stepladder and two good hammers—just in case your friend decides to help you out. "

"No such luck. 'Nita said she may have gotten me into this, but it's up to me to get out of it!"

Windy chuckled, "Some friend you have there!"

"Besides," Cassie said, "She has a hot date tomorrow night and can't risk chipping her nails."

Windy smiled his lopsided, dimpled grin and said nothing.

After nailing two boards into place, Cassie felt she had the hang of handling the hammer. The siding was heavy to lift, and she had to place each board on a cinder block to hold it at the right height to nail into the wall studs. Cassie began to seriously doubt she had the strength to do the job, but wouldn't admit defeat until she had at least tried.

"Thanks, Windy, wish me luck!"

"I'll stop by next week if I get a chance, to see how you're progressing. But don't hesitate to call if you want Don and me to put you on our schedule." And with a wave, he climbed into his truck and headed down the road.

"Well, Joey boy," she said as she nuzzled the fur on her tabby friend, "I guess it's another Friday night with just the two of us."

Cassie was up bright and early the next morning, determined to nail the siding on the corncrib. She secured the ladder in place, hefted an eight-foot section of siding from the pile Windy had had delivered from the lumberyard, and balanced it precariously on the cinder block. She managed to pound a nail in the top, just as Windy had shown her then climbed back down from the ladder to hold the board securely against the one next to it while hammering a nail in the bottom to keep the wood in place. She pounded two more nails on either side of the bottom nail and repeated the procedure at the top. The thought of climbing up and down the ladder twice for each board was daunting. She lifted another board and continued as before.

By ten o'clock in the morning, Cassie's shoulders ached and she rested on the pile of siding to survey her work. She had nailed seven boards into place. Though not perfect, she felt pride in her accomplishment. She shed her long-sleeved cambric shirt and massaged her forearms while watching Joey chase a butterfly near the pond. Rivulets of sweat trickled down her chest disappearing into cleavage barely covered by the too-small tank top she had picked up at the Goodwill store.

Cassie shifted a kerchief holding her hair from falling across her face, retied it at the nape of her neck, and picked up another board. She carefully sat the siding on the cinder block then began to reset her ladder. In her peripheral vision she saw the board shift and reflexively turned to catch it. Instead, her footing slipped and she fell with a thud to the ground. She barely had time to lift her arms to catch the board before it landed on top of her. As Cassie shoved the heavy board aside she noticed a pair of men's sneakers standing near her shoulders.

Her eyes followed the crease of new jeans upward past a crisp button-down lemon yellow shirt to see a dark pair of Foster-Grants looking down at her. The sun glinted off Jaimé's bronzed skin as he hovered over her. Cassie pulled her kerchief over her face and groaned. If only she could dig a hole and crawl in! A cool breeze skittering across her midriff diverted her attention to her tank, which had slipped up exposing her stomach. As she tugged it into place, Jaimé stooped down and lifted the scarf from her face.

"Are you okay?" he asked. Mirth vied with concern as he helped Cassie slowly ease herself to a sitting position.

"I think the only thing permanently injured is my pride." Cassie hunched her shoulders, entwined her fingers on her knees, and rested her forehead on her hands. In spite of herself, she had watched in vain for Jaimé every day for a month.

Why now, Lord, why now? She peeked up at Jaimé. Yep, he was still there—gorgeous, every hair in place, shirt freshly ironed. She ducked her head against her hands again.

"Ah, Cassandra, I realize this may not be the best time, but I've brought someone to meet you."

CHAPTER FOUR

Oh yeah, it could get worse, Cassie thought. Resigned to a fate of total embarrassment, she asked, "Could you please hand me that shirt over on the stack of boards?"

"Ah, *querida,* I prefer that wisp of material you are wearing now. But since my children are in the car waiting, I'd best do as you ask."

"Your children?" Cassie's head popped up—*much worse!*

Jaimé helped Cassie to her feet and touched his fingers to her chin tilting her face toward him. He rubbed a smudge from her cheek, "Don't worry, you look beautiful!"

"Now I know not to believe anything you say!"

While Cassie brushed off what dirt she could from her jeans, Jaimé retrieved his children from his sedan.

Cassie waited as Jaimé walked toward her, attempting to still her rapidly beating heart. His arm rested comfortably on the shoulder of a tall boy of eleven or twelve, a mirror image of his father. Jaimé's daughter hid behind him, poking her head around his waist for a furtive look at Cassie. They stopped a few feet from where she stood.

"Cas, I'd like you to meet my son Benjamin Alvarez. Ben, this is Cassandra Alexander." Cassie extended her right hand and

Ben returned her gesture with a firm handshake.

Jaimé pried his daughter from behind him and draped his arms around her shoulders pulling her back against him.

"And, this is Christina. I'm not sure why Tina's putting on the shy act today."

"Hi Tina." The child's round face, nearly black eyes, and tawny skin spoke of a native heritage. She appeared to be seven or eight years old, younger than what Cassie had thought. "You must favor your mother," Cassie said with a smile.

"My mother's dead and I don't want another one. Me, papa, and Ben do just fine. We don't need anyone else." The girl's sharp eyes skewered Cassie, warning her not to disrupt their lives.

"*Kreees-tina!*" A Latino inflection sharpened her father's reprimand, causing Tina to avert her eyes and stick out her lower lip.

"That's okay, Tina. Your dad and I are friends—nothing more. No one can replace your mom, and I have no intention of trying." Though Cassie looked at Tina as she spoke, her words were also intended for the child's father.

With a cautionary glance at his daughter, Jaimé turned to Ben, "What do you say, son. Think we could help this lady out?"

Ben was still of the age that an invitation to use a hammer with his dad rated above even the best video game. His eyes lit up, but he tried to be nonchalant as he said, "Sure, dad. We might as well give it a go."

"Jaimé, you're not dressed for this sort of work! You don't need to help, really!" Cassie protested.

Ben looked from his father to Cassie then back to his father again. Not willing to trust the decision to either of the adults, he dropped his guise of indifference, "Please, papa, can we? I promise not to get too dirty!"

"How can I say 'no' to such an eager plea, Cassandra? Looks like you're stuck with our help whether you need it or not!" Jaimé smiled as he picked up a hammer from on top of the stack of siding.

After asking Cassie to show to his son the best technique for nailing the siding boards to the support studs, Jaimé allowed the boy to climb the ladder while he stooped down to nail the bottom of the board into place. Cassie gave her aching shoulders a rest, holding the board being nailed snug against the one beside it until Jaimé and Ben fastened it securely in place.

Tina hung close to Jaimé sending scowls Cassie's way whenever she thought her father wasn't looking. After a while, Cassie made a point of checking her watch. "Gosh, it's almost noon. Think I'll make us a picnic lunch. I sure could use some help!"

Tina looked from Cassie to her father. Cassie felt a little guilty at the dilemma she had caused for the girl. Going with Cassie could be an adventure, but the child obviously did not want to betray the memory of her mother—or chance allowing this stranger to wedge her way into their lives.

"I don't have anything fancy—just cold meat sandwiches, fruit and maybe some chips." Cassie hesitated waiting for Tina to make up her mind.

"That sounds great, Mrs. Alex...er...Cassie," Ben chimed in. Cassie had bonded with Jaimé's son early on, and urged him to call her by her given name.

Slack-eyed Joe chose that moment to emerge from the tall grass edging the pond. He paused halfway to the barn when he saw all the commotion. He looked quizzically at Cassie with his one good eye, then proceeded over to Tina and rubbed against her legs.

"Joey, you traitor, picking a cute young girl over me. And I've spent the past two weeks feeding you! Isn't that just like a fickle male." Cassie crossed her arms against her chest and feigned indignation, bringing a hint of a smile to Tina's face.

"You may as well pick him up, because he won't let you alone unless you do."

"What's his name?" the child asked as she held the tabby tightly.

"A friend named him Slack-Eyed Joe because of his bad eye. I call him Joey."

The cat squirmed free of the girl's grip and raced toward the house. He stopped when he reached the deck and looked back toward the barn as if to cajole them to hurry. "Looks like our Joey is hungry for a bite of lunch, too!" Cassie said.

With a backward glance at Tina, Cassie started walking in the direction of the house. After a moment, she noticed the girl's shadow several steps behind her.

She slowed her pace allowing the child to come closer. They entered the house through the side door leading directly into the kitchen. After filling Joe's bowl with fish-shaped kibbles, Cassie grabbed a loaf of wholegrain bread from the breadbox and a bag of thin-sliced roasted turkey, a head of lettuce, and bottles of catsup and mustard from the refrigerator.

"Tina, would you mind starting the sandwiches while I clean up a little bit? You can wash your hands at the kitchen sink."

"My papa doesn't like bread with seeds in it," the girl declared.

"Those are just sesame seeds sprinkled on the top. Your father can pick them off if he wants to," Cassie replied patiently as she headed to the bathroom.

When Cassie emerged in clean clothes and freshly applied make-up, Tina had made three sandwiches and lined them up on the counter. Cassie complimented her on her work while slipping two more slices of bread from the bag and placing lunch-meat between them. She fit the sandwiches into plastic containers then washed four peaches from the fruit bowl. Rummaging in the walk-in pantry, she pulled out a picnic-basket-sized box with handles cut into the sides. She took a bag of potato chips from an upper shelf and put it into the makeshift basket.

"You need plates and silverware," Jaimé's daughter instructed.

"You're right, and napkins, too." Cassie placed the assembled picnic items in the box, along with four cans of cold soda pop.

"What are we going to sit on?"

"Sit on? I'm a little rusty at this picnic stuff. I guess we do need a blanket or something." Cassie soon returned with an old bedsheet and placed it on top of the items in the box.

"Gosh, this is pretty heavy. You wouldn't want to help me, would you?"

Tina let out a sigh of obvious exasperation, "You're just trying to trick me into liking you, but it's not going to work. I'll help you but I'm not going to like you, *not ever.*"

It was Cassie's turn to sigh, but she was determined not to give in to the child's petulance. Calling a silent truce, they carried the box out to where Jaimé and Ben had just finished nailing up another board.

"Great! I'm about starved. How about you, Ben?" Ben had already peeked under the sheet to check out the goodies below.

Jaimé gave Cassie an appreciative double take—she had changed into a hot-pink gauzy blouse with beige Bermuda shorts, and taken time to twist her hair into a knot at the nape of her neck, tied with a pink and green flowered scarf.

"Just a second," Jaimé jogged over to his car and grabbed a bag from the back seat. "A little something for dessert," he said as he placed the sack on top of the sheet.

"Why don't we see if we can carry that box the rest of the way, Ben. Cassie can lead the way to her favorite picnic spot."

"You know, I can't remember the last time I was on a picnic. Maybe high school?" Cassie mused. "However, there's a great place down by the stream."

They walked past the pond, startling bullfrogs that jumped with a "redeep" into the water, and through the small woodlot that bordered the stream separating Aunt Nell's property from the McAlister's fields. A massive oak hugged the bank, shading a large circle with its branches. Cassie instructed Jaimé and Ben to place the box by the trunk of the tree. They smoothed the sheet beneath the spreading limbs, and Cassie asked Tina to help her pass out the food.

They sat cross-legged, enjoying their sandwiches while listening to the birds twitter as they flew from tree to tree. "Hear that rat-a-tat? There must be a woodpecker nearby," Jaimé noted.

"Can we wade in the water, papa, please?" Ben pleaded, wiping the last of the potato chip crumbs from his face. "We'll eat our peach later, promise!"

"Sure, why not? Just don't get too wet!"

With the children distracted, Cassie and Jaimé ate their fruit in silence. Jaimé watched the juice from the succulent peach trickle down Cassie's chin before she caught it with a napkin. He pitched his seed into the woods, while Cassie nibbled at what remained of her fruit. He edged closer to her, until they sat hip-to-hip, facing each other.

As she licked the remnants of the peach from her lips, Jaimé took the pit and tossed it to the grass along the edge of the sheet. Bracing his right arm beside Cassie's left leg, he leaned in close to her, with only the slight summer breeze separating them.

Desire clouded his eyes as he searched hers for a sign of resistance. Instead, she closed the gap between them. Their lips met in a tentative reacquainting, each tasting the sweet, sticky residue of fruit juice on the other. Her breath fired his as their kiss evolved into a scorching heat fueled by long-deprived desires. They pulled back slightly with their foreheads still touching.

"My sweet Lord, Cassandra, I need you so much," his words came in ragged gasps.

"I know, I know. I've tried so hard not to want you," she trembled as her heart tried to keep pace with her breathing.

"Papaaa!" They broke apart abruptly looking in the direction of the stream where Tina stood watching them, arms akimbo. She splashed to the bank and tromped up to the blanket, announcing her disapproval of their kiss with each step.

"Ah, guess this is as good a time as any for dessert," Jaimé suggested, casting a look of resignation toward the woman at his side. He pulled a box of chocolate-iced doughnuts from the bag he had retrieved from the car and handed one to Tina. "Go get your brother and ask if he would like a doughnut, too."

Tina eyed him suspiciously then glared at Cassie. "Go on, scoot, or I'll put that doughnut right back where it came from." Jaimé was betting on his daughter's love of chocolate to buy him another minute or two of privacy with Cassie. Tina cast them a reproachful look as she slowly walked back to the stream, calling loudly for her brother.

"Now where were we," Jaimé said softly as he sidled back over to Cassie.

She placed two fingers on his lips and sighed, "No, Jaimé, Tina's right. She needs you. What we feel is just leftover lust from long ago. We can't let it interfere with your relationship with your children."

"Damnation, Cassandra, you know there's something between us that needs to be settled, whether it's a simple case of 'leftover lust,' as you call it, or...more."

By the time Tina returned with Ben in tow, Cassie had the picnic remnants gathered up and Jaimé was shaking leaves off the sheet and folding it.

As the afternoon wore on, Cassie replaced Ben on the ladder driving nails into the top of each board.

"Cassie, look what we found!" Ben scurried up in a fast walk from the beach area of the pond. Cassie stepped down from the ladder just as he approached the barn. She peeked into his cupped hands to see a small polliwog flopping about. "What is it?" Ben asked.

"It's called a tadpole or a polliwog, a baby bullfrog," Cassie explained. "When I was a child, I would scoop out pools in the mud along the edge of the pond to keep tadpoles in. You better get this little guy back in the water, though, before he dries out."

Tina inspected the polliwog with skepticism, "If that's a baby frog, where's his legs?"

Cassie cocked her head toward Jaimé, "What sort of environmentalist father hasn't taught his children the life cycle of a frog?"

"We were getting to that, we just hadn't made it there yet," Jaimé laughed as he put his board down and walked over to where Cassie stood huddled with his children over the hapless tadpole.

"Let's get this fellow back in the pond and we can talk about how he trades his tail in for legs." Jaimé looked at his Rolex, "In fact, it's getting pretty late and your *abuelo y abuela* will be waiting for us." He turned to Cassie, "My parents are expecting us for dinner. Why don't you join us?"

"I couldn't impose on your family, Jaimé."

"That just goes to show how little you know about Latinos—food is always plentiful and guests, always welcome. My folks would be insulted if they thought you stayed away because you didn't want to impose!"

"But I'm a mess!"

"No more excuses. Two more boards will finish the corncrib, then we can all clean up for dinner."

After a quick shower, Cassie donned a pale green sundress with a square neckline and full skirt. She slipped on a pair of white sandals and lamented the loss of her diamond and emerald necklace and earring set, as she inserted cheap green rhinestone studs in her ears.

The children had each taken a turn in the bathroom, washing up to the best of their abilities. Jaimé opted to wait and shower at his parents' home, where he had a fresh change of clothing. He did take advantage of the few extra minutes while his children and Cassie were occupied to call ahead and notify his mother that he would be bringing a dinner guest, much to her delight.

The drive to Jaimé's parents' home was filled with a discussion of frogs, toads, and other creatures the children had encountered that afternoon. Cassie nervously folded and unfolded her hands in her lap as she listened to Tina and Ben's chatter and their father's patient explanations of pond life. She had known Jaimé's parents tangentially since her childhood, as they had all attended the same church, but though they had spoken in passing, she had never met them as the guest of their son. Soon after Jaimé left for the Marines, they had moved to Bowling Green to be nearer to the University where Dr. Alvarez taught and from which he had since retired.

Jaimé pulled up in front of a newly constructed condominium in the ironically-named subdivision of Cedar Hills. Much like the gated community from which Cassie had recently moved, the only cedars in the area had long ago been sacrificed to cornfields and the hills were perfectly-formed manmade mounds.

Ben and Tina jumped from the car and raced up the sidewalk to tell their grandparents about the frogs, while Jaimé walked around the front of the sedan to open Cassie's door. Sensing her unease, he smiled his assurance, "Don't worry, *querida*, you'll do just fine." Better than fine, Jaimé thought as Cassie stood, smoothing non-existent wrinkles from the skirt of her sundress.

A tall, slender, balding man waited at the door and was joined by a petite woman in an apron by the time Jaimé and Cassie approached the stoop. "*Señora Alexander, ¿Como estás?*" Jaimé's mother greeted Cassie warmly. Cassie searched her limited recollection of her high school Spanish classes for the correct response, "*Estoy bien, gracias.*"

"Come in, come in," Jaimé's father stepped aside so that they could enter the house. Despite the bland exterior of the condominium, the bold colors within reflected the richness of the Mexican culture of Jaimé's mother. A brilliant blue paint trimmed with an equally daring green adorned the foyer. The border continued into the living room, where a woven tapestry of bright reds and yellows hung on pale adobe walls above a dark brown leather davenport. Matching overstuffed chairs flanked the fireplace opposite the couch. Arched walnut bookcases lined the far wall, while a large portrait of Our Lady of Fatima dominated the near one.

"Mom, Dad, you remember Cassandra Alexander, don't you?" Jaimé asked. "Cassandra, I'd like to introduce you to my parents, Juanita and Gregorio Alvarez."

"I do hope I am not intruding," Cassie began, but Juanita Alvarez raised her hand and shook her head, "*No, no. Se lo hago con mucho gusto!*"

Jaimé wrapped an arm lovingly around his mother's waist. She seemed engulfed by his large frame as he smiled down at her. "Mother said 'It is our pleasure.' She's been in this country nearly sixty years, and still prefers to speak Spanish. However, don't let her fool you, she comprehends *Inglés* very well, right *madré?*"

The twinkle in her eye confirmed her son's statement, and Cassie made a mental note to heed his warning.

Mrs. Alvarez excused herself to finish dinner preparations, refusing Cassie's offer of assistance by suggesting that she join the men in the living room instead. The aromas of cumin and pepper sauces emanating from the kitchen reminded Cassie that their picnic had been several hours and many barn-siding boards ago.

"I need to catch a quick shower if you don't want me to compete with the smells of mother's cooking," Jaimé said as he opened a door that evidently led to steps to the upstairs bedrooms.

Cassie listened to his footsteps as Jaimé crossed the floor above. A picture of him undressing and stepping into a steamy shower slipped unbidden into her mind, and she shook her head slightly to free herself of the image. She glanced up to see Dr. Alvarez looking at her quizzically. She closed her eyes, silently praying that he couldn't read her thoughts.

"So, Cassandra," Jaimé's father spoke her name with the same soft lilt as did his son. "Jaimé said that you have moved out to your aunt's farm? Such a delightful lady, your Aunt Nell. I heard she had moved to Pleasant Valley after her stroke. How is she?"

Relief flooded over Cassie, as she mentally thanked Aunt Nell for once again coming to her rescue. "I wish I could say that she is fine, but she's holding her own against the ravages brought on by her stroke. Her doctors say that as long as her mobility continues to improve, there is still hope for a near-full recovery. I would like to be able to move her back to the farm once I get settled and she's completed her physical therapy regime."

Gregorio Alvarez nodded slightly as though assessing her answer. In truth, he found Cassandra Alexander to be much better company than the twitterhead that showed up at their door a few weeks ago looking for his son and ended up inviting herself to dinner.

Cassie asked Dr. Alvarez how long he had known her family, which led to his revelation that he had emigrated from the island country of Aruba to the states for graduate school, and met both his wife and Cassie's parents and Aunt Nell soon after taking a teaching position at the University.

"So very long ago. And here I am, retired with grandchildren, and content to live in the cold and wintry Midwest for the rest of my days," he chuckled and shook his head. "Though, at times, my old bones do miss those tropical breezes!"

They were in the midst of an involved discussion about Cassie's new job, the function of the public library versus the University library, and the effect of digitization on each, when Jaimé returned to the living room, his wet jet-black hair slicked back. The slight yet sophisticated crest of silver at his temples arrested Cassie's attention, and she missed Dr. Alvarez's last comment until he said, "Don't you think so, Cassandra?"

"I…um…" Cassie stammered searching for a credible response to a question that had completely flown by her. This time Juanita Alvarez was her savior with the announcement that dinner was ready.

The children ran in from the back veranda, skidding to a halt when they reached the arched entrance to the dining room. Eyeing the adults as though waiting for a reprimand, they walked with exaggerated politeness to the table.

"*Bueno, mijos, sientesé,*" their grandmother complimented them, then directed them to sit down.

When they were all settled in their places, Jaimé's father said grace. His mother then passed a tureen filled with spicy chorizo sausage soaking in a tangy tomato sauce with sliced onions, bell peppers, and zucchini squash, followed by a bowl of Spanish rice.

Cassie inhaled the fragrant aromas as she ladled a small helping onto her plate.

"*Más, más,*" Mrs. Alvarez encouraged her to take more.

"You may as well give in, Cassandra. You wouldn't want to insult my mother," Jaimé cautioned.

Setting aside manners that had been drilled into her throughout her life dictating that a lady only took small portions at a formal table setting, Cassie readily spooned another ladle of the luscious chorizo mixture onto her plate. The marvelous smells had her mouth watering in anticipation.

"Ah, Cassandra, *Yo…I…mees* seeing *su madré a San Jude's.*" Mrs. Alvarez began.

"You miss Mrs. Mikhailov's chocolate cakes at the bazaar." Dr. Alvarez teased his wife. Then, to Cassie he commented, "We enjoyed your mother's company when we attended St. Jude's. But, since moving to Bowling Green, we've joined the parish here."

"Unfortunately, mother seldom attends church anymore. After we lost my father, she seemed to lose interest," Cassie commented.

"Such a tragedy." Gregorio Alvarez shook his head. At Jaimé's questioning look, his father went on, "Cassandra's father fell while working at O'Shay's. They never determined for certain what happened, did they?"

Cassie took a deep breath and released it slowly before answering, "He had worked maintenance for O'Shay's since before I was born. He patrolled the catwalks once a day, every day, checking the machines to ensure that they were working properly. The official report simply says that he tripped and fell," Cassie hesitated before finishing her tale, "though Sheriff Crenshaw implied that he believed my father jumped to his death. Billy Joe only gave the accident site a cursory once-over before writing his report. Too afraid he would find something that would lay the blame on Paul and O'Shay's, I assume." Cassie barely contained the edge in her voice. Though she had never been close to her father, and even less so after her marriage to Paul, Billy Joe Crenshaw's dismissal of his death was a canker that festered just below the surface of her skin. She hadn't spoken of it to anyone in years and, looking around the table, instantly wished she had tempered her remarks.

"Please excuse me for going on so, I don't know what came over me!"

With a sympathetic smile, Mrs. Alvarez patted Cassie's hand reassuringly before censuring her husband, "Gregorio, *la comida no es el tiempo para esté.*"

"You are right, I am upsetting our guest. Dinner is not a time to discuss such terrible events."

Jaimé observed the interchange in silence, trying to recall what he had heard about the death of Cassie's father. It happened within months of Paul's taking over O'Shay's—within months of the death of Paul's own parents. Though curious to find out more about both accidents, in deference to Cassie and his mother, Jaimé chose to let the subject drop until after dinner.

They took their coffee to the more comfortable chairs in the living room. Tina insinuated herself between her father and Cassie on the couch, giving Cassie a smug look of defiance. Ben disappeared up the stairs, holding a small video game player, while his grandparents settled into easy chairs near the fireplace.

Jaimé took a sip of steaming black liquid before turning toward his father, "Do I recollect you telling me that Mr. & Mrs. Alexander were killed in a car accident?"

"Yes, as I recall, it happened in February, five or six months before Cassandra's father fell."

He nodded in Cassie's direction, and she picked up the story, "The brakes gave way in their Mercedes. Paul and I had dinner with them the night before. Charlie had mentioned that the brakes were sticking and that he needed to take the car into the shop the next day. Phoebe, Paul's mother, wasn't supposed to be with him. All we could conjecture is that she must have asked him to drop her off somewhere on the way to the service station."

Cassie drew in a breath, looking past the others, and focused on a large aloe vera plant in the corner of the room. "An early morning ice storm had left the roads fairly treacherous, and as they approached the highway the Mercedes skidded through the stop sign and under the bed of an eighteen-wheeler. The top of the car was sheered off. Both of Paul's parents were killed instantly." She dropped her gaze to her hands, folded in her lap.

Jaimé's mother spoke softly in Spanish to her husband, who then translated for Cassie. "My wife expresses her sympathy for all of your losses that very sad year."

Cassie nodded. She looked at Jaimé, then at his parents. "Oddly enough, the hardest death for me to handle was Uncle Clem's heart attack." After a moment she added, "Maybe because it was the last."

"Uncle Clem?" Jaimé questioned.

"Clement Jones. He was Aunt Nell's handyman and companion. I used to be his tag-a-long on the farm. He was the one who spent time teaching me about tools and animals and even how to drive a tractor."

Jaimé nodded, and not wanting to cause Cassie further stress, seized the opportunity to veer the subject away from that fateful year, "He must have done a great job, because this lady can definitely handle a hammer." Jaimé proceeded to tell his parents about the events of the day.

Tina scooted closer to her father, while glaring at Cassie, no doubt thinking about the kiss she had interrupted earlier in the day. Cassie prayed the child would not see fit to inform her grandparents of the indiscretion she had witnessed and was rewarded by Tina clamping her lips together while possessively wrapping her arms around her father's bicep.

A bit later Jaimé rose, saying that he needed to get Cassie home—they still had a lean-to to side tomorrow.

"Jaimé, I'm the one who undertook this job. There's no need for you to give up Sunday with your family to help me," Cassie protested.

"*Por favor*, no worry," Jaimé's mother interceded.

"We have already promised to take the children shopping tomorrow," Gregorio Alvarez explained.

"And I'd do anything to escape an afternoon in the mall—even spend the day nailing on barn siding!" Jaimé added with a conspiratorial smile.

Cassie felt a little hoodwinked, but even she had to admit that she needed help with the barn. It was spending an entire day alone with Jaimé that concerned her.

"I'll ride with you when you take Mrs. Alexander out to her house, papa. That way you won't have to drive home alone." Tina offered with a sly look back at Cassie as they walked to the foyer.

""No, *mija*, it is time for you to get ready for bed. We have a big day ahead of us tomorrow." Her grandfather took Tina's hand, staying any further objections the child might have had.

After thanking Juanita Alvarez again for the delicious meal, Cassie allowed Jaimé to escort her to his car.

Silence fell between them as Jaimé backed his sedan out of his parents' driveway and maneuvered the side roads to Bowling Green's Main Street. Silence followed them as they navigated their way out of town. The silence stretched out and threatened to snap as the waning light of the summer evening faded into the horizon.

Finally, Jaimé flipped on the radio. The piercing voice of a classic rock jock cut through the air before he punched another button. The last bars of a country ballad played out as he switched to another channel. A cello solo led into a full string orchestral piece, and Jaimé let the music ease the strain of the silence into a more relaxing quietude.

Cassie spoke first, "I enjoyed meeting your family today, Jaimé. But..."

"No 'buts'" he interrupted. "Not tonight, princess. Let's just accept today for the gift that it was and see where tomorrow takes us."

"Jaimé, you know as well as I that there can't be anything after tomorrow." She inclined her head toward the night sky, fidgeting with an earring as she continued, "Your life is with your children in Canada. Even if I wanted to, I couldn't leave mom or Aunt Nell. And I don't want to.

"For nearly half a century my life has been ruled by others— first by my father and then by Paul. I need to prove, if only to myself, that I can survive on my own. Besides..." Cassie thought about Paul's phone call alluding to her possible incarceration, but evaded mentioning it, "...I just started my job at the library and am committed to restoring Aunt Nell's farm so that she can live out her life there and not at Pleasant Valley."

Wagner's "Ride of the Valkyries" blasted from the radio, and Jaimé flipped the knob to "off." Knowing any assurance he gave her would ring hollow, he let silence again settle over them like an enveloping fog.

As soon as Jaimé parked the car in Cassie's driveway, she opened her door and jumped out. Jaimé caught up with her as she hurried to the house.

"Cassandra…"

She stopped but did not turn toward him. A galaxy of stars dotted the black sky above. The chill of the evening sent a shiver through her body. She felt the heat of Jaimé's hands shoot through her as he drew her back against his warmth. He bent his head and gently kissed the top of hers.

"Ah, *querida*, what are we going to do? You are, of course, right. Tina needs to be in Canada among people who at least in some way resemble her. I won't have her growing up as the outcast like I did. And you need to be here with your family."

His acquiescence was a hollow victory for Cassie. She felt an ache growing in the center of her being. How could she endure losing him again? Yet she couldn't allow him to entangle himself further in her problems.

"I'll be back tomorrow," he whispered into her hair.

She knew she should protest. Demand that he stay away. Yet she didn't have the strength to refuse him this one last time. She reasoned that she couldn't finish the siding without his help, and that she wouldn't be keeping him from his family. In the end, she gave a slight nod of her head before pulling from his grasp and running into the shelter of her aunt's home.

Cassie dressed carefully in the morning, trying to find an outfit that would be suitable for the work ahead, yet flattering. She told herself that she just wanted to look nice for a friend. She settled on a sleeveless white eyelet blouse and a pair of khaki slacks. She coiled her hair at the nape of her neck, applied a modest touch of make-up, and waited.

At 11:00, she and Joey surveyed yesterday's efforts with satisfaction; at 11:30 she walked back to the house to check the answering machine; at noon, she nibbled at a light lunch; at 12:30 fear began to creep into her belly that perhaps Jaimé had reconsidered his offer; at 1:00, she'd given up and began tidying the house, her disappointment too keen for her to muster any enthusiasm for tackling the lean-to by herself.

The crunch of tires against the gravel of her driveway caused her to drop her dust cloth in the midst of polishing a coffee table she had found at a garage sale. She tried not to appear too anxious as she scurried to the door.

The sight of Billy Joe Crenshaw emerging from his sleek black Corvette convertible stopped Cassie in her tracks. Quickly regaining her composure, she hastened down the walk, unwilling to wait for the sheriff to approach her.

"Cassie, darlin', what cha doin' movin' way out here in the Boonies?" Billy Joe exaggerated his Kentucky drawl as he leaned against the door of his sports car. His slight build and thinning hair gave him a resemblance to Mayberry's bumbling Barney Fife, but Cassie knew better than to underestimate the calculated malevolence that lay just below his veneer of civility.

The appearance of another car in the drive deflected any retort with which Cassie may have responded. Jaimé eased out of his dark sedan, hesitating a moment before recognizing another nemesis from his school days.

"Well, well, Jimmy Boy. Fancy meeting you way out here! Heard you were in town a spell back, but thought you had split by now."

Jaimé quelled the urge to knock Billy Joe Crenshaw's cocky chip off his scrawny shoulder; instead he turned to Cassie. "This yahoo bothering you, Cassandra?"

"Watch what your saying, Jimbo, I wear the badge around here."

"Then seems to me you should be off chasing the *bandidos*

rather than harassing a law-abiding citizen." Jaimé stepped closer to the sheriff, so that he was able to look down on the man where he slouched against his car.

Billy Joe Crenshaw pulled himself to his full height, but was still a head shorter than Jaimé. He looked as though he were going to say something else, however had reconsidered. Instead, he opened the door to his convertible and slithered onto the seat. Looking past Jaimé, he addressed Cassie, "You should really pick your company a little better, sweetheart. I'll be back when the macho *Mejícano* isn't so intent on flexin' his muscles."

Jaimé took a step back as the sheriff revved his motor and peeled around the curve of the U-shaped driveway.

"Some lawman he is. Didn't even buckle up his seatbelt," Cassie scoffed as she took a deep breath, trying to steady her jangled nerves.

"What do you suppose he wanted?" Jaimé mused.

Remembering what Paul had said, Cassie hedged, "Probably just as you said. He was bored and wanted to do a little harmless harassing. Who better to pick on than his best drinking buddy's ex-wife?"

"So Paul and Billy Joe are still thick as thieves, eh? How long has that wuss been sheriff, anyway?"

"Yep and way too long," Cassie replied to both questions before quickly switching the subject, "I thought maybe you had changed your mind and opted for shopping over manual labor."

"Shopping for school clothes with those kids *is* manual labor. I gave the folks free reign over my charge cards as well as my undying gratitude for undertaking the task," he quipped, then explained his late arrival. "Mom likes it if I go to Mass with the family when I'm home. She's afraid I've neglected the children's Catholic upbringing, and it's especially obvious on Sunday mornings that she's right. So, I had to listen to her lecture me through brunch at a breakfast buffet, which has left me with a lot of aggression and a few extra pounds to work off on that barn back there." The crinkle around his eyes and hint of a smile undercut the seriousness of any altercation he may have had with his mother.

They gathered the hammers and nails from the barn and moved the stepladder to the back lean-to. Cassie helped Jaimé restack a dozen boards from around the corner of the barn to their current worksite. She climbed the ladder to nail the top of the first board, while he held it securely in place. Jaimé casually watched Cassie step from one rung to the next.

"Mmm, nice," he commented as the stretch of the khaki clung to her derrière, earning him a glare from the top of the ladder. "Didn't anyone tell you that it's not protocol to iron your slacks before working on a barn?" he jibed flashing her a killer grin as he pretended to examine the crease in her pants.

Cassie turned her head away so he couldn't see the blush she felt rushing through her. *Drat him, how was she supposed to pound nails with Jaimé looking at her bottom end. It'd serve him right if she dropped her hammer on his hard head.* Instead, she grabbed the rubberized handle covering the metal shaft of the tool and whacked the first nail with, perhaps, a little more gusto than was necessary.

They moved in like fashion from board to board. Jaimé would toss an occasional tease Cassie's way and she served one back to him in kind. Their repartee made the time pass quickly, and they were nearly halfway done when Jaimé suggested they take a break.

"Whew, I thought you'd never stop," Cassie laughed as she perched at the top of the ladder. Jaimé steadied the base as she turned to step down the rungs. Once again the sway of her derrière diverted his attention. As a way to keep his hands occupied, he loosely placed one on either side of her waist ostensibly to assist her as she stepped to the ground.

She turned when she touched down and found herself trapped between his arms. He lifted his hand to brush a stray strand of hair from her face and she rested her cheek lightly against his open palm. He gently massaged her shoulders while nudging her closer to him. The ache between her shoulder blades drifted lower and she surrendered herself to his touch. She lifted her face and met his lips with a thirst that could only be quenched by one man.

Her breath came in labored sighs as he eased her blouse from the waistband of her slacks. She thought about stopping him. Knew she should stop him. Knew she was powerless to stop him. One by one he released the buttons of the cotton top until it fell loose around her forearms. His kisses strayed down her cheek to her enchantingly lovely long neck—the graceful neck of a princess—his porcelain princess. He caressed his way to the sensitive spot at the well of her collarbone before once again seeking her lips.

His hands wandered across her exposed midriff, then gently teased the rise of her breasts where they edged the lace of her brassiere. He reached around her back and with one deft stroke released the clasp on the stretch of satin. He bared her breasts to the sunlight, while carefully backing her up against the newly installed siding of the barn. He looked into the green and gold-flecks of her tigress eyes and read only desire. She arched against him as he lowered his head.

"Cas! Cassie where are you?" Fear quickly supplanted desire as Cassie tugged her blouse together. In her rush to reassemble her clothing she didn't know whether to curse or thank her best friend. She had just tucked her shirt back into her waistband when Anita rounded corner of the barn. She stopped abruptly looking first at Cassie, then to Jaimé.

"Whoa, didn't mean to interrupt anything," she said taking a step backwards.

"It's okay, 'Nita, you didn't interrupt anything that should've been happening." Cassie said as she tried to bring her heart back to a steady cadence. Jaimé raised his eyebrows in her direction and opted to remain silent.

"I, ah, was just stopping by to see if you wanted to go out for pizza later on or if I should bring one by. I called, but I guess you were, um, occupied…."

Cassie had collected her wits enough to answer, "Yeah, climbing up and down this ladder. I can't wait until Windy stops by to see our progress. Oh, that's right—speaking of the man, how was last night?"

Anita gave her friend a dreamy look and just smiled.

"Ooh, this looks good. We'll talk over pizza tonight, but I'm going to be too beat to drive anywhere and they don't deliver this far out. Would you mind terribly…?"

"Already got it covered. I'll be back in a few hours. You two can get back to, ah, whatever it was you were doing." With a wink toward Jaimé she disappeared around the side of the recently constructed corncrib.

Jaimé leaned against the barn with his arms crossed. "I suppose it would be asking too much to pick up where we left off?" he queried with one eyebrow cocked at Cassie.

In response, Cassie hefted another length of siding from the pile they had assembled.

"I thought so," Jaimé sighed in resignation as he moved to help her.

They labored in quiet synchronization for the next few hours, keeping a steady rhythm in their work. They were careful to avoid physical contact unless necessary. Those few times when their fingers brushed as they lifted a board or they accidentally bumped into one another, a searing heat would paralyze them for an instant.

The sun had dipped low in the west when they nailed the final board into place. Cassie's arms ached as never before and her calves complained with each step she took. As they stashed the ladder, hammer and nails in the barn, Cassie admitted, "I don't know how I can repay you, Jaimé."

To his hooded glance and half-grin she replied with a smile of her own, "Okay, anything but that…. However, if you would like to join 'Nita and me for pizza, I'm sure she'll bring enough—it's a Pisanello's special."

"Nah, you two have girl-talking to do. Unless I miss my guess, 'Nita's going to be bending your ear about this Windy character. Oh, and when you see him next week, tell him he frames out a damn good barn." Jaimé rubbed a smear of dirt from her cheek then bent to place a tender kiss on her lips. Using all of the willpower he could muster, he backed toward his sedan, unwilling to take his eyes off of Cassie as she stood immobile in the middle of the driveway. Slack-eyed Joe rubbed her ankles and she stooped to pick up the cat, holding him close to keep her from running to Jaimé. He hesitated as he opened the car door, gave her one last searching look then disappeared into its dark interior.

By the time 'Nita returned with the pizza, Cassie had showered, dressed in a pair of old sweats, and was uncorking a bottle of inexpensive merlot.

"Hot pizza, sweats, and cheap wine—comfort food, comfort clothes, and comfort nectar. What more could a girl want?" 'Nita asked as she placed the brown corrugated pizza box on the kitchen counter. *Jaimé!* Cassie's response was immediate and unbidden. The thought was so intense Cassie wondered if she had spoken aloud, but Anita had already begun a monologue about her date with Windy.

CHAPTER FIVE

august

Cassie loved her job at the library. She had become especially fond of shelving books in the children's section, stopping a few minutes here and there to help a youth find what she or he needed. On the Thursday after Cassie and Jaimé had worked on the barn, she stooped down beside an ambitious five-year-old grappling with a large volume of Disney stories.

"That's a pretty big book, Rosalita, may I help you carry it to your table?"

The petite dark-eyed girl nodded as she handed the book to Cassie.

"Would you read a story to me, *Señora Alesander, por favor?*"

With an inherent sense of loss, Cassie hugged the book against her breast—she had never before been asked to read to a child. As she and Paul had no siblings, her life had been devoid of nieces or nephews—which was just as well. Watching other children grow up after her baby had been ripped from her womb would have been unbearable. She studied the small face before her.

Would her little one have resembled this Latina child or would it have inherited her own fair skin? She closed her eyes to will her thoughts in another direction. When she opened them again, Rosalita was giving her a wary look.

"Are you okay, *Señora Alesander?* 'Cause if you don't want to, my mommy can read me a story. Or I can even jus' look at the pictures by myself!"

Cassie laid the book on the table by where the child had been sitting, "Maybe I can read to you another time; right now I do need to do some shelving." She blinked her eyes rapidly as she turned away from the girl.

Cassie had finished shelving the books and was straightening the volumes on a bottom shelf when she sensed someone watching her. She pivoted her head to look over her shoulder then grabbed a ledge to gain her balance. Jaimé stood at the end of the aisle, dressed in a charcoal gray business suit.

The man looked great in denim, she thought, *but in a suit, he was drop-dead gorgeous.* His white shirt provided a striking contrast between his dark skin and tailor-fit jacket. A smartly patterned black tie was knotted neatly at his throat, drawing her attention to the total maleness of his Adam's apple. Cassie remained locked in position, mesmerized as her eyes traveled his finely sculptured face to meet his penetrating gaze. She felt heat seep through her as he moved down the aisle toward where she crouched, her hand still clutching the shelf.

He stopped in front of her, raised a quizzical eyebrow, and shot her a heart-stopping grin. Cassie shoved completely inappropriate fantasies of what they could do in the more remote stacks of the library out of her mind as she accepted his proffered hand to assist her in standing. She immediately realized her mistake, as he stood so close that her breasts grazed the front of his jacket. She sucked in her breath, taking a quick step backward, only to be stopped by the wall behind her.

His eyes turned to liquid smoke as he angled his head toward her.

"Jaimé!" Cassie regained her senses in the nick of time. "This is a public library! Are you going to find me another job when I'm fired for scandalizing preschool children?"

It was Jaimé's turn to take a deep breath. He studied her momentarily before stepping aside to allow her to pass by him. As he reluctantly followed her down the aisle, he watched the gentle sway of her hips in her trim gray slacks. A pastel pink silk blouse skimmed gracefully from her shoulders down the seductive slope of her back and disappeared behind the thin black belt that encircled her slender waist. He thought about how easily he could slide the tail of slippery satin from where it was tucked beneath the swell of gray material that draped the rounded curve of her bottom then chastised himself for allowing his attention to drift in that direction.

Once they were in the safety of the open room, Cassie turned to Jaimé. Placing the book cart strategically between them, she asked with a slight tilt to her lips, "Was there something specific that you came here to tell me, or did you just randomly choose this time and place to ensure that my libido was fully functional? Because I can tell you right now, Jaimé Alvarez, that suit has definite possibilities...."

"The suit? How about the *hombré* in it, Cassandra? Does he have possibilities?" Jaimé rested the palms of his hands on the book truck and leaned forward as he let the question fall between them.

A college student sitting at a table nearby glanced up from the books spread out before her, and Cassie moved to the end of the cart. Jaimé lifted his hands so that she could maneuver the book truck out of the way.

As he followed her past the rectangular tables, he asked quietly so that only she could hear, "Can we go someplace and talk for a few minutes? I really don't want to cause you any trouble at work, but something has come up and I'd rather not discuss it here."

She parked the cart beside another, consulted her watch, then angled her face toward him. The intense seriousness with which he looked at her caused her to acquiesce without further questioning.

"It's nearly time for my lunch break. Let me check with Evelyn to see if I can take a little longer, if necessary."

Cassie ducked into an office behind the front desk and returned within seconds. "It's been a slow day, she said we could take as long as needed."

They walked in silence to his car. Cassie slid into the front seat and waited patiently for him to walk around to the driver's side. She was on edge to find out what he wanted to say, though a part of her dreaded hearing his news. She knew in her heart that he would eventually leave, but she wasn't ready—not yet.

He drove to a small bar/restaurant on the edge of town, *Tía's Taverna*. Cassie had been by the place many times, but had given it little attention.

"It doesn't look like much on the outside, but *Tía* Juana cooks a mean burrito," Jaimé said as he opened the door for Cassie to get out of the car.

"*Tijuana*? You are joking, aren't you?" Cassie asked, grateful for even a borrowed moment of levity, but Jaimé only cast her a sideways glance and shook his head, as he placed his hand on the small of her back and steered her toward the door. A neon light blinked off and on above them as they entered the darkened interior.

A well-rounded Hispanic woman greeted them from behind a long polished wooden bar. "Where you been keepin' yourself, Jimmy Boy?" The woman pronounced "Jimmy" as though the "J" were an "H." "I heard chu were home, but you no come to visit your *Tía*."

Jaimé bent over the bar to give her a quick kiss on the cheek, before apologizing, "*Lo siento mucho, Tía,* I've been busy with meetings…work, you know…."

"Ah yes, my Jimmy, I can see that," she nodded with a not altogether approving look toward Cassie.

"*Tía,* this is a very good friend of mine, Cassandra Alexander. Cas, this is my mother's twin sister, my Aunt Juana."

"Hah, Alesander. I know that name. You married to that big lummox oaf who causes nothin' but trouble. Why you bring this *gringa* lady with you, Jimmy?"

Cassie looked from Jaimé to his aunt, before interjecting, "So, you've met my former husband? He seems to leave a memorable impression wherever he goes."

"*Sí*, that one is bad, *muy mal*, a snake in the grass. He comes into *Tía* Juana's next time, my Pablo will show him the bottom end of his boot." The woman took a large drink of amber liquid from a mug on the bar, "You want *Tía's especial burrito*, Jimmy? *Es* spicy good wit' *mucho* cilantro. I know my Jimmy boy likes his cilantro."

"Sounds great to me," Jaimé replied, "Cassandra?"

"I'm sure it's wonderful, but do you have anything less... filling?"

"*Sí, la quesadilla es nuevo en el menú,*" *Tía* Juana said, assessing the *gringa* woman.

"*Bueno, gracias.*" Cassie thanked Jaimé's aunt.

"Could we have a couple of *Dos Equis* with that, *por favor, Tía*?" Jaimé asked.

"Would you make mine an iced tea—I have to go back to work this afternoon." *Tía* Juana huffed at Cassie's request, but turned to pour their drinks as they made their way to a booth covered in cracked red vinyl near an empty pool table in the back of the room.

They sat opposite one another. Cassie tucked her feet along the side of her seat to prevent making contact with Jaimé's under the table. *Tía* Juana delivered their drinks, and they each took a sip without speaking.

Jaimé leaned against the back of the booth and braced his hands against the edge of the table. "I've spent the first part of the week at the Cleveland office. We've hit a hitch in the negotiations with some big companies that have been polluting Lake Erie. Unfortunately, they're on the Canadian shore..."

"...and you're the white knight that's been chosen to slay the fire-breathing dragons," Cassie concluded.

"In case you didn't notice, this white knight's a little tarnished, and fire is the least of what these iron dragons are belching out.

It appears to be a real cesspool over there. I just hope we can find the right weapons to either force them to clean up their act or put them out of commission."

"It isn't anything dangerous, is it?"

"Nah, nothing like the good old days when we faced down the oil and timber companies with the First Nations. Now those timber guys were some bad dudes—not a bucket's worth of scruples among the lot of them. This'll be a cakewalk in comparison."

Cassie wondered at the incidents to which Jaimé had alluded. She'd never thought of a lawyer as a precarious profession and blanched at the notion of Jaimé in jeopardy.

"Hey, there's nothing to worry about, really," Jaimé assured her, "but I do find the fact that you're concerned for my welfare encouraging…."

Cassie shook her head and laughed, then asked, "When do you have to leave?"

"Tomorrow."

"So soon?" It slipped out before Cassie had a chance to hedge her response.

Jaimé reached across the table and lightly caressed her hand, "Ah, *querida*, so you will miss me then, eh?"

"Don't flatter yourself too much, Jaimé Alvarez," However, she left her hand where it was on the table.

A slight cough brought their attention to *Tía* Juana, who was standing at the side of their booth with hot plates of savory-scented steaming food. They quickly drew their hands back so that the stout woman could place their selections before them.

Cassie closed her eyes and inhaled the fragrant spices, missing the wink that *Tía* Juana gave her nephew.

Cassie waited until Jaimé's aunt returned to the bar before sampling her *quesadilla*. She took one small bite and then another, enjoying the smoky chipotle flavor, before the full force of the pepper sauce hit her. Her eyes began to water as a searing heat burned her lips and scorched her throat. She quickly grabbed her ice tea and swallowed a decidedly unladylike gulp. She searched frantically in her purse for a tissue, before Jaimé handed his handkerchief across the table.

"*Tía* Jauna!" The immediate appearance of Jaimé's aunt with a foil of soft flour tortillas in her hand confirmed his suspicion that she had been watching for Cassie to bite into the *quesadilla.*

"Here, eat this." *Tía* Juana instructed Cassie. Then to her nephew she sniffed with derision, "Such a *gringa.*"

"*Tía,*" Jaimé's voice held a note of controlled warning.

"*¿Qué?*" At his aunt's feigned innocence, Jaimé sat back, crossed his arms over his chest, and put on his best intimidating lawyer stare.

"Hah, you no scare your *Tía* Juana," she scoffed, but retrieved Cassie's plate with the offending *quesadilla.* "Here, *Señora* Alesander, I will make you another." Then, to Jaimé, "The *gringas*, they have no spice. No fire. Not like the *Mejicana señoritas!*"

"Take my word on it, *Tía*, this is one *gringa* you don't want to mess with!" Jaimé countered.

"Actually, I'm not that hungry, anyway. If I could just have a refill of my ice tea, I'll be fine." Cassie conceded.

"Just bring a second plate, *Tía, por favor*, this burrito is *muy grande*—there's plenty for both of us." Then to Cassie, Jaimé said, "I'm really sorry about that...."

"There's no need to apologize, Jaimé. Your aunt just wants what's best for you—and, in her eyes, that's not me."

"Yeah, but in my eyes you're damn near perfect. Doesn't that count for something?"

"You're leaving tomorrow, Jaimé, for how long? A month? Two? Three? I've said before, your life, and your children's, are in Canada, mine is here."

"I know, I know." Jaimé took her hand in both of his, "but I can't let go. Promise me you'll be careful while I'm gone. I've never trusted Paul. Not then, not now. I think he's capable of...I don't want to think about what he is be capable of doing. Just don't antagonize him into..."

"Doing what, Jaimé? He can't hurt me any more than he already has." Her barren womb ached as she recalled the words her former husband had written across their wedding picture. He had defiled her in ways that Jaimé would never know. What further harm could he do?

"Just promise me, okay? Maybe I can't have you. Maybe life just doesn't have happily-ever-afters like in the movies. But, if that... if Paul harms you in any way, I'll make sure he regrets it 'til his dying day."

The intensity in Jaimé's eyes frightened Cassie and she shivered involuntarily. "I'll be careful, I promise. I'll have 'Nita to protect me, and now Windy's taken to hanging around. They seem to use the farm as a rendezvous place. They're both getting so comfy there, it's almost like having roommates.

"By the way, Windy was quite impressed by our barn-building prowess. He figured he'd come back and see one or two more boards up. 'Nita and I had him going for a while, until we confessed to having help from you and Ben."

"Nice change of subject, princess. I'd be jealous of this guy if I weren't so grateful to have someone else keeping an eye on things out there."

Tía Juana brought Cassie's tea, and Jaimé placed half of his burrito on the empty plate his aunt left on the table. The intimacy of sharing lunch settled over them and they ate slowly, their glances meeting across the table and holding between bites. Cassie licked the lingering tang of cumin from her bottom lip, and Jaimé's gaze dropped to her mouth.

"You were supposed to be fat and matronly, dressed in polyester with sensible shoes."

"What?"

"I would go to the high school reunion, see you, realize I had been in love with a fantasy all these years, and go back to Ottawa a contented man."

Cassie lowered her eyelashes, then looked up at him with an unaffected coquettishness. "And?"

"I'm returning to Ottawa anything but contented. I think I

was better off with the fantasy. Now that I know the reality, know that my princess still exists, how can I walk away again?"

Cassie suppressed the urge to plead with him to stay, suppressed the urge to run home to pack a bag, suppressed the urge to beg to go with him. Instead, she concentrated on steadying her heart, feeling it slowly breaking once again.

They finished their lunch methodically and walked to the bar to pay their bill.

"So, Jimmy, you are leaving for Canada again? Next time you don't wait so long to visit your *Tía* Juana. Your cousin Ernie is in the Marines, you know, just like you were. And my Mariá Anna is a new mama. I am *seis* times a grandma now. See, aren't they *precioso?*" Jaimé's aunt brought a photo from under the bar with six smiling children of various ages.

Jaimé and Cassie admired the portrait. A particularly beautiful girl of seven or eight caught Cassie's attention. The child looked so much like Jaimé, Cassie couldn't take her eyes from her.

"Ah, that's my little Angela. She is Pablo's youngest. Such a challenge, that one is! So full of *travesura.*"

"That's 'mischief'," Jaimé provided the translation for Cassie, "and I can't imagine a granddaughter of yours being mischievous, *Tía!*" he teased, glad to be back in her good graces.

"Mischief, yes." *Tía* Juana looked sheepishly at Cassie, "I guess I may have put one or two extra peppers in your *quesadilla, Señora Alesander.* You are lucky you are no more married to that bad man. I don' blame you for wanting my Jimmy!"

Cassie only laughed, as she couldn't lie to Jaimé's aunt and deny her attraction to him. "I've always thought that it's not authentic Mexican cooking if you can't taste the peppers. I just wasn't quite prepared for them to be so...um...*caliente.* I think," she looked at Jaimé for confirmation, "if I recall from my Spanish classes, that means 'hot'?"

It was *Tía* Juana's turn to laugh. "This *gringa*, maybe she's not so bad." Jaimé looked from one woman to the other, amazed that Cassie was able to win over his crusty aunt so easily. He gave the older woman an affectionate hug and paid their bill, promising to stop by the next time he was in town.

The afternoon had turned sultry, with the sun glinting off the hood of the lone car in the small parking lot. Jaimé slipped on a pair of dark glasses, and Cassie caught her breath as he smiled down at her. He wrapped his arm around her shoulders and drew her close to his side.

"I like your aunt. She has spirit," Cassie said as they walked as one toward his dark sedan.

"That's not all she has...." Jaimé rejoined as he opened the passenger door. Cassie lowered herself onto the front seat, and he felt an immediate chill where her warmth had been.

When he climbed in the driver's side, he reached for her hand. "Could we take just a little longer?"

Cassie nodded her assent. Jaimé drove the short distance to the old Lower Eastside neighborhood where they had grown up and pulled his car to a stop along the curb of the back road that skirted the river.

"Is our path still there?" Jaimé asked.

"I...I've never been back. I...I just couldn't...." Cassie faltered.

They got out of the car and walked hand in hand until they found the familiar trail, worn smooth by the footsteps of children and, perhaps, other young lovers sneaking away for a romantic tryst. They eased down the path single file, with their fingers linked, until they reached the bank of the river. She swallowed hard over the lump in her throat as memories washed over her. "This probably wasn't the best of ideas."

A blue jay scolded from his perch on a low branch of a cottonwood, while a squirrel chattered from a cluster of leaves high in a maple along the river's edge. Cassie focused on a tangle of roots from a tree that was slowly being undercut by the flowing waters. She inhaled the familiar scents of the river—the slight musk of fish intertwined with the fecund aromas of rotting wood and lush undergrowth. Their movement startled a great blue heron and he spread his massive wings, rising like a prehistoric pterodactyl only to land again some twenty yards upriver.

"Cassandra..." Jaimé said her name softly as he stepped behind her, drawing her to him. She leaned her back against him, then slowly turned and melted into his arms. The sun glistened through the trees as she glanced up at him, and he lowered his mouth to hers. The sensuous urging of her soft lips sent desire coursing through him, escalating their kiss from tentative to frantic...hungry...searching.... Their tongues danced the dance that their bodies could not, and when they pulled away, each gasped for the breath that mingled between them.

"I could come over tonight...."

"No, Jaimé, no!" she said with more emphasis than she had intended. "Unless you can stay this time, don't come. I don't have the strength to let you go as it is. How could I after we...if I let you...No, I won't love you again!"

The vehemence of her words splashed on him as palpably as though she had doused him with a bucket of cold river water. *She would not love him again.* He had no right to ask it of her, but was powerless to step away. He held her loosely against his chest subconsciously memorizing the scent of her hair, her taste on his tongue, the feel of her breasts as they heaved against him. He caressed her lips with a tender kiss, and with a sigh, shifted his gaze to the cloud-strewn sky that hovered above the trees on the north bank of the river—north, toward Canada.... Taking her hand in his, they slowly retraced their footsteps back to the road.

Jaimé parked in front of the library in the same space that they had vacated such a short time ago. He covered Cassie's hand with his, tracing the length of her slender fingers, as they sat side-by-side staring straight ahead.

"When will you be back?"

"I don't know. I plan to enroll the kids in school as soon as I find out whether I'll be at the Ottawa office or in Toronto. I imagine it'll be Toronto, as that's closest to the polluters in question. The Christmas holidays will be the children's first extended break."

Cassie closed her eyes and leaned back against the smooth leather seat. "That's over four months away." She thought of Paul and the trial that would most likely be in her near future. "Anything could happen in four months."

He shifted so that he could face her. "It's not so long, Cassandra. We've waited thirty years…."

She ran her free hand along the coil of her tightly bound hair, and looked out the window. "It doesn't matter, does it? It all comes back to the irresistible force—that would be you—meeting the immovable object—me. What a quagmire!" She turned slightly toward him and gave him a half-smile. "You are definitely irresistible and I am about as immovable as that building over there." She inclined her head toward the library. "And, no matter how many quick trips you make to Northwest Ohio, that irresistible body of yours belongs in Canada."

"Ah, *querida*, you are so wrong. There's only one place this body belongs." Jaimé glanced around to ensure that no one was watching then bent over to graze her lips for one final bittersweet kiss. He straightened back up and quickly exited the car. Cassie was still leaning against her seat when he opened her door. She looked up at him, reluctant to step into the emptiness of the oppressive August afternoon. After a moment, she slid her feet to the ground and placed her hand in his.

They stood looking at each other, letting the heat of the day soak into their skin. He chucked her lightly under her chin, staying his hand just an instant, "Here's lookin' at you kid."

"Yeah, right, you remember how *Casablanca* ended, don't you?" She gave him a halfhearted smile. Cassie lowered her lashes then raised them again, tilting her head toward the only man she had ever truly loved. "Bye, Jaimé." She stepped back from his grasp, squared her shoulders, turned and walked with a determined stride to the sidewalk, not stopping to look at him until she reached the library. He was still standing by the open car door watching her when she slipped through the entrance to the building.

CHAPTER SIX

september

"I'm fine, Aunt Nell, really." Cassie tried for the hundredth time since Jaimé's departure to convince her aunt that she wasn't ill. She was positive Aunt Nell didn't have any magic tonic in her bag that would cure what ailed her. They sat across from each other at the end of a long table under a large striped carnival tent at the Labor Day picnic Pleasant Valley put on for its residents and their families. Cassie's mother had gone to the food table for dessert for herself and Nell. Cassie had declined her mom's offer to pick up a piece of pie or a chocolate brownie for her. Her appetite had dwindled to the point that she had to force herself to eat anything.

"I've been thinking, Aunt Nell." Cassie said, in an attempt to divert the conversation away from herself before her mother returned to the table. "You've been making steady progress, getting stronger all the time. You said yourself that you've been able to use the walker for longer periods of time."

Aunt Nell took the bait, "You bet! Yesterday I was able to go from the far end of the east wing to the main desk. 'Course it took me near half an hour to do it," she chuckled. "They still won't allow me to use the walker to go out, though—just inside along the hallways."

"Well, what I would like to see happen is for you to be ambulatory enough to move to the farm with me by next spring. I've been toying with an idea for a small business there and could use your help. What do you think?"

Before Nell could respond, her sister placed two slices of fresh peach pie on the table between them. "Well, aren't you looking like the cat that ate the canary. What'd you do, Cas, tell her that old Elmer Wainright over there was sweet on her?"

"Get real, Martha Jane," Nell retorted, "my radar may be rusty, but Elmer? Puh-lease! Besides, this is better than a man—Cassie's going to spring me from this joint, right, Cas?"

"We'll work on it, Aunt Nell, we'll work on it!"

"Have you heard from Jimmy?" 'Nita asked, as they watched Windy and Don spray a coat of bright green paint over the newly-constructed barn doors that they had hung the previous day. The two women sat on the glider on the deck of the farmhouse, sipping lemonade and enjoying a beautiful Indian summer afternoon.

"Not since that call the first week. You know, when he said they had arrived in Toronto. He wanted to check out the schools and find a place to live." Slack-Eyed Joe lay curled up between them, with his head resting on the side of Cassie's leg. She absentmindedly rubbed her finger along the nub of his nose, and he rewarded her with a contented purr.

A crash and yelp from the direction of the barn startled them all. Joe sprang from the swing to investigate the source of the noise. Before Cassie and 'Nita could do likewise they heard Windy shout "Dang it, Johnston, you're just lucky that bucket didn't land on my head."

"Ooh, green on red...not good!" 'Nita laughed. "Maybe the guys could use a little lemonade to cool them down a tad." They rose to get the pitcher from the house.

"Speaking of Windy, how are things going?" Cassie asked as

she filled two tall plastic glasses with ice.

The sparkle in her friend's vivid brown eyes answered Cassie's question before 'Nita said anything. "I just can't believe that that gorgeous hunk of manhood is in love with an overweight..."

"Voluptuous..."

"Yeah, right, *voluptuoso chicana* like me!"

"Wait a minute! Did you say the 'L' word? Or, rather, did *he* say the 'L' word?"

"Uh huh. I've been meaning to ask you something all afternoon. Would you consider...ah...being my matron of honor?" 'Nita waved her left hand exhibiting the distinctive flash of a diamond in front of her friend.

The ice cube tray Cassie had been holding clattered to the floor as she grabbed 'Nita's hand to examine her ring. "What? You've been sitting on this the entire afternoon without even dropping me the slightest hint?"

"I dropped plenty of hints. You were just too lost in Toronto to notice."

"I'm sorry, 'Nita. I've just had a lot on my mind, I guess."

"*No problema, amiga,*" 'Nita assured her friend, "but you still haven't answered my question!"

"Of course! I would be thrilled to be your matron of honor! ...Ah, this doesn't mean I have to wear some gosh-awful pastel poofy-sleeved gown, though, does it?" Cassie laughed as she filled two more glasses with lemonade.

When the men had finished for the day and Don had driven off in his pick-up, Cassie popped a pizza in the oven to celebrate and discuss the upcoming nuptials. Anita and Windy had selected the Saturday after Christmas as their wedding date.

"That doesn't give us a lot of time, but the church and hall have both been booked," Windy said between bites of pepperoni.

"How about a caterer?" Cassie asked.

Anita answered, "The family—aunts, cousins, everyone pitches in to make the food. My mom's so excited, she's started making tamales and freezing them already!"

They talked a while longer before Windy suggested that, as he had "an early day tomorrow," he and 'Nita should be leaving.

As Cassie walked with them to the sunporch, Windy said, "I wish you'd let me install new doors in the house, Cassie. Anyone could bust out one of these little windows, reach through, and unlock the door. It just isn't safe."

"I'll be fine." At 'Nita's rolled eyes, Cassie agreed to at least think about it. She watched them stroll to the car, arm in arm. Windy bent down to give Anita a quick kiss before opening the door for her.

Cassie locked the door and turned away from the intimate gesture. She disposed of the empty pizza box, rinsed their plates, and stacked them in the sink.

Though she was excited for her friends and shared their joy, she was having trouble keeping her green-eyed monster at bay. With a heavy heart, she dragged herself to the living room, turned on the television, and popped a rented copy of *Casablanca* into the VCR.

october

Cassie's entire body ached as she drove home from the library. She had spent the morning rearranging the tables in the children's area so that they were closer to the book stacks. In the afternoon, she shifted the volumes in several sections of shelving that had become cramped for space. *Perhaps it was time to start acknowledging that she wasn't a spring chicken anymore,* she thought with a groan as she pulled into her driveway.

Before entering the house, Cassie walked to the mailbox

along the road. She popped open the hinged door to the large metal container, revealing several envelopes stacked inside. She pulled them out, glancing at the top one—another plea for money from a worthy charity. *Sorry, guys, can't get water from a turnip,* Cassie thought as she relegated the letter to the bottom of the pile. Next was the bill from the electric co-op. *They probably won't swallow the "water from a turnip" line,* she laughed to herself and shuffled the invoice under the last letter. The third envelope was fairly thick and more the size of a card. She studied the small, neatly slanted script before reading the return address.

Toronto, Canada! A letter from Jaimé!

Cassie hurried back to the house, fumbled with her keys to open the door, tossed the rest of the mail on the table, sank onto the couch, and slit open the envelope with Jaimé's letter inside. She studied his precise handwriting before reading on.

> *Dearest Cassandra,*
>
> *You are with me wherever I go. I see you in the stranger walking down the street, hear your voice in the middle of a crowded room and turn to look for you. I miss you.*
>
> *Unfortunately, things are not going well with our cases. The paper mill we are pursuing continues to dump toxic waste into Lake Erie, despite our having an injunction served against them. And though we've traced raw sewage flowing into the lake to a town along the shore, litigation is moving at a snail's pace. At times, it seems that fighting the status quo is a losing proposition.*
>
> *But, enough on that. Tina and Ben continue to do well in school. Tina has a newfound best friend and has blossomed from a shy daddy's girl to an outgoing tomboy. I'm not sure which I prefer—she was much easier to keep track of when she was clinging to my leg whenever I wasn't at work. Now I need to call her friend's mother to find out my daughter's whereabouts.*

Cassie reread the last sentence with a tinge of jealousy. Tina's best friend's mother? Was Jaimé trying to tell her something? The longer he stayed away, the more she felt him slipping through her fingers. Then she read the first paragraph again, reassuring herself that he still cared about her. The letter continued:

> *Ben has instructed me a number of times to be sure to tell you about his science project on the life cycle of a frog. His teacher declared it to be the best in the class and has submitted it to be presented at a district science symposium. Ben said the project was all due to finding the tadpoles in your pond, and insisted that I send you a photocopy of his report.*
>
> *Though Ben enjoys his classes, he frequently drops not-too-subtle hints that he would rather be living in the States. For the first time in many years, it has a certain appeal to his father as well....*
>
> *The hour is late and I have a brief to prepare first thing in the morning. I must finish this and get it into an envelope so that I can post it on my way to the office.*
> *Take care of yourself, My Love.*
> *Jaimé*

"My Love," Cassie said the last two words aloud. She held the letter tight against her breast and let tears trickle unimpeded down her cheeks. Never before did the miles between them seem as insurmountable as at this moment.

Cassie waited until the weekend to pen her reply, cherishing the tenuous thread the unanswered letter held to Jaimé. She could visualize him waiting for her response—but once her letter was sent, she would be the one to check the mailbox daily in anticipation of an answer.

A bright sun poured through the crisp October air Saturday morning as Cassie fired up the old green John Deere riding mower that Windy had resurrected for her from the odd and end bits of machinery and tools her Uncle Clem had amassed in the back of the barn. The ignition made a grinding sound for an instant before the engine sputtered to life. Cassie retied the kerchief that held her hair in place then backed the mower out of the barn.

As she lowered the blade and began to cut swaths across her front lawn, she thought, as usual, about Jaimé and contemplated her reply to his letter. After a few hours, she killed the motor and went into the house to fix a small lunch. She gathered up a blanket, a writing pad and pen, and carried them outside with the food. She crunched through the early autumn leaves that had fallen from the cottonwood trees by the pond.

She waited for the plop of the frogs into the water but was greeted only by the honking of geese overhead, winging their way southward. Cassie surmised that the frogs must have retreated to the bottom along with the fish, to wait out the winter ahead. She had read in Ben's report that they burrowed into the mud in the depths of the pond and lowered their body temperatures to that of the water overhead.

Cassie took the path that led to the old oak tree along the bank of the creek. Leaves lightly tinged with red and gold clung to its branches awaiting their transformation to the brilliant colors of fall before cascading to the ground below. Cassie spread her blanket out in the same grassy spot where she had picnicked with Jaimé and his children just a few short months ago.

The brook babbled over the rocks covering its bottom. Cassie marveled at the power of water to wash the stones smooth over time. *Time, all things in due time,* she thought. *But, how much time did she have? How much time until she was called to account for the missing money from O'Shay's?* She dispelled the worrisome thoughts from her mind and concentrated on recalling the words she had composed for Jaimé's letter while mowing the lawn that morning.

> *Dear Jaimé,*
>   *Your letter was like a draught of fresh water after a long drought,* she wrote, then crossed it out after deciding it was too

melodramatic.

How are you and the children? She scribbled a line through that, thinking it too impersonal.

Thank you for your letter—it was a bright spot in a long week. Better, she thought, as she transcribed her words to a fresh sheet of paper.

> *Last weekend I conned 'Nita and Windy into help-ing me rip up the old shag carpeting in the dining and living rooms and the main stairway. I had pulled it up in a few places and discovered it covered beautiful hard-wood floors. Windy sanded the floorboards and poor 'Nita spent a day on her hands and knees helping me oil them to a rich shine. Talk about a test of friendship! Now the challenge will be finding affordable area rugs.*
>
> *Then Evelyn, Beth, and I completely rearranged the children's section at the library. I think it will greatly enhance our ability to meet the needs of our younger pa-trons. I was pleased that Evelyn liked several of my sug-gestions. Guess what else? She surprised me on Wednes-day by offering me the position of Circulation Assistant! I had interviewed for the job last week, but didn't think I would be selected as I knew several graduates from area universities were also applying. Though it doesn't pay a lot, jobs are very hard to come by these days. It's fulltime with a small raise, but I am most excited about having health benefits again—something you Canadians don't have to worry about!*
>
> *Please thank Ben for the copy of his report. I enjoyed reading it, and it helped explain why I didn't hear frogs jumping into the pond as I walked by this afternoon. I am glad that Tina has made the transition to school in Toronto and has found a new friend.*

Cassie felt a little ambiguous about her last sentence—if Tina wanted to live in the USA, as well as Ben, perhaps Jaimé would consider moving back to Ohio.

> *I know you will prevail over the polluters in Lake Erie, Jaimé. I'm sure they will be as unable to resist your charms—and legal persuasions—as I am.*

Cassie reconsidered this line, but as it was near the bottom of the page, she left it as written. She continued:

> *I have been reading quite a lot about the Great Lakes ecology. Now that I have a ready access to the library, it's so easy to find information on just about everything.*
>
> *I am hoping to save enough to buy an inexpensive laptop. Internet access is fairly cheap here through the local provider, and one can research just about any subject with Google. Not to mention, e-mail is such an easy and convenient way to keep in touch, and now everyone's talking about Facebook. I hardly even know what that is! I never used the computer at O'Shay's for anything but accounting spreadsheets. I've since discovered there are even computer software programs to help set up small businesses!*

Cassie sat back and took a long drink out of her water bottle, then munched on a baby carrot and a celery stick. She debated on whether or not to tell Jaimé about her dream for the farm. He might think her foolish or, at best, naïve. However, if she valued his opinion she would have to trust him enough to know he wouldn't laugh at her.

> *The reason that I am interested in the small business software is that I have been thinking about converting the acreage behind the barn into an herb and flower garden. Anita and I have enjoyed shopping at small boutiques this fall looking for flowers and decorations*

for her wedding. Oops! Did you know about 'Nita and Windy's upcoming nuptials? More about that later. Anyway, these little shops all have clever displays using dried flowers and herbs. Ela's Herbary downtown offered a few evening workshops this fall and much to my surprise, I discovered that I have a talent for creating dried flower arrangements! I thought that, perhaps, if I could grow herbs and flowers to market, as well as making arrangements of my own to sell, I might be able to eventually support myself and the farm with the venture.

I could use Uncle Clem's tack shed for a shop—he ran a business there for years doing harness repairs and other leatherwork, so it's set up for a small workshop and store. I was hoping that perhaps Aunt Nell could manage staffing the shop for as long as she is able—just answering the phone and taking care of the few walk-in customers that we might have. I am convinced she will be able to move home with me by spring. Anyway, it's a bit of a pipe dream now, but I have been thinking about it a lot (keeps my mind off a certain lawyer up north).

Now to 'Nita and Windy. Did you hear that they were engaged? It's been nearly a month now. They are planning to get married the Saturday after Christmas. Is there any chance that you and the children will be home over the holidays? 'Nita's been a basket case—she doesn't want to wear a traditional white gown, so we've gone to every clothing store within a hundred miles looking for just the right dress. If I hear "I'll know it when I see it" one more time, I may throttle her!

Cassie reread the last paragraph, pleased with the way she worked in asking Jaimé if he would be home for Christmas without making a big deal of it. Then she thought about how to end the letter. She had considered long and hard what she felt she needed to say—especially with her future being so uncertain.

I didn't mean to prattle on so long. I do miss you, Jaimé. But I cannot let myself love you. Not when our lives are separated by so much more than just the miles between us. I treasure your friendship—you will always hold a special place in my heart. Please do take care and keep in touch.

Yours,
Cassandra

Cassie folded the letter and tucked it inside its envelope. She ate a few more bites of her lunch then packed it away in a bag. She stood, pulling the blanket up with her and shaking the leaves and grass off of it. When she emerged from the woodlot, wintry clouds had blotted out the sun rendering a chill to the air. She wrapped the blanket around her shoulders and hurried back toward the house without glancing at the pond as she passed by.

CHAPTER SEVEN

november

"Paul, what are you doing here?" Cassie hissed as her former husband leaned nonchalantly on the end of the circulation desk.

"I came to ask you out to lunch." He raked her up and down with his eyes, letting his gaze rest on her breasts. Cassie crossed her arms over her chest, protecting herself from his leering stare.

"How dare…I can't believe…the audacity…! The only place I'd go with you is the door to latch it after you slithered out," Cassie sputtered before slamming her hand down on the counter.

"Now, is that any way to treat the man who could hold the key to your future, Cas-hon?" Paul said with a menacing edge that mocked the endearment.

"I don't know what you're talking about, and what's more, I don't want to know. Would you please just go away?"

Paul glanced over Cassie's shoulder at the woman in the office behind her. She seemed to not be paying attention to what was happening at the front desk. He shot his hand out and caught Cassie's arm by the wrist.

"Maybe you'd better try being just a little nicer to me, sweetheart. After all, you're the one in hock for one point five million. You'll look real cute in an orange jumpsuit." He yanked on Cassie's arm dragging her face to within inches of his, "I might just have to help me to a little of your...ah..." he glanced down at her breasts again, "assets before the ladies at the pen get to you."

"Ladies at the pen? The penitentiary? Oh my God, Paul, you are sick, really sick!"

"Cassie, is there a problem out there?" The concern in Evelyn's voice carried to the outer office.

Paul dropped Cassie's arm and she immediately began to massage it. Evelyn emerged from her office as he stepped away from the circulation counter.

"This isn't the last you'll hear from me, dollface, so you better watch your step!" He nodded toward Evelyn then turned on his heel and heaved out the front door nearly knocking over a young mother and her daughter on their way in.

"Who was that man and did he hurt you?" Evelyn asked.

"The man I made the mistake of marrying thirty years ago— then repeated the mistake each year after by staying with him."

"That's Paul Alexander?"

"The one and only, thank you God!"

Evelyn took Cassie's wrist in her hand and turned it over. The imprint of Paul's fingers still circled her arm.

"If I ever see him walk through those doors again, I'm calling the police—no questions asked."

"Thanks, Evelyn. I'm so sorry about bringing my personal life into work."

"I didn't notice your bringing Paul Alexander into the library. Besides, I don't mind when it's that handsome lawyer friend of yours. Just where has that man been hiding himself?"

"Toronto, Canada. He was just in the states on business this summer and for a brief visit with his parents."

"Yes, uh huh—don't think you can get away with that dismissive little shrug, Cassandra. There was something very special about that man—mark my words, he'll be back!" Evelyn smiled at her employee and gave her hand a reassuring pat before returning to her office.

Her time with Jaimé seemed a distant memory as Cassie stood staring at the door through which her ex-husband had just exited. She took a deep shuddering breath before returning to the cart of books that she had been scanning into the online computer system.

When Cassie finished her shift at the library that afternoon, she stopped by Anita's apartment for another evening of what was becoming the search of the century for the elusive "I'll know it when I see it" dress.

"I think we've found it!"

"Whoa, 'Nita. Found what? *The* dress?" Cassie said with a slight guilt-tinged relief at the thought of having an evening to herself that wasn't completely absorbed by her friends' wedding.

"Well, not exactly, but Jeanne at work told me about this lady in Findlay who designs and sews gowns. Jeanne said the woman has a knack for finding styles and material that compliment your figure and coloring. She, Jeanne that is, went to this one wedding where the bride was even fatter..." At Cassie's gasp, Anita added, "Well, she didn't exactly say that, but I know that's what she meant. Anyway, that's beside the point because Windy likes me just the way I am. He says skinny women, like *some* of us in this room, just don't have enough...um..." Cassie raised her eyebrows and grinned at her friend, who was trying to delicately worm her way out of repeating what Windy had said without offending her closest confidant and wedding consultant, "...well...voluptuosity...."

"Voluptuosity? Did he *really* say 'voluptuosity'?"

"Well, no, but you know what I mean...wait a minute, Alexander, you're enjoying watching me squirm *way* too much!"

Cassie snickered, holding her hand over her mouth to keep from laughing. Anita then began to shake with suppressed chuckles. The two friends looked at each other, collapsing to the floor in a fit of giggles completely out of proportion to their witticisms. When one stopped, gasping for breath, the other would laugh even harder. They slowly regained their composure sitting cross-legged facing each other.

"Oh my heavens, that felt good!" Cassie was the first to eke out a coherent sentence. "I haven't laughed like that since…well, since we were kids."

"Yeah, well, we'll see how good it feels when we try to get all this voluptuosity up off the floor!" 'Nita's dry observation sent them into another spate of laughter, releasing them both from weeks of tension.

Cassie wiped tears from her eyes with the back of her hand, "I feel like Uncle Albert, you know, in *Mary Poppins*? Didn't he end up laughing to death or something like that?" She dried her hand on her pants as she went on, "I can just see the headlines now, 'Old Ladies Found Collapsed on Apartment Floor: Coroner Suspects Death by Laughter.'"

"Hey, who're you calling 'old'? Gosh, it feels great to just let go once in a while!" Anita took her friend's hands in hers and they held each other's gaze with just inches separating their faces. "It's nice to see that you've loosened up your laces enough to realize that, Alexander. Look at you, you're hair could *almost* be called a mess."

Cassie started to raise her hand to strands of hair that had worked free from the coil at the nape of her neck, then stopped with a quick half-smile. "I'm learning, 'Nita. I'm learning."

Cassie lowered her lashes then looked at her companion's beautiful, cherished face. "You are my dearest, most special friend, 'Nita. What am I going to do after you're married? You'll be caught up in the throes of being a newlywed, and as it should be, Windy will be your new best friend. Oh crap, I sound like a sniveling baby. Besides, you'll probably have to visit me at the 'Big House' in Marysville, anyway."

"Cassandra Grace Mikhailov Alexander, that's just enough of that! You are *not* going to prison!"

Cassie beamed a manufactured smile at her childhood friend, "You're right 'Nita! How selfish of me to even bring up the subject on this momentous evening! And we were having such a good time. Forgive me for turning maudlin on you. Now, about that seamstress—did you get a phone number?"

"Better than that. I called her and we have an appointment at 7:00 this evening."

"7:00? That barely gives us an hour and a half to grab a bite to eat and get to Findlay! It's at least an hour's drive if there's no delays on I-75!"

Anita tried to evoke a genuine smile from her comrade, "An hour and a half *to get this voluptuosity up off the floor*, grab a bite, and drive to Findlay, that is!"

Cassie laughed, "That's just what I mean, you can bring me out of a funk faster than anyone. I will miss you dearly, my friend. Now, what'll it be—Arbys, Mickey D's, Burger King, or Wendy's?" she asked as she helped 'Nita to her feet.

Anita groaned, "When this is all over, I am *never* going through another 'bun 'n run' so help me!"

Sitting in the gaily-colored booth at the nearest fast food outlet, Cassie nibbled at her grilled chicken sandwich.

"No wonder you are just skin and bones, girl. You eat like *you're* the bride-to-be, while I make the major sacrifice trying to resist gobbling down a supersized pack of fries." Anita commented from her vantage point across the table from Cassie.

After a moment, Cassie said, "Paul came into the library to-day."

"He what? When's the last time you saw the bast...?"

"I don't know, I ran into him with the bimbette a few weeks ago at the grocery. He was ripping on her, and I just wanted to get away. He saw me, but didn't say anything. I did something I've never done before—left my half-full cart in the aisle and ran from the store as soon as they were out of sight."

"What'd he want today?"

"Just to make trouble for me at the library, I guess. And, to remind me that a bright orange jumpsuit was in my wardrobe fu-ture." As usual, Cassie choose not to mention the sexual innuendos her ex-husband had displayed that afternoon, falling into her old habit of not revealing his perversions to anyone, even 'Nita. *Besides*, she thought, *maybe she had just imagined the looks he gave her. After all, why would he want anything in that way from her when he has an overly endowed fashion doll at his disposal?*

"*Cosa del Diáblo!*" Anita swore. "If we didn't have this appointment tonight, I'd get Windy to replace that door for you right away. A door with windows just isn't safe out there in the country, Cas!"

"Yeah, and how often have you left your apartment unlocked saying 'the only ones locks keep out are honest people' or something to that effect?"

"Listen, Alexander, it's not fair to use my words against me," 'Nita rejoined, "Besides, I don't have a deranged ex-husband running around threatening to kill me."

"That's a little drastic, 'Nita, Paul may have…" Cassie stopped before saying *played the lecher*, quickly amending it to, "…come into the library, but he didn't threaten my life."

"Whatever…but I am going to talk to Sam about this."

"Sam? What happened to 'Windy'? There isn't any 'Trouble in Paradise,' is there?"

"No, never, at least not until I get the matching ring on my finger," 'Nita laughed as Cassie dropped her jaw, "I'm only joking—I just like to use the name 'Sam' once in a while. I don't know, it makes him more, well, mine."

They finished Anita's last fry and tossed their sandwich wrappings and drink cups into the trash bin on their way out the door.

"A whole week without dress shopping!" Cassie assured herself as she left work the next day. The session with Carol Francis turned out better than they could have hoped. The seamstress selected an antique-white velvet material for Anita with just enough red trim to highlight the bride-to-be's creamy latté complexion. For Cassie, Carol suggested, in keeping with the holiday theme, a green velvet design with simple yet elegant lines. The best part was that their first fitting wouldn't be until the following week! 'Nita and Windy had an appointment that night with the priest who was performing their ceremony, so Cassie was free from all thoughts of the wedding for at least one evening!

Darkness had eased over the landscape as she finished her errands and headed out of town. A brisk wind threatened to blow in the first snow of the season. Cassie flipped on the car's heater and was rewarded with a blast of warm air. She had forgotten to buy a pair of gloves when she picked up a next-to-new coat at Goodwill last week but vowed, as she extended her chilled fingers to the dash vents, she would remember tomorrow.

Though Cassie could now afford to do a little shopping for new clothes with her small income, she had become addicted to the Goodwill store, amazed at what people discarded—things that she wouldn't have thought twice about buying in an upscale department store prior to her divorce.

She drove the miles to the farm in peaceful contemplation, thinking about what she would prepare for Thanksgiving dinner for her mom and Aunt Nell. It would just be the three of them, and Cassie was looking forward to a relaxing afternoon of Scrabble and, perhaps, a game of Canasta.

Cassie pulled into her driveway and turned off the motor. She hesitated before leaving the warmth of the car's interior. The cold damp air soaked through her outer wrappings and into her skin as she scurried up the walk. Slack-eyed Joe was waiting at the doorstep to be let into the house.

"Brrr, fella, this is the kind of night that chills you to the bone," Cassie said as she reached down to pick up the furry feline, "Mmmm…better than a muff!" She warmed her hands on his belly before inserting her key into the lock. The door pushed open with ease, as though the latch hadn't caught. *Strange, I was sure I had pulled the door tight this morning,* she mused.

Once inside she nuzzled her cold nose into Joe's ruff. "Not a bad nose-warmer, either," she grinned before the cat squirmed from her grasp and ran to his food bowl.

"Just like a man—think of your stomach first, then, if it so pleases you, you may bask in my attention."

The phone rang as she filled Joe's bowl with fresh kibbles.

Cassie felt a chill run up her spine and turned automatically to see if someone was standing behind her. As she answered the call she walked to the dining room to flip on the light switch there.

"Hey Cas, it's me, Anita."

"Hi 'Nita. Aren't you supposed to be meeting with Father Harrman this evening?"

"Yeah, we're leaving in a few minutes. Windy was wondering if we could stop by afterwards so that he could check out your door and maybe talk some sense into you about changing it."

"Tell our hero 'thanks' but you guys don't need to drive all this way tonight. Even I know that replacing a door isn't a five-minute job, so there's nothing he could do about it until the weekend anyway. We can discuss it civilly over pizza on Friday night, if that suits your man."

Anita relayed Cassie's message to Windy and his reply back to her. "He says that you are one of the most stubborn women he knows…next to me, that is. We'll bring the pizza on Friday—pepperoni and mushrooms for us and one of those fancy California whites for you."

After she hung up the phone, Cassie surveyed the contents of her refrigerator in an attempt to scavenge an easy dinner. She opted for a small tub of yogurt and a slice of fresh rosemary bread from the loaf from the bakery she and 'Nita had patronized in Findlay the day before. She poured a glass of skim milk, picked up an extra saucer for a treat for Joe, and carried everything to the coffee table in the living room.

The hairs on the nape of her neck stood on end, and she glanced around the room. She flipped the switch that lit up the open stairwell, taking the first few steps to the upstairs before retreating back to the safety of the living room.

Cassie chastised herself for foolishly giving in to the power of suggestion, after 'Nita and Windy's warnings. She popped *Dirty*

Dancing, her favorite feel-good movie, into the videocassette player, relieved that she had, at the last minute, rejected *The Postman Always Rings Twice* when she had stopped by the video store on her way home. She poured a little milk in Joe's saucer and settled back for a quiet evening.

"I do love Patrick Swayze's moves in this flick," she said to her furry companion as Jennifer Gray and her family unloaded their station wagon after arriving in the Catskills.

"You used to love my moves a lot, too, Cas-hon. Let's see if we can dance that old dance again. Whaddya say, babe?"

Cassie jumped, dumping her milk in a puddle on the hardwood floor. "Damn you, Paul, how did you get in here?" She felt her heart race to her throat as she turned to face the man lounging against the closet door, now ajar. Memories of her former husband's depraved assaults on her held her momentarily petrified. *Think, Cassie, THINK!* she commanded herself. *Damn, why did she tell Anita and Windy not to come out to the farm!*

"I need to get a towel to clean this up before we can discuss anything." The excuse sounded lame even to her ears.

Paul grabbed her forearm and drug her to him, "I'm not that stupid, sweetheart." He shoved her aside, "I'll get somethin', but don't you move." He returned with a bath towel before Cassie could do more than pick up the glass.

He handed her the towel and pushed her toward the floor. Cassie caught her balance and dropped the swath of terrycloth over the milk, knowing that if she allowed Paul to get her in a prone position she would be much more vulnerable to his attack.

As she wiped at the spilled milk with her foot, she attempted to hone her senses. She studied his once handsome face, noting that it had become flaccid and blotched. His eyes were watery and bloodshot—for once, his abuse of alcohol could work in her favor. She surveyed his clothing: A thin short-sleeved dress shirt—a definite plus! In her subconscious, she heard Johnny and Baby in a duel of words. Paul yanked her toward him as the legendary music of *Dirty Dancing* poured into the living room. He ground his erection against her, forcing her to him in only the barest semblance of rhythm.

"C'mon, Cas-hon, I know you can do better than that," he rasped in her ear before dragging his mouth across hers, forcing his tongue between her lips.

Cassie felt her stomach churn, but did her best to seem to relax in his arms. "You like that, don't you Cas? You always liked things rough." He clamped his hand on her breast, causing her to cry out with pain. With his thumb and forefinger, he pinched her nipple through her sweater. She tasted the bile that rose in her throat as his breath grew rapid in her ear. "You want it, tell me how much you want it, baby."

Fear licked about her like flames, and she fought against an ensuing panic. She took a deep breath, struggling to maintain control. She drew her hands up along his forearms, casually caressing the soft flesh underneath.

"Oh yeah, baby, whatever the Spic's been givin' you, I can give you more of. You know I can," he panted, his breath moist against her cheek. "You feel how much I've missed you, don'cha sweet thing?" As he pressed her to him, he stumbled just slightly before grabbing her to regain his balance. She knew it was now or never.

She gritted her teeth and in one swift motion grabbed hold of a chunk of flabby underarm skin with her left hand, pinching with all her might.

"Owwwwww, let go, bitch!" Paul howled.

"Okay," Cassie said. And with a rush of adrenaline she gave a sharp poke to his Adam's apple with the three middle fingers of her right hand jamming them into his windpipe. As Paul raised his hand to stop her, she caught his ring and index fingers in a full grip, and, using both hands, forced him backwards. He tripped over Slack-Eyed Joe, who had slunk up behind him growling, and went sprawling to the ground, where Cassie rendered him helpless by stomping on his groin.

Paul doubled over in agony and Cassie grabbed the poker from the fireplace, brandishing it at him. "Get out of my house.

Get the hell out of my house! If you ever try to touch me again, so help me, I will kill you!"

Paul scrambled half-crouched to the door, "You'll regret this, bitch," he called as he limped toward the driveway.

Cassie waved the iron tool in the air and shouted after him, "Not in your lifetime, you…you…." She couldn't find a name despicable enough for the man who fled into the night from her wrath.

Cassie managed to close and lock the door before she crumpled to the floor. Slack-Eyed Joe padded up to her and licked her arm.

"Oh, Joey boy, he's gone! We did it!" After a few minutes, she crawled to the table and reached up to where she had left the phone.

"'Nita? Oh, thank God, you're home. Listen, something's happened. Could you and Windy come out here tonight? Please? … No, I'm okay, just a little shaken. Just come as soon as you can. And, could you either spend the night, or could I come over there? Oh, and do you have anything like brandy? I could definitely use something a bit stronger than lemonade!" Cassie hit the button to disconnect the call, her body quaking too violently to talk further.

By the time Windy and Anita came flying into the driveway, each in their own vehicle, Cassie had regained control over her breathing and her heart had settled back into its proper cavity in her chest. She met them at the door, throwing her arms around both at once.

"It was Paul. I don't know how he got in—he didn't break a window around the doorknob. You were right, 'Nita, locks are for honest people."

"That son of a …"Windy looked at the two women who had become so important to him as he hugged them close. "Son of a gun," he finished half-heartedly.

They moved into the kitchen and while Cassie reassured Anita that she really was okay and that Paul hadn't harmed her, Windy retrieved a glass from the cupboard. He filled it with an apricot brandy that he pulled out of a paper sack he had been carrying. "Here, drink a little of this."

He found two more glasses and filled them as well, handing one to his fiancé. "Let's go into the living room and I'll light a fire. I think I, for one, need to sit down before I hear any more."

Windy took a long match from the tin box that hung near the fireplace and lit the wood that Cassie had already stacked in the brick opening behind the glass doors. Slack-Eyed Joe immediately took possession of the hearthrug, grooming himself and preening as though he knew he had just played an important role in saving his mistress. Windy reached down and scratched the cat between his ears, eliciting an immediate and loud purr.

Cassie and Anita curled up on opposite ends of the davenport, sharing Aunt Nell's large afghan between them, while Windy angled the bentwood rocking chair so that he was near Anita but could still watch and listen to Cassie.

Cassie picked up the remote and clicked Patrick Swayze back into his little black box. "That's what really ticks me off about all of this," Cassie ranted, "now I won't be able to watch *Dirty Dancing* without thinking about Paul!"

"Okay, Cas, enough stalling. What happened tonight?"

Cassie began her story with the drive home and finding the door to the house ajar. "What a dumb-blonde move" she chastised herself, "the first rule of safety is 'if a previously locked door is mysteriously unlocked, don't go in.' You see it in the movies all the time! I'm the first one to shout 'Run!' to the airheads on the screen, but they always go on in. Just like I did! Maybe next time I'll cut them a little more slack."

'Nita shook her head as Cassie continued, "And, then, when you called, I felt like something wasn't right. You know how you get a chill down your spine when you get spooked? I should have told you to come over right then."

"Good observation, Sherlock, just a little late..." Anita jibed, but then countered, "But, I know you, you wouldn't have asked us to cancel our appointment with the Rev because you had the creeps."

"You're right, I suppose. Anyway, I gathered a small dinner."

'Nita had picked up the remnants of Cassie's makeshift dinner and wiped up the rest of the spilled milk while Windy lit the fire. "You call a yogurt and bread 'dinner'? Honey, that's not even a good snack! Maybe you had better go easy on that brandy until you get some food in your stomach."

Cassie took another sip of the warming liqueur. "There's no way you are getting this out of my hands tonight, and there's no way I could eat anything else, honest!"

Windy gave his fiancé a cautionary glance, and Anita sat back in her seat. "Okay, no more interruptions from 'the mouth,' I promise."

The bantering with Anita had been just what Cassie needed to settle her nerves, so that she was able to recount her story. When she had finished, Windy and Anita stared at Cassie in mute astonishment.

"Wow! Remind me to never do battle with you, woman! That's incredible!" Windy sat straight up in the rocker, in awe of Cassie's description of her counter-attack on her ex-husband.

"Holy Toledo, Xena Warrior Princess, where did you learn all that stuff?" Anita gushed.

"From a self-defense class they held at the library a few weeks ago. It just seemed like a good idea, now that I am on my own. I was supposed to find someone to practice the moves on so that they would become automatic if I ever needed them. I had intended to ask you, Windy, but instead I just replayed them in my mind as I drove to work or while I was doing some simple tasks at the library. I guess I owe that young officer who taught the class a huge 'thank you'!"

Windy shook his head in amazement then said, "Speaking of officers, you need to contact the sheriff and file a complaint against Paul Alexander."

"For all the good it will do!" 'Nita sneered.

"Why?" Windy gave his fiancé a quizzical look.

"Because our esteemed sheriff, Billy Joe Crenshaw, is a bosom buddy of my ex-husband. I doubt that he would file a report even if I made one." Cassie supplied.

"You're not serious, are you? If you let him get away with this without filing a complaint…"

"It will be an exercise in frustration and futility, trust me on this, Windy," Cassie interrupted with a flat voice, taking another long sip of her brandy. "But ask me again tomorrow, and maybe I'll feel differently."

They sat in silence watching the flames dart around the logs in the fireplace. Cassie felt the soothing liqueur coat her jangled nerves and yawned.

"Are you guys sure you don't mind spending the night? I hate to be a namby-pamby about this, but I really do appreciate it!

"The hide-a-bed is as uncomfortable as…well, it's darned uncomfortable to sleep on," Cassie continued, "but what I do when I want to have an all-night movie marathon is to pull the mattress off of the frame and lay it on the floor in front of the fireplace. It's real cozy."

"Sounds romantic to me," Windy draped his arm around 'Nita's shoulders, pulling her snug against him.

"Hmmm, just keep the noise down…" Cassie clapped her hand over her mouth, "Did I really say that? I think it must have been the brandy talking! I'll get you a set of sheets and a comforter, and put out towels in the bathroom. I'm afraid I don't have any pillows for you, but you're welcome to use the ones that go with the couch. I'll bring down some pillowcases."

"Thanks, Cas, but I brought my pillow along with me." Cassie glanced back as she ascended the open staircase to see Anita wrapping her arms around her intended, laying her head upon his shoulder.

'Nita and Windy took the bedding Cassie offered, insisting that she lie down before she fell down. Cassie gave scant attention to her usual nighttime routine, barely running her toothbrush across her teeth, before climbing into her bed. She pulled her woven coverlet up to her chin and, with the murmurings of her friends in the living room to keep her company and Slack-Eyed Joe curled at her feet, she fell into a deep brandy-induced stupor.

By the time Cassie awoke in the morning, Windy had left for work, sparing her a lecture about calling the sheriff's office to report Paul's attack. Anita stood at the stove, removing a whistling teakettle from a burner. "Omigosh! What time is it?" Cassie said in a momentary panic. "Nine-thirty? I was supposed to be at the library half-an-hour ago!"

"Not to worry, Sleeping Beauty, I called your boss. That Evelyn Maples is one cool lady—intuitive, too. I told her that you were shook up after finding an intruder in your home last night, and right away she asked if it had anything to do with your no-good ex-husband.

"I hope you don't mind, but I gave her a quick rundown of your encounter with Paul. Anyway, after I assured her that you were okay, she was delighted that you were able to use the tactics you learned in the library's self-defense class to ward off the scum's attack. We both would have loved to see him crawling out the door after you toasted his…ah…family jewels!"

Cassie gave her friend a sleepy grin, "Thanks, 'Nita. I truly don't think that I could have faced the people at the library today."

"How about a cup of tea and a little breakfast?"

"Tea sounds marvelous, and I could use a few carbs to soak up that brandy. It sure hit the spot last night, but I'm feeling a little queasy this morning."

They chatted over a plain omelet and dry toast, rehashing the events of the previous evening. Cassie thought to ask Anita about the meeting with the parish priest, and the conversation followed the less alarming course of wedding preparations.

"How can I thank you and Windy, 'Nita? I don't know how I ever thought that you wouldn't be there for me after you got married—instead, I'm getting two friends for the price of one! You don't need to hang around and baby-sit me today, though. I'm sure Paul won't be back—especially not in the light of day. After all, skunks are nocturnal animals."

"Okay, if you really think Paul won't bother you, we'll be back by dark."

"On second thought, unless you guys plan to move out here, I'm going to have to stay by myself sooner or later. You know the old adage about biting the dog that bit you—not that I plan to bite Paul, mind you—I might get rabies! But, the sooner I face staying here at night alone, the better. I promise I'll be careful tonight and keep the phone close by—your cell number is the first one on my speed-dial."

Reluctantly, Anita agreed. "But you better not let anything happen to you, girl—I don't want to have to scare up another matron-of-honor at this late date. I'd never find anyone skinny enough to fit into the dress Carol is making!"

Cassie walked with Anita to her car. The mercurial autumn climate blew in a spring-like breeze as the temperature skirted the sixties.

"Can you believe this weather? Yesterday I would have predicted a snowstorm, today I look like a fool in my lined jacket." Anita draped the parka over her arm, obviously enjoying the sun as it bore down upon her sweatshirt.

"It's almost as though Mother Nature knew…." Cassie inhaled the warm spring-like air.

"Yeah, uncanny, huh?" Anita opened her car door and tossed her jacket inside. She straightened and hugged her friend. "You take care and call if you need anything. An odd feeling…a strange chill…*a-ny-thing*, you call!"

With Cassie's assurance that she would strap the phone to her waist and keep it with her at all times, Anita climbed into her car and drove it around the drive. Cassie watched as 'Nita stopped at the end of the far lane before pulling out of the driveway, and then as her taillights disappeared down the long, straight country road.

CHAPTER EIGHT

"This is a day the Lord has made, let us be glad and rejoice," Cassie sang an improvised melody to a favorite psalm, as fluffed-up sparrows sitting on the electrical wire overhead joined in chorus enjoying their reprieve from the fast-approaching winter.

Though there was much to be done around the farm, Cassie decided to act like she did when she was a girl, and the radio had just announced a school closing due to snow or fog: curl up all day with a good book.

She walked to the barn to retrieve an armful of logs for an afternoon fire. The urge to watch over her shoulder persisted in spite of her bravado to Anita just a few minutes past. She hated living with the fear that Paul might return at any moment, despite her best efforts to quell it. She hurried back to the house with her load of wood, determined that her decision to stay inside and read by the fire was motivated by a need to relax rather than anxiety over being too exposed outside in the open.

Cassie locked her door, and though she felt foolish doing it, braced a chair under the doorknob. She stacked the kindling she had collected in the fireplace, carefully arranging smaller logs over the top and a large wedge of dry maple over all. She struck a long fireplace match against the rough side of its box and lit a pre-made fire-starter. The dry kindling blazed around the logs, and in just a few seconds their bark caught fire.

Cassie ducked into her bedroom to get the paperback she had been reading—a romantic comedy by an author that she had just recently discovered. Slack-Eyed Joe lay sleeping against her pillow and elevated his head slightly when she turned on the light to find her book. Opening his one good eye, the cat gave her an annoyed look before stretching out his front paws and easing himself to all four feet. He pranced off the bed and marched to the living room, commandeering his spot on the hearthrug.

Cassie pulled her rocker over near the fireplace. She wrapped herself in the comfort of Aunt Nell's afghan and opened her book to the page marked by a strip of scrap paper. Eventually, Joe deigned to climb up on her lap and allow her to ruffle his fur.

After a few hours, Cassie put her book down just long enough to nudge Joe off of the afghan and put another log on the fire. She took a second short break midday to fix a light lunch. She finished the novel she had been reading and selected another from her burgeoning "to be read" shelf that she had filled with books from the Friends of the Library sales. This time she opted for a genre that she hadn't yet tried—a paranormal featuring vampires. Though the *Twilight* series was all the rage, she wasn't sure if she was willing to "suspend her disbelief" enough to become engrossed in the story, but the blurb on the back cover had captured her attention so she thought she would give it a try.

Joe, she noticed, had moved back into the bedroom at some point during the afternoon. This time he slept undisturbed, with his paw covering his eyes. He had rolled himself into a ball and curled his long tail around the perimeter of the half-sphere formed by his body. Cassie slipped back out of the room while her feline friend chased mice through his dreams.

She nestled into her rocker, propping her feet up on the footstool. She found the well-written book in her hands to be as captivating as the blurb had promised and was soon caught up in the life of a four-hundred-year-old vampire and his modern-day love interest. She tossed another log on the fire, not noticing as the twilight outside her large picture window turned to darkness. Toward the end of the book, she flagged her page and rolled her shoulders and neck to work out the kinks that had developed from sitting so long in one position.

The black of the moonless night outside the living room window pricked her apprehensions as she put her last log on the fire. She walked to the kitchen and opened a can of comfort food—Chef Boyardee ravioli—and dumped it unceremoniously into a pan. She warmed it slowly and when it was thoroughly heated she took the pan and a fork back to the living room.

Cassie decided that she was too on edge to finish her vampire novel and switched the television to the local news. "Pretty scary stuff," she said to no one in particular and got up to pop an old Jimmy Smits tape into the VCR. The actor's uncanny resemblance to Jaimé had Cassie checking out all of his old movies. Truth be told, she even tried to find reruns of *NYPD Blue* on the oldies channels on TV—especially that one episode she had heard about where you could see Jimmy Smits' naked butt. She had enough of a prurient curiosity to want to catch that show in particular....

She had tried, with less than stellar success, to keep thoughts of Jaimé at bay throughout the day, so had chosen to give her desires a feeding frenzy instead. She absentmindedly minced at the aromatic little pasta pockets of beef, swirling each in the tomato sauce clinging to the bottom of the pan before bringing it to her lips as she fast-forwarded through the previews and promotions. She set her pan of unfinished ravioli aside as she settled in to watch the opening scenes of *Old Gringo.*

Cassie jumped at the ringing of the phone lying beside her on the couch. She clicked the pause button on the remote, suspending Jimmy Smits in mid-sentence.

"Hello…" Cassie said tentatively into the mouthpiece.

"Cassandra?" Jaimé's voice floated from the receiver.

"Jaimé?" Cassie responded, relief and pleasure sending her

pitch an octave higher than its usual controlled tones.

"Does that mean you're happy to hear from me?" His laughter was apparent over the phone lines.

Cassie attempted to modulate her voice, "Uh, well..." then she, too, laughed, "Would you believe me if I said 'no'?"

"Huh-uh," His voice softened, "I've missed you so much, princess. I never realized how cold Canada was before."

"Me, too. I mean I've missed you. I've never been to Canada...."

"We'll have to fix that...."

The phone lines went quiet for a moment as they each savored their contact, tenuous though it was.

"Cas...."

"Yes?"

"There's something I have to know...."

Cassie took a deep breath, apprehensive of what would come next but knowing the time had come for honesty. She clicked the VCR remote and Jimmy Smits disappeared into a black void.

"Why didn't you write back to me?" His question caught Cassie off-guard.

"You mean to your last letter? You should have received mine a week or so ago!"

"Not now, then. Back when I went to Harvard. I wrote you letter after letter, but you never wrote back."

"What? What are you talking about? What letters?" Cassie moved to an upright position and leaned into the phone, "I never heard a word from you! You didn't call, you never wrote!"

"You never received any of my letters? Your mother never told you I called? I can understand your father's reaction—he read me the riot act and told me to never phone you again. But, your mom?"

"...never told me you called. You have to believe me, Jaimé, I never knew you tried to contact me. I thought you had found someone else—some sophisticated east coast..." the full impact of what Jaimé said fell on her like molten lead, "Oh my God, nooooooooooooooo! No no no no no no no no no!"

Jaimé heard silence then the wrenching words, "It can't be, it can't be," pounded over and over across the miles that lay between them. "Cassandra! Honey, what is it?" Jaimé thought he caught the word "baby" in between wracking sobs. He waited helplessly for her weeping to stop. At last he heard a keening moan followed by a loud hiccup.

After a quivering sigh, she said, "Wait a second…" He heard her blow her nose in the background. After a few minutes she returned to the telephone.

"Sorry…I'm so sorry…oh, Jaimé, I'm so sorry I doubted you. It's all my fault…our baby…it's all my fault…."

"Whoa, Cas, let's start at the beginning. What baby?"

Silence again rode the lines.

"When you left," Cassie began tremulously, "I was pregnant. I waited for your call…your letter…. My parents must have intercepted them…. I should have known then…I should have trusted you…."

"Pregnant? My sweet Lord, Cassandra." He hesitated, not wanting to ask his next question. "What happened to our baby?"

"I didn't tell anyone, not even 'Nita. If I had, maybe she would have gotten in contact with you. Maybe everything would have turned out differently. Maybe…. Anyway, I was sick a lot at first and after several weeks, my mother guessed my secret. She must have told my father, because he went ballistic. He had yelled at me often in the past but had never struck me."

"Oh God no." Jaimé said, anticipating her next words.

Her voice went flat, "When I returned home from my job at O'Shay's that night, he met me at the door. As soon as I opened the screen, he jerked me into the house and started shouting, half in English, half in Russian. He slammed me against the wall and kept yelling about you…in words I could never repeat. I fell and he kicked me in the stomach and, I think, would have killed me then and there if mom hadn't intervened. She fell onto the floor in front of me. He raised his arm to strike her, then lowered it to his side and stormed out the door."

"Cassandra, sweetheart...."

She continued in a monotone, "Paul had been calling the house since you left, but I kept refusing his advances, which rubbed against his pride. He picked at my father at work, saying how he, Paul, was too good for me and where did I come off turning him down. My father had been pushing me to date Paul since way before you and I were...together. As I just recently found out, it had something to do with an asinine Russian princess fantasy he had about me. I think he was truly delusional."

"You miscarried?" Jaimé's incredulity rang across the phone lines.

"No, not then at least...I don't know for sure what happened."

"Tell me about it." His voice held the even tones of controlled anger.

"Paul called again the next day to ask me to go to dinner. My father accepted for me."

She waited an instant before continuing in the same monotone as before. "Paul drove me to a dive restaurant on the outskirts of Toledo. After dinner, we walked to the car. My father was sitting in the front seat. Paul opened the door to the back seat and pushed me in then climbed in beside me.

"My father drove to a back alley nearby and parked the car. Paul crawled out and pulled me with him. I didn't know what they had planned but I feared for my—for our—baby's life. I fought Paul as he pulled me down the sidewalk and twisted my arm from his grasp, but I fell backward. I remember hitting my head on something and...."

Cassie sucked air into her lungs to keep her tears at bay, "...and the next thing I remembered was waking up in a hospital recovery room. It wasn't until later that I learned that I had not only lost our baby, but had hemorrhaged in the process, and the doctors had to perform an emergency hysterectomy to save my life."

"Cassandra, no...."

"Yes. I had not only destroyed our baby, but also lost all chances of ever having another."

Cassie continued, "They kept me in the hospital for several days until I…I tried to…I pulled the IV out of my arm and ran to the top floor of the hospital. There was a helicopter pad on the roof and the door had been left unlocked. As I stumbled toward the edge, a paramedic saw me and ran over to pull me back. They kept me in the psychiatric ward for observation for another month. They pumped me full of sedatives and anti-depressants, and by the time I left, I was engaged to Paul and our wedding date had been set."

"Damn him to hell!" Jaimé cursed Paul Alexander, then chastised himself, "How could I not have known…how could I have loved you so much and not have known you were in such danger?"

Cassie went on as though he hadn't spoken, "Mother never knew that my father had been involved in what had happened to me. She just knew that I had miscarried and had a hysterectomy. She was drinking a lot back then, and pretty oblivious to what was going on around her. I avoided 'Nita. Wouldn't talk to her when she called. I've never told her…never told anyone what happened…until now."

Cassie began to recite details as though they were fresh in her mind instead of buried under thirty years of rubble, "I gave up hope on ever having a normal life—gave up hope of ever seeing you again. I went to social engagements with Paul and his family, allowing his mother to outfit me as she pleased. Though Phoebe Alexander considered me beneath her stature in the community, I wore clothes well and so, became an acceptable accessory for her son. I guess all of the money my father spent on schooling me in poise and etiquette finally paid off—for him, anyway. Phoebe dove into the wedding preparations with the dervish of a…a…Tasmanian devil, with little input from me or my mom."

Cassie held her next words in her throat momentarily before allowing them to spew forth, "A few weeks before our wedding, Paul drove me to a seedy motel…you know, one of those broken down shacks along the highway. I was alive but felt more like a walking zombie—an empty shell. I let him take me into a room.

He ripped the zipper to my dress in his haste to get it off. He threw me on the bed and raped me. I don't remember fighting him. I don't remember doing anything but lying there. When it was over, he slapped me and said I was a lousy...a lousy...." Cassie stopped, refusing to repeat what Paul had said.

"He dropped me off at home. My father sat on the couch watching TV and didn't even bother to look up at me. Mom had passed out at the kitchen table. I ran to the bathroom, locked the door, hung my head over the toilet bowl and retched. After I had vomited everything out I tore off my dress and threw it across the room. I turned the shower water on as hot as I could and just stood under its cleansing force.

"Only I couldn't get clean. I couldn't rid myself of the stench of what I had permitted Paul to do to me. I hadn't fought him. I was still engaged to him.

"I turned off the water and stood naked in the bathtub. After a while, I toweled myself dry. I went into my bedroom and dressed in one of my best suits. I dried my hair and applied fresh make-up. Then I opened the medicine cabinet, removed the bottle of my mother's sleeping pills and swallowed each, one by one.

"I assume my father found me when he tried to go to the john. I guess there weren't enough pills left to.... Anyway, when I woke up, I was in the emergency ward of a hospital with tubes pumping my stomach. I remember how the ugly institutional green walls seemed to close in on me as I tried to pull on those tubes. Someone subdued me with a shot, and I don't remember anything else about the next few days. I never even found out the name of the hospital that I was in—nothing about it was familiar."

Cassie's voice took on an even tone as she continued her recitation, "Phoebe Alexander must have pulled some powerful strings to keep her son's fiancé's attempted suicide from reaching the local news.

"Funny thing is, I could never figure out why Paul wanted to marry me—why anyone would want to marry me—after all that I had done. He did say that I had solved the problem of having little brats running around the house. But he never seemed to want me, not really, even after he had me." The hint of wistfulness seemed out-of-place, and evaporated as she went on, "I was barely released from the hospital in time for the final fitting of my wedding dress, an exquisite pearl-encrusted gown that Phoebe had ordered from an exclusive New York designer's line.

"I hated myself for wanting to wear the beautiful dress. Hated myself for going through the sham of a rehearsal dinner. Hated myself for blaspheming my marital vows in God's house. Hated myself as I put on the façade of a new bride while I danced with Paul at the reception.

"At the hotel on our wedding night, I locked myself in the bathroom of our suite, while he screwed our maid-of-honor—a distant relative Phoebe had selected because she would look right in the photos—in a room across the hall.

"Guess that set the tone for the next thirty years. Pretty pathetic excuse for a life—I should have ended it back then."

Cassie waited for Jaimé to fill the silence that followed her final admission. She tried to remember when she had last heard him speak. She couldn't blame him if he had hung up the phone in disgust after she confessed her complicity in the death of their child. When she was just about to press the "end" button on the phone to disconnect the call, she heard a faint sound from the receiver.

"Jaimé?" she asked tentatively.

"I'm here," came the barely audible response.

Long moments passed before she heard his voice again, "Sweet Jesus, Our Lord protect us, my Love. I don't ever again want to hear you talk about ending your life! What happened wasn't your fault—*it wasn't your fault*! I've never before wanted to kill another human being, but if your...if Paul Alexander crossed my path right now, I can't say what I would do."

Jaimé took a deep breath, "If it weren't for Tina and Ben, I'd be on the road tonight driving home to you, Cassandra. I don't know what will happen between us, but promise me you will never attempt anything so desperate, and so incredibly selfish, again because there would be many more lives than your own that you would take with you."

Cassie laid her forehead against the phone, absorbing what he had just said and remembering sitting along the bank of the Maumee just this spring staring down at the murky waters. "I won't Jaimé, I promise. I have a lot more to live for now."

She stopped to wipe the tears that streamed down her cheeks, "I could never have dreamt of your forgiveness," she finally whispered into the receiver, exhausted but exonerated by the one she had most offended.

"Go to bed, darling, and sleep. I am with you."

When they finally terminated the invisible line that had connected them, Jaimé lay awake for hours reliving all that Cassandra had told him, while Cassie fell into a deep and dreamless slumber.

"Mother, we've got to talk," Cassie called her mom from the library staff phone the next day. "Can I bring dinner by this evening?" At her mother's assent, she responded, "Good, I'll pick up a 'to go' order of Happy Family from Wong's on my way." Cassie hung the phone back on its cradle, smiling to herself at the irony of the name of her mother's favorite Chinese dish. "We may not be such a 'Happy Family' when I get through with you, Martha Jane Mikhailov." She said to no one in particular.

Cassie's day was filled with meetings—first a staff meeting and then a district conference at the Wood County Public Library in Bowling Green that afternoon. The day dragged on as memories that Cassie had held at bay for nearly a lifetime cascaded over her. Though she had been interested in the topics offered at the afternoon workshops, she found that once she was seated in the room among the other librarians, she couldn't concentrate on the Power Point sessions offered by the speakers.

It had been one long week, with the dress fitting on Monday, Paul's "visit" on Tuesday, and Jaimé's call last night—she could hardly muster the energy to face her mother tonight, much less take notes on the current presentation on electronic journals. Fortunately, both presenters provided extensive hand-outs replicating each screen they projected from their computer, so Cassie would be able to review their main points another day.

The conference ended early, and by 4:30 the tantalizing aroma of Happy Family wafted through Cassie's Festiva as she drove toward her old Lower Eastside neighborhood. The closest available parking spot to her mother's apartment was in front of the adjacent building, and Cassie pulled into the empty space. As she reached across the seat to pick up the take-out bag from Wong's, she saw her mother's door open and a tall, elderly man with wavy white hair step out. He turned back into the apartment, apparently in response to something her mother said, and out of Cassie's line of vision. He reappeared a few minutes later whistling, and walked with the aid of a cane to a highly polished burgundy-colored Cadillac parked in front of her mother's apartment.

Hmm, wonder who that was? Cassie thought to herself as she balanced the bag containing the carry-out boxes while she pushed her car door shut. He looked familiar, and she tried to recollect where she might have met him as she walked to her childhood home. Her mother had the door open before Cassie could ring the bell.

"You're here early," she said with a touch of chagrin, blowing smoke from the cigarette balanced between her fingers over Cassie's shoulder, "I didn't expect you until after five!"

"Our meeting let out a little after four. I didn't think you would mind if I came on over." Cassie replied.

"No, no of course not," her mother hedged. "Mmm...that 'Happy Family' sure smells good!"

"Mom, who was that man leaving your apartment?" Cassie asked as she sat the bag on the Formica table top, slipped off her coat, and draped it on the back of a kitchen chair.

"Man? What man?"

"You know, the dapper-looking white-haired man who just climbed into the Cadillac parked out front." Cassie tried to keep her exasperation with her mom from her voice, as she had bigger fish to fry with her mother tonight than the identity of that strange man.

"Oh, he was just asking for directions to another building." Martha Mikhailov avoided looking at her daughter as she busied about pulling plates and flatware from her cupboards, the ubiquitous cigarette dangling between her lips.

Cassie knew that her mother was dodging the truth but chose to let the subject drop. She poured herself a glass of milk and sat it on the table, noting her mother's partially empty beer bottle sitting beside an ashtray full of lipstick-stained butts. She moved the ashtray to the counter before opening the white pasteboard container of rice and lifting the clear plastic cover off the disposable aluminum pan holding the "Happy Family" of seafood, pork, chicken and Chinese vegetables in a tangy sweet and sour sauce.

Her mother made a show of sniffing the steam as it rose from the pan before spooning the concoction over the rice on her plate. "Ahh, it's been a long time since I've smelled anything that good!"

"Okay, Mom, I'm letting the subject of the man at your door drop, you don't need to go overboard about the dinner."

Martha Mikhailov gave her daughter a guilty smile, "Well, it does smell delicious!" They ate in silence, each deep in her thoughts. As Cassie let a delectable scallop melt in her mouth, she watched her mother across the table and wondered at her secrets.

"Mom, there's something I have to know."

Martha glanced warily at her daughter but said nothing.

"The fall before I married Paul, did a man named Jaimé Alvarez try to contact me?"

Cassie's mother blanched and choked on a bamboo shoot. She coughed and took a long swallow of beer before answering, "That was such a long time ago, sweetie. I hardly remember those days."

"Mo*therrr*..."

"Okay, okay. I told your father that we shouldn't interfere. I said that you had a right to talk to the boy." She looked carefully at her daughter with eyes yellowed by smoke and alcohol, "Was he the one who…"

"…fathered my baby? Yes."

"And you've been seeing him again? I heard talk around about how people had seen the two of you together over the summer. Are you sure that's a good idea, dear?"

"A good idea? I guess it's a moot point, since he's living in Toronto with his children. Besides I'm not talking about now, I want to know about that fall thirty years ago. So, Jaimé did try to contact me."

Cassie's mother fidgeted with her fork, stirring a piece of chicken back and forth on her plate. "Maybe, once or twice."

Cassie took a deep breath. Though she knew Jaimé had told her the truth, her mother's admission hit her like a blow to her solar plexus. When she regained her equilibrium, she asked, "What happened to his letters?"

"Your father burned them—he only wanted the best for you!"

"Don't! Don't defend him, mother! He didn't give a rat's ass about me! He was certifiably nuts, living in some fantasy world that he had created. It had nothing to with me and everything to do with his illusion about himself. I was just a pawn in his make-believe world—but you, you were my mother! Why didn't you tell me…?"

"Don't you understand after all these years, Cassie? I couldn't go against your father's wishes any more than you could. You let him mold you into the daughter he wanted. I could never be the wife he thought I should be, but I couldn't openly defy him. It would have just enraged him even more." Martha Mikhailov pleaded for her daughter's understanding and forgiveness.

Cassie sat back in her chair, defeated, and looked, really looked, at her mother. Vestiges of the beauty she had been still clung to her wrinkled and whiskey-weathered face.

"Why did you marry him, Mom?"

"It was such a long time ago and I was so young and ready to take on the world. Your father had just recently emigrated to this country from Hungary, where his family had been living since the Russian Revolution. He was so handsome—like that Omar Sharif guy in *Dr. Zhivago*—not the made-for-TV remake they did a while back, but the real one, you know, with Julie Christie.

"He had made his way to St. Louis where your grandfather met him while working on the waterfront. He was so independent, so alone, and he swept my heart away the first time your granddad brought him home for dinner. He was, oh, such a romantic! And much to your grandparents' dismay, we eloped that spring." She took another swig of beer before continuing with a voice turned hard, "It wasn't until after we moved to Ohio that his...his controlling side came out."

"And I married Paul," Cassie said, "and history repeated itself. Except my baby died and I couldn't have another."

Martha Mikhailov avoided looking at the woman across the table, hooding other long-buried secrets from her perceptive gaze.

They each made a show of eating, the act of lifting their forks to their mouths and laconically chewing each bite occupying minutes that would have, another time, been filled with idle chit-chat.

Cassie cleared their plates from the table, spooned the leftovers into an old cottage cheese container from the cupboard, and fit it in amongst the clutter that filled her mother's refrigerator, knocking over a salad dressing bottle that crashed to the floor.

"Don't you think it's time you cleared some of this junk out of here?" Cassie said with an unaccustomed edge to her voice, as she stooped to pick up the offending bottle.

"It's not my refrigerator that you are upset with, dear, but if it will help, I'll get to it this week."

"You're right. Your 'fridge is your business," Cassie said closing the door with more force than necessary before turning abruptly and grabbing her jacket. "Listen, I think I'd better go." She swung her coat over her shoulders, jabbing her arms into the sleeves in one angry motion.

"Cassie, I'm sorry, I really am." After a moment, Martha Mikhailov called to her daughter's retreating back, "Can...can I still come out to the farm for Thanksgiving?"

Her mom's plaintive plea caught Cassie off-guard. She shifted around to face the apprehension that had formed in the older woman's rheumy eyes, and Cassie's anger dissipated. She walked to her mother and wrapped her arms around her stooped shoulders. "Of course you're coming to my house for Thanksgiving dinner— You may not be perfect, but you're the only mom I have!"

Cassie felt her mother's shoulders stiffen slightly as she bent her head back to look up at her daughter, "Oh, Cassie, dear...."

"It's okay, mom. We'll talk later. I love you." She gave her mom a quick peck on the cheek and then slipped out the door. It wasn't until she was walking to the car that she remembered that she hadn't mentioned Paul's "visit" to the farm. *Just as well*, she thought, *the evening had been exhausting enough.* Besides, there was no need to worry her mother unnecessarily.

The brisk November winds blew swiftly from one day to the next. Autumn gave way to wintry skies as the Thanksgiving holiday approached.

Windy had installed a steel door at the entrance to the farmhouse. Though Cassie understood the need, the big unpainted gray door not only offended her aesthetic sensibilities, it was also a daily reminder of Paul's incursion into her home. However, she faithfully locked its deadbolt when she left for work in the morning and was grateful it was there when she returned home each evening. She was more cautious now, aware of all movements around her as she walked to her car from the library or the grocery. Prickles of paranoia would catch her off guard in the middle of the day, and she would give her surroundings a wary visual search, expecting Paul to appear at any moment. That she had experienced no repercussions from her counter attack against her former husband left her even more on edge.

Her Thursday evening phone calls from Jaimé did little to ease her mind. While their conversations verged on the mundane, the underlying thread of tension added to Cassie's stress. For their relationship to evolve beyond a friendship, one or the other would be forced to put their personal desires before the good of their family—an unlikely prospect for either of them. She found that as much as she looked forward to each call, once they disconnected from one another, she felt little inclination to do anything but sit on the couch and stare into the night.

Cassie relegated thoughts of both Paul and Jaimé to the back-burner as, on the Wednesday before Thanksgiving, she stopped to pick up the small, fresh turkey and pint of oysters that she had ordered from the local meat market. She hummed as she jostled with other last-minute shoppers at the grocery store. Her excitement at preparing her first Thanksgiving dinner as a free woman percolated through her as she smiled at the frazzled clerk ringing up her grocery bill. A light snow floated against the windshield as she drove home, recounting her menu in her head: turkey, dressing (both bread and oyster), gravy, thick whole-egg noodles, ambrosia, jellied cranberry sauce (the kind that when you open both ends of the can plops out in a cylinder and that Phoebe Alexander refused to allow near her table), Brussels sprouts, and pumpkin pie—everything her Aunt Nell used to make for Thanksgiving dinner on the farm when Cassie was a child. Paul had always insisted that she prepare epicurean dishes for their dinners with his family—roast duck á l'orange, cranberry dressing with water chestnuts, and tortes for dessert. Her only salute to her days of *Bon Appetit* cooking would be smashed yams and russet potatoes with garlic cloves rather than the traditional mashed potatoes—no need to give up *everything* gourmet!

By the time her mother arrived with Aunt Nell the next day, the aroma of roast turkey wafted through the house. Cassie hurried out the door to help her mom with Aunt Nell's wheelchair. However, much to Cassie's surprise, Aunt Nell had pushed open the car door and braced a folding aluminum walker on the drive in front of her before her niece could reach the end of the walk. The older woman pulled herself up off the seat using the walker and proceeded to take hesitant steps toward Cassie.

"Aunt Nell! You've been snookering me! You've completely

graduated from the chair!" Cassie clapped her hands together and stepped aside as her aunt proudly made her way up the walk. Cassie's mother walked behind Nell, her smile revealing her pleasure at her sister's progress.

Once inside, both Cassie's mother and aunt exclaimed over the wonderful smells. Cassie had set the table with her mother's wedding china, which she had borrowed earlier in the month. She had even polished Martha's silverware to a bright, gleaming shine and placed knives, forks and spoons beside the plates. A linen napkin, crisply starched and ironed, lay by each place setting.

"So fancy for just the three of us!" Aunt Nell said, admiring the table.

"Hey, nothing's too good for the Gibson Girls!" Martha Gibson Mikhailov declared to her sister, as she wrapped her thin arm around her daughter. They stood together in a camaraderie that had been absent during the years of Cassie's marriage.

"Now, you two sit down while I do the finishing touches and serve dinner. Everything's ready and waiting."

Slack-Eyed Joe slipped into the kitchen as Cassie carved the turkey, waiting patiently for her to drop a morsel onto the floor. He watched as she carried bowl after steaming bowl of food to the table, and not to be dissuaded, followed her to the dining room as she filled three wine goblets with a top-shelf chardonnay.

Sizing up the situation, he sidled over to Aunt Nell and rubbed against her chair. Giving a furtive look at her niece, Nell snuck a sliver of turkey from the platter and lowered her hand to the waiting feline. Joe quickly ate the treat, licking his benefactor's fingers to get the last bit of juice.

As Cassie took her seat at the head of the table with her mom and aunt at either side, Joe scurried underneath and gently pawed Cassie's mother's ankles. Martha bent to look under the table.

"Joey," Cassie admonished, "Are you begging?" Then to her guests, she said, "Don't encourage him, he's a reprobate when it comes to stealing people food."

As though he understood his mistress's words, Slack-Eyed

Joe slunk over to the doorway and plopped down in the middle of the rag-rug that served as a runner. He placed one paw over the other, and rested his chin on his legs, keeping a dejected watch for any scrap that might be tossed his way.

"Poor baby," Cassie consoled, "You'll get your Thanksgiving salmon later."

The women then joined hands, taking turns giving thanks for the blessings they had received through the year. Before Cassie spoke, she silently put Jaimé's name at the top of her list.

Though conversation meandered from topic to topic, Cassie noticed her mother and her aunt exchanging furtive glances. Finally, she could contain her curiosity no longer. "What is up with the two of you? I'm feeling just a little left out here!" Her smile belied her mock-offense.

"Cassie, dear," both women began at once.

"You start," Martha Mikhailov nodded to her sister.

"No, I think it's your place," Nell Gibson deferred.

"One of you, just tell me what's up!" Cassie exclaimed with a good-natured impatience.

"It's a long story, sweetie," her mom began. "But Nell and I have talked it over and decided that it was time that you knew... our secret."

Cassie cut off a bite of turkey from the slice of breast on her plate, slowly chewing it while she waited for their great mystery to be revealed.

"Oh, how do I begin?" Martha sent a perplexed look across the table to her sister.

"You always were the timid one," Nell chastised back. "Cassie, dear, this is the way of it. You remember back when I was in my twenties...."

"Well, of course, she doesn't remember that, Nell. You're getting senile!" Martha interjected.

"Hush, sister, and let me tell the story, or do it yourself. Now, as I was saying, when I was in my twenties I worked in the USO canteens and ended up in Hollywood. Ah, those were the days, I danced from morning 'til night!"

"You're daft, Nell. Let *me* tell the story," Martha interrupted again.

"Okay, one of you tell me what you're talking about, and do it soon!" Cassie declared as she popped a small Brussels sprout in her mouth.

"Okay, sweetie, I'll cut to the chase, as they say—what Nell is trying to tell you is that, well…your father wasn't really your father."

"*What?*" The sprout nearly shot back out before Cassie's hand flew to her mouth.

"Leopold Mikhailov didn't father you, it's as simple as that."

"Mother, there is nothing simple about telling me that the man that I had always thought sired me, didn't…. If not him, who?"

"Well, now, that's not for me to say…."

"Mo*therrr* …"

"I hate it when you take that tone with me, Cassandra Grace! It's not my business to say who fathered you because…well, because…I'm not your mother."

Cassie's fork clattered onto her fine china plate. "Okay, this isn't funny anymore. What in the H-E-double-hockey-sticks are you talking about?" She glared, dumbfounded, from one woman to the other.

"Martha, you are going about this all wrong. You never did have a way with words." Nell shook her head, "What your moth… what my sister is trying to say is that, she's not your mother—I am."

"*Get Out!*" Both women gave Cassie a startled look as she took a sizable gulp of chardonnay before quickly amending her statement, "No, I don't mean 'get out' as in 'leave' I mean 'get out' as in 'What in the *hell* are you talking about?'"

"Well, dear, that's what I was trying to tell you," Nell Gibson said with an exaggerated patience. "Back when I was a chorus girl in Hollywood, I met this most marvelous man—oh how he could dance! Given half the chance, he could have out-stepped Fred

Astaire and Gene Kelly both at once! He took a shining to me—I was a bit of a looker back in the day—and, well, you know how it is, one thing led to another and…."

"…I was conceived?" Cassie asked, incredulity covering every nuance of her face. She took a deep breath and heaved it out, while bracing her back against the chair, looking from one sister to the other. She shook her head in disbelief, and said the first thing that popped into her mind, "No wonder I love to dance!"

"You do get it honest, dear."

"But how?" Cassie turned to her mother—at least the woman she had assumed was her mother.

"Your father…er…Leo had very romantic notions of what being married meant. He stuck me up on a pedestal—well, you know, not really, but, whaddya call it? Figuratively speaking. When it came to the more…ah…earthy aspects of lovemaking, he was, well, thoroughly disgusted. He thought a woman should just lie there and be a receptacle of his…."

"*Mother!* There are some things a daughter doesn't need to hear—no matter how old she is…and…" Cassie hesitated searching for the right words, "…no matter if she isn't really your daughter. This is way too bizarre—are you sure *Candid Camera* isn't hiding somewhere behind the curtains?"

"No, dear, now do get serious," Martha admonished. "As I was saying. Your fa…Leo…wasn't into the carnal side of marriage. He soon took to sleeping on the couch—you remember that." Indeed Cassie could not recall a time when her parents had shared a bed. "When Nell phoned me to say that she was 'in the family way,' we decided that I was in a better situation to raise a child than she was, and to be honest, I was so lonely that the thought of a baby to keep me company had me jumping at the idea. We concocted what our father called another of our 'hare-brained schemes.' But, he and our mother agreed to help us.

"The first thing I needed to do was to get Leo tanked, so I brought home a bottle of top-shelf vodka. It took nearly the whole bottle until he passed out. The next day, I convinced him that he had seduced me and we had made mad, passionate love. He denied it, but in a few weeks, I announced to him that I was 'expecting.' It was a simple matter to deceive him using pillows. He never saw me na…" at Cassie's raised eyebrows she amended, "without clothing, and had as little to do with me as possible after I told him that I was 'in that way.'"

Nell picked up the story, "When it came close to my time, we met at your grandparents house in St. Louis. Much to Leopold's apparent relief, Martha said that she wanted to be with her mother when she delivered. When it came time to go to the hospital, I assumed Martha's identity—we were close enough in age and appearance to pull it off as they didn't have all the rigmarole they have these days—and, the rest, as they say, is history!"

"Not quite—there's one big gap in this preposterous tale," Cassie looked from one woman to the other. "Just who is my father? Some ne'er-do-well fly-by-night wham-bam-thank-you-m'am jerk?"

"Not exactly…." Nell Gibson shifted uncomfortably in her seat. "I eventually resumed a relationship with your real father, and when I told him about you, he at first became angry, but then agreed that we had done the sensible thing at the time, taking your best interests to heart. Mind you, we had no idea that Leopold would become so overbearing with you. We had assumed that he would ignore you as he did Martha, and that she would be free to raise you as she saw fit.

"However, after a time I missed my baby too much and had to be near you. So, your grandparents bought me this farm. They wanted me to find a place in town, but I had this idyllic notion about life in the country."

"You gave up your career for me?" Cassie asked with a note of wonder.

"Pshaw, it was the least I could do. Besides, I wanted to be a part of your life, if only as your aunt."

With a dogged determination, Cassie again asked, "But what about my birth father?"

"Well, after a while, he, too, wanted to have a part in raising you. He had broken his leg in a fall from a stage and needed a place to recover. I invited him to move to the farm to recuperate...and he never left."

"Uncle Clem? Uncle Clem was my father?"

Nell nodded.

"Oh my good heavens! But why?...No, don't tell me. I have to think about this. Why don't the two of you go on into the living room, where you can discuss how well you think this all went. I'll light a fire and then clean up the table. I'd like to have a little time to myself, if you don't mind."

Cassie paid no attention to the hushed voices in the living room while she gathered up the remains of the meal and carried them to the kitchen. She put the leftovers into containers and methodically washed and dried the dishes, her mind churning through the gamut of emotions ranging from shock to anger to awe.

In the end, Cassie cut three wedges of pumpkin pie and placed them on dessert plates and prepared three mugs of herbal tea. She took a can of whipped cream from the refrigerator and shook it vigorously. She squirted a healthy dollop on each piece of pie then picked up the lid to cap the dispenser. Slack-eyed Joe strutted into the kitchen, eyeing the canister in his mistress's hand.

"Oh, what the heck," Cassie told her furry companion, and shot just a smidgen of whipped cream along the rim of his food bowl. Joe sniffed it suspiciously then took a tentative taste before lapping up the swirl of confection with gusto. The cat lifted his butterscotch head imperiously, demanding more. He pawed Cassie's leg and peered up at her with one green eye causing her to relinquish, giving him another small squirt.

She then looked at the lid and back to the long white nozzle dripping a trickle of white. Shrugging her shoulders, she held the canister aloft above her open mouth and released a steady stream of creamy foam, letting it slide down her throat before easing her finger from the dispenser. She swallowed the last bit of whipped cream and with the grin of a Cheshire cat, capped the container and returned it to the refrigerator.

Still licking her lips, Cassie put the pie and the mugs of tea on a tray and carried them into the living room, followed by a very contented yellow feline. Her mother and aunt watched her warily from their perch on the davenport as she sat the tray on the coffee table and gave a plate and mug to each. She took a slice of pie and cup of tea for herself and sat down in the rocker opposite the couch.

"I've been thinking," Cassie began, taking a bite of pie, chewing it deliberately, and chasing it with a sip of tea, "assuming all that you have told me is true and, incredulous as it sounds, I have no reason to doubt you...the tyrant that I thought was my father, wasn't—what a relief to know that not a drop of his princely Russian blood has tainted my veins!

"What's more, the man that I loved, respected, and—though it sounds almost incestuous to say so now—had a crush on throughout my entire childhood, actually *is* my father."

The sisters exchanged looks of surprise before turning their attention back to Cassie as she went on, "Plus, I not only still have the mother who raised me, but also found out that the aunt whom I treasured as a second mom really *is* my mother."

She took another bite of pie, taking time to savor its rich texture, and grinned at the women on the couch, "The way I see it, I couldn't be any luckier if I'd just won the Powerball lottery! In fact, any amount of money pales compared to the gift I've just been given. The only thing that upsets me is that it took you so long to tell me the truth!"

They finished their dessert in a companionable silence by the warmth of the fire, letting its glow settle over the momentous events of the day. The older women prepared to leave as dusk fell outside. As Cassie walked the sisters to their car, she was startled to realize that her mother wasn't reaching immediately for a pack of cigarettes from her purse. "Mom, you haven't had a cigarette all day!"

Martha Mikhaliov smiled smugly at her daughter, "'Bout time you noticed—I'm on the patch!"

"This is very nearly the biggest shock of the day—whatever brought this on?"

"I had an appointment with Doc Patterson last week, and he said I needed to give up the smokes or I might not see my eightieth birthday."

Cassie laughed, "He's been harping at you to quit for years, what made you decide to listen to him now?"

"No need to be a smart-aleck, Cassandra." Martha chided her daughter, then added with an air of mystery, "Besides, that's not the only change I'm thinking about making, but don't ask me anymore questions yet—I'll tell you when I'm ready."

"Aunt Nell?"

"Don't look at me, I seldom have any idea as to what my sister is talking about!" She shrugged her shoulders while leaning heavily on her walker.

As they had reached the end of the walk and the air was brisk, Cassie temporarily let her mother have her way. She wasn't sure if she could handle another surprise tonight, anyway! She gave each woman a heartfelt embrace then helped her Aunt Nell into the car. After seeing them safely down the road, she quickly returned to the house to await Jaimé's call—he wasn't going to believe what she had to tell him....

CHAPTER NINE

december

Cassie strung fat kernels of white popcorn interspersed with fresh red cranberries in various patterns on long strands of heavy green thread. As she finished each string, she draped it on the Christmas tree that Anita and Windy had insisted she put up last weekend. They had shown up at her door on Saturday with the small white pine, a sturdy stand, and several boxes of miniature colored lights. The rest, they said, was up to Cassie. Windy fastened the tree into the stand, and under Cassie's direction, sat it by the large picture window across the room from the fireplace, so that she could still safely make a cozy fire and yet enjoy her festive little tree.

She had spent that evening stringing the lights on the pine, interweaving them, where possible, toward the trunk to give the tree depth. Though she hadn't intended to decorate for the holidays, she was taken with the small tree, and Monday morning had found her searching through the library's books on handmade ornaments to find ideas for simple decorations that she could craft on her limited budget.

Cassie sat back on her couch to admire the sparkly white

cutout snowflakes, red construction paper cone Santa Clauses, and tinfoil stars that adorned her tree. She had splurged on a box of painted glass ball ornaments that caught her eye at the Dollar Store, as well as an assortment of antique colored aluminum icicles she had found at Goodwill and that now danced merrily in the air currents whenever the furnace kicked on.

The Kris Kristofferson/Dyan Cannon remake of *Christmas in Connecticut* flashed from her TV screen and she laughed at the mishaps caused by Tony Curtis's bumbling character while waiting for her weekly Thursday evening phone call from Jaimé.

She had just stepped back to admire her latest addition to the festive little tree when the anticipated ring sounded from the phone on the coffee table.

"Hello!" She tried to temper the excitement in her voice.

"Hey, Cas, it's me."

"Nita?"

"Yeah, you were expecting maybe…oh, shoot, it's Thursday— I know who you were expecting! Sorry, kiddo, but I'll make this short." Anita promised before continuing, "Mom Alvarez just called me."

"Jaimé's mother? Is everything okay?" Cassie asked, worry tingeing her question.

"Fine, or will be if you could help us out. She and the doc— Jaimé's father—work at a soup kitchen up in east Toledo once a month. I know it's short notice, but I was supposed to help out on Saturday and I'm swamped with last minute stuff for the wedding. I don't know what I was thinking when I agreed to go up with them! Anyway, if you could take my place in the serving line, I'd be eternally—well, maybe not that long—grateful!"

"Saturday? I was going to head up to the Maumee Bay Market to do a little Christmas shopping anyway and that's in the same general vicinity, so I don't see why not. Should I call Dr. Alvarez for directions?"

"Sure, that would be great. Thanks, Cas—once again, I'm in your debt!"

Cassie laughed as she bid her friend goodbye and good luck with her wedding preparations. She sat back on the couch pondering 'Nita's call when the phone rang again. This time Jaimé's voice sauntered over the line, and she pulled her afghan around her and settled in for her weekly 'fix' from Canada.

Cassie turned off of the Interstate, following Dr. Alvarez's directions through the unfamiliar streets of East Toledo. She pulled up in front of an old red brick church nearly hidden amidst the surrounding large, boarded-up but once opulent homes. The church sat back from the road, fronted by a cracked stretch of concrete that evidently served as a loading zone. She noticed a parking lot across the street and pulled into one of the many empty spaces. She locked her car and skirted the rusted and bent chain-link fence that must have at one time served as security for the lot.

A few young men loitered among the fast food wrappings and other debris scattered around the entrance to the church, and Cassie hesitated before approaching the steps.

"You lookin' for the soup kitchen?" A muscular young black man dressed in just a tee-shirt and jeans, tossed a cigarette aside and looked her in the eye without smiling.

"Yes...yes I am" Cassie replied.

"You go in over there." He pointed to a stairwell at the side of the building leading down to a basement door. Cassie surveyed the others standing around watching her. If the door at the bottom of the stairs was locked, she would be trapped and at the mercy of an attacker or attackers. She nodded and thanked the man as she walked calmly toward the stairway, still undecided as to what she was going to do. Much to her relief, when she approached the stairs, Dr. Alvarez opened the door below and greeted Cassie warmly. She turned and waved to the young man who had directed her to the stairwell and hurried on down the steps.

Dr. Alvarez introduced Cassie to the other volunteers and to the staff at the soup kitchen. Green beans simmered in huge pans on the eight-burner gas stove. Aromas of Italian spices seeped from five electric roasters filled with goulash and lining a wide shelf adjacent to, but six or so inches below, the serving counter. A commercial-grade dishwasher stood in the corner, awaiting its crucial role in the feeding of the hungry.

After giving Cassie a brief overview of how the soup kitchen operated, Dr. Alvarez suggested that she serve green beans next to him, while he ladled goulash onto the clients' plates as they passed through the line. Mrs. Alvarez put various desserts donated by individuals and outdated baked goods from companies around the city onto small plates at the end of the counter.

While waiting for the food line to open, Cassie filled a large fruit bowl with bananas, apples, and oranges that had been collected from the members of the Alvarez's home parish, then busied herself stirring the goulash in the roasters.

"I understand that you met my sister-in-law," Gregorio Alvarez commented to Cassie, his smile turning his face into an older version of Jaimé's.

Cassie laughed, "We didn't get off to such a great start, but I think we made our peace before Jaimé and I left."

"She paid you a high compliment. I believe her exact words were 'That Alexander woman isn't so bad for a *gringa*'!" Dr. Alvarez's smile deepened causing laugh-lines to fan out from the corner of his eyes. Cassie tried not to stare at him, but he so resembled Jaimé that she found her gaze drawn back to his face.

"I hope to meet her again. I'll have to get Anita to join me for lunch at *Tiá's Taverna*."

Gregorio Alvarez's response was lost in the commotion of their first customers, two teenagers jostling to be in the front of the line.

"No need to push, boys, there's plenty for everyone," Dr. Alvarez said with good humor as he dished a generous spoonful of goulash onto a plate and handed it to one of the teens.

"Green beans?" Cassie offered, using a set of tongs to lift the hot beans out of their steaming pot.

They bantered with the clients as they came through the line,

Cassie feigning hurt when someone rejected her offer of beans. She was amazed when, midway through serving, she realized that she was thoroughly enjoying herself. Many of the people, and especially the men, going through the line gave Cassie a good-natured teasing either about her beans or some little idiosyncrasy about her appearance. She chatted briefly with the mothers with small children and listened to an older woman's complaints about her health, all the while helping to keep the line moving along.

The two hours of serving passed with extraordinary speed. Cassie found that the minute she turned from her station to either refill the fruit bowl or ask the volunteer cooking the beans to bring over another pot when she was running low, more patrons would be waiting for her return. She also kept the food in the roasters stirred and assisted with swapping out an empty roaster for a full one when needed.

When the last helping of goulash had been served, they washed the large pans and aided with spot-drying the plates and other dishes as they came out of the dishwasher.

"You did a magnificent job, Cassandra," Jaimé's father said as he dropped pieces of flatware into their proper holders.

Cassie smiled as she stretched to relieve the ache that had developed between her shoulders, "Thank you. The pleasure was, indeed, all mine—I'd love to help again if I'm needed."

Jaimé's mother joined them and overheard Cassie's comment. "*Muy bueno!*" She said as she reached up to pat Cassie on the shoulder. She spoke to her husband in Spanish, and he translated for Cassie. "We would be honored if you and your mother would join us for Christmas dinner, if you don't have other plans."

Their invitation momentarily overwhelmed Cassie. "Are you sure we wouldn't be imposing?" she asked with anticipation. But then her expression fell as she thought about Aunt Nell. It would be rude to ask to have her included, and there was no way she would spend Christmas away from her aunt, especially this year.

"Is something wrong?" Gregorio Alvarez asked.

"I'm afraid we will have to decline, Aunt Nell is…"

"…invited to join us, as well, of course!" Jaimé's father finished Cassie's sentence for her.

"In that case, I think I can speak for mother and for Aunt Nell when I say we would be delighted to accept your offer. May we bring an appetizer or some other contribution to the dinner?"

"*No, no es necessario,*" Jaimé's mother answered. "*Jest yorsels.*" She spoke the last phrase in a heavily accented English.

Jaimé's parents walked with Cassie to the parking lot where they parted ways with assurances that she would see them on Christmas Day.

Cassie mentally added Dr. and Mrs. Alvarez to her Christmas shopping list as she steered her Festiva toward the Maumee Bay Market, a unique conglomeration of shops in the old warehouse district along the river. She was still astounded by the "high" that working the soup kitchen gave her—enhanced, of course, by being with Jaimé's parents. She felt closer to Jaimé today than she had since he left for Toronto. And in just a few weeks, he would be home! She would be spending Christmas Day with Jaimé *and* his family!

She lucked out, finding a vacant parking spot directly across from the Market. She had no idea what she was shopping for, and as with Anita and the long-suffering search for a wedding dress, trusted that she would know the perfect gifts when she saw them.

Her first purchase was easy—a Peace Frog tee-shirt for Ben. She bought a cute little catnip-filled mouse for Joey, and found a darling life-like molded vinyl babydoll for Tina. It cost more than she intended to pay, but was irresistible, with a rounded tawny face that could easily have resembled Tina as a baby. For the first time, Cassie didn't feel the deep sense of loss that had overwhelmed her in the past when she saw such a realistic doll.

She walked from shop to shop searching for just the right gift for Jaimé and for his parents, but she was at a loss as to what to buy. She decided to look at the mall for a sweater for her mother and a new nightgown for Aunt Nell. She laughed to herself, acknowledging that she would always think of Martha Mikhailov as her mother, and Nell Gibson as Aunt Nell, regardless of her birth relationship to either woman. Both were equally dear to her and she could not love either of them any more than she already did.

At last she gave up her search, tucked the bag with the tee-shirt and the mouse under her arm, and cradling the doll as if it were a real baby, crossed the street back to her waiting car.

It was Evelyn Maples who accidentally provided her with the idea for the perfect gift for Jaimé's parents on the following Monday. She had a catalog for the Heifer International charity on her desk, and as Cassie paged through it, she decided to buy trees for a third-world country in their honor. As she and Anita had made a pact not to exchange presents due to 'Nita's fast-approaching wedding, Jaimé's was the only gift she had yet to buy.

Cassie and 'Nita had their final dress-fittings with Carol on Wednesday, with less than a week until Christmas and two until the wedding. Cassie dabbed a tissue at the corner of her eye, when her best friend emerged from the changing room in her bridal gown. The dress fell to a tea-length with long draping sleeves ending in two-inch cuffs. Along with accenting the gown in red velvet, Carol had talked Anita into letting her take several yards of the red material to create a hooded cape that fell just below the hem of the bridal dress. The cape was trimmed in a soft white faux fur that Carol assured them had never been attached to any animal. With the long-stemmed red roses that 'Nita had chosen for her bouquet, the effect would be stunning.

The green velvet of Cassie's dress clung to her form as it flowed from its empire waist. Cassie's gown was tea-length as well, with full, flowing sleeves caught in a deep cuff. The sleeves were sliced from the cuff to the shoulder, exposing her arms as she walked. The bodice had a square neckline cut just above the rise of Cassie's breasts and with just enough material on either side of her chest to connect the dress to the draped sleeves. Cassie would carry one long-stemmed white rose to accent the deep green of her gown.

'Nita's excitement as they left the dressmaker's was infectious and they drove to Dietsch Brother's ice cream shop to celebrate with a hot fudge sundae. Anita took a spoonful of whipped cream and swirled it in fudge sauce before bringing it to her lips. "Now this is true heaven. This will be the last fattening thing I eat until after the wedding. That gown fits like a glove!"

Cassie anchored her spoon in her maple-nut ice cream and opened the clasp to her leather purse. "I have something for the closest friend I will ever have," she said and handed Anita a long box tied with a red velvet ribbon. Anita tugged the strip of velvet off and removed the lid from the box. A strand of gleaming pearls lay on a bed of satin with a small elegant ruby poinsettia caught in the middle of the necklace. Matching ruby earrings with tiny pearls at their core lay in the center of the box.

"Cassie, omigosh! They're beautiful! I couldn't—they're too much! You can't afford…"

"Hush, they're your wedding present from me, mom, and Aunt Nell. We pooled our resources and used all of our wiles to find what we hoped would be the perfect jewels to set off your gown."

"They are awesome, truly. I will cherish them for the rest of my life." Anita reached across the table and gave her friend a spontaneous hug, very nearly giving the Winnie-the-Pooh appliqué on the front of her sweatshirt a taste of whipped cream.

The next evening, Cassie sat curled up on the couch with a new novel, sipping hot chocolate while Slack-Eyed Joe lay across the back of the davenport just above her head. His contented purr blended with the Christmas music softly harmonizing from Cassie's CD player. Her little tree twinkled gaily in the window, while logs crackled in the fireplace across the room.

The jangle of the phone caused Joe to lift his head as Cassie reached for the instrument laying on the coffee table.

"Cassandra?" the usual lilt was missing from Jaimé's voice as he spoke her name.

"What's wrong?"

He gave a quick chuckle, "Do you know me so well that you can tell something's not right just by how I say your name?"

It was Cassie's turn to laugh, "Scary, huh?"

"No, not at all. But, I do have some bad news. We're at a crucial stage in our negotiations, and there's no way I can leave Toronto at this time."

Cassie's silence gave voice to her dismay.

"Cas?"

"Your parents will be so disappointed!"

"I hope they aren't the only ones...."

"Oh, Jaimé, I was so looking forward to seeing you."

"I was looking forward to doing a lot more than that with you...!"

Cassie swallowed to get past the lump that had formed in her throat. She would not cry, she wouldn't. Instead, she asked, "The children?"

"I was able to get tickets for them on the train to Windsor. Mom and dad will pick them up at the station Christmas Eve."

"You'll be all alone for Christmas?"

"I'll probably be poring over the fine print of a half dozen government regulations while you're sharing Christmas dinner with my folks. By the way, you knocked their socks off at the soup kitchen last Saturday. They're as smitten with you as I am."

If you were really smitten with me, you'd be here Christmas Day, Jaimé Alvarez, Cassie thought, but aloud, she said, "They were so gracious to invite mom, Aunt Nell, and me to join them for dinner. We're all looking forward to spending the day with them." *Not as much as I was before you called*, she mentally added, but said nothing further.

They talked a short while longer, but their conversation was stifled by the frustration created by this latest chasm that had sprung between them.

Cassie became more dejected with each passing moment until she finally broke down and said, "You know, Jaimé, maybe we should just throw in the towel. This isn't working—at least not for

me. I don't want to live the rest of my life from week to week waiting for a phone call. Your work and your life are in Canada; mine
are here. I foolishly thought I could handle a long-distance relationship, but I was wrong." What she wanted to say but didn't, was
how very badly she needed him to be with her, needed to feel the
security of his arms around her. The strain of the past few months
had her so tightly strung that Jaimé's call had devastated her beyond her power of resiliency, snapping the small vestige hope that
she had cradled deep within her.

"Is that what you really want, Cassandra?"

"Yes, yes it is," she lied, then hit the button disconnecting the
call.

"What do you mean, Nell Gibson has been moved?" Cassie
questioned the young woman at the receptionist's desk after stopping by her aunt's room the next day on her way home from work
and finding it devoid, not only of its occupant, but also all of her
belongings.

The pretty young brunette tried to maintain a straight face,
but finally dimpled a mischievous smile at Cassie, "Your aunt's
been transferred to the rehabilitation wing. She's made such wonderful progress since summer that the administration decided she
would be better served staying in the wing with the short-term
residents who receive more intensive therapy. To be honest," the
woman leaned toward Cassie conspiratorially, "I think it's because
of your generous offer to have her move in with you. The doctors
really want to get the residents back into their own homes whenever possible."

"Oh, Jennifer, I can't thank you enough! And I think my
aunt's progress is due to the wonderful encouragement the pa-
tients receive from the staff here!"

As Cassie hurried down the hall she nearly bowled over Julie
Klotzenmeier exiting one of the rooms.

"Cassie! I haven't seen you all fall—where've you been keeping yourself? No, come to think of it, after helping you move into

your aunt's place, I know what you've been up to—cleaning and painting!"

Cassie laughed, "The farm's really shaping up—you and Arn have to stop out when you have time between your grandchildren and caring for your mom. How is she doing?" Cassie inclined her head toward the room that Julie had just left.

"Alzheimer's is the pits—she wanted to know if I was the nurse come to give her a bath today." Julie shook her head and then asked about Cassie's aunt. They chatted briefly about the vagaries of aging, before Julie changed the subject, "By the way, Cas, what's up with the Latin lover?"

"Jaimé?" Cassie asked innocently. "He left for Toronto at the end of the summer. I talk to him now and again, but there's nothing more than that. Long-distance relationships are way too complicated to maintain."

"Yeah, right. You're lips say 'no, no' but there's 'yes, yes' in your eyes!" Jules jibed.

Cassie laughed off her friend's astute observation and, wishing her a Merry Christmas, headed back down the hall in search of Aunt Nell.

Christmas Eve dawned with a heavy snow blanketing the countryside. Cassie awoke early and padded to the kitchen to brew a cup of tea and drop a slice of whole-grain bread into the toaster. The wet flakes clung to one another as they floated by the window, drifting against the house. In spite of her malaise after Jaimé's phone call, Cassie felt her spirits lift as she watched the crystals of moisture tumble to the ground while memories of building snow forts and skating on the pond with 'Nita swirled in her head.

Slack-Eyed Joe ambled into the kitchen, looked up expectantly and demanded with a loud "me*ooow*" that his bowl be filled when Cassie didn't immediately stop what she was doing to attend to his needs. "Alright, already!" Cassie laughed, popping open a can of Salmon Supreme and spooning a bit of the aromatic food into the impatient feline's dish. Joe took three bites, licked his lips, and pranced back into the dining room from whence he came.

"You are one spoiled rotten cat—a far cry from the mangy critter that came begging at my door six months ago," Cassie chided with a good-natured grin. Talk about changes, she could hardly remember the woman she had been before moving to the farm. She poured herself a cup of tea, spread a thick coat of cherry preserves on her toast, and carried both into the living room.

"This snow reminds me of the Christmases I spent on the farm," Cassie told her long-haired friend as she settled on the couch. Joe immediately jumped onto the cushion beside her and climbed upon her lap. "I'll try not to coat your fur with gooey jam," Cassie said as she took a bite of toast while rubbing the cat between his ears.

More often than not, Cassie and her mother would spend her Christmas break from school on the farm, while her father traveled back to Europe to visit with his family. He had never adjusted to life in America, often speaking with such a thick Russian accent that only Cassie or her mother could interpret what he said. Cassie had recently found out that he spent much of his time abroad searching through old records in dank archives trying to prove his family's connection to the Romanovs. She never questioned her father's annual trips—his sojourns simply meant a reprieve from his temper and a truly merry Christmas with her Aunt Nell and Uncle Clem. Funny, she thought, her best times during her childhood were spent with her real parents and the woman she would always consider her mother.

Cassie had just flipped on the television set, inserted *White Christmas* into the VCR and curled up on the couch with Joe snuggled against her, when she heard the crunch of tires on the driveway. She scooted the cat off of the couch and stood up, surveying her outfit, if one could call it that, with dismay. She hadn't expected company, so had dressed in an old pair of sweatpants and a ratty cast-off sweatshirt. She peered out the window and was able to discern two cars through the snow. Her heart sunk and her hands flew to her mouth as she recognized the black and yellow of the sheriffs' patrol cars.

She walked with trepidation to the door, opening it just as Billy Joe Crenshaw was about to knock on its wooden frame.

"Cassandra Grace Alexander?"

"You know who I am, Billy Joe," Cassie said, annoyance covering the fear in her voice. She towered above the slight-built man as she stood, arms akimbo, on the door stoop.

The two patrolmen who had stopped a few steps behind the sheriff smirked in silence as their boss whipped an envelope from his heavy navy blue coat and waved it under Cassie's nose. "I have a warrant to search these premises."

Cassie took the envelope and opened it slowly. She had no idea what a valid search warrant looked like. She tried to read the words written on the papers in her hand, but couldn't focus on the legalese that surrounded her name. She knew she should call an attorney; however, she had sworn off the only lawyer with whom she had any familiarity. Besides, she had nothing to hide.

"Could I just take a moment to change?" Cassie asked.

"Sorry, suga…," Billy Joe Crenshaw glanced in the direction of his deputies and amended, "…er, m'am, but I can't allow you to be in the premises unaccompanied." He grazed her from head to toe with a single glance, "'Course, I'd be glad to accompany you," he finished in a low Kentucky drawl that only she could hear.

"I'll just get my coat and boots—perhaps one of those nice gentlemen would be willing to escort me to the closet to retrieve them," Cassie said looking past the sheriff to the deputies behind him.

"Moran," the sheriff cut a curt order, "see that Mrs. Alexander doesn't leave your sight. Sergeant Diedrich and I will start searching the outbuildings."

The auburn-haired man who accompanied Cassie mumbled his apologies for interrupting her on Christmas Eve.

"That's okay, Officer…Moran, is it? Billy Joe Crenshaw just needs to find little ways to be a big man." Cassie reassured him then asked casually if he had a family.

"Yep, two little girls," he answered with pride.

"Well, I know you would rather be spending the day with your family so we'll try to get this over with as soon as possible."

When they finally joined the sheriff and the sergeant, the two men had tugged open the barn doors and stepped inside.

"Check the haymow first—leave no board unturned!" Billy Joe directed. As he looked toward Cassie, his subordinates raised their eyebrows at each other and shook their heads in obvious amusement. After fifteen or so minutes, they returned to the main level of the barn empty-handed.

"Just what do you hope to find, Billy Joe?" Cassie's curiosity got the better of her.

"Money."

"Money?"

"Money. You know, the green stuff you embezzled from your former employer!"

"You've been listening to Paul again. Read my lips, Billy Joe, I didn't take any money!" Cassie protested. Her brash words couldn't prevent a shiver of apprehension from passing through her, causing her to draw her arms protectively around herself.

The center channel of the barn had a poured concrete floor, but the stalls still retained their dirt flooring. A groundhog had excavated holes in two of the stalls before Windy had evicted him last summer. Sergeant Diedrich stuck the handle of a rake as far into each hole as possible to verify that they were not manmade.

"Why does that stall over there have a false floor?" The Sheriff asked pointing to an enclosure with rough boards covering the bottom.

"That's where Uncle Clem kept his old tiller, push mower, and the like. I guess he wanted to store them up out of the dirt."

"Moran, over here! Pry those boards up, pronto!" The sheriff commanded, rocking cockily back and forth on his heels with his thumbs hooked in the waistband of his pants, pulling his jacket apart in the middle.

The deputy grabbed a crowbar that had been hooked over

the half-wall of the stall and began working on the first board. He forced the old piece of wood up, using the tool as a lever and pushed on it, breaking it in the middle.

"Billy Joe! There's no need to wreck the floor—I'm not hiding any money!" Cassie exclaimed as the splintering board mimicked her frayed nerves.

Officer Moran pried another board loose, this time taking care not to break it. As he pulled a third plank from the false floor, he stopped and stooped down to investigate something he had evidently spied in the hole he had created. He bent on one knee and reached into the cavity with his right hand. Unable to grasp whatever he had found, the deputy knelt on both knees and stuck his left hand into the hole as well. He strained to pull a long, shallow cardboard box through the gap where he had removed the boards. He brought it to where Cassie stood with Billy Joe and laid it on the floor at their feet.

"Open it," the sheriff directed. Sergeant Diedrich walked over from where he had been searching a large tack box. All eyes were focused on the pasteboard box from which Deputy Moran peeled a length of clear sealing tape.

"No, no! It can't be!" Cassie uttered in shock as the officer revealed three rows of neatly stacked bills.

"It's a coat box, Miz Alexander—a pretty ritzy logo on it, too. Have you ever seen this box before?" the sheriff asked.

"Yes, yes, of course, it's from a jacket that Paul bought for.... But I didn't know it was there! I didn't hide it, I didn't!" Cassie cried, despairing in the knowledge that she may already have said too much.

All three men stared at her—Billy Joe Crenshaw wearing a look of smug derision, while Sergeant Diedrich and Deputy Moran held only disappointment in their eyes.

"Take this box to the office and secure it, the sheriff commanded his men, "We'll need to count the cash when I get there." Then to Cassie he said, "I'd advise you strongly to not leave the county. I'm sure you'll be hearing from the judge before too long."

Cassie remained in the barn well after the patrol cars had disappeared from her view. She thought about all of the people she had let down, starting with her Aunt Nell—how could she move to the farm if Cassie was in jail? Who would take care of Joe? The once feral cat had come to depend on Cassie. And the farm! After all of their hard work, what would happen to the farm? So much for her plans to start a dried-flower business. What would Tina and Ben think? Ben might give her the benefit of the doubt, but Tina would most likely be quick to assume her guilt. And, of course, there's Jaimé. In spite of their last phone call, she couldn't squelch her feelings for Jaimé. If she thought a long-distance relationship with him in Canada was difficult, adding the barriers of metal bars, and all that they represent, would make it nearly impossible.

Cassie walked slowly back to the house, her thoughts a jumble of self-recrimination. She went through the motions of wrapping presents, fashioning elaborate bows from remnants of holiday-patterned material that she had purchased from the local fabric store. She realized somewhere near midday that she had forgotten to eat lunch, but the thought of food turned her stomach. She made a cup of powdered chicken bouillon and sipped it while standing in the kitchen looking out the window toward the pond and the woods beyond. She couldn't fathom being incarcerated. After spending decades as a virtual prisoner to Paul's demands, her taste of freedom had been all too brief.

She set her cup carefully in the sink. Her energy sapped by despair, she retreated to her bedroom, climbed into her bed, and took refuge under her large down comforter, pulling it up over her head to shroud her in a blessed darkness.

When Cassie emerged from her cocoon, several hours had passed. Night had overtaken the day, leaving the house ensconced in black. As Cassie's eyes adjusted to the dark, the glow of the moon on the snow served as a beacon from the window.

The chill of the evening seeped through her, and she felt a restless need to escape the confines of her house. She quickly changed to a pair of black slacks and a warm cable-knit sweater. She pulled on woolen socks and black leather boots. She hadn't bothered to hang up her coat that afternoon and grabbed it from where she had draped it over a dining room chair.

The Festiva creaked its resistance in the sub-zero temperatures, as Cassie opened the door and dropped down on the cold vinyl seat. She turned the key and was rewarded with a sputter and then a whine as the ignition sparked the engine. She plowed through the snow that swept over her driveway, easing onto the road.

She passed the McAlister farmstead. Each spruce had been festooned with bright lights, turning her neighbor's home into a wintry fairyland. An illuminated Santa dangled from the edge of the roof, and a concerned Rudolph perched precariously above him. Cassie had laughed at the humorous scene when she had dropped off an array of holiday cookies to Mack and Liz the week before, but now she took little notice.

She drove down one country lane to another, drifting as aimlessly as the snow that coated the pavement ahead of her. When she turned onto the river road, she allowed the car to navigate to the same parking lot to which she had driven that early spring night a seemingly lifetime ago.

She killed the engine and sat in the car staring toward the Maumee. When the air in the Festiva chilled, she stepped out into the night. Snow deadened her footsteps as she walked purposefully toward the familiar precipice that loomed above the frozen river.

A cold wind whipped against her face, tearing her hair free from its bondage. She held her coat together fighting the force of the gusts blowing across the icy wasteland below. No stars shone down upon her on this night. It would be such a simple matter to cast herself into the eternal darkness. She wouldn't have to cope with an enervating trial, wouldn't have to deal with life behind bars, wouldn't have to face Paul or that worm of a sheriff, wouldn't have to worry about a love lost.

Jaimé…what had she promised Jaimé? His words from that fateful night when she had told him about their baby replayed themselves in her memory: *Promise me you will never attempt any-thing so desperate, and so incredibly selfish, again because there would be many more lives than your own that you would take with you.*

The strength of his words pushed her back from the edge. She must go on...ending it now would only serve to prove her guilt. Paul and his cronies would win without a fight. Prison was still only a possibility—death, a finite reality. If her being incarcerated would let down those who depended upon her, what would be the conse-quence of plunging into the icy depths below? Jaimé was right, the only problems her death would solve would be her own: everyone else would have to cope with the effects of her selfishness.

Cassie stepped again to the edge, carefully peering into the inky blackness below. She thought about water—the ending...and the beginning. The genesis of life took form in the sea.... Chris-tians renewed their life through baptism of the water.... Water in the womb breaks, ushering a new life into the world.... She searched the heavens for her new beginning, and found it in a single star flickering through the haze of crystallized water. She remained motionless for a moment longer, letting the flakes fall on her upturned face, and wishing that Jaimé, too, would look up to see the bright Christmas star that shone on both of their lands.

She retraced her footprints to her car, knowing where she needed to be. She headed the Festiva toward town, skirting her old neighborhood, and pulling into the closest available spot two blocks away from St. Jude's. She hadn't been to church since her wedding day, but now joined the throngs of parishioners and visi-tors who were drawn to the majesty of Midnight Mass.

The choir heralded the joy of the season as Cassie stepped through the massive ornately-carved wooden doors, blocked open to admit the crowd. As she entered from the vestibule, an usher signaled her to a rear pew, already crowded with people. Cassie shook her head, preferring to stand in the back of the church. She smiled to herself as she remembered her Uncle Clem's wry whis-per one Christmas Eve when one too many persons had been es-corted to their bench, "It appears that the usher is the only one who doesn't know how many folks will fit in a pew!"

She let the familiar rituals of the service lull her into a cleansing peace, emboldening her spirit as she prayed to a God that she thought had forsaken her. Prayed for strength to face the trials that lay before her. Prayed for the wisdom to appreciate the blessings that had been bestowed upon her—with or without Jaimé Alvarez at her side.

CHAPTER TEN

Cassie passed through a winter wonderland as she drove to Bowling Green on Christmas Day. A bright sun glinted off the diamond-studded snow, forcing her to don dark glasses. Her gaily-wrapped packages were spread from front seat to back, adding to Cassie's festive mood.

She waved to the McAlisters as they climbed into their SUV with their two teenage children and laughed at the sheer joy of being alive. She was at peace with her decision to end her relationship with Jaimé, at least until their situations changed. Life was too precious to waste pining for what wasn't meant to be. She would enjoy this day and let tomorrow bring what it may.

Several cars were parked in front of the Alvarez home, as Cassie pulled in behind her mother's aging Oldsmobile. Dr. Alvarez and a tall man that had to be Jaimé's brother emerged from the front door before she could gather the packages from her car. Cassie greeted Jaimé's father and was introduced to Jorgé, Jaimé's older sibling. They retrieved the boxes from the back seat and walked with Cassie back to the house.

A bevy of children scurried about the living room as Jorgé set the packages that he carried beside the pile of presents that already circled the Christmas tree and returned for those that Cassie held. Cassie smiled affectionately as she recognized Tina chasing a younger girl to the stairwell door. Ben quick-stepped into the living room, skidding to a halt when he saw Cassie. He ran to her and then hesitated. Cassie opened her arms and he threw his young limbs around her, bending his head back to look up at her to tell her about his frog project.

"Just a moment, Benjamin, let Cassandra get her coat off!" the boy's grandfather reprimanded with a smile. Jorgé held Cassie's deep red wool wrap while she slipped her arms out of the sleeves. Cassie drew Ben back into her arms for a quick hug, assuring him they would discuss his frog project later.

Jaimé's mother stepped out from the dining room, her hands, arms, and apron splotched with flour, followed by two younger women, both equally coated in white.

"Tamales—" Jorgé explained with a chuckle, "Each Christmas they magically transform an ordinary kitchen into a war zone." He introduced his wife, Haiyin, a small delicate-featured woman of obvious Chinese descent, and his sister, Elida, a younger version of her mother.

Elida sized up Cassie with a challenging grin, before introducing her husband, Matthew, who occupied one end of the couch, bouncing a toddler on his knee. "That little one is our grandson, Eddie." Jaimé's sister explained. "Our daughter, Angela, is upstairs at the moment with the baby—little Stephen was born in September. Our son-in-law, Andrew, instigated a snowball fight with Jorgé's youngest, Jimmy, out in the back yard. I don't know if such activities are allowed in this hoity-toity neighborhood, but I'm not going to be the one who tries to stop them!

"Speaking of my other brother's namesake, I understand you are an old friend of Jaimé's?" Elida's less-than-subtle attempt to extract her middle sibling's relationship to their latest guest washed all of the family names that Cassie had carefully chronicled from her memory.

"Yes, we, ah, knew each other in high school and renewed our...acquaintance this summer. Jaimé and the children helped me rebuild the corncrib on the barn on my aunt's farm. I saw that she and mother must have arrived?" Cassie deftly changed the subject, looking around the room to locate her aunt and her mother.

"They decided to stay out of the fray, choosing to remain in the kitchen where the children are forbidden to go." Elida supplied, curiosity sparking her dark brown eyes, but letting the topic of her brother and Cassandra Alexander drop for the moment. "However, little did they know of *mi madre's tamale tradición!*"

Juanita Alvarez laughed at her daughter, and invited Cassie to join the women as they prepared the meal. The aromas of cumin, chili powder, and garlic blended with the unique smell of cornhusks, wafting through the dining room and beckoning them to the kitchen. Two steamers of tamales simmered on the stove, and when Jaimé's mother opened a lid to ensure that the pot had sufficient water, the smell of a tangy meat combination set Cassie's mouth to watering.

Martha Mikhailov removed a stack of cornhusks that had been soaking in the sink, and laid them on a towel to dry, while her sister attempted to master the art of covering the husks with *Masa*.

"Aunt Nell, I'm not sure whether there is more batter on you or on the cornhusks!" Cassie exclaimed.

Cassie's aunt turned toward her niece and waved her dough-covered hand menacingly, with a feral gleam in her eye.

"You better get ready to duck, Cassandra," Jaimé's sister warned with a hint of mischief. "Your aunt has learned quickly that flying *Masa* is also a *tamale tradición!*"

Cassie backed up, holding her hands palm side out, as though to stave off her aunt's threatened dough-missile. "Maybe I could fill the tamales after you cover them…" she said in an attempt to placate the older woman. As Cassie began her task, she found it impossible to resist sampling a bit of the meat mixture,

"Hmmm…what's in this? It's scrumptious!"

"*Madré* has never allowed us to help her prepare the meat—though, she has promised to bequeath the recipe to us in her will," Elida said, giving her mother a quick hug. "She creates the mixture on Christmas Eve and has it ready for us to start the tamale ritual bright and early Christmas morning! Woe to the daughter—or daughter-in-law—" she nodded toward Haiyin, "who fails to arrive by 9:00—in the morning, mind you, after being up half the night putting together a bicycle or whatnot—to help with the tamales!"

When the first batch of steaming tamales had drained and cooled slightly, and the second had been dropped into the pots, the family was called to the dining room. Rice, refried beans, shredded lettuce, cubed tomatoes, and a variety of hot sauces, guacamoles, and salsas, were already assembled on the large polished cherry wood dining room table that had been expanded by several leaves and covered with an embroidered holiday cloth.

The children were served at card tables, while the adults gathered with anticipation around the big table. Cassie was seated between her mother and Elida, with Aunt Nell occupying the chair between her sister and their host. Juanita Alvarez took the seat at the opposite end of the table from her husband, where she could readily access the kitchen when needed.

Cassie had just bitten into her first hot tamale and was savoring the pungent taste sensation, when the front door opened then closed again. Juanita Alvarez excused herself from the table and hurried to the living room. Forks were laid to rest, while those remaining at the table waited expectantly, trying to overhear the hushed tones emanating from the foyer. Then a cry rang out from the children's area, "Papa!" Tina jumped up and ran to the living room, with Ben close at her heels.

Cassie sat frozen to her chair, unable to control the rapid beating of her heart. After what seemed to be an eternity, Jaimé followed his mother through the arched entrance to the dining room, an arm wrapped around each of his children.

"We didn't think you would be here!" Tina exclaimed.

"I couldn't miss Christmas with my little princess, now could I?" He smiled at his daughter before looking toward the woman across the room.

Cassie gripped the edge of her chair to keep from flying to

Jaimé's arms. A dusting of snow covered the broad shoulders of his charcoal gray overcoat. A dark plaid wool scarf lay indolently around his neck, dangling down the front of a powder blue cashmere sweater. The sweater's V-neck revealed the starched white collar of a linen shirt and blue silk tie expertly knotted at his throat. Cassie lifted her eyes to meet his piercing brown gaze.

Jaimé greeted his father, siblings, and the others at the table one by one, introducing himself to Cassie's mother and Aunt Nell, while never letting his eyes stray far from those of his porcelain princess. Though, over the past months, he'd discovered the strength that she kept hidden behind her fragile exterior—he was the one who had fallen apart when the airwaves went dead after their last phone call.

He shrugged out of his coat, which his mother insisted on taking to hang up. He pulled each of his children back to his side in a brief hug before urging them to return to their places at the card tables.

He locked his gaze with Cassie's and walked slowly around the table oblivious to the others who watched in silence. As he passed the back of each chair, its occupant looked at him with either an amused or a perplexed smile, but he paid them no heed. When he finally stood behind Cassie's seat, he placed his hands gently on her shoulders and lowered his lips to the top of her head. "Cassandra," was all he said.

Cassie lifted her hands to cover his and inclined her head to allow his lips to meet her temple. She felt his warmth against her back as he straightened, and leaned into it.

Elida quietly picked up her plate and flatware and moved it to the space her mother had made at the end of the table. Jaimé nodded his appreciation as his sister brought a clean plate to place before him, and he sat down in the chair she had formerly occupied.

"Thought so," she grinned as she patted Cassie's shoulder.

Cassie and Jaimé took every opportunity to clasp hands under the table while they finished their meal. If Cassie freed her fingers to take a bite of food, Jaimé rested his hand on her knee, as though he needed the reassurance of physical contact with her. Their mood infected the rest of the group, and a lighthearted banter bounced around the table.

When the last tamale had been devoured, the women cleared the table, insisting that Cassie remain with Jaimé. Cassie's mother and Aunt Nell were also shooed from the kitchen, and took up stations on the divan beside their daughter.

After the plates and flatware had been stacked in the dishwasher and the leftovers covered to await the next batch of tamales, the children were summoned for the distribution of presents. They gathered in a semi-circle on the floor around the tree with gleams of anticipation lighting their faces.

Andrew played Santa, selecting a gift from under the tree, reading the name of its recipient, and handing the present to the designated person. Ben tore the wrapping off of the package from Cassie and held his Peace Frog shirt up to show everyone. As Cassie had chosen a larger size to allow for growth, he immediately slipped it on over his sweater, flashing Cassie a huge grin.

Cassie received a beautiful pastel green Merino wool sweater from Jaimé's parents. Juanita Alvarez spoke in Spanish to her son, who translated, "Mother selected the color because you looked so beautiful in green when you came for dinner last summer. What mom doesn't yet know is that you are beautiful in any color!" Jaimé added so that only Cassie could hear.

Dr. and Mrs. Alvarez were delighted with Cassie's selection of her gift to them, beaming their approval at her. And, though Tina put it aside until after opening all of her other presents, she finally unwrapped her gift from Cassie, her scowl making it apparent that she did not intend to like whatever the box held. However, when she pulled out the darling babydoll, her eyes lit up and she immediately pulled it to her chest. Then realizing what she had done, she cast a furtive glance toward the woman who occupied the seat beside her father. Though Cassie's heart lurched in triumph as she watched the child's initial reaction to the doll, she tried to give Jaimé's daughter a passive, non-threatening smile.

When Jorgé handed Cassie a small, elongated box wrapped in silver paper with a lacy gold bow, Cassie quickly read the tag and looked to the man at her side. Jaimé's smile was neither passive nor non-threatening, but rather, promised of things to come. Cassie tugged the ribbon off the side of the package and carefully slit the tape that held the paper together, revealing a velvet-covered jewelry box within. Looking again to Jaimé, she gently opened the case.

"My heavens...it's...it's...exquisite!" Lying against the satin inset of the box, a slender gold chain held an emerald teardrop pendant with an array of diminutive diamonds forming a delicate arched setting connecting the pendant to the chain. Two smaller emerald teardrops had been fashioned into matching earrings, dangling from gold wires.

"To replace the ones you 'lost' when you moved," he whispered in her ear.

Touched by his remembrance, Cassie exclaimed in dismay as she closed the case on her sparkling jewels, "Oh Jaimé! I don't have any gift for you!"

"Ah, but you do! And I fully intend to unwrap it as soon as we are alone...." Jaimé's whispered vow created a nearly palpable heat between them.

The remainder of the afternoon passed with excruciating slowness for Cassie. Her skin tingled wherever Jaimé touched her. Her face ached from failed attempts to keep her feelings from being transparent to the others gathered in the living room. Jaimé left her side for a short while to accompany his children upstairs to see the presents 'Santa' had left them at their grandparents' home—gifts he had shipped to Bowling Green weeks ago. When Jaimé left with his children, Martha Mikhailov seized the opportunity to say what a pleasant man he was. She started to apologize for her role in thwarting her daughter's earlier relationship with Jaimé, but with a shake of her head, Cassie quieted her mother.

"Things happen as they are supposed to happen. If there is anything that I have learned over the past several months, it is that it's futile to worry about what's done, and a waste of the present to worry about what might come. Today has been a very special gift, and to be able to spend it with both of you," Cassie held her mother's hand and reached across her to squeeze that of Aunt Nell's as well, "and with Jaimé, is more than I could have hoped for."

An early dusk was settling into darkness when Jaimé returned to the living room. He walked over to Cassie and reached his hand down toward her. "Are you ready to go? If it's okay with you, we'll leave your car here and I'll drive you home."

Cassie felt a blush creep up her neck and cover her cheeks as all action in the room ground to a halt, and everyone looked in her direction. She raised her head to peer into the depths of Jaimé's smoldering gaze and felt the thrill of emotions held at bay. After only a moment's hesitation, she put her hand in his and allowed him to help her up from the davenport.

Ben still wore his Peace Frog tee-shirt and Tina clutched her doll, as their father assured them that he would return tomorrow. "And Cassandra, too?" Ben asked. Tina looked at her father warily as he reminded them that Cassie's car would still be here, so he would be sure to bring her back with him.

Jaimé held Cassie's wrap as she slipped her arms into its sleeves and then put on his overcoat. They bid *Feliz Navidad* and Merry Christmas to their families before stepping into the darkness.

Jaimé put his arm around Cassie's shoulders and pulled her close to him. He looked down at her with a tempting half-smile and bent his head to graze a kiss across her lips, "Just an appetizer for what's to come," he promised.

Anticipation filled the front seat of Jaimé's sedan as he drove out of his parents' subdivision and down the side roads to Main Street. The four-lane highway was nearly deserted, creating the appearance of an avenue of wonder meant just for them. The downtown had undergone a massive renovation at the turn of the century, and dark green faux-Victorian streetlights illuminated the roadway. The street was flanked with glittering white lights wrapped around fledgling trees that lined the sidewalks fronting the restored late nineteenth-century buildings. Clusters of wet snowflakes cascaded in the beams of their headlights as they drove past the vintage Cla-Zel Theatre, recently renovated into a pub and concert venue.

Cassie read with delight from the marquee, "Jaimé, look! They're playing *It's a Wonderful Life* on the old screen!"

Jaimé brought her hand to his lips and agreed, "Indeed it is a wonderful life," and again, as if for reaffirmation, "indeed it is."

They drove the snow-covered roads to Cassie's farm in an expectant silence, casting glances at one another with barely-contained desire. Finally, Cassie said with a nervous laugh, "You do look like the veritable cat that ate the canary, Jaimé Alvarez!"

He shot a sidelong look at her before returning his attention to the road, and said with a sly grin, "Not, yet, princess, not yet...." And, for once, Cassie did not mind the royal title.

Jaimé followed the faint tracks Cassie's Festiva had made earlier that day through the snow in the driveway, pulling close to the sidewalk so that she would not have to step into the wet slush. He hustled around the front of his sedan, opening Cassie's door before she had a chance to do so herself. She laid her hand in his as he helped her from the car. He then placed his palm on the small of her back as he escorted her to the house.

Cassie handed Jaimé the keys, and he opened the door, following her inside. She turned on a few lights and hung her coat in the closet while he returned to the car to retrieve his overnight bag. Once back inside, he dropped the black duffle in an out-of-the-way place, unzipped it, and pulled a bottle of champagne from its interior.

When Cassie looked at him with mock suspicion, he flashed her his trademark killer grin, and simply said, "I was betting on getting lucky...!"

Cassie placed his overcoat on a hanger next to hers, the sight of their garments hung side-by-side filling her with a sudden whim of nostalgia for what might have been. She focused her mind on the present as she heard the unmistakable sound of a popping cork coming from the kitchen.

"I don't have any champagne flutes. Think these wine glasses will do?" Cassie asked as she pulled two crystal goblets from the top shelf of her cupboard and sat them on the table. Jaimé filled each glass with the effervescent liquid, and they carried them along with the bottle to the living room.

It was Jaimé's turn to look at Cassie with suspicion, as he saw a mattress, complete with sheets, pillows, and a comforter, spread on the floor in front of the fireplace, and wood stacked on the grate awaiting the strike of a match.

Cassie again felt a blush creeping over her cheeks, "I was planning a Christmas night film fest—solo. See," she pointed defensively to a pile of videos lying beside her television set, "they're all there—*A Christmas Story, White Christmas, Christmas in Connecticut*—both versions, *Elf, It's a Wonderful Life*, even the *Grinch* …"

"Whoa," Jaimé laughed, "So this is how you spend your nights?"

"Well, until now…" she lowered her lashes and gave the man of her dreams a sultry 'come hither' look that would have done Mae West proud, as she backed toward her CD player. She turned her back on him just a moment to activate the disk in the tray. Dean Martin's whisky-smooth voice sauntered seductively from the speakers, "Chestnuts roasting on an open fire…."

"Okay, I can take a hint," Jaimé said as he put the champagne bottle on the coffee table. He edged around the mattress, sat his wine glass on the mantle, extracted a long match from the tin holder beside the fireplace and knelt on one knee in front of the pile of wood. He struck the match and held it to the kindling. In an instant, flames licked around the central log. He tossed the stick of the match in on top of the blazing wood and turned toward the love of his life.

He retrieved his glass and skirted the mattress, stopping within a foot of where she stood. He lifted his glass to hers in a silent Christmas toast and they each took a sip of the sparkling wine. Jaimé then slid Cassie's glass from her hand and sat it along with his beside the green bottle on the coffee table.

"There's something I've been wanting to do for a long time," he said as he gently took her face in his hands. Cassie caught her breath as he began to work her ash blonde hair free from the chignon she had carefully coiled that morning. Hairpins fell noiselessly to the floor as he loosened their grip on tresses smoothed into submission. He ran his fingers through the length of her hair, spreading it out to its full extent and then letting it fall free to her shoulders.

He opened his arms and Cassie stepped within their beckoning circle. He pulled her to him and they swayed to the rhythm of "White Christmas." Their eyes locked—brown held green as their movement slowed. His head dipped, she raised on her toes, and their lips met midway in a soft meshing of flesh.

Their pulses quickened in unison as their kiss deepened into a starved frenzy. He suckled her bottom lip; she devoured his upper. Tongues darted in and out and breaths followed in sharp gasps. Bing Crosby crooned from the stereo as Jaimé eased the soft material of Cassie's cardigan off of her shoulders and tossed it aside. His hands traveled to the scalloped edge of the shell that she wore underneath. He slipped the bit of woven cotton over her head. However, as he reached for the spaghetti straps of her green satin camisole, her hands stayed his.

He held his breath until she reached up to loosen the Windsor knot of his tie, lifted the loop she had formed over his head, and walked over to the rocking chair to carefully drape it over the back. He watched motionless at the graceful sway of her bottom as she kicked off her pumps and scooted them under the chair before returning to him to continue her ministrations. She took hold of the bottom ribbing of his sweater and, with his help, pulled it up and over his head. Then, deliberately, button by agonizingly slow button, she teased open his shirt until she came to the place where it met the waistband of his slacks.

She hesitated before unbuckling his black leather belt and pulling it from its confining loops. She dropped it to the floor then worked the fastener that held his waistband together. He groaned as she eased the tail of his shirt free from his pants. She took each of his arms, one by one, and unbuttoned the cuffs, lightly massaging the sensitive underside of his wrists with her thumb. Reaching up, she peeled his shirt from his shoulders, baring his smooth chest for her eyes to feast upon.

"Not fair," he finally said, as he took over, spilling the straps of her camisole from her shoulders and aiding the slip of silk to slide over her narrow hips. She wore a matching lacy green brassiere, above which the rise of her breasts flowed in tantalizing slopes toward her shoulders.

He then unbuttoned and lowered the zipper of her gray wool slacks and let the slippery lining assist in their pooling around her ankles. She stepped out of the puddle of material and, inserting her fingers under the elastic band of her panty hose, inched them down her long slender legs revealing the high cut of her bikini panties.

"Lady, you are killing me," he growled as he watched her striptease.

"Hush, you deserve every ounce of misery you get for that phone call last week." She declared mercilessly as she carefully released the zipper to his pants and eased them to the floor.

"Red and green plaid boxers? Really, Jaimé," she teased.

"I didn't think you were the thong type..." He raised an intrigued eyebrow.

"Hmmm...no...boxers are fine, just fine," she said as they lowered themselves to the waiting mattress.

He lay gently on top of her reveling in the feel of her body beneath him. He kissed her forehead, the tip of her nose, each cheek, and finally, caressed her waiting lips. They melted together, their hands exploring all of the exposed skin they could reach. When they broke apart to catch their breath, he propped himself up on his elbow and rolled half on his side while still covering as much of her body as he could without crushing her.

"I can't believe I'm here—after all of the years of waiting and wondering and wanting, you are with me, more beautiful than before." His words caressed her in places his body could not reach.

"I'm not beautiful, Jaimé. There are scars and wrinkles and cellulite...."

"Ah, *querida*, do you think I care about little things like that? Those are..." he searched for the right words, "...badges of courage on the road to wisdom. If I wanted a flawless ingénue, I would have...well, I haven't wanted one for a long, long time." He lowered his lips to hers and kissed her reassuringly before leaning back again on his elbow.

With his free hand he reached under her back.

"It opens in the front"

"Hm?"

"The clasp is in the front."

He chuckled as he unhinged the fastener to her bra, allowing the strip of material to fall apart. He let his hand wander, gently kneading the fullness of her breasts. He stopped as his fingers encountered an unnatural dimpled indentation in her skin and looked at her quizzically.

She turned her head from him, sighing deeply.

"Cassandra?"

"I had a lump removed."

"Sweet Lord, a tumor?"

She nodded her head.

"Malignant?"

Again she nodded. "It was nothing, really. I'm three years out, so I'm practically in the clear."

"Three years ago? You didn't have to have a mastectomy? Did you undergo radiation? Chemo?"

"Yes, no, yes, and no," she answered, amusement crinkling around her eyes.

"Cassandra, this isn't funny! I want to know all about it! My God, I could have lost you!"

"Yes, silly, you could have. And I could have lost you any number of ways as you clambered about Canada chasing bad guys!" She pulled him down to her and rubbed her lips tenderly against his. "But I didn't," she said intermingling her breath with his, "and you didn't. And that's all that matters right now." She kissed him again, and then arched her body against his, "so quit stalling!"

They consummated their love by the warmth of the fire, emerging from under the downy quilt only long enough to add another log when the blaze threatened to die down to embers.

Cassie giggled in the middle of the night when she felt a brush of fur against her back as Slack-Eyed Joe bellied under the sheet beside her, "I think Joey's jealous—he's never known me to share my bed with another male."

"Mmmm..." Jaimé responded half-asleep, "You better not have." He nibbled at her lips as she snuggled against him, "Damn, woman, you keep this up and I'm going to need to get out the Viagra. There's only so much a man my age can do!"

"Yeah, but you're doing it just fine without any help," she said in a sated voice. Her laugh turned husky with desire as he moved against her, proving again his need for her.

They slept late in the morning, until Slack-Eyed Joe nudged the covers against Cassie's back and meowed, demanding his breakfast.

"Hmmmfff...Go away, Joey," Cassie said sleepily as she waved her hand toward the source of her annoyance, trying to bat the pestering feline away.

She turned back to the warmth at her side and found Jaimé looking down at her, "Mornin', sleepyhead," he grinned.

"Ahhh," she sighed with a purr of total contentment that would have done Joe proud. Her lips met his in a soothing waltz—until their tongues got involved. Then the dance evolved into a heated tango, the rhythm traveling the length of their torsos and climaxing into a primal homage to the morning.

He lay over her, his bodyweight braced on his elbows and forearms, "Heaven would be to wake up every morning with you at my side. You are so incredibly beautiful!"

"Hush, my love," she placed her finger on his lips, "I know what I look like in the morning, and it isn't beautiful!"

"Then you're not seeing yourself from this angle. If I weren't on the downside of fifty, I'd show you again just how lovely you are." He held her prisoner between his arms and molded his mouth against her protesting lips.

They showered together in her old clawfoot tub, luxuriating in lathering each other with a slick layer of soap and letting the warm water rinse over their naked bodies. He bent to kiss her as the water pelted his back and splashed over onto her shoulders. Their embrace deepened as he brought her against him.

"I don't think this is either safe or possible," she laughed as he tried to lift her to him. "Besides, I learned all about shrinkage on *Seinfeld*."

It was Jaimé's turn to laugh, "You are such a romantic!"

After giving their bodies a final rinse, Jaimé turned the faucets to stop the flow of water. They stepped out of the tub and leisurely toweled each other dry. He captured her in the large stretch of terry cloth, using it to pull her to his aroused body.

"I'll show you what shrinkage can do," he whispered in her ear and then lifted her hips to settle her over his waiting tumescence.

It was nearly noon before they found themselves sitting across from each other at the kitchen table—Jaimé drinking a mug of steaming black coffee while Cassie sipped gingerly at her cup of piping hot tea. She had wrapped her well-used body in a worn pink ankle-length chenille bathrobe, while Jaimé had donned a pair of sweatpants and a Cleveland Browns jersey missing its sleeves.

Cassie pondered telling him about the money Billy Joe had found in the barn Christmas Eve but was unwilling to cast a pall over their perfect morning. She would deal with the consequences of the discovery, she decided, after 'Nita and Windy's wedding on Saturday.

"A penny for your thoughts...." Jaimé said, watching her

closely.

"Ah, the price has gone up. Inflation, don't you know!" She teased, in an effort to distract him.

"Name your price," he challenged.

"That could be dangerous," she countered.

"Okay, princess, you win. But I will find out eventually!"

"Yes, yes you will…." *Just not today*, she thought with resignation as she took another sip of her tea.

They dressed in her bedroom, the act of clothing themselves nearly as provocative as disrobing. He leaned against the doorjamb of the bathroom while she applied her make-up.

"So it's true!" he exclaimed.

"What?"

"Women do hold their mouths open when they put on mascara!"

"Where did you hear that?"

"I don't know, I think I saw it in a book called *Imponderables*—great late night reading…when there isn't a sexy blonde around to distract you, that is…." He wiggled his eyebrows and gave her a lecherous grin, which caused her to smear her mascara under her eyelid.

"Keep that up, and you're outta here, Alvarez!" Cassie threatened as she wiped the offending black smudge from her face and attempted to reapply her mascara.

They were still laughing and teasing each other as they put on their coats and headed out the door to make the drive to Bowling Green. They stopped short when a sheriff's cruiser pulled into the driveway and parked behind Jaimé's car.

CHAPTER ELEVEN

Cassie and Jaimé waited while Billy Joe Crenshaw and Deputy Moran stepped from the car.

"Well, isn't this interestin'! Din't know you were back in the area, Jimmy Boy!"

Jaimé moved slightly in front of Cassie and looked down at the sheriff as though he were a slug sliming up the sidewalk. "What do you want, Billy Joe?"

"That's Sheriff Crenshaw to you," the officer drew himself up to his full height, but still fell several inches short of the man before him. "And I came to talk to Cassie there."

"So talk," Jaimé didn't change his stance.

The sheriff fidgeted, then looked back at the junior officer still standing by the squad car. "Moran, bring those cuffs!"

"What th'...." Jaimé started to say as Billy Joe whipped an envelope from his coat pocket.

"I have here a warrant for the arrest of one Cassandra Grace Alexander for the embezzlement of one-million-five-hundred-thousand dollars from the former O'Shay's Catsup Factory." The sheriff puffed up his chest as he barked to his deputy, "Cuff her!"

Jaimé snapped the envelope from the sheriff's hand and tore it open. He turned to Cassie, confusion clouding his eyes, "They found fifty-thousand dollars in the barn? Why didn't you tell me?"

"Mrs. Alexander?" Officer Moran reluctantly dangled the handcuffs from his fingers.

Fear lined Cassie's face as she looked toward Jaimé while the deputy slipped the cuffs around her wrists, snapping them shut. "I didn't want to ruin our Christmas. I thought I would have more time...."

Billy Joe Crenshaw grabbed Cassie's elbow and pulled her toward the waiting vehicle.

"Jaimé, the wedding! 'Nita and Windy...." Cassie called frantically.

Shell-shocked, Jaimé stood in the middle of the sidewalk, still holding the offending warrant in one hand while reaching toward Cassie with the other.

"I'll tell them...I'll get you out, Cas!" Then, to the sheriff, he said, "If you harm a hair on her head, you scum bucket, I'll...."

"Better watch what you say, Jimmy Boy, or you'll be sharing a cell with your whore here. But, then, you'd probably like that jus' fine," the sheriff taunted as he shoved Cassie in the patrol car and slammed the door shut.

Cassie held her head in the palms of her cuffed hands as the sheriff sped toward the county jail, not wanting to look at the back of Billy Joe's head. The blur of the electric posts as they whizzed by the window caused Cassie's stomach to vault into spasmodic convulsions. She held her hand tight to her mouth. It would serve Billy Joe Crenshaw right if she retched all over the back seat of his patrol car, but she didn't want to give him the satisfaction of knowing how rattled she truly was.

The sheriff parked in front of the Justice Center and hauled Cassie out of the back of the cruiser. "By the way, the judge set bail at a hundred-thousand smackeroos, so unless your boyfriend has a lot o' loot stashed away—or you told him where the rest of the money you stole is—you'll be cookin' in our little ol' steamer for a good long while," he gloated.

Once in the station, Cassie was asked rudimentary questions

and endured the humiliation of being fingerprinted. Under the watchful eye of a middle-aged female officer, she was directed to change into a jumpsuit faded to a pale peach color and deposit all of her personal belongings into a wire mesh basket.

The woman then ordered Cassie to follow her down a long hallway. Cassie nearly crumpled when she heard the clank of a metal gate closing behind her. Instead, she forced herself to remain upright and summoned the stamina to move one foot after the other until the officer stopped before a small cell. She opened the barred door and motioned for Cassie to enter the cubicle. Panic swept through her and with it the urge to run, but feet of lead held her fast where she stood. The deputy nudged the recalcitrant inmate toward the opening and Cassie stumbled through. With an unsympathetic sneer, the officer pulled the door tight and walked back down the hall. Cassie collapsed on a sparse cot as the latch clicked securely in place and she heard the crisp footfall of the woman fade away.

In less than twenty-four hours, Cassie had soared into the heavens and spiraled into the depths of an iron-barred hell. Lying back on the cot, she curled herself into a fetal ball and gave way to the sobs that she had been holding at bay since Billy Joe Crenshaw forced her into his patrol car. Day turned to night without Cassie acknowledging its passing. She left untouched the plate of food slid to her through a slot in the bars.

For perhaps the first time, Cassie began to truly comprehend what life in prison would mean. The only sounds she heard were hard and metallic. Gone would be the giggling of little children as they ran through the library—the song of the wren trilling to his mate from the branches of the mountain ash outside her living room window—the chorus of bullfrogs emanating from her pond on a summer's night. She wouldn't be able to pop the Beach Boys in her CD player when she was feeling down, or a Jimmy Smits movie in the VCR when her need for Jaimé was especially keen. *Jaimé*—she thought about the man who had, once more, become so dear to her. *How would he ever trust her again? And how could she go on without him after last night?*

Despondency sank into despair as seconds whittled away at minutes and minutes crawled into hours. And in the bleakest of those hours just before the dawn, she dropped into a fitful sleep.

Jaimé's heart lurched when he saw the woman that the corrections' officer brought forward from the hall beyond the reception area of the Justice Center. At first glance, he had thought that the deputy had released the wrong person. Cassie stood subdued, with head bowed and shoulders stooped. Gone were the proud thrust of her chin and regal posture that Jaimé had come to know so well. A dingy oversized orange prison jumpsuit hung loosely on her thin frame, while strands of unkempt hair straggled around her mascara-streaked face.

"Cassandra, darling," he said as he quickly closed the gap between them. She made no response but slumped limply into his arms, allowing him to cradle her against his chest but not raising her eyes to meet his.

"Here's your things, Mrs. Alexander," the deputy held out the basket containing Cassie's clothing. Cassie stepped out of the shelter of Jaimé's arms, accepted the basket, and held it as a barrier between them. Still refusing to meet his gaze, she backed away and retreated to the changing room that she had used the previous day. She emerged almost immediately, dressed in her own clothes, but just as disheveled as before.

Jaimé said nothing as he pulled her close to his side and held her there as they exited the building. They walked through a biting sleet to his black sedan. He kept his grip on her while he fished in his coat pocket for his keys. He felt her weight so fully that he feared she would slide to the ground if he let go. He eased her down onto the seat and pulled the strap of the seatbelt across her, securing it at her hip.

As Jaimé lowered himself into the driver's seat, Cassie turned away toward the window. He started to speak, but inadequate words caught in his throat forming a jagged-edged mass. He worked his Adam's apple until he swallowed the granite lump, sending shooting pains directly to his heart. He backed the car slowly out of its space and forced all of his concentration onto navigating the icy roads.

Cassie sat as though frozen in place during the drive to her farm, not reacting even when the back end of Jaimé's sedan fish-tailed as he attempted to negotiate the turn onto her driveway. She placed her hand listlessly in his as he reached down to help her from the car. A thin veneer of ice had coated the sidewalk, and Jaimé held Cassie tight against him to prevent her from falling on the treacherous surface.

He slipped her key from her purse and let Cassie into the security of her home. Still holding on to Jaimé for support, Cassie silently urged him toward her bedroom. Jaimé tugged her coat from her shoulders and tossed it on the bed. He pulled back the bedcovers and when she sat down, he knelt before her to free her feet from her black leather boots. He then helped her slip between warm flannel sheets. She drew the comforter up past her chin, so that only the top of her head was visible above the soft shell she had formed. Wordlessly, he bent and kissed her tangle of hair before backing slowly from the room.

Cassie awoke to the sound of voices speaking in low tones from somewhere outside her bedroom door. She felt like she had just crawled across the Sahara after being dumped by her camel. Her throat was parched and her head throbbed. The tantalizing aroma of simmering chicken reminded her that it had been over a day since she had last eaten. She attempted to sit upright, but a lightheaded and queasy sensation sent her immediately back to her pillow. She listened to the drone of the voices as they carried through the open door to her room. Her ears perked up when she detected Jaimé's distinctive tones.

"I've talked to Harvey Walton. He's the best criminal lawyer in the area." He spoke softly, so that Cassie had to listen carefully to understand what he said.

"What are we up against?" asked another, somewhat louder, male voice Cassie thought she could identify as Windy's.

"Evidently Crenshaw and his deputies uncovered a box with fifty-thousand dollars in the barn. It had to have been planted there some time ago, as it was coated in dust. I have no doubt that Paul Alexander had his dirty hands involved in its getting there, but the only fingerprints that could be lifted from the box were those of Cassandra and the deputy who found it."

"It had to be that shyster," Anita's voice shot through the dusk, "but, to tell the truth, I didn't think Paul had the brains to think about something like fingerprints."

"You've got a point there, 'Nita. Walton's office is trying to get access to Cas's computer—that's what started this whole snowball on its downhill roll—but the only thing they will give him is the auditor's report showing the million and a half shortfall. He's having that analyzed as we speak," Jaimé said before further explaining, "The real wildcard is the testimony of some guy name Craig Herman. According to Harvey, the prosecutor seems to think this Herman guy is her ace-in-the-hole."

"Craig Herman?" Anita asked.

"Yeah, I think that was his name. You know him?"

"Sure—you remember him. The quintessential nerd, complete with thick black-rimmed glasses, who kept the basketball stats in high school." Anita supplied.

"I was a wrestler, remember? We ate basketball players for breakfast and spat them back out for lunch." Jaimé joked half-heartedly. "But, yeah, I do vaguely remember him now. What's he got to do with O'Shay's?"

"Paul hired him after the old man died. Cassie said he was Paul's..." Anita searched her memory for the right word, "Oh, shoot, what did she call him?"

"Lapdog. I said Craig was Paul's lapdog."

All eyes turned in unison to the bedroom door.

"Cas! Jees, you look like hell!"

"Thanks, 'Nita, leave it to my best friend to not pull any

punches!" Cassie stood in the door wrapped in her comforter. She reached her hand up to smooth hair that hadn't been touched by a comb in over twenty-four hours. What was left of her make-up had been rubbed anywhere but its original location.

"Um, sorry, Cas—It's just that next time I tell you that you need to let your hair down a little, maybe you shouldn't take me quite so literally...."

Cassie shook her head and flashed a tentative grin at her closest friend—only 'Nita would understand that Cassie needed a laugh more than a hug. Had Anita uttered so much as a word of sympathy, Cassie might have lost the thin veneer of composure she had worked so hard to regain.

The pull of Jaimé's gaze drew her attention to the end of the dining room table where he sat with Anita and Windy on either side, and she sent him a sheepish smile before looking down at her rumpled clothing. "'Nita's right, I think I'd better take a shower," she said glancing back at him.

"Hmmm, I think I'll help.... You'll excuse us, guys?" Jaimé slowly peeled himself off of his chair and walked over to where Cassie stood, taking hold of the comforter where it draped around her neck.

Anita and Windy raised their eyebrows at each other. "Guess that's our cue to scram, sweetie pie," 'Nita laughed. "Don't forget, rehearsal dinner in just two days!"

"Oh my gosh, Anita! The wedding!" Cassie poked her head around Jaimé's broad shoulders, "How could it have slipped my mind, even for an instant!"

"How, indeed?" It was Anita's turn to shake her head and grin at her friend as she once again looked at Cassie's disheveled state. "You just take a long hot shower and get some rest, okay?"

"I'll take care of that," Jaimé assured her. He bent down to plant a kiss on Cassie's lips but was met by the palm of her hand in front of her face.

"No swapping spit until I find a toothbrush. And, mmm, could I have a bowl of whatever smells so good before I bathe?

Oh, and water…definitely a glass of water!"

"You know, Alexander, when they write the definition for 'resilient' in the dictionary, your picture should be there!" Anita marveled, "You bounce back better than a red rubber ball!"

"We'll see you both Friday evening at six at St. Jude's," Windy laughed and called to them, as he ushered his fiancé out the door, then poked his back in. "Oh, and we brought your car back, Cas, and parked it in the driveway."

Sitting on the couch in her living room a few hours later, Cassie cradled a mug of hot chocolate between the palms of her hands. She licked the tip off of a swirl of whipped cream before it dissolved into the steaming liquid. Freshly showered and swathed in her comfy, worn chenille bathrobe, she leaned her damp hair against the soft wool sweater that covered Jaimé's chest. Blue-tipped flames chased each other around a dry cedar log in the fireplace, while Jack Nicholson sparred with Diane Keaton on the television screen in a scene from *Something's Gotta Give*.

"So, it doesn't look good for me, huh?" Cassie tilted her head up toward Jaimé. He answered her with the flick of his tongue catching the residue of sticky sweetness from her tempting lips. "Mmm…." The contented sound arose from her throat as his hand slid up the side of her robe and cupped her breast through the ridges of cotton. The ball of his thumb circled the sensitive nub causing heated waves to ripple through her body.

She arched her back against him before leaning forward to place her cup on a coaster on the coffee table. She then turned into his embrace, molding herself against him as she tugged on his bottom lip with the faintest grazing of her teeth, seducing his mouth by nibbling her way around its perimeter. He licked her lips, "Ahhh…chocolate…" he smiled as his fingers worked at the knot in the tether that cinched her chenille robe together, until only skin lay against him.

"One of us," she said as her lips brushed against his, "has way too many clothes on."

He gently pushed her back until she sat upright on the middle couch cushion, then stood and, with record speed, divested himself of his clothing, including burgundy polka-dot boxers.

"Now who's the one who's overdressed?" He asked as he extended his hand to hers and drew her up to his sculpted naked body.

She took a step back and ogled him from head to toe, "It just isn't right—no fifty-year old man should look this good!" She gave a throaty growl and rubbed her hands down his well-muscled torso, resting them on the curve of his lean hips. Her eyes wandered downward and she smiled her delight at the power she had over his body.

She removed her hands from his waist and placed them on the collar of her robe, slowly separating the material and letting it fall in a pile of fabric at her feet.

He nudged her back to the edge of the couch, and she sank down onto the overstuffed velveteen cushions. He looked into green eyes glazed with passion and pulled himself over her readied body. They came together, man and woman, propelled by the desire to heal and to nourish each other's deepest needs.

When they had spent their passion and their hearts had slowed as one to a steadied pace, she slipped behind him and spooned against his back. She dragged the afghan off the top of the davenport and spread it over of them, nestling between his warmth and the rise of the couch. They laughed in unison as Jack Nicholson stumbled across the screen in hospital garb. He bent over, mooning the audience as his gown split down the middle.

Cassie blushed as she remembered searching for the *NYPD Blue* episode with Jimmy Smits' bare butt. Shaking the memory, she asked, "So how bad is it?"

"The movie? It's a fun flick."

"No, real life—my life…."

Turning toward her, Jaimé brushed wisps of hair from her forehead and dusted the top of her head with his lips before answering, "I'd be lying if I said we were sitting pretty."

"Who's this Harvey guy I heard you mention to 'Nita and

Windy? Why can't you be my lawyer?"

"Harvey Walton is the best criminal lawyer around, and I want you to have the best. I know environmental law—give me the big logging companies or the outfitters who want to hunt on First Nations' lands and I can find the legal precedence to fight them. But, my *querida*, I don't trust myself to fight this one."

He nuzzled her cheek and slipped a kiss on the side of her mouth, "There's too much at stake for me. They say a 'doctor who treats himself has a fool for a patient'; this is the same thing. I couldn't be as dispassionate as I would need to be to go after Paul Alexander—he might goad me into beating him to a pulp on the witness stand. And, that would not be a good thing for our case, trust me!"

"Okay, so this Harvey guy is that good, eh?" she asked.

"What's this 'eh' stuff, I'm the only Canuck around here!" he teased before answering her question, "They call him Harvey Wallbanger, because that's what the prosecutors want to do whenever they draw a case that he is defending."

He soothed her worries with kisses before asking, "Cas?"

"Hmm?"

"What can you tell me about Craig Herman? After talking to the DA's office, Walton seems to think that they are planning to use his testimony as the linchpin against us."

"Craig? As I told 'Nita, he was Paul's lapdog. He's tall and awkward and sort of bumbling. Paul hired him to serve as my assistant, but I think that was just a ruse, because the guy was a blithering idiot when it came to computers. He barely knew how to turn one on, much less figure out how to manipulate a spreadsheet. He had my desktop so screwed up one time, I had to call our systems guy to straighten it out.

"I lost nearly a day's worth of computations, but luckily I still had the raw data to work with so I was able to reconstruct my tables. To be honest, I think Paul just wanted him around as an ego trip—all he had to do was wiggle his little finger and the Craigster would jump without even asking 'how high'!"

"Okay, assuming the guy's just an innocent toady, what could he possibly have against you?" Jaimé held her close, slightly muffling his words as he tucked her head under his chin.

"I dunno. Craig always acted a little standoffish toward me. He had this way of holding his head up just a notch and looking down at me over his nose that would have been insulting if he didn't look so ridiculous when he did it. I figured it was because I was married to his hero and that Paul probably wasn't as flattering as he might have been when he talked about me to Craig. The Craigster and I didn't communicate too much, but then, I didn't interact much with anyone at the plant. My office was isolated from the main part of the factory, and Paul didn't like me talking with the hourly workers.

"I sound like such a wuss. I should have told him to go flush his head in the toilet a long time ago. I don't know why I let him walk all over me like that!"

"Paul Alexander doin' a swirlie on himself—now that's an image I could live with!" Jaimé chuckled into her hair. "Don't beat yourself up too much, princess, between Leo Mikhailov and Paul Alexander, it's truly a miracle that you survived, much less turned into the incredible, beautiful, sexy woman that you are!"

He rolled over letting his weight press against her. She felt the total maleness of him grow heavy against her abdomen. He leaned his forearms on either side of her head as he lightly crushed her breasts while covering her mouth with his.

"Hmm…I don't think I could manage an instant replay…at least not for an hour or two…." he gently blew in her ear as the tip of his tongue traced its outer shell.

He scooted behind her and pulled her against him. They lay spooned together as the movie credits rolled down the screen.

"What a dolt I am!" Cassie turned her head to look at a startled man at her side. "I forgot all about calling the library! Evelyn expected me back at work today!"

Jaimé smiled at her, "Not to worry—I stopped by yesterday and talked to your boss. She's a great lady, and told me to tell you that you can get back to her when all of this is straightened out. Evidently Paul has already made an impression on her, eh?"

"Yeah, he was his usual smooth self—a real ambassador of charm," Cassie said, then added, "How about you? When are you expected back in Toronto?"

Cassie felt him stiffen against her back, "You think I'm going to bail on you again, don't you? I had hoped that you would have a little more faith in me by now, *querida*."

Cassie shifted her head in an attempt to see his face, "I just thought that the trial—I mean the one in Toronto, not mine—and the children's schooling...."

"There's only one trial that concerns me right now—they can get someone from Ottawa to cover for me up north. As for Tina and Ben's classes, I'll work something out with their teachers. You're not going to shake me quite so easily this time, Cassandra."

Cassie scrunched her body around so that she was facing Jaimé and nestled her head against his chest. "I do love you, Jaimé Alvarez, you know that, don't you?"

He rested his lips on the top of her head, silently absorbing the full extent of her words.

She tilted her head back to look up at him, "Well?"

He gave her a lopsided grin and kissed the tip of her nose, "If you haven't figured out by now that I am head-over-heels in love with you, Cassandra Grace Mikhailov Alexander soon-to-be Alvarez, you are not the brightest bulb in the chandelier!"

Cassie batted at her lover with her free hand, giving him a gentle rap on his shoulder, before the impact of what he had said sunk in. She jerked her head up to search the depths of his mesmerizing brown eyes, "Is that a proposal? If so, it's the most cockamamie, backhanded one I've ever heard!"

"And just how many proposals have you heard? No, don't answer that. I don't think I want to know. And, yes, I guess it was a proposal—just not quite in the way I had planned. I was going to do the dinner, fine wine, down on one knee, roses in hand kind, but this one just sort of slipped out."

"Just sort of slipped out, did it? Well, before you have a chance to reconsider, I accept!" Cassie sunk her lips into his, but when they broke apart to gasp for air, she added as an afterthought, "You can still do the dinner and roses bit, though."

Even though she could little afford to do so, Cassie called Evelyn Maples to request the remainder of the week off from the library. Against her supervisor's protests that Cassie should stay home the following week as well, she assured the older woman that she would be at work bright and early Monday morning.

When the telephone rang mid-morning, Cassie thought it was Evelyn again, but instead, Jaimé's voice carried through the receiver. He had driven to his parents' home to check on Tina and Ben soon after eating a light breakfast a few hours past. "Cas, the children want to spend the night with me tonight."

Though she was disappointed, she had no intentions of interfering with Jaimé's relationship with Tina and Ben. "Of course they do! They need to spend time with their father, too!" In her attempt to hide her true feelings, she nearly chirped out her reply.

"The least you could do is to fake sounding a little letdown or dejected!"

"Okay, in truth I was faking sounding upbeat. After last night, I'll be devastated not to have you here with me, but I do understand that the children need to see their father."

"Whoa! Who said I wouldn't be there with you? We were planning a pizza party and all-night movie fest in front of the fireplace! Ben can't wait, and little Tina is doing a poor job of trying to hide her excitement. If you say 'no,' it'll break all of our hearts!"

Cassie chuckled, "I guess I can't be responsible for that, now can I?"

"I was hoping you would see it our way. We'll pick up the pizza..."

"...and I'll stop by the library to borrow a half dozen movies. Are there any special ones that Tina and Ben would like to see? They'll have to be on VHS, though—I'm still saving for a DVD, or maybe even one of those Blue-Ray players"

"You know what's available—why don't you just surprise us?"

Cassie could sympathize with Tina, as she, too, was having a hard time containing her excitement at the evening's prospects. She had just put the finishing touches on her make-up and hair, when she heard the grind of tires on the stone driveway. Cassie hurried to the window, her heart doing a triple beat with fear that Billy Joe had returned. Instead, a portly man in an expensive over-coat stepped out of a late-model BMW. He reached back through the open car door, pulled out a dark fedora, and perched it jauntily on a crisp steel-gray crew cut.

The stranger didn't look at all familiar to Cassie—and this was one man she was certain she would remember having met. His demeanor demanded that he be reckoned with. She waited impatiently as he covered the distance to her front step in several confident strides, barely giving him time to knock before swinging the door open.

"May I help you?"

The man looked startled to see her standing in the doorway as he lowered his balled fist.

"Shouldn't you be a bit more cautious about whom you allow into your home?" Cassie felt the man's shrewd blue eyes assessing her as he awaited her response.

"I've learned to take care of myself, Mr. ..."

"Walton, Harvey Walton."

"Harvey Wallbanger? The lawyer?" Cassie asked then covered her mouth with her hand as she realized she had blurted out the man's nickname.

The hint of a smile came more from his eyes than his mouth, but put Cassie at ease just the same. "My apologies, Mr. Walton, but your reputation has preceded you."

"Then you must be Cassandra Grace Alexander."

"One and the same."

"And you are aware that Jaimé Alvarez has asked me to look into the charges of embezzlement that have been brought against you?"

"Yes, Jaimé has assured me that you are the best criminal lawyer in Northwest Ohio. Please, won't you come in?"

He stepped across the threshold, stopping to survey the interior of Cassie's home. "I like these old farmhouses, they have character—personality, you know—the stories these old walls could tell...."

"Why, Mr. Walton, that crusty exterior is all a sham, deep down inside you have a soft heart!" Cassie shot the lawyer a winning smile.

This time the corners of the attorney's lips took on a slight curve, but he chose to gloss over her observation, "In Northwest Ohio? What do you mean the best criminal lawyer in Northwest Ohio? I'm the best damn lawyer in the state—maybe even the entire Midwest, and don't you forget it!"

Cassie laughed as she took Harvey Walton's coat and hung it on the hall tree. He dropped his hat on the dining room table as they passed it by on their way to the living room.

"Would you like something to drink? A cup of coffee or water?"

"Water will be fine—I'm off caffeine, doctor's orders."

Cassie quickly retrieved two glasses of ice water from the kitchen. When she returned, Harvey Walton had settled his substantial frame on the center cushion of the davenport.

Cassie stationed herself halfway back in the bentwood rocker, impatient to hear what the lawyer had to say.

He visually sized her up before asking, "I have one question for you, Ms. Alexander: Did you steal money from O'Shay's Catsup Factory?"

"No, I wouldn't dishonor Charlie Alexander's memory like that!"

"Yeah, but would you do it to sink Paul Alexander's future with a blond bombshell?"

"I'd hardly call the bimbette a 'bombshell,'" Cassie muttered more to herself than to the lawyer.

"Pardon?"

"Mr. Walton, my ex-husband is perfectly capable of screwing up his future without any help from me. I work as a library assistant, buy my clothes at secondhand stores, most of my furniture is compliments of garage sales—do you see any money around here?"

"Well, there was that box Sheriff Crenshaw found in the barn...."

"I honest-to-Pete do not know how that money got there! Well, I have a suspicion—Paul is the only other person who would have had access to that particular box."

"Unfortunately, yours were the only fingerprints on the box, other than the officer's who found it."

"Listen, Mr. Walton, you can either believe me or not." Cassie's voice took on a strident tone as she scooted to the edge of the rocker, leaning forward with her elbows resting on her knees and her hands clasped tightly, "If you're going to be my lawyer, I'd prefer you trust that I am telling you the truth."

"That's what I am attempting to establish," the lawyer replied.

"What, that I am telling the truth?"

"No, whether or not I am going to be your lawyer.... I don't like to lose, Ms. Alexander, and truth be told, the deck is not only stacked against you—you're barely in the game. If we're to have a chance of winning this case, I need to be convinced of your innocence."

"And how do I do that? If you question my word, my integrity, perhaps I should find another attorney."

The stout man surveyed Cassie with a keen eye. She tried not to flinch under his steady perusal. She moved slightly as oak slats cut into her derrière, perching ever closer to the edge of the chair. As she shifted her weight, the rockers shot back and upward on the hardwood floor, dumping Cassie on the braided rug in front of the coffee table with the rocking chair on top of her.

For a man of his girth, Harvey Walton literally sprang to her assistance, righting the rocker from where it landed on Cassie's shoulders. Cassie peered up at the lawyer as she sat, legs spread-eagled in front of her, on the rug.

"Cassandra Grace, is it?" The lawyer's eyes crinkled with mirth and a grin split his rounded face. "I think maybe I'll take your case, after all, Gracie. It could be good for a few laughs, if nothing else."

Too embarrassed to take offense at his cavalier attitude and relieved that he agreed to be her attorney, Cassie accepted his proffered hand to help her stand.

Cassie paced restlessly as she waited for Jaimé to arrive with the children. She had a half-dozen videos stacked on top of her VCR. Evelyn had suggested a Harry Potter movie and Cassie had selected a few Disney features as well as another favorite, *The Adventures of Milo and Otis*.

She had spent better than an hour with Harvey Walton that morning, inspecting the barn and the outbuildings. He had found it curious that the sheriff stopped his search immediately after finding the box with the cash in it. "You would have thought he would have given the house a thorough going through. It's almost as though he left as soon as he found what he had come after. I may have to do a little checking on our good Sheriff Crenshaw." The attorney departed with a promise to contact her if he uncovered any new leads.

Cassie carried a cup of tea into the living room and flipped on the television. As she ejected last night's movie from the VCR and slipped the tape into its case, memories held in check throughout the day careened into her mind, ricocheting between her head and her heart—Jaimé had proposed to her last evening! It wasn't exactly a proposal from the pages of a romance novel, but nonetheless, he had asked her to marry him—and she had accepted! She felt a little guilty for not calling Anita to share her news with her best friend, but it was still too fresh and tenuous for Cassie to say anything. Besides, what if Jaimé changed his mind? What if he had only spoken in the heat of passion? What if, after thinking it over, he decided there were too many problems between them to surmount?

The tension of the past week had left Cassie feeling exhausted and lethargic that morning, so Jaimé had risen before her and was showered and dressed by the time she had forced herself to roll out of bed. He had not mentioned the proposal again, only suggesting that she take a long hot bath after he left. In spite of her self-reproach that she was "borrowing trouble," by the time she heard Jaimé pull into the driveway, over an hour later than they had planned, she had convinced herself that he regretted his hasty proposal. After the strain of waiting, she was tired and irritable, and in little mood for the evening ahead.

Ben came charging up the walk while Tina sulked behind her father. Jaimé greeted Cassie with a perfunctory kiss on her cheek while his daughter glared at her rival with her chin jutting out in an unspoken challenge.

Cassie took the children's coats and hung them on the hall tree, while Jaimé returned to the car to retrieve the pizzas. Tina had wrapped her babydoll in a blanket and held her close, while she waited by the door for her father's return, refusing to talk or even look at Cassie. Ben, meanwhile, had made himself at home in Cassie's living room, adding two videotapes that he had brought with him to the stack on the VCR.

"Harry Potter! Cool! What's this Milo and Otis one? Can we watch it first?"

"Sure, whatever you want—it's your evening," Cassie tried to muster enough enthusiasm to keep her bad mood from becoming noticeable.

They ate pizza sitting around the coffee table while Dudley Moore narrated the story of Milo, the adventuresome cat that was whisked down the river in a box, and Otis, the loyal dog who valiantly tried to rescue his friend. Tina watched intently as the pair stumbled into one misadventure after another. Ben ducked his head when both the cat and then the dog found mates who bore them litters.

As the two animal families finally made their way back to the farm, Tina critiqued, "That was dumb."

"Hmm, is that why you haven't finished your pizza?" Her father asked noting the half-eaten slice of pepperoni that lay forgotten on a plate in front of the girl. Tina gave Cassie a surreptitious glower from her perch beside her father on the couch as she picked up the now cold pizza and began to gnaw on its crust.

Though the movie had become a favorite of Cassie's, she had found herself drifting in and out of sleep as she rocked back and forth in the bentwood chair. The cute little animal pair had managed to lift her spirits somewhat and the pizza's spicy aroma had enticed her to nibble on a slice.

Ben and Jaimé had each devoured several wedges of the pie, and the boy was selecting their next movie while coaxing his father to light the fire, without seeming to notice either his sister's petulance or Cassie's muted energy level.

Ben stretched out on the braided rug, immediately immersed in the escapades of Harry Potter, the boy wizard. Jaimé tugged the fire screen together to catch any wayward embers from the crackling blaze he had lit, and stopped behind Cassie's rocker on his way back to the davenport.

"There's room for one more on the couch," he said, his words falling lightly on the top of her head.

Cassie cast a glance over to where Tina glared at them from her seat on the middle cushion.

"I'm not so sure about that," Cassie replied, "I think it might be best if I stayed right where I am."

Jaimé stooped down on one knee beside her chair and took her hand in both of his. Cassie caught her breath—would he propose again, with his children as witnesses?

"Is everything okay, Cas? You've hardly spoken all evening. You look beat—maybe tonight wasn't such a good idea after all."

She knew she was being foolish to be so disappointed—knew her disillusionment was born of the cumulative effects of the past week—knew she should just hold her tongue—but wisdom did not prevail.

An edge honed by frustration sharpened her voice, "Yeah,

you're right. It's been a long day. Why don't you pull the mattress out so that you and the children can enjoy the videos. I'll get the sheets and blankets and then I'm going to be the proverbial party pooper and go to bed."

His gaze probed her deliberately passive face before he acquiesced. Much to Ben's chagrin, his father captured Harry Potter in suspended animation with the flick of the remote, while commandeering Ben to help shift the coffee table out of the way so that they could pull the daybed out from the bowels of the couch. Jaimé untied the straps that secured the mattress to the frame, hefted the bedding on its side, and then while balancing the mattress with one hand indicated to Ben to assist him in folding the frame back into the body of the davenport.

Cassie returned with sheets, a coverlet, and pillows just as Jaimé and Ben were positioning the mattress on the floor in front of the fireplace. A sudden *dejá vu* threatened to overwhelm Cassie as Jaimé glanced up to catch her staring at him. A quiet acknowledgment passed between them, soothing, just a bit, her self-inflicted pain.

After they had covered the mattress with sheets and blankets, Cassie gathered up the remnants of the pizza party. She carried the box and the plates to the kitchen, stashing the remaining few pizza slices in the refrigerator. They had planned to pop corn, and as Cassie heard Harry Potter spring back to life, she retrieved the popcorn and canola oil from the cupboard. *No need for the children to be disappointed as well*, she thought to herself.

As she heated the oil in a large, heavy saucepan, Jaimé ambled into the room. He leaned against the doorjamb, nearly filling it with his well-muscled six-foot frame. He waited while she added the popcorn to the sizzling oil, dropped the lid in place, and proceeded to shake the pan over the burner. The sound of exploding kernels filled the room, muffling the silence that hung between them.

Cassie dumped the fluffy white corn into a big aluminum bowl, doused it liberally with salt, drizzled melted butter across the top, and handed the metal dish to Jaimé. She then poured two glasses of lemonade and motioned for him to follow her to the living room.

"Wow! Can we really eat popcorn in bed? That's phat!" Ben exclaimed.

"Fat?" Cassie asked.

"Yeah, phat—you know, cool!" the boy explained.

Cassie gave Jaimé a perplexed look and he laughed, "We're just out of it, I guess. Be careful not to spill your lemonade," he instructed his children.

"Where are you going?" Tina asked as her father walked toward the arch that separated the living and dining rooms.

"I'll be in the kitchen helping Cassandra...uh...clean up the pizza mess."

"I thought she was going to bed," Tina baited her father with a sullen look.

Cassie stood back, not wanting to be a pawn in the game between father and daughter, but reluctant to follow through with her earlier plans. Slack-Eyed Joe chose that moment to make his entrance. He strutted over to the mattress, looked over the children with one amber eye, and without warning, pounced directly onto the mound of blankets covering Tina's soft belly.

"Oomph!" the girl gasped as the air whooshed out of her lungs.

Unconcerned with any discomfort he may have caused, the feline settled his tawny mass of fur on top of the child, eliciting an unexpected giggle from her.

With his daughter distracted, Jaimé slowly backed from the room, grabbed Cassie's hand, and pulled her toward the kitchen. When they were out of the view of the children, he drew her to him and assuaged her disillusioned weariness with his very reassuring lips.

"Now are you going to tell me what's been eating at you all night?"

But she couldn't, not without revealing her insecurities about him. He had done everything to prove his love, and yet, tonight she remained unconvinced.

Instead, she told him about Harvey Walton's visit that morning.

"There's several things that don't add up when it comes to our esteemed sheriff—like how did he know where to find the money hidden in the barn? Unfortunately, we have less than a month to find out." Their arms remained loosely locked around each other as her questioning look was reflected in the brown depths of his eyes.

"Your trial date has been set for January 26. I found out when I stopped by the courthouse today." What he didn't tell her is that they had drawn "Hang-em Harry" Harrison as the presiding judge. He tried to hide the concern that had settled in the pit of his stomach when he read the docket that afternoon.

"Dad, Tina spilt her lemonade all over the floor!"

They broke apart, each automatically responding to the call from the living room while still dwelling on the trial that loomed ahead. Cassie grabbed a dishtowel and tossed it across the room to Jaimé who sprinted through the dining room in time to see a puddle rapidly enlarging itself as it was being fed from a still-tipped glass.

"I told you to be careful with your lemonade," he scolded as Cassie dropped a bath towel on top of the wholly inadequate and thoroughly soaked dishtowel.

"I'll bet that Joe was responsible—that cat has never learned to mind his manners!" Cassie offered in Tina's defense.

Tina and Ben exchanged wary glances before the girl lowered her eyes and shook her head. "Papa's right, I was being careless."

"It's my fault, too," Ben admitted, "We were having a little tiny pillow fight, and...."

"A pillow fight? With a fire right behind you in the fireplace? Benjamin, I thought you had more sense than that!" Jaimé reprimanded his son.

"It was just a little fight—we were careful not to get close to the fire, honest!"

"Tell you what," Cassie interjected, "I borrowed a few games from the library today, too—is anyone up to a rousing rendition of *Clue* or *Sorry* or maybe a little *Yahtzee* or *Life*?"

The roll of dice, slap of cards, and click of tokens moving across game boards punctuated the remainder of the evening, while movies provided background entertainment. They popped a second pan of popcorn, only this time they used the long-handled popper that Cassie had found for a quarter at a garage sale and took turns shaking it over the open fire.

Toward midnight a pair of very sleepy children trooped into the bathroom, brushed their teeth, then snuggled under the blankets by the fire. Shrek had just rescued Fiona from Prince Charming's cloying grasp as Jaimé once again led Cassie from the living room and into the kitchen.

"I think that big green ogre has the right idea," Jaimé said as he slid his arms around her waist and rested his hands on her supple bottom.

"And just what might that be?"

"Taking his woman back to the swamp to live Happily Ever After."

"Hmm…well, all of this area was once part of the Great Black Swamp…."

"Think we could find our 'Happily-Ever-After' in this swampland, princess?"

Her kisses told him she thought it might be so.

CHAPTER TWELVE

Cassie walked slowly down the aisle to where Windy and Don Johnston stood waiting. The prospective groom wore a smile that stretched from ear to ear as he clasped and unclasped his hands behind his back. Jaimé sat in the back pew of St. Jude's admiring the swish of silk as Cassie's rehearsal dress rustled back and forth across her hips with each step that she took.

When Cassie at last assumed her place at the front of the church, she turned just in time to see her best friend begin her march down the aisle on the arm of her aging father. Henry Morales could only navigate his stooped body with the aid of a wheeled walker, but he made his way proudly beside his youngest daughter.

The parish priest led the bridal party through the basics of the nuptial mass. Nervous laughter tittered through the cavernous building as Anita answered, "I do," before the clergyman had finished reciting the prelude to the question. When the priest invited the couple to kiss at the conclusion of the rehearsal, Sam Windmiller took his bride-to-be in his arms and bestowed upon her a reverent caress that bespoke the lifetime of devotion that he offered her. A hush filled the air, as those present acknowledged the love that swelled between this man and this woman and encompassed those few fortunate enough to bear its witness on this, the eve of their wedding.

From her position near the altar, Cassie searched for Jaimé in the dim recesses of the church. He was, as she knew he would be, watching her. Their eyes met and held across the empty pews.

After the recessional, they adjourned to *Tia* Juana's for an informal rehearsal dinner. The tavern had been reserved for Anita and Windy's family and friends, and many well-wishers waited in the parking lot for the entourage to arrive from the church. A light snow filtered through the streetlights as Jaimé pulled his sedan in a space beside Windy's cherry red pick-up. The flare of bottle rockets and the pop-pop-pop of lady fingers pierced the air, heralding their arrival. The festive atmosphere was contagious and Cassie laughed as Jaimé tucked her into the shelter of his arm.

They were immediately approached by a medium-height, well-muscled Hispanic man of thirty-five or so, "Hey, Jaimé, *primo mío*, are you going to introduce me to your *señorita* here?"

"Easy, cousin, you have your own *mujer*—you had better hope I don't talk to Mariá Anna, or your *suegra*, *Tía* Juana."

"Ah, man, you hit hard—you tell my mother-in-law I was eyeing your *gringa* and she'll have me in the Marines beside Ernie before the night's over!"

Several others greeted Jaimé and welcomed Cassie as they progressed through the waiting crowd into the tavern.

Champagne and other libations flowed freely as they enjoyed a first-class buffet, including *Tiá* Juana's now famous fire-eating *quesadillas*.

"I can't eat another bite," Cassie groaned as she polished off a *sopapilla*, licking the lingering cinnamon and sugar from her fingers.

With a sly smile, Jaimé took her hand in his, "Here, let me do that for you." He slipped one sticky digit into his mouth and let his tongue wash away the sweet concoction from her skin.

Cassie held her breath as the warmth from her finger rushed throughout her body. "How long do you think we need to stay before we can make a proper exit?" The raise of Jaimé's eyebrows suggested that another part of his anatomy was coming to attention as well.

Cassie lowered her eyelashes, and began "Um, Jaimé, there's something we need to talk about…" However, just then the loud chink of silverware against a glass brought the notice of those gathered in the restaurant to the bridal couple. Windy placed the requisite kiss on his bride's lips, then requested that the best man and matron-of-honor join them at their table.

Reluctantly, Jaimé stood and helped Cassie from her chair. He escorted her to the front of the room and gave her a brief but territorial kiss before handing her over to Don Johnston. A snicker traveled through the area around the bar where his relatives had clustered, and he cast them a mock-threatening glare before returning to his table.

Anita and Windy presented a gift to each of their attendants along with a verbal expression of their appreciation for their friendship. Windy told the crowd about how he and Anita had met at "Barn Again!" and, much to Cassie's surprise, invited everyone to her farm to check out the end results of the workshop. Cassie smiled and reiterated the invitation as she tugged the bow from her package and opened the decorative box.

Tears welled in her eyes for the first of what would be many times over the weekend as she held up a bracelet of fine gold with an emerald setting to match the necklace and earrings that Jaimé had given her on Christmas Day.

"How did you know? I didn't even have time to show you…."

"A 'little birdie' gave me a hint," Anita teased as she was engulfed in a hug from her best friend.

Windy presented Don with the perfect handyman gift—a small engraved all-purpose tool in 14-carat gold that had been attached to a keychain.

After toasts were made to the bride and groom and their families, Jaimé slipped up to reclaim his date. Cassie bent over and whispered to Anita and Windy, who both smiled and nodded.

Windy stood and shook Jaimé's hand, "Just have the lady to

St. Jude's by noon tomorrow for the photo shoot—and make sure she's well-rested!" The men exchanged conspiratorial grins as Jaimé replied, "Yeah, you too, buddy...."

Cassie shook her head as Anita laughed, "Boys, they never change—problem is, 'You can't live with them...'"

"...and living without them is not an option!" Cassie added her twist to the age-old adage. She leaned into Jaimé's strong frame as he drew her back against him. "We'll see you tomorrow, promptly at noon."

They stopped on their way out of the restaurant to bid farewell to Anita's and Windy's parents. As they approached *Tía* Juana, the older woman stepped out from behind the bar to embrace both Jaimé and Cassie.

"You take care of this *gringa, sobrino—¿Le dijiste del dinero?*" Jaimé's aunt shot her nephew a look that demanded he maintain their secret.

"*Desde luego que no, Tía. Yo se lo prometo!*" Jaimé protested while suspicion clouded Cassie's features.

"Forgive us, *Señora* Alesander, my nephew and I, we come to an understanding, that is all. You look *muy bella*—very beautiful—this evening!"

"*Gracias, Tía. La comida estada muy buena,*" Cassie complimented the proprietor on the buffet that she served. A wary look slowly overtook *Tía* Juana's round face as she, too late, recalled that Cassie possessed at least a basic knowledge of the Spanish language.

Jaimé just shrugged his shoulders and rolled his eyes at his aunt, knowing the questions would come fast and furious when he and Cassie stepped out into the parking lot.

Indeed, no sooner had Jaimé closed the door behind them than Cassie turned on him, "'*¿Le dijiste del dinero?*' What money haven't you told me about? You'd best spill it, Jaimé Alvarez, because you will have no peace until you tell me what that was all about!"

"You heard me promise my aunt that I wouldn't say anything.

Can't you just trust, princess, that this is all for your own good?"

"No, I'm sorry, Jaimé, it's not that I don't trust you or your aunt—you know that. But I'm a little gun-shy when the subject of money comes up these days. And I don't need you to patronize me—if it's truly for my own good, I have a right to know about it!"

They had reached the car, and he unlocked the door and opened it so that Cassie could slide into the passenger's seat. When Jaimé had settled into the driver's side, Cassie grabbed the keys from the ignition. "We are not moving until you tell me what's going on, Mr. Alvarez!"

"Uh-oh—Mr. Alvarez, is it? You've got me between the proverbial rock and a hard place."

"Yeah, well, I know where the soft places are, too, and you aren't getting near any of them until you 'fess up!"

"You don't play fair, you know that, don't you?" He sent her a sidelong glance and let out a deep sigh. "You tell *Tía* Juana that I said anything, and the next Corona she serves me will be spiked with *habañeros!*"

"You think I can't outdo *habañero* peppers? Trust me, unless you come clean right here, right now, in this parking lot, you won't be safe anywhere—day or night!"

"Ouch! Okay, Lorena, you win!" He leaned back against the seat and let his fingers trail along the back of her neck. The halogen lighting in the parking lot played havoc with the night-shadows, casting a surreal pattern across her face, "I couldn't get my hands on enough cash to post your bail—so *Tía* put the *Taverna* up as collateral."

Cassie bolted sideways in her seat, "She did *what?*"

"She used *Tía's Taverna* as collateral for your bail. It took a while to get the paperwork approved—that's why you had to spend the night in Billy Joe's hellhole."

Cassie sat back against her seat, dumbfounded. "I was so relieved to be out of there, and things have been so hectic since—I wondered where you got the money, but never remembered to ask when we were together. I assumed...I don't know what I assumed.

Certainly not that your aunt would offer the *Taverna* for my freedom! I have to thank her!"

"Haven't you been listening, *querida?* For my sake, you can't let *Tía* Juana know that I said anything. Besides—it's only for a month. Once we clear this up and nail that thieving bas... *diablo* that you were forced to marry, her money will be returned. She called it an investment in her favorite nephew's future!"

Cassie leaned back against the smooth leather of her seat, pondering this latest unexpected turn of events, before turning the conversation to the subject she had intended to bring up earlier in the evening.

"Jaimé, the other night when you..." His fingers caressed the sensitive area at the base of her neck and she leaned into their touch.

"...When I asked you to marry me?" He finished.

"You didn't ask just because we..."

"Just because we made love?" He again surmised her thought.

The almost shy glance she gave him tugged at his heart and he brought his lips to hers as though to reassure her of his love.

She drew away from his embrace just a whisper's length, when she spoke, "If you truly want to marry me, I don't think you should spend the night at the farm."

"What are you saying?"

"That you should drive back to your parents' home tonight."

Their breath still warmed each other in the chill air as he said, "Let me get this straight—if we just make love, I can stay the night. But if I intend to marry you, I have to drive back to Bowling Green?" He closed the distance between them, heating the atmosphere with his kiss.

Again she broke away, sighing deeply. "Please hear me out, love. If I am to one day be your wife, I need to have the respect of your family, and especially your children. How can that happen if they know we are sleeping together every night? I'm so torn—I know each night with you is precious. I know that we may only have a few weeks left before I'm..." though she thought it, she could not say the word *incarcerated*, "Loving you…being loved by you is the most marvelous gift I could have received. If I…if I…" she again stumbled over the words, "…go to prison, your love will be enough to sustain me through the years."

She stopped a moment to collect her thoughts before going on. "But I don't want our act of love to be born in desperation. I want to be able to come to you freely. When I take you as my husband, I don't want to be burdened with conditions mandated by the state.

"If, God forbid, Harvey Walton cannot find evidence to clear my name, then I will do what I must. If you still want me, I will marry you when I am a free woman."

This time it was Jaimé who leaned back against his seat and forcefully exhaled the air that he had pent up while listening to her speak.

"It's getting cold in here. Don't you think you'd better give me the keys so that I can start the car?" He knew his words came out clipped, the harsh tones fueled equally by disappointment, frustration, and a growing realization that she was right. As much as he wanted to rush to the farm and ravish her by the firelight, he reluctantly ceded that, even though he had spent the previous night in the living room with his children, they were beginning to ask questions. And if there was anything that his princess deserved, it was respect.

As she laid the ring of keys in his extended palm, he turned his head toward her. "You know the only reason I'm ticked off is because you're right, don't you? That, and the fact that this boner is making me damned uncomfortable, and now I know the only cure I'm going to get tonight is a cold shower."

She bent over and let her lips tease his. She playfully flicked her tongue along the pout that had extended his lower lip then worked her way between his clamped teeth. Finally, he laughed and kissed her thoroughly. They broke apart, each breathing hard, but allowing their foreheads to remain touching.

"There's something to be said for good old-fashioned making

out!" A twinkle danced from her eye and landed on her smile as she licked her lips seductively.

"Yeah, easy for you to say—you don't have this thing throbbing between your legs," he lamented. She resisted the urge to reach over and caress the object of his concern. *Perhaps this respect thing is a little overrated* she thought as she placed her left hand firmly under her thigh, pinning it to the seat.

He eased back toward the steering wheel, inserted the key into the ignition and fired the engine. "Anyone comes out and sees these steamed up windows will think we couldn't wait to get back to your place," he said as he turned the defrost on high.

At nine o'clock Saturday morning, Jaimé found himself speeding down the country roads that he had just traversed the night before. Cas wasn't expecting him for another hour, but he had woken up early, stiff, out-of-sorts, and alone in the twin bed he had slept in every night for the first eighteen years of his life. True to his word, he had taken a cold shower when he came in last evening.

His mother had hummed while she prepared breakfast and his father cast questioning glances at him over the pages of the *Toledo Blade*. Ben and Tina had bombarded him with questions when they came running down the stairs to find him sitting at the dining room table.

"Why didn't you stay at Cassandra's last night?"

"Is she mad at you?" "

"When can we go back?" "

"I really *did* like Milo and Otis!"

"Maybe next time we can take some of our games?"

"Can't, dummy, they're in Toronto!"

"That's just about enough from both of you! Christina, apologize to your brother for calling him a 'dummy,'" Jaimé had tried to keep his irritation in check as he nursed an incipient headache with a cup of strong hot coffee.

Much to his mother's chagrin, he had eaten only a few bites

of breakfast before taking his leave, assuring his children that they would be able to return to the farm again soon. "Cassandra and I will see you all at the wedding this afternoon," he responded to his father's unspoken question.

His headache threatened to become full-blown as he swerved to miss a large pick-up that came barreling towards him smack down the middle of the narrow paved road. *What the hell is Paul Alexander doing out here?* He thought as he pressed on the accelerator, concern vying with the pain that creased his forehead.

He sped into Cassie's driveway, sending loose stones flying, and had barely pulled the keys from the ignition switch before rushing up the walk to the door. Cassie appeared behind the glass window wrapped in her aged chenille robe as he banged his knuckles against the door.

"I'm getting you a doorbell," he barked as he barged through the doorway.

"Jaimé, what in heaven's name are you doing here now?" she asked, ignoring his demand.

"Was Paul Alexander just here?" He knew it was a crazy notion, fed by fear, frustration, and a latent *machismo*, but he had visions of her former husband worming his way into Cassie's bed after she closed the door on Jaimé the previous night.

"What? Jaimé Alvarez, what are you talking about?"

"He damn near ran me off the road just a half-mile back. Are you telling me he wasn't here?"

"Do you honestly think I would lie to you about Paul? Because if you do, you're not the man I thought you were and you can just turn around and hightail it back to town."

Jaimé pressed his fingers against his throbbing temples. He knew he was being a jerk, but couldn't figure out how to extricate himself from the hole that he had so efficiently dug.

"No, I know you wouldn't lie to me. I was just so worried when I saw him coming from your place…"

"Jaimé, I told you, he wasn't here. He knows what he'll get if he tries anything with me."

She poured him a cup of steaming black coffee as he asked, "What do you mean by that?"

Cassie hadn't told Jaimé about Paul's attack earlier in the fall, and now wrestled with whether or not it would reassure him or cause him to insist that someone stay with her. The fact that Paul had been driving by her house rattled her and she steeped herself another mug of ginger peach tea.

She sat down across from him at the small kitchen table, inhaling the fragrant scent of her drink. "In the interests of honesty and full disclosure, Paul was here..." His head popped up, as though expecting the worst.

"...back in October or November. He thought he would pay me a little surprise visit..." Cassie went on to relay the events of Paul's calamitous attempted assault, finishing with his tripping over Slack-eyed Joe and Cassie's well-placed kick. "So you see, I don't think he would have the intestinal fortitude to take on Joe and me again—he's way too much of a coward. Besides, everything's on his side with the court case—why would he want to jeopardize that?"

"All I know is that the man is a slithering snake—the kind that gives even reptiles a bad name. Why didn't you tell me before now that he attacked you?"

"You were in Canada—there wasn't much you could do to protect me, so I didn't see any reason to worry you. Besides, like I said, he hasn't come around since then."

"Until today, that is," Jaimé countered.

"Until today," Cassie reiterated, worrying her bottom lip.

Jaimé dropped Cassie off at St. Jude's just as the anachronistic Angelus bells rang out twelve chimes, supposedly calling laborers to noon prayer much as they had for the past hundred years. Windy came down the wide span of steps from the church entrance to meet them while Jaimé retrieved the small suitcase containing Cassie's make-up and personal items from his trunk.

"Jees, Jaimé my man, Cassie looks well-rested, but you..."

"Don't say it—I had a rough night...." Jaimé sent Cassie an accusatory look as she swallowed a guilty grin. Windy watched the exchange, but wisely chose to make no further comment on it.

"I have an errand to run and need to pick up my suit at mom and dad's. I'll be back in a few hours," Jaimé pressed a quick kiss on Cassie's lips before handing her luggage to Windy and heading back around the car.

"What was that all about?" the prospective groom asked as they watched Jaimé's sedan peel across the parking lot.

Cassie just smiled and said, "Boys will be boys," then turned to join Anita who had been waiting just outside the massive doors to St. Jude's.

Jaimé sat between his two children in a pew with his parents as the organist played the cue for Cassie to begin her walk down the aisle. Anita's younger brother, Davíd, had ushered them to a seat near the front of the church, allowing Jaimé a vantage point where he could watch with pride as others admired his princess— a role for which Cassie had seemingly dressed. The green velvet of her gown flowed effortlessly from its fitted bodice, emphasizing the swell of her breasts, before falling loosely around her slender hips. The necklace with which he had gifted her on Christmas Day lay against the creamy texture of her skin, while the earrings accentuated the glamour of her blonde hair, which had been swept into a sleek French roll.

"Wow, Dad, Cassandra's even prettier than Fiona," Ben whispered, then amended, "when she wasn't an ogre, I mean." Jaimé smiled at his son and nodded his agreement, not unaware of the fact that, rather than reassuring Ben, his unexpected return home the night before had been a source of concern for the boy.

Tina said nothing, but shifted closer to her father as Cassie drew nearer to their pew. Cassie gave them all a brief smile before returning her concentration to the white runner that stretched out before her. When she turned to face the back of the church, the organist pumped an enthusiastic wedding march out of the aging instrument, signaling the bride's entrance....

It was hours later that the wedding party and their guests gathered at the Moose Lodge on the edge of town for the reception. Anita and Windy had invited Don's wife and Jaimé to join them at the head table, and the three couples were basking in the afterglow of a perfectly executed ceremony. They had finished their buffet and the plates had been cleared. Many toasts had followed Don's initial salute to the bridal couple.

Anita's nephew served as the DJ, and as he inserted the "Hawaiian Wedding Song" into the CD player, he invited the bride and groom to the dance floor. As the music transitioned to "You Are So Beautiful," the best man and matron of honor joined the bridal couple.

Jaimé stifled a whiff of jealousy as Don Johnston's agility on the dance floor belied his size. He and Cassie appeared to be rapt in an animated conversation as they effortlessly glided around the floor. When he was nearly at his wit's end, Don's wife, Daun, an attractive brunette with a keen sense of humor, nudged him.

"What do you say we take a turn on the floor. Then, before you actually skewer my husband, we can quietly exchange partners."

With a sheepish grin, Jaimé asked, "Was I being that obvious?"

"Nah, only to me and a few hundred others in the room," she chided him with a laugh as they walked to the dance floor together.

They managed a few turns around the perimeter of the floor before easing toward Cassie and Don. When they were within reach, Jaimé winked at his partner and tapped her husband on the shoulder. "I think your wife wants a word with you...."

Jaimé quickly whisked Cassie into his arms, vowing to keep her close for the remainder of the evening. Others joined them on the dance floor as the DJ increased the tempo to a *cumbia*. After a few songs, several teenage boys requested a Latino rap artist and immediately dropped to the floor in a contest of intricate hiphop moves.

Jaimé escorted Cassie to the edge of the floor, dodging flying hands and legs. "I think this is our cue to sit this one out. Before you know it, they'll be playing the 'Chicken Dance' and the 'Hokey-Pokey'!"

"What? You're not going to 'Hokey-Pokey' with me?" Cassie feigned indignation as Jaimé eased her in the direction of the guests assembled at the various tables.

"Let's say hello to your Mom and Aunt Nell, then maybe you'll get me back on the dance floor."

The two ladies were seated with Jaimé's family, enjoying the festive evening. Jaimé gave each a quick kiss on their cheek in greeting.

"Oh, Cassie dear, it flutters my heart to be kissed by such a handsome young man!" Aunt Nell purred.

"Careful, Aunt Nell, you don't want to give him the big head!"

"You don't think I'm handsome, eh?" Jaimé challenged her with lifted brows.

"Oh, you're handsome enough, all right—it was the young part I was questioning!" To those sitting at the table, she explained, "This fuddy-duddy won't even do the 'Hokey-Pokey' with me!"

"Not do the 'Hokey-Pokey' at a wedding party? Why it's a downright sacrilege, isn't it, sister!" Nell said with a reproving lift of her chin and a twinkle in her eye. "If I were just a little more spry you wouldn't find me sitting back here!"

They chatted a little longer with their families before their attention was diverted to the area where a three-tiered cake stood suspended on white plastic pedestals above a small working fountain. Two spun-sugar staircases led from either side of the lower tier to a pair of smaller cakes. Rose petals lay strewn on and about the iced confections. Anita and Windy stood behind the cake, holding a knife festooned in ribbons.

"I heard that Anita's sister made the cake," Cassie's mother said.

"Yes, amazingly, the entire reception was catered by her extended family," Cassie confirmed.

Jaimé's mother smiled, "*Sí, ese es nuestro costumbre.*"

"It's the Latino way," Jaimé loosely translated.

Windy and Anita fed each other a bite of their wedding cake, each smearing a bit of the icing on the other, much to the delight of the children gathered around them.

Cassie suggested that Ben and Tina walk with her and their father to the cake table where Anita's cousins were slicing a rich chocolate confection with a raspberry filling. Ben was out of his seat before Cassie finished her sentence. Tina held back a little longer, but wasn't about to be left behind when her father and Cassie followed Ben across the room.

Cassie chose a piece of traditional white cake with buttercream icing for herself while Jaimé opted for the chocolate. The children returned with their cake to their table, as Jaimé and Cassie joined the rest of the bridal party at the head table.

Jaimé pulled Cassie's chair out for her, but rather than sitting down beside her, he stepped behind where Windy and Anita were seated, bent down and spoke in a low tone so that Cassie could not hear. She watched with suspicion as both the bride and groom broke out in huge smiles and nodded their assent.

Anita walked over to her nephew with a request. He checked his playlist, and turned to his stash of CD's. The opening bars of "Unchained Melody" followed the bride to her chair, as her new husband refilled the champagne flutes at the head table.

The clatter of a fork falling to the floor drew their attention to the end of the table where Jaimé stood from his chair, moved it out of the way, then genuflected as though to retrieve the utensil from where it had fallen. Instead he knelt before Cassie, taking both of her hands in his. He waded into the sea-green of her eyes as the confusion he detected there gave way to wonder.

Windy chinked a spoon on the side of his water glass drawing the attention of all the assemblage to the head table.

A hush spread through the room as Jaimé drew in a deep

breath and slowly let it out again, "Cassandra Grace Mikhailov Alexander, I have loved you for as long as I can remember. My life will never be complete unless you are a part of it."

He released her hand long enough to draw a small box from the breast pocket of his suit and flip it open. Nestled in a bed of silk lay an antique gold ring with a large square-cut diamond set in a bed of exquisite diminutive emeralds.

"Will you accept this ring as a token of my love and consent to be my wife?"

A collective breath was held throughout the room as Cassie stared, speechless, from the ring to the face of the man who held it and back to the ring again. Tears welled in her eyes, blurring her vision and threatening to pour over her carefully applied mascara.

"Oh, Jaimé," was all she could say.

She shifted her gaze from the beautiful man who knelt before her to the throng of friends and relatives gathered in the room. Her heart swelled as she absorbed the enormity of Jaimé's gift—to proclaim his love before all present, especially given her current status in the community.

"I promised you wine and roses...." He began, his confidence waning as he awaited her response.

"Jaimé Alvarez, you are my destiny," she spoke softly to the man who offered her his life, his trust. "If you will have me regardless of what the fates may bring, I promise to love you until my dying day." Then, louder so that those nearby could hear, she said, "Yes, I will marry you."

"Good, because this kneeling is getting damned uncomfortable," he teased as he slipped the band of gold on her left ring finger.

"She said yes!" someone close by shouted, and a spontaneous round of applause spread from table to table.

As Jaimé took his chair, Anita moved over to hug her friend. She brought with her the small bridal bouquet that she intended to toss to the single women in attendance and presented it to Cassie. "The fates have decreed that you, *mi amiga,* have this. I cannot wait to dance at your wedding!"

"Speaking of dancing," Jaimé interjected, "I believe we were interrupted the last time we tried our turn at this song, princess. 'Nita, would you and your bridegroom care to join us on the dance floor?"

Throughout the remainder of the evening, Cassie caught herself staring at the glint of the diamond ring on her left hand, reminding her that one day she would marry the most handsome man in the room.

Jaimé and Windy stood together as the groom waited for his bride in order to take their leave for their honeymoon. From across the room, Cassie admired the fit of Jaimé's black jacket over his well-toned frame. A renegade feathering of dark hair strayed across his forehead as he inclined his head toward the shorter groom. He had discarded his tie, and undone the top button of his white shirt allowing her to fixate on the hollow at the base of his Adam's apple. His bronze skin contrasted against the white of his collar, and the masculine line of his lips accentuated his strong face as he smiled at something Windy had said.

Cassie let her gaze drift to where he had tucked the fingers of his right hand into the pocket of his slacks as he casually leaned against a doorjamb. It traveled the length of crisply creased trousers to polished wingtips. He was all man…and he was her man. The delicious sweetness of being loved oozed through her as she skimmed over to take her place beside him.

He immediately held out his arm and drew her to his side— his inviting smile and possessive glint in his eyes letting her know that she could not so easily brush him off on this night.

Anita emerged from the ladies' room dressed in a casual suit, and soon after, the bride and groom departed amidst cheers and applause.

Cassie and Jaimé tarried at the reception a while longer, accepting congratulations and basking in the pleasure of officially being a "couple" among their family and friends. Much to Aunt Nell's chagrin, she and Cassie's mother had left soon after Jaimé's proposal. To everyone's—except her sister's—amusement, Martha Mikhailov had declared, "You know I don't like driving late at night, Penelope. Besides, I've got to get you back to the old folks' home before they lock you out and I have to take you home with me."

Tina was sleeping, her head resting on her grandfather's lap, as Cassie and Jaimé sat down, once again, beside his family.

"I think you should stay at Cassandra's tonight," Ben instructed his father.

"Oh you do?" Jaimé ruffled his son's hair as he shot him a questioning look.

"Yes, well, since you are engaged and Cassandra's going to be our mom now, I think it would be okay."

"She's not going to be my mom, not ever," came a sleepily belligerent voice from Gregorio Alvarez's lap.

Temporarily ignoring his daughter's protest, Jaimé told his son, "We'll see what Cassandra has to say about it. Maybe, since it's so late, she'll let me sleep on the couch, just for tonight…."

Cassie slipped in beside Jaimé's father and gently brushed her hand along Tina's round cheek. "I promise, Tina, that I will never try to replace your mother. Even after I marry your father," she stopped to savor those words, "you may call me 'Cassandra' just as you do now."

Tina gave Cassie a skeptical look with one sleepy eye then closed it again without responding.

After they bid his family goodnight, Jaimé retrieved their coats.

"It's hard to believe that tomorrow is New Year's Eve. It hasn't even been a week since you returned from Toronto. So much has happened, it seems as though a month has gone by." Cassie said as they walked out into the night.

Jaimé's overcoat flapped open as a brisk wind caught them unprepared. He put his arm around her shoulder and pulled her to him to protect her from the biting gusts. *Beware the winds of change*, he thought then wondered why the ominous words had passed through his mind.

As they walked around the back of his car, he noticed it leaning toward the right. He immediately glanced down at the tires—both were flat.

Cassie followed his line of vision, "Oh no, Jaimé, Paul...."

"I can't imagine that he would do his own dirty work, but I'm sure he's behind this." It was then that they saw the words scrawled across the doors in crude, nearly indecipherable white letters: "Spic go home" and below that, "Die bitch."

Jaimé hustled Cassie back into the hall before quizzing some of the men that had gathered off and on all evening outside the door to smoke. Jaimé's car had been parked only a few spaces from the entrance, but no one had seen anything suspicious. The men fanned out around the parking lot searching for clues to the vandalism, while word of it spread quickly within the hall.

Cassie feared that Jaimé's friends and family might blame her for involving him in her plight or because she was a *gringa*, but everyone closed around her offering their support. *Tía* Juana came up to Cassie where she sat with Jaimé's parents, "We'll find out who did this. You are one of us now, and we take care of our own."

When Cassie returned to the parking lot, two police cars sat with their lights flashing red and blue strobes into the night. One officer stooped down beside the slashed tire of Jaimé's sedan while another jotted notes on a clipboard. Cassie was relieved that the city police had responded to the call, rather than the sheriff. Though when she said as much, one of Anita's older brothers commented that it depended on the officer—not all of the town's finest were colorblind.

"Look what we found hiding in the bushes," Davíd called out as he and a cousin held two young teenagers by the scruffs of their necks and forced them across the parking lot. "These two little *amigos* have white chalk all over their coats."

The two boys—one a short, skinny redhead and the other, taller, with long, unkempt blond hair—scowled at the men who held them captive. "You better let us go, you greasers, or the cops'll haul your asses to jail," the blond muttered.

"That so?" The policeman with the clipboard walked over to where the boys were struggling to get their footing. "And why would we haul these fine gentlemen off to jail, when, as they pointed out, you have chalk all over you. If you were just a little smarter, you might have thought to dust yourselves off!" He shook his head as the boys began to beat their hands against the incriminating white marks on their jackets.

"It's a good thing you boys used chalk—there may not be any permanent damage to Mr. Alvarez's car. But the tires, now those are pretty expensive. He's a lawyer, you know, so don't think you're going to get off easy!"

Jaimé had stood to the side, letting the policeman do his work. But now he strode forward, towering over the teens to add effect to the officer's threat.

"This is Mr. Alvarez. It's his car you vandalized. Now, he wants to know why you did what you did." The policeman was powerfully-built and nearly as tall as Jaimé—together they provided a formidable front. The boys stole a glance at each other before the redhead confessed, "A big guy gave us each fifty bucks. He told us what to write. He wanted us to use paint, but we couldn't get any." The blond tried to jab his cohort but Davíd grabbed his wrist and twisted it behind his back.

"We'll let these kids cool their heels downtown," the officer said to Jaimé. "We'll be in touch if we find out anything else from them."

"You'll book them overnight? I'd like to have my lawyer ask the boys a few questions." Jaimé replied.

"A lawyer's lawyer? You kids are in big trouble!" the policeman said to the teens then to Jaimé, "They'll be at the Juvenile Detention Center at least until tomorrow. Beyond that, it depends on what we find out and what charges you intend to press."

While the one officer was interrogating the boys, the other had called a garage to repair Jaimé's tires. After photographing the vandalized side of the sedan, he helped wipe the chalk from the doors.

All the while, Cassie watched the proceedings from under the awning that sheltered the door to the hall. She had welcomed the company of Anita's brother, who had stayed with her as others came and went. When they observed the officer helping to clean Jaimé's car, he grudgingly admitted that these two *policias* just might be all right.

The midnight hour had long since come and gone before Jaimé pulled his repaired sedan into Cassie's driveway.

"I am staying for what is left of the night, no arguments."

Unnerved by the events of the evening, Cassie knew she would have begged him not to go. With her right hand, she traced the outline of her ring through her thin leather gloves. A chill settled through her as she felt the shadow of her former husband loom menacingly over her newly rediscovered love.

Though bone-weary, Cassie and Jaimé slept little during the night. Near dawn, Cassie awoke from a fitful dream to find the bed beside her cold and empty. She slipped on her robe, and made her way through the darkness to the dining room. She spied Jaimé beyond the arched doorway, dressed in a pair of sweatpants, standing by the Christmas tree. The sun creeping over the eastern horizon cast him in silhouette as he stared out the window.

They had held each other close throughout the night, but had both been too unnerved to make love. *This is what Paul wants*, she thought, *to keep us on edge—his own little form of terrorism. Well it's not going to work!* She walked over to where Jaimé stood and wrapped her arms around his bare torso. He turned into her embrace, holding her tight against him.

"I've been thinking, *querida*, maybe it would be better if I left. My presence here is just antagonizing Paul to the point where he is becoming irrational. I wouldn't want to live if he harmed you because of me."

"Hush! We are not going to give in to Paul's intimidation. Tomorrow starts a new year—it will be our year, not his!" She put her hand on the nape of his neck gently nudging his lips to hers.

"I'll be fine, at least until after the trial. For the time being, I am convinced Paul is all smoke and no fire."

Cassie withdrew her arms from around him and toyed with the engagement ring on her left hand. She tossed him a coy glance and lightly ran her fingers up his bare chest, "Now, isn't there something we should be celebrating, rather than looking like old Joe just drank our last saucer of milk?"

"I've said it before, and I'll say it again, you are one amazing lady, Cassandra Grace Mikhailov Alexander…"

"…soon to be Alvarez," she finished as she pulled him to her once more.

"Harvey talked with the boys. They were either unable—or too afraid—to identify Paul as the one who paid them to trash my car."

Cassie and Jaimé sat at the small kitchen table, lunching on a salad and bowl of soup. Cassie tossed the baby carrot she had been nibbling back onto her salad plate. "Why can't we get any of the breaks? It would have been so easy for those kids to point the finger at Paul!"

"He'll slip up yet. Everything can't continue to go his way."

Cassie sat pensive for a moment then scooted her chair back from the table. "I've got something to show you. It may be nothing, but perhaps Harvey will be able to use it." Cassie disappeared into her bedroom. She bent down and pulled her suitcase out from where she stored it under her bed and opened it. There in the bottom lay the pieces of the wedding photograph on which Paul had scrawled the same words he hired the teens to write on Jaimé's car.

She carefully withdrew the picture fragments from the luggage and returned with them to the kitchen, "Do you think this will help our case any?" She showed Jaimé the desecrated photo.

The first thing Jaimé noticed was the vacant look in the bride's eyes. Her lips were molded into a forced smile that reached no further than the upturn of her mouth. Then, as he assembled the pieces, he read the words "Die Bitch" written in a black marker across the white bridal gown.

"My sweet Lord, Cas, why didn't you show me this before?"

"I didn't want to worry you. I had stuffed it in the bottom of a suitcase and had nearly forgotten about it—that is until I saw the words written on your car last night. I know this doesn't prove that Paul hired those kids, but maybe Harvey can make something of it."

They planned to spend New Year's Eve with the children at Jaimé's parents' home, and on the way, stopped by Harvey Walton's office to drop off the torn wedding photo.

"Interesting," the lawyer commented as he pieced the photo together on his desk. "We might be able to use this to show malicious intent on the part of your former husband. Too bad we don't have a police report to accompany the snapshots you took that day. Or" he continued as he shot a look of frustration toward Jaimé, "a sheriff's report on the scumbag's attacking you last month. Breaking and entering, assault, attempted rape…"

Cassie bit her lower lip, regretting not following Windy's advice, as the lawyer went on,

"You said that Paul Alexander assaulted you while you and Jaimé were dancing at your high school reunion last May. Do you think anyone who witnessed that would be willing to testify at your trial? It's a long shot, but if Paul took the money, it may behoove us to validate his antagonism toward you—to establish a motive for framing you."

"I don't know who was near enough to overhear what he said. Let me think about it and ask a few friends. I'm sure 'Nita was at the table across the room with Arnie and Jules," Cassie said as she looked toward Jaimé, who shook his head.

"I was focused on Paul—and you, of course." To the attorney he said, "We'll ask around. At least if Paul thinks we are checking with others in an attempt to tie him to last night's vandalism, it might prevent him from further harassment of Cassandra."

Harvey Walton stretched his substantial frame against the back of his oversized leather desk chair, and picked up an unlit cigar. He pointed the end of the tobacco-wrapped stogie toward Jaimé, "Sounds like you're as much of a target as Gracie here."

"Gracie?" Jaimé's gaze shifted from Harvey to Cassie then back to the lawyer again. "Gracie?" he repeated.

The portly attorney and the slim, sophisticated suspect simply exchanged conspiratorial glances and said nothing.

CHAPTER THIRTEEN

january

Cassie returned to the library Tuesday morning, striving to fall back into a normal routine. Evelyn welcomed her, though questioning the wisdom of not taking more time off after her ordeal of the week before.

Soon after the library opened, Jaimé appeared with Ben and Tina in tow. He had e-mailed their teachers, who had sent instructions for assignments for the children. Ben's teacher suggested that they find a formal setting to work on their studies for at least part of the day, and Cassie had volunteered the library, where she could assist them if needed. Evelyn had concurred, so Cassie set the children up at a table close to the circulation counter where she was sorting books onto carts. Jaimé said he would pick up the children at lunchtime, and his parents would supervise their studies during the afternoon.

As Jaimé was leaving the building, Dolores Tyler whipped through the door. Though a slight woman in her mid-seventies, the town matriarch was a force to be reckoned with. Bedecked in a black wool coat with a mink collar and matching pillbox hat, she marched past Cassie with a haughty lift of her chin and straight into Evelyn Maples office, where she loudly demanded that the library director close the door.

Cassie continued to sort the books that had been returned over the long holiday weekend, but kept an eye on Evelyn's door with a sinking sensation in her stomach. Dolores Tyler had been a close associate to Paul's mother, and Phoebe Alexander had insisted that Cassie join their bridge club soon after her wedding. Dolores had always treated Cassie with a mild disdain, and since the death of Cassie's mother-in-law, had done little to disguise her scorn. Cassie's current concern had nothing to do with cards or with Phoebe Alexander, however—Dolores Tyler was a very vocal member of the Library Board of Trustees.

The hands on the clock slowly marked off the minutes until the library director's office door swung open again and Dolores Tyler strode across the area behind the circulation counter to where Cassie stood.

"Cassandra, you really must stop keeping company with that Mexican boy. Why Paul allowed you to continue your association with that Morales girl during your marriage is beyond me, and this is what it's come to—why, you're acting like you are one of them! Surely you realize people are talking."

Cassie slowly filed the book in her hand while mentally counting to ten.

"People, Dolores?" Cassie knew it was a mistake to bait the woman, but she had been forced to swallow Dolores Tyler's condescension for too many years. "What people?"

"Don't get impertinent with me..." the older woman began, but Cassie cut her short, pointing the index finger of her left hand at the mink that encircled the society matron's withered neck.

"...And, if by 'that Mexican boy' you are referring to Jaimé Alvarez, I am exceedingly proud to be his fiancé." She flashed her diamond ring between their faces before returning her hand to its former position. "You may not be aware of the fact, but he is an internationally-renowned attorney who graduated with honors from Harvard."

She took a breath before continuing, "Oh, and his father is from Aruba—that's in the Caribbean, not Mexico. But his mother's family is from Nuevo Laredo, which *is* in Mexico. They immigrated to America—legally, so save your snide remarks—and I, for one, admire their industry and perseverance to become successful in a country where they had to learn to adapt to a different culture and language, in what was most likely a not-so-welcoming environment. I doubt, Dolores, that either you or I could have done as well." Cassie thought about *Tía* Juana—in more ways than just skin tones, Dolores Tyler paled in comparison.

"Now, if you will excuse me, I have work to do," Cassie abruptly turned back to the cart of books she had been sorting.

"Well, I never..." Dolores Tyler huffed. "You'll rue this day, Cassandra Alexander, mark my words." With that she stormed from the library, leaving the scent of her expensive perfume to linger as a reminder to Cassie of her own intemperate outburst.

Cassie's anger dissipated as fast as it flared. Her knees shook as she realized the enormity of what she had done. She had no doubt that Dolores Tyler had demanded that Evelyn dismiss her, and Cassie knew she had just added fuel to the trustee's fire.

She sunk her elbows onto the counter and buried her face in her hands. After a minute or two, she felt a thin, yet surprisingly strong, arm around her shoulders and lifted her head to see Ben standing beside her.

"Don't cry, Cassandra. Do you want me to call my dad? He'll take care of that mean old witch."

Cassie smiled at the boy, "No, I'll be okay, but thank you—I'm sorry we interrupted your studies." She walked with Jaimé's son back to the table where Tina sat watching with apparent curiosity.

"Is there anything I can help you with?" Cassie offered. Ben shook his head, while his sister eyed her with suspicion.

As Cassie stepped back to the counter, she saw Evelyn standing in her office door. Cassie gave her supervisor a look of resignation before crossing the restricted area to where she waited.

"I really blew that one—I am so sorry, Evelyn."

"You can guess what Mrs. Tyler wanted."

"My head on a platter, I presume."

"Well, she wasn't quite that drastic. But she did point out, in her signature imperious way, that she did not think you were the proper example to set for the young people who come in to the library."

"And I did everything I could to confirm her allegations."

"You didn't say anything that shouldn't have been said to the old biddy years ago. Perhaps, if more people had the courage to stand up for their principles, she wouldn't be allowed to fly around on her broomstick intimidating whomever she pleases." The library director took on an expression of regret, "However, we do have to deal with the fact that Dolores Tyler is a prominent member of the Library Board and a very generous benefactor to our Friends of the Library group."

Evelyn Maples gave Cassie a reassuring smile, before continuing, "Let me give Jack DeVry a call. He's the Board's chair this year. Maybe I can bend his ear before Dolores knocks on his door."

When Jaimé returned to pick up Ben and Tina at noon, Cassie refrained from telling him about her encounter with Dolores Tyler. He invited Cassie to join him and the children for lunch, but she declined explaining that she and Evelyn were the only staff members working the afternoon shift.

Evelyn had still not been able to contact Jack DeVry by five o'clock that afternoon, and Cassie left with a sinking sensation that Dolores Tyler had succeeded in planting the seed of her dismissal in the minds of the library trustees.

Though the events of the past several days had left Cassie exhausted, she decided to pay her mom an impromptu visit on her way home. When she approached her mother's apartment complex, she noticed the burgundy Cadillac once again parked in front of Martha Mikhailov's door. Cassie pulled into a spot a few spaces down from the late-model car. The curtains were drawn and lights were out in her mom's apartment, and when Cassie rang the doorbell, no one answered. She waited a few minutes and pushed the bell again, thinking, perhaps, her mother had been napping. When her mother still did not come to the door, Cassie walked back to her car, concern vying with curiosity. As she backed from her parking place, she thought she saw the edge of the drapery in the window fall back into place. *What in the world is she up to now?* Cassie thought as she turned her Festiva toward home.

Jaimé called soon after she had washed her dinner dishes and stacked them in the drainer to dry. Slack-Eyed Joe tagged her to the living room as she settled on the couch, the rhythm of her fiancé's slight Caribbean accent acting as a balm to her jittery nerves.

"I hear you had a bit of a rough day," he said as she took a sip of water.

She swallowed before answering, "I figured Ben would tell you all about it."

"I don't want you to lose your job because of me."

"If I lose my job, I'll have Paul to thank, not you. Besides, I am trusting that small-minded people like Dolores Tyler are in the minority on the Library Board."

"Dolores Tyler? Was that who brushed by me when I was leaving the library?" Jaimé gave a dark chuckle, "You stood up to Dolores Tyler? She and Herb own half the town! Ben told me pretty much what went on, and I am proud and grateful that you defended me and my family…."

"I couldn't just stand there and let her talk that way!"

"I know, that's why I love you, *querida*, I just wish I could have seen Mrs. T's face when you lambasted her!" They laughed together and talked for a while longer before hanging up. Cassie held the phone against her cheek well after the dial tone had signaled that her invisible connection to Jaimé had been severed, not allowing her mind to travel into their future.

On Wednesday morning, Cassie arrived at the library early, after a nearly sleepless night. She had dressed carefully, so as to present the most professional image possible in case another member of the Library Board chose to make an unannounced appearance.

When Jaimé arrived with the children, it was all she could manage not to skirt the counter and run into the security of his arms. Several times during the previous night she had questioned her self-imposed chastity. But even more than his lovemaking, she missed Jaimé's companionship. He had become her friend and her confidant—she hadn't realized how much she had come to depend upon him until she lay awake near dawn with only her thoughts and a one-eyed cat for company.

She forced herself to walk at a normal pace to the table where Tina and Ben were opening their backpacks and pulling out their textbooks, along with computer print-outs of their daily assignments.

Jaimé slipped up beside her, and after looking around to ensure that no one was watching, put his arm around her and placed a chaste kiss upon her forehead. She inclined her head toward him and, for just a moment, allowed herself to lean into the strength of his embrace.

"Dinner tonight, just you and me," he whispered. "Your place, my treat."

"Jaimé, you promised…." She began.

"I promised not to stay the night…. I'll tuck you in at ten o'clock, and then drive back home like a good boy."

"Hmmm…sounds like a workable compromise to me."

Cassie stepped away from her fiancé as the library door swung open. A tall, attractive man in a dark suit and gray overcoat cast a glance toward them and nodded before heading to Evelyn's office.

"Oh drat. What next?"

"Who's that guy?" Jaimé asked.

"Jack DeVry, the chair of the Library Board."

Jaimé looked to the closed office door, "Think he's talked to Mrs. T?"

"I don't expect he would be here otherwise."

"I wish I could stay, but I doubt that would help any."

Cassie shook her head. Jaimé lightly fingered the line of her jaw, "You're too strong for them to break you, Cas. Just keep your chin up."

"Yeah," Cassie gave him a half-smile, "it gives them a better shot...."

Jaimé chuckled as he instructed his children to do their homework.

"I'll see you tonight, princess—six o'clock."

Jaimé had no more than left the library before Evelyn Maple's door opened, and the director stepped out. She summoned Cassie with a smile and the crook of her finger. As Cassie approached the circulation counter, Evelyn took a few steps toward Cassie and asked her to find Beth, the young clerk who had been shelving in the stacks, to cover the desk.

When Cassie returned, Evelyn asked her to come into her office.

"Cassie, you've met Jack DeVry, haven't you?"

Cassie had served on a charity board with the trustee a number of years back and had developed an appreciation for his level-headed and well-thought-out decisions. Cassie nodded and extended her hand to her former acquaintance, who stood when she entered the room. "How are you, Mr. DeVry."

"Mr. DeVry? Please, Cassandra, there's no need for formalities. Do sit down." As Cassie took the chair at an angle to Jack DeVry and across the desk from her supervisor, she assessed the man at her side. He had aged since she had last seen him. Though balding, his engaging smile remained the same, putting her at ease.

"A member of the board, whose name shall remain anonymous," he gave the women in the room a wry grin, "called an emergency meeting of the trustees last evening."

Cassie sighed as he continued, knowing that she was the main item on the agenda. "Evelyn has filled me in on yesterday's interaction, and I must admit, I wish I had been here to see you take the lady in question down a peg or two. That woman's been a pain in our side for longer than I care to remember.

"However, as Evelyn has also pointed out, the *grande dame* is a pillar of local society and heavy contributor to the library, and in these tenuous financial times, we can't afford to lose her patronage."

"I know, Jack, and I truly am sorry I let my temper get the best of me." Cassie apologized.

"You've been under tremendous strain, Cassandra. The embezzlement charges—which, I might add, I do not for one minute believe—have got to be taking their toll on you. And, I am told, congratulations are in order! I haven't had the pleasure of meeting your intended, but I hear he is quite formidable in a courtroom. He's built a reputation for taking on the big guys and winning."

"Thank you, I don't know what I would have done without the support of Jaimé and his family these past several months."

"But…"

"But, the fact still remains that certain board members do not consider me to be a proper library employee…," Cassie finished, looking directly at the man across the room.

"I would like to be able say that the remaining members of the board unanimously supported you. However, Dolores Tyler still carries considerable weight with the others."

"Am I being relieved of my position, Jack?"

"No, not yet, at least. The board voted four to three to retain you conditionally."

"The conditions being?"

"That you work in the stacks only—not at the front desk, and that you not work in the children's area."

"She said I'm not fit to be around the children? That viper!" Cassie's temper flared once again before she quickly tamped it down. She needed her job, not just for the income, but also to keep her sanity while waiting for her trial at the end of the month.

"Please inform the board that I agree to their terms." Cassie said, defeated. "Thank you, Jack, for all that you did on my behalf." Cassie, for the first time since the conversation began, looked across the desk at the Library Director. "And, thank you, Evelyn, for your support. I assure you that if I feel I am being a detriment to the good of the library, I will tender my resignation."

"I am sure there will be no need for that. I just regret that that…woman has cost me one of my most effective and valuable front-desk workers. However, on the bright side, maybe we'll catch up on those trucks of books that need shelved. That Bethany's a sweetheart, but you can shelve circles around her."

After taking her leave from the director and the trustee, Cassie walked over to where Tina and Ben sat watching her, books open before them and pencils stilled in their hands.

"You must have done something *really* bad!" Tina accused.

"Why do you say that?" Cassie asked, forcing a smile she didn't feel.

"Because, in my school, only the bad kids get sent to the office," she said smugly.

This time Cassie's smile was genuine, "Some people think that I did, I guess."

"Yeah, but a person is innocent until they are proven guilty," Ben declared.

Spoken like the son of a lawyer, Cassie thought as she put her hand on Ben's shoulder. "That's the way it's supposed to work, but unfortunately, it doesn't always happen that way. I need to shelve some books in the back of the library. Is there anything I can help you with before I go?"

Ben had been puzzling over a map of Africa in his workbook, and Cassie spent a few moments helping him match the names of some of the smaller and more confusing countries to their locations. As expected, Tina refused her offer of assistance.

At precisely six o'clock that evening, Jaimé's headlights slashed through the darkness that had already cloaked the countryside. Cassie's heart thrummed a rapid cadence as she waited impatiently at the door while he turned into her driveway. The car ground to a halt and the driver's door opened. Cassie forgot to breathe as Jaimé unfolded his long, lean body from the front seat of his sedan. He wore the brown leather jacket and blue jeans that he had on earlier in the day, rather than the charcoal gray overcoat and dress pants that she had become accustomed to seeing on him.

She swung the door open before he had traversed halfway up the walk and flung herself into his arms when he was still a step away from her.

"Now that's what I like, a woman who plays hard to get," he laughed as he nuzzled his cold nose against her warm neck. They stepped into the house, and he kicked the door closed with the sole of his shoe.

She unzipped his jacket and thrust her hands against the cabled texture of his sweater, pulling him to her. Their lips merged together, fed by a hungered desire. His hands roamed her back, pressing her tight against him. Their mouths broke apart as they sucked in a deep breath. He held her head between his palms and placed a kiss on her forehead.

"My sweet Lord, how I have missed you, woman," he sighed.

"No more than I, you," she replied bringing her lips to meet his once again.

"I have dinner in the car," he said.

"That's not what I'm hungry for..." she teased.

"It's KFC, in honor of that first night, when I found you here, vacuum in hand."

"Oh, Jaimé," was all she could say.

He made a quick trip to the car, returning with the steaming hot chicken.

"Think maybe it needs to cool down a little?" she asked, as she took the bag from his hand and walked into the living room.

He hung his coat on the hall tree as he passed by it. "Yeah, think so," he said as he surveyed the room. The daybed mattress was in its place, with a fire crackling behind. A bottle of wine sat on the coffee table, flanked by two glasses. "Theme from a Summer Place" drifted from the CD player.

"Terrible movie, but a great soundtrack," he said as he retrieved the bag from her and sat it beside the wine bottle on the coffee table. He pulled her into his arms and began swaying to the beat of the music.

Their movement slowed, then stopped as his hands strayed from her back to the top button of her powder blue silk blouse.

"You know, I have wanted to do this since I first saw that row of buttons at our class reunion. I sat across from you, imagining my fingers undoing each little pearl, one-by-one until your breasts lay bare before me." As he spoke he loosed one button after another from its eyelet.

Cassie drew in a breath as his fingers grazed the rise of her breasts. She let it out slowly as she countered, "Yeah, right, you sat there holding hands with Melanie-the-Bit...oops...I mean that sweet Melanie Adams."

"Hmm, jealous, eh?"

"Maybe...but not for long. She came into the library a few times to try to taunt me—she definitely had her talons out for you. Did you really invite her to have dinner with your family?"

He had reached the place where her blouse was tucked into the waistband of her skirt and was searching for the fastener that held the material together. He nibbled at her neck, gently blowing on the moisture his tongue had left behind, sending a shiver of anticipation through her body.

"Invite Melanie? No, she showed up at the door as we were about to sit down to dinner, and my poor hapless father felt compelled to ask her to stay. The only thing she succeeded in doing is making him appreciate the fact that you could carry on a conversation that wasn't totally centered on yourself."

"So you've broken it off with Mel completely then?" she asked as she teased his earlobe, exuding a breath of warm air.

"Uh-huh," he said freeing her blouse from the confinement of her skirt and easing the offending swath of navy down over the satin of her slip. "She is history. In fact she is ancient history. Predates the written word."

Cassie stepped out of the circle of navy and kicked it aside, before taking her turn removing his sweater. His white undershirt molded itself to his chest and she rubbed her hands against the soft cotton, caressing the taut male nipples she encountered under the thin layer of material.

Their foreplay continued as first her blouse and then her slip were layered on top of her skirt. He stooped to peel her nylons from her long, slender legs.

He stood and drew the white cotton of his undershirt over his head. She slipped her fingers under the waist of his jeans and pushed the brass button free of its hole. She carefully lowered his zipper, letting the backside of her fingers rub against him. He took over, shoving his jeans to the floor.

"SpongeBob? Really, Jaimé darling, SpongeBob SquarePants boxers?"

"My Superman Underoos were in the laundry." The boyish look he gave her nearly undid what little self-control she still possessed.

He unclasped the wisp of satin that had restricted the softness of her breasts from his touch. He gently kneaded his thumb against the indentation from her lumpectomy. Small red veins radiated from the artificial dimple and he traced one to the dusky rose of her waiting nipple. He brushed his thumb over the rigid circle before slipping the straps from her shoulders. He then hooked his thumbs on the elastic band that held her panties to her hips and drew them downward until gravity relieved him of the task.

She tugged SpongeBob and Squidward to the floor, as she lowered herself to the muslin sheet covering the mattress.

Thursday afternoon found Cassie shelving in the stacks in the back of the library. She was humming to herself as she overheard two women talking a few shelving ranges away. At first their words passed in an indistinct blur over her head, but she stopped abruptly as they began to fall in sharp waves around her.

"I can't believe they still let her work here. Did you hear that she spent a night in the slammer last week?" The disembodied voice of an older woman carried across the open top of the book ranges in the throaty rasp of a chain-smoker.

"Serves her right for what she did! Dad put in over 35 years at O'Shay's. It nearly killed him when the plant closed," a younger woman said.

"Yeah, and all because of the greedy ice queen. That's what we called her. Miss Holier-Than-Thou, too good to talk to any of us commoners."

"I hear she's taking up with that lawyer from the Lower East-side. Probably trading a roll in the hay for free legal advice. As if she couldn't afford the best lawyer in town with what she stole from us." *So much for innocent until proven guilty*, Cassie thought as the younger woman's nasal tones reached her.

"I'll give her some free advice alright—she'd better keep her high and mighty ass out of my way or I'll kick it to the moon."

"You and the rest of the county what got laid off when O'Shay's closed. There'll be some big-time celebrating when that bitch gets sent upriver!"

"Yeah, if she's lucky maybe she'll find some butch girlfriend to replace her Casanova when she's in the tank," the older woman snorted as she let out a wheezing cough.

Cassie put her hands over her ears, blocking out the remainder of the women's conversation, and slumped noiselessly to the floor—where Evelyn found her some time later, still sitting with her knees bent, and her head ducked into the circle formed by her arms.

"Cassie! Cassandra, good heavens, what happened?"

Cassie shook her head without raising it from the shelter of her arms. She heard the book cart move, as Evelyn knelt down in front of her.

"Cassie, please tell me what's wrong!"

It took all of Cassie's strength to lift her head. "Would you call Jaimé," she finally managed to choke out in a barely-audible whisper, "Please?" When Evelyn asked again what had happened, Cassie just said, "Later," and sunk her head against her arms, hiding her face from her employer.

Jaimé arrived a short while later and Evelyn directed him to a back door where he could slip Cassie out of the library without drawing the notice of the patrons. During their drive to the farm, he didn't press Cassie about what had occurred that afternoon. She leaned into his shoulder as they walked to the house and clung to him when they got inside.

He peeled her away from him long enough to remove their coats and toss them aside. Then he urged her into her bedroom, much as he had the week before, wondering how many more blows she could absorb before crumbling. He gently removed her clothing and wrapped her in her comfortable old bathrobe before leading her to the living room. He helped her ease down onto the couch, covered her with her Aunt Nell's afghan, and went to the kitchen to heat a cup of hot chocolate in an attempt to soothe her.

When he returned with the steaming mug, Slack-Eyed Joe had wound his tawny yellow frame into a ball and nestled up on Cassie's lap. She scratched his head and ran her hand along his soft fur as Jaimé sat down beside her. He carefully handed her the cup of hot liquid and she inhaled the rich chocolate scent.

"Ahhh…you really are what the doctor ordered," she said in weary appreciation, finally trusting her voice enough to speak. She blew across the top of the mug, sending brown ripples outward toward the cup's rim, before gingerly taking a sip.

"Ready to tell me all about it?" Jaimé asked while scratching Joe between his ears.

"I think so," she answered with a tentative quaver in her voice.

After she concluded her rendition of the women's conversation, Jaimé let out a pent-up gust of air, "My sweet Lord, what next?" He took the mug from Cassie's hands, and pulled her against him, much to Joe's obvious chagrin as he let a growl rumble forth before launching himself to the floor.

"Ouch! Joe!" Cassie exclaimed as she sat up to examine the skin beneath her robe for claw marks. The cat glanced back at them with an annoyed one-eyed glower before stretching and ambling over to the fireplace, where he curled up and resumed his nap on the hearth, oblivious to any pain he may have caused.

After ascertaining that Joe had not drawn blood, they both

chuckled at the feline's antics, breaking the tension that had built during her retelling of her afternoon.

The classic movie channel featured a series of John Wayne movies, and they spent the evening immersed in the Duke's brand of *machismo*. And, in spite of her earlier resolve, Cassie acquiesced with little resistance when Jaimé offered to spend the night.

The next morning, Cassie called Evelyn Maples and tendered her resignation, promising to stop by the library with a full explanation that afternoon. Restless, Cassie coaxed Jaimé to help her scour the barn, yet again, for evidence they might have missed previously, while rehashing any and all facts that could possibly be pertinent to Cassie's case.

As promised, after lunch they drove into town so that Cassie could meet with Evelyn Maples. While Cassie was talking with the library director, Jaimé settled in a comfortable chair in the area where the newspapers were kept and picked up the *Blade* to pass the time. As he perused the front page, a headline toward the bottom caught his attention.

"*El Diáblo!*" he swore out loud. He read the accompanying story, flapping the paper open to page two. He dreaded showing Cassie the article, but knew she would see it sooner or later. The timing had all the earmarks of Dolores Tyler's handiwork, and he bristled at the vindictiveness of the wealthy dowager. He folded the paper and reread the headline: "Local Librarian Key Suspect in O'Shay Embezzlement Case," with a smaller typeface just below declaring, "Over 200 Employees Lost Jobs When Catsup Factory Closed Its Doors."

CHAPTER FOURTEEN

Jaimé spent the weeks before the trial reading law books and legal briefs searching for any angle to aid in Harvey Walton's defense of Cassie. He also poured over the newspaper accounts of the deaths of Paul Alexander's parents and Cassie's father. When Harvey finally managed to obtain them, the sheriff's reports on both accidents proved to be sanitized beyond any hope of substantiating Jaimé's suspicions that Paul had been involved in some way. Nevertheless, he could neither shake the feeling, nor the chills that it gave him in the dark of the night.

Though Harvey hired an independent systems analyst and an accountant to comb through the auditors' reports, they shed little light on what had happened to the missing million-and-a-half dollars, only showing that the money had not been accounted for and where the discrepancies occurred within the print-outs of Cassie's computer files. Try as they might, they could not gain access to the computer itself—the machine was under lockdown somewhere so deep in the bowels of the justice complex that even Harvey's inside connections could not locate it.

"Our esteemed sheriff's probably taken a sledgehammer to it," Harvey had grumbled after yet another unsuccessful trip to the Justice Center.

On January 19, just one week before the scheduled trial date, Judge Harrison informed Harvey that neither Cassie's wedding photo, the testimony of witnesses of Paul's assault at the class reunion, nor the vandalism to Jaimé's car were admissible as evidence in the embezzlement case, saying that they were irrelevant. In the judge's words, "Paul Alexander is not the subject of this litigation: your client is."

Though he had been ambivalent about doing so, Harvey had filed for subpoenas for both Sheriff Crenshaw and Deputy Moran, only to find that the prosecutor's office had beaten him to the punch. Their deposition statements substantiated his fear that their testimony would further incriminate Gracie. His only hope would be to undermine the veracity of their stories, and he doubted that "Hang-em Harry" would allow that in his courtroom.

On January 25, the day before the trial was scheduled, Cassie and Jaimé sat on worn leather chairs in Harvey Walton's office. Reams of paper lay scattered about his desk, along with open legal books.

"I don't know, Gracie. You're a tough cookie to defend," the attorney said as he shuffled through the disarray that covered his desktop. "I finally got the background check on that Craig Herman guy, and he's as squeaky-clean as a baby's butt after a bath—not even so much as a parking ticket on record. He does have a degree in accounting from a community college, but it pre-dates the age of computers. He's mostly worked in bookstores and led a pretty mundane, low profile life—takes care of his elderly mother, goes to church on Sundays—hell, he was even a Boy Scout! I was sure we'd be able to dig something up on him!

"Then there's your 'ex'" the lawyer continued. "A real pillar in the community—struts around at the charity balls while he pulls wings off of flies for his private jollies. But, again, there's nothing official in the records on him. My guys did see a couple of real unsavory characters go into his place, but we haven't been able to tie anything to him.

"I just don't know, Gracie, I just don't know..." He slapped the file in his hand back on his desk and shook his head.

"But I'm innocent! Where's the justice if I go to jail and Paul goes free?"

"I'm not sure justice is what Judge Harrison cares about. God, I hate that bastard! Every door I try to open, he slams shut. I would be tempted to think that your 'ex' has Harrison in his pocket, except that I'm nearly certain, for all his faults, the judge can't be bought."

"He just has a tendency to decide who's guilty or innocent before he hears a case—and, in his mind, I'm guilty," Cassie supplied.

The two lawyers exchanged glances and looked down at their hands. Jaimé pushed back his chair and jumped up in obvious frustration. He walked over to the wide picture window and stared at the bleak winter scene before him, hands braced against his hips. He turned to face the woman with whom he was determined to spend the rest of his life, refusing to acknowledge the truth behind her words then shifted his gaze to Harvey Walton.

"Why the hell couldn't we have drawn Gary Swartz or that new woman who recently joined the court, Marsha What's-her-name?"

They left Harvey Walton's office as the afternoon sun sank low in the horizon. The lawyer was flipping through a stack of files searching for a rabbit in a silk top hat when they closed the door.

"All rise, the Common Pleas Court is now session. Judge Harold Harrison presiding!" The deep baritone of the bailiff's voice bounced off the courtroom walls, finally traveling, as though through a long tunnel, to where Cassie was seated at the defendant's table. With Harvey Walton on her right and Jaimé on her left, she felt herself standing. Breathing, normally a reflexive bodily function, became a deliberate exercise. She focused on the slight man in the black robe seated behind the massive wooden desk. Cassie jumped involuntarily at the sharp rap of his gavel.

Small beady eyes bore through Cassie as the judge read

the charge against her, their intensity delivering a silent verdict of "guilty" as he stated the maximum penalty of ten years in the women's penitentiary. Almost as an afterthought, he asked, "How do you plead?"

"Your Honor, my client pleads 'Not guilty,'" Harvey Walton responded as Cassie attempted to form the words with trembling lips.

As the prosecuting attorney, a petite, shapely blonde woman in her mid-thirties, presented her impassioned opening statement, Cassie, for the first time, scanned the faces of the jurors. Most were women, with only two or three men scattered in their midst. One lady, Cassie noticed, could possibly be Hispanic and one appeared to be African-American. All were intent on the prosecutor's delivery and several nodded as her voice rose in a crescendo that successfully emulated a Baptist preacher at a revival meeting.

"...and consider now the plight of the 239 people formerly employed by the O'Shay Catsup Factory! Over 200 honest, hardworking people left jobless! Two-hundred families left without a breadwinner! Children going to bed hungry! Friends, neighbors, family members—few in this town, nay in this county, have not felt the sting of O'Shay's closing! All due to the greed of one woman—" The lawyer turned, extended her arm, and pointed directly at the defendant's table, "the accused, Cassandra Grace Alexander." When the lawyer spoke her name, Cassie flinched and shrunk back in her seat, as though struck by a physical blow.

She barely heard Harvey Walton's opening statement. Though he ably argued her innocence and attempted to open the juror's minds to other possible perpetrators, Cassie feared that he had not been as persuasive as the prosecuting attorney. She became convinced of the fact when the judge smiled as Harvey returned to his seat.

After the opening statements, the bailiff informed the assemblage that court would recess for lunch, and resume at "precisely one o'clock in the afternoon." The jury filed out and then Cassie stood up. With Harvey Walton on one side and Jaimé on the other, she managed to rise from her seat. As she turned to leave, her heart sank—the courtroom was filled, with standing-room-only along the back wall. Her mother and Aunt Nell, Anita and Windy, Julie and Arnie, and a few additional friends, along with Jaimé's parents, *Tía* Juana, and other relatives occupied the cluster of seats directly behind the defendant's table. However, the courtroom was predominately packed with her former co-workers from O'Shay's. Several had grouped around Paul, while others openly glared at her with undisguised hostility.

Cassie pivoted back toward the front of the courtroom and dropped down on the nearest chair. "Dear God, they hate me! If they had a rope, I'd be dead."

The next hour and a half passed at an excruciatingly slow pace. After the court cleared substantially, they managed to slip into an unoccupied conference room across the hall. Anita and Windy brought lunch back for Cassie, Jaimé, and Harvey Walton, but they ate little, and stole back in the courtroom before many spectators returned from their break.

At exactly one o'clock, the bailiff brought the room to attention, and the low rumble of conversation gave way to silence.

Paul was the first witness called to the stand. Under the conducting skills of the lady prosecutor, he played the jury like a Stradivarius. Cassie clasped her hand over her mouth to keep from crying out when he either distorted the truth or outright lied with the expertise of a trained thespian.

Harvey Walton had little recourse in his cross-examination, knowing that swearing an oath on the Bible had no influence on Paul Alexander's penchant to twist or invent facts to suit his purposes. The lawyer's only hope was to snare the witness in the web of deceit he was weaving.

"You're telling us, Mr. Alexander, that even though you were the CEO of O'Shay's, you had no way to access the files of your accountant? Surely you knew how to obtain the password to open my client's computer! What would have happened if she had been struck by a truck while crossing the street? Would the financial records of your entire company have been locked in her computer *ad infinitum?*"

"Objection! The counselor is badgering the witness!"

"Sustained! Mr. Walton, you may be able to push your considerable weight around in other judge's courtrooms, but not in mine. You will restrict your questioning to one inquiry at a time, and refrain from asking the witness to repeat answers already given."

"If it please Your Honor…" Harvey Walton began.

"It does not please me. Do you have any further questions Mr. Walton?"

"I have no further questions at this time," the lawyer sent a parting glare at the witness before returning to his seat.

Sheriff Crenshaw was brought to the stand to testify to finding the coat box filled with money in Cassie's barn, dodging, with the aid of the prosecuting attorney, Harvey Walton's cross-examination as to why the sheriff did not continue searching further after discovering the one cache of bills.

Deputy Moran substantiated the sheriff's testimony, adding that, "Mrs. Alexander objected to his ripping up the flooring where the money had been hidden." He also confirmed that Cassie admitted that she had had previous possession of the coat box in which the money had been found.

With a smug arch of her well-shaped eyebrows, the prosecutor called her final witness for the afternoon: Craig Herman.

The tall, gangly man rose and approached the bench. When he swore to tell the truth, the *whole* truth, Cassie felt a flicker of hope. For all his faults, Cassie believed that Craig Herman would not lie under oath.

The prosecutor asked Craig routine questions, establishing his relationship to the accused and his position at the O'Shay plant.

"Could you, Mr. Herman, describe what happened two years previous, on the afternoon of June 17?"

Craig looked at Cassie and then in the direction of his former boss. He lifted his chin slightly and began, "I approached Mrs. Alexander as she was sitting in her office at her computer desk, and

I asked her to give me the new password she had installed on her machine so that I could access the entries made the previous day."

"Had you had access to the computer files previously?"

"Yes, but Mrs. Alexander chose to change the password so that only *she* could use the files."

"But you were her assistant. Wouldn't it be logical for you to have access to the financial records?"

Craig let his gaze shift to Cassie as he said, "Yes, it would seem so. But Mrs. Alexander never approved of her husband's hiring me. I think she felt threatened by my...."

"Objection!" Harvey was on his feet, "The witness cannot say what my client did or did not feel!"

"Overruled. Sit down, Mr. Walton," the judge declared, then bid the witness to continue.

"As I was saying, I believe Mrs. Alexander felt threatened by my presence at O'Shay's and the trust her husband placed in me. She became more and more protective and secretive of the records she was keeping."

Craig gained confidence as he continued, "On the day in question, Mr. Alexander directed the defendant, his wife, to give me the password to the files. She not only wouldn't give me the password, but she refused to give it to him, as well."

"Let me get this straight, Mr. Herman. The defendant refused a direct order from the CEO of the company—the company for which she was the sole accountant—to relinquish the password to access the financial records of said company. And, within two years—within the time span of two short years—the company, O'Shay's Catsup Factory, was bankrupt and independent auditors discovered a one-point-five-million-dollar discrepancy in the financial records—the financial records for which only one person, the defendant, had the password to access."

The prosecutor walked toward the jury as she spoke, then deliberately shifted her attention back to the judge, "No further questions, Your Honor."

Cassie expelled a long breath, closed her eyes, and hung her head. With one look at her reaction, Harvey Walton knew Craig Herman had told the truth. "Your Honor, I would like a brief recess to confer with my client prior to cross-examining the witness."

"Denied."

"He continually jumbled my files," Cassie whispered to her attorney. "I had spent the entire day repairing the damage he had done and was too angry to give him access to my computer again, regardless of what Paul wanted."

Harvey Walton's cross-examination of Craig Herman was riddled with objections from the prosecutor, all sustained by the judge. Finally, the lawyer who was accustomed to doing the battering walked back to his seat bruised and bloodied by a woman half his size.

Harvey called Anita to the stand, both as a character witness and to substantiate Paul's previous antagonistic actions, but each attempt was overruled with strong warnings from the judge.

Evelyn Maples attested to Cassie's exemplary work habits, impeccable professionalism, and honest disposition, citing a number of examples before being cut off by the prosecutor.

Under ordinary circumstances, the attorney knew that Cassie would be her own best defense. But Judge Harry Harrison did not qualify as "ordinary circumstances." However, they were left with little recourse. "Can you do it, Gracie?"

Cassie closed her eyes then nodded her head. Jaimé reached over and covered her left hand with his right, as Harvey rose to address the judge.

Jaimé leaned against the back of his chair and tried to assess Cassie objectively in an attempt to see her as the jurors did. Her walk first drew his attention: she carried herself with an elegance that spoke of self-confidence, but could, as it was so many years ago when she had been tagged the "Ice Princess," be interpreted as aloof. She wore a forest green, brushed-wool suit jacket with matching slacks that fit as though they had been tailored to her specifications, though Jaimé knew she had found the outfit at one of her secondhand shops. Her hair had been drawn back in one of her signature chignons, and black leather pumps completed her ensemble. The total effect was one of classic refinement—an effect that would have had him swelling with pride under any other circumstance, but now he worried that the jury might be put-off by a perceived arrogance.

"Cassandra Grace Alexander, do you swear to tell the truth, the whole truth and nothing but the truth, so help you God?" The bailiff's sharp tones rang through her ears as she placed her hand on the Bible and answered in a steady voice, "I do."

Cassie turned and faced the courtroom. She studied the audience with a slight uplift of her chin before taking a seat in the large red leather and polished wood chair reserved for witnesses.

Harvey Walton approached her, stopped several feet short of where she sat, and drew his hands together behind his back. "Would you please tell the court, Mrs. Alexander, did you or did you not embezzle one-and-a-half million dollars from the O'Shay Catsup Factory?"

Cassie looked at the jurors and then directed her answer to the throng of former O'Shay employees who filled the better part of the courtroom, "No, I most certainly did not. As I told you before, Mr. Walton, I respect the memory of Charlie Alexander too much to do anything to endanger his business."

"Counselor, you will instruct your witness to answer only the questions put to her, and not add further embellishment," the judge interrupted.

Cassie shot a quick look of disbelief at the judge before turning her attention back to her lawyer as he asked, "Mrs. Alexander, for how many years were you the primary accountant for the O'Shay Catsup Factory?"

"I have worked on the finances at O'Shay's since Charlie Alexander hired me soon after my graduation from high school. I was promoted to head accountant five years later, and served in that capacity for nearly twenty-five years."

"Thank you, Mrs. Alexander. And when was Mr. Herman hired as your assistant?"

"Five years ago, soon after Charlie and Phoebe Alexander's untimely death."

"Had you ever had an assistant accountant prior to this time?"

"Yes, years ago. But once we installed a workable computer system, the responsibility for the financial records for O'Shay's was mine alone—until Paul hired Craig."

"When Mr. Herman was hired by your husband as your assistant, were you allowed to interview him?"

"No, Paul hired Craig Herman without my knowledge."

The Prosecuting Attorney jumped to her feet, "Objection! I fail to see in what way this line of questioning pertains to the case at hand!"

"Sustained."

"Your Honor, I am trying to establish…" Cassie's lawyer interjected.

"Mr. Walton, are you hard of hearing? Did I not just say, 'sustained'?"

A deep red crept up Harvey Walton's neck as he clasped his hands tightly together. Through clenched teeth, he asked, "Could you please tell the court, Mrs. Alexander, why you refused to give the password to your computer files to Mr. Herman?"

Cassie looked toward the judge, then at the jury, and finally to Craig Herman. "Though Mr. Herman professed to have a knowledge of computers, he had muddled my records so thoroughly that my computer crashed, and I had to have our systems expert help me restore the information. When Mr. Herman asked for the password to my files, I refused in sheer self-defense."

"Are you saying that Mr. Herman sabotaged your files?"

"Objection!" the prosecutor called, but Cassie went on without taking notice, "No, no, I think it was done in complete innocence…." Much to Cassie's surprise, the prosecutor sat back down in her seat.

Harvey continued to question Cassie, more often than not eliciting objections from the prosecutor—all of which were sustained by the judge.

After a particularly strident objection, he gave a barely perceptible nod of his head to his client. "No further questions, Your Honor."

The slender blonde prosecutor approached the witness stand. "Mrs. Alexander, could it have been possible that your husband hired Craig Herman as your assistant to keep an eye on you because he suspected that you were stealing from the company?"

"Objection!" Harvey Walton shouted while Cassie sat dumbfounded in her chair.

"Overruled! The witness will answer the question."

"Paul? Suspect me? You should have asked him that question." Cassie looked to where her former husband sat with the bimbette at his side. "Or maybe you could just ask him where the rest of the money is?"

The judge rapped his gavel, "The witness will refrain from any such outbursts or be subject to Contempt of Court charges."

Cassie glanced down at her hands, drew in a deep breath, held it while she consciously counted to ten, then exhaled slowly.

"I apologize, Your Honor," she said in even tones.

Cassie raised her head until her eyes locked with those of the woman before her. When she glimpsed the almost feral glimmer of conquest in their lioness-gold depths, a shiver of dread seeped through her.

"No further questions," the prosecutor purred.

"The jury is returning," Windy poked his head in the door of the small conference room where Cassie sat surrounded by Jaimé, Harvey Walton, and Anita. Fear, followed almost immediately by resignation, passed across Cassie's face as she stood and smiled, "It's almost a relief that this will finally be behind me. Whatever happens, Harvey, I know you did the best for me that any attorney could."

"We'll appeal, Gracie. We've got all manner of evidence to show the judge was prejudiced—the way he handled your testimony alone should get us another trial. Any other judge would've let us…."

"It's all right, Harvey," she stopped the lawyer mid-sentence. Then, placing her hand in the crook of Jaimé's elbow, she calmly said, "I'm ready."

A silence cascaded over the crowded courtroom as Jaimé escorted Cassie to the defendant's table.

"Will the defendant please rise?" the bailiff instructed Cassie, and she stood tall and erect.

"Has the jury reached a verdict?" The judge asked the elderly woman who served as the foreman.

"We have," she replied, without looking at Cassie. The bailiff took the small sheet of paper from the juror and handed it to the judge.

Judge Harrison opened the folded slip of paper, read it, held it in his hand for a full minute, then addressed the room.

"In the case of Cassandra Grace Alexander versus the State of Ohio, the jury finds the defendant…" the black-robed magistrate paused, glanced toward Cassie, then smiled back at the paper in his hand, "…guilty as charged on all counts."

Though she thought she had prepared herself for the verdict, Cassie slumped back under the weight of the judge's words. Jaimé threw his arm around her and pulled her against him for support.

"Bail is continued and raised to one-hundred-fifty thousand dollars. This matter is set for pre-sentence investigation. Court is adjourned until sentencing, three weeks from today."

A numbness overtook Cassie as she walked with leaden steps from the courtroom. Though she had no idea how, Jaimé was arranging to cover her additional bail, giving her blessed freedom until the sentencing. Her Mother and Aunt Nell sat motionless in their chairs in shell-shock. Neither had spoken since the judge had rendered the verdict. Jaimé caught up with Cassie, who was being escorted from the courtroom by Harvey Walton, and tucked her elbow in his hand just as she passed by Paul. Her ex-husband had secured what appeared to be his final revenge, but neither Cassie nor Jaimé spared him a second glance.

A cacophony of photographers' cameras flashed as they swung the courtroom doors open and Cassie raised her arm to block her eyes from a momentary blindness.

"Mrs. Alexander, over here!" a newswoman called as she shoved a microphone in Cassie's face. "What's your reaction to the verdict?"

"What? No!" Realization of what was happening dawned slowly upon Cassie. "Go away! Leave me alone!"

Jaimé turned Cassie away from the woman, pushing her microphone to the side. He elbowed his way through the crowd, shielding Cassie from the brunt of the media's intrusion, as well as the catcalls from her former co-workers, while negotiating the cascade of courthouse steps. His dark sedan sat waiting at the curb, with Windy at the wheel.

Cassie slid into the back seat then turned to Jaimé, "Mom and Aunt Nell! Someone has to help them through this mob!"

Jaimé gave a dark chuckle, "If anyone could handle these guys, it's your aunt with your mother covering the left flank!" Cassie smiled through her tears, and Jaimé gave her a brief kiss on her forehead. "That's my girl. We'll get through this thing together."

Jaimé made sure Cassie was securely locked in the car before pushing his way back through the mass of reporters and former O'Shay employees. Halfway up the steps he was stopped short. *Tiá* Juana had split the crowd, swinging her large purse in front of her like Attila the Hun wielding his sword. Pablo came next with an irate Aunt Nell on his arm, hobbling down the stairs while raining invectives on anyone within earshot. Martha Mikhailov marched at the back of the parade, surrounded by Jaimé's parents. Jaimé stationed himself as the rear guard, following the group back down to the sidewalk.

Two more cars had pulled up to the curb behind Jaimé's. Jorgé and Davíd stepped out of the drivers' seats and opened the passenger doors for the entourage. By prearrangement, they all headed to *Tiá* Juana's to regroup and strategize.

Sleet spat against Jaimé's windshield as he drove toward the farm. While a bright winter sun had shone over the courthouse earlier in the day, a brisk wind had blustered in a billowing snowstorm by late afternoon. As darkness fell, the snow had grown heavy, covering the narrow country roads with a treacherous sheet of ice and slush.

At Cassie's insistence, Jaimé pulled the car up beside the barn. He drew the collar of his overcoat around his neck as he ducked into the wind to open the doors to the structure before escorting an exhausted Cassie from the protection of the sedan.

"Are you sure you want to do this now? We've searched the barn a hundred times. Besides, whatever might be here will wait until morning. We'll be able to see better then, *querida.*"

Cassie flicked on the switch to the two bare overhead light bulbs that hung from the rafters high above as Jaimé slid the doors shut behind them, leaving a small gap between the two. The dim illumination cloaked the interior of the barn in a surreal glow. She shook her head at the man she loved with all her heart, "I couldn't sleep now if I wanted to. I have to do something. In just three short weeks, I could go to prison for who knows how long!"

She took a deep breath, "Prison, Jaimé! Do you know what happens to women like me in prison?" Her voice rose in a crescendo, the imagined horrors of incarceration feeding her desperation. "There has to be an answer somewhere in this barn. That's the way it always happens in the movies—you go to the crime scene and find a clue to the perpetrator's identity. This is where Billy Joe found the money. Maybe Paul or whoever planted it dropped a matchbook or a receipt with a phone number or something and we just haven't searched in the right place for it."

"I wouldn't spend too much time lookin', sweetheart." Paul stepped out of the shadows of the stall nearest the door. "Move over there dollface, and take your Spic lover with you."

Jaimé started toward his nemesis, but Paul stopped him with a slight movement of his hand. "C'mon, big boy, let's see what you can do against this." He waved a snub-nosed pistol in Jaimé's direction. "Nothin' would give me greater pleasure than to put a bullet right between your eyes. 'Course then I'd have to kill your whore here to make it look like a lovers' quarrel. And, it'd have to be a real close range so's to make it look like a suicide. Messy, messy...." Paul's face took on a maniacal hue in the dim light, and Jaimé backed up instinctively putting Cassie behind him.

"Not that it will do you any good," Paul continued, "'Cause I'm going to have to shoot you both anyway. But you could buy some time while I tell you a little story. I wouldn't want you to go down without knowing the full extent of my brilliance. You shouldda fought harder to hang on to me, Cas-hon—but thanks to you and the Craigster, me and the little woman are gonna live a long and happy life in Belize.

"Speaking of the boy, you can come on out now, Craig. The show's about to begin!"

Craig's lanky form emerged from the stall where Paul had been hiding. He looked warily at his former boss. "You didn't tell me there was going to be any shooting. I thought we were just going to get the rest of the money so you could give me my share!"

Paul sneered in Craig's direction and aimed the gun at him. "You always were a sucker—what makes you think I'm going to share anything with a dimwit like you? Move on over there with them—Now! You don't think I could let you hang around as a witness, do you Craig, my man?"

The instant Paul diverted his attention to Craig, Jaimé lunged toward him. At the last second, Paul turned and fired. As the gun exploded, Jaimé stumbled backward, falling on the straw that lay strewn about the barn floor.

"Jaimé! No! Oh my God, No!" Cassie dropped to her knees, drawing his head onto her lap.

His eyes flickered open as he mustered a lopsided grin. "So much for..." he closed his eyes and took a shaky breath, then fluttered them open again, trying to focus on her face, "...for 'Happily-Ever-Afters,' princess."

"Shhh, darling, don't worry." She gently rubbed her thumb

along the contours of his jawline. His breathing became more shallow, then he gasped for air.

"Some...some hero I turned out to be." She felt him shudder, then fall heavy against her as he slipped from consciousness.

"You bastard! You filthy bastard!" Cassie hurled the words at her former husband as she cradled the stilled body of her fiancé against her bosom. She choked back a sob, swallowing her fear and her fury, as her eyes raced about the barn in search of a weapon. *Think, dammit, THINK!* She focused on two pitchforks that leaned against the stall beyond where Paul stood. Perhaps she could signal to Craig....

"Sticks and stones..." Paul scoffed at her, as he pointed the gun at his hapless co-conspirator. "Now, Craigster, let's fill the good lady in on your little part in this play."

"I'm so sorry, Mrs. Alexander, I didn't know it would end this way!"

"Stop your sniveling," Paul interrupted, "and get on with it!"

"I...I created a duplicate set of records for O'Shay's. That's what the auditors saw. I replaced your computer files with mine."

Cassie looked up at the harmless-appearing man with whom she had shared an office space for years. "But how? Why? I thought you didn't know anything about computers!"

"I've been working with computers since they used punch cards. It was easy to hack into your security system. Even a beginner could have done it." He hesitated for a moment, "Why? Money, partly." He turned his face toward Paul, "And, because you were my friend. I trusted you!"

Paul gave a snort as he pulled the trigger of the gun again. Craig slammed back against the riding lawnmower, leaving a trail of blood down its green hood as he slumped into a lifeless pool.

Bile rose in Cassie's throat as she tore her gaze from Craig's limp body to the ghoulish gleam that distorted the face of the man who loomed above her.

Jaimé's flesh grew cool and clammy against the palm of her hand, and she began to rock back and forth emitting a keening moan. She wanted to close her hands over her ears and shut out the voice that hammered down on her. Wanted to scream at the demonic figure to take her life too. Wanted blessed oblivion to end the nightmare whose seeds were spawned in the blasphemy of that long ago wedding day.

Instead, the man with whom she had stood at the altar on that fated day stooped down in front of her, presumably to get the satisfaction of watching her reaction at close range as he said, "But there's more, Cas-hon, just wait until you hear the rest of the tale!"

Cassie steadied her swaying, holding Jaimé's head against the flat of her stomach. She forced herself to look evenly into the eyes that blazed not a foot from hers.

"My old man thought you were the cat's meow. You could do no wrong. No matter what I did, whether it was the high school football championship or getting a new account at the business, it was never good enough. He took such a shining to you that I thought when I married you, I would finally mean something to him."

His foul breath reeked of alcohol and stale tobacco, as he lanced aged, festering wounds and let their poison ooze forth. "But, there you were, still the Ice Princess with her prim skirts and every hair in place, treating me like I had rabies, and doin' everything right in the eyes of the old man. He kept making more money and you were right there at his side getting the credit that shouldda come my way. You wouldda thought that you were his kid instead'a me.

"Well, I got him. He paid for what he did to me, all right." He laughed as the enormity of what he had done washed over his ex-wife.

"The accident...?"

"Accident? What accident?" He gave Cassie a malevolent smile before continuing, "Course, my mother wasn't supposed to be in the car that day. I hated that—she's the only one who ever really gave a shit about me."

He leaned back on his heels with the appearance of complete

satisfaction with what he had done. "And, you know what else? Your daddy's fall...."

"You killed my father? Why? He treated you like the son he never had!"

"Seems your daddy got to snooping a while after the old man's accident. He caught the Craigster messing around with your computer and confronted him. That stupid piece of dung over there didn't know enough to keep his mouth shut. So, when the boy told me about his meeting with your daddy, I had no choice but to have him take a..." he snickered, "long walk off a short rail."

Rage swept through Cassie—she shot her arm out and shoved the flat of her hand into Paul's face, knocking him off balance. The gun fired into the air as two figures came rushing through the gap in the doors. One plowed on top of the prone gunman, and the other grabbed the pistol from his loosened grip. Sam Windmiller sat on Paul's chest and grabbed his collar with both hands lifting his head a few inches above the floor.

"You rotten son of a..." he spat at the man beneath him. "I'd love to smash your ugly face, but you aren't worth it...you aren't worth it. You'll spend the rest of your sorry life behind bars for what you've done!" He then dropped Paul's head letting it crack sharply on the concrete beneath it.

"Somebody call 911!" Cassie shouted as she buried her head in Jaimé's thick black hair, not looking at the dark stain that was spreading through his topcoat.

"They're on their way. I dialed them on my cell as soon as we heard the gunshots." True to 'Nita's word, the shrill symphony of ambulance and police sirens pierced the night air. In a matter of minutes, an EMT squad had gently lifted Jaimé onto their stretcher.

"Is he...? Will he...?" Cassie asked through the knot that had formed in her throat.

"He's weak, extremely weak. Whoever shot him was a damn poor marksman. At that range, your friend here should have died instantly. He's lost a lot of blood, but we're getting a pulse. Not a strong one, but we'll take what we can get."

Cassie watched the ambulance skid out of the driveway with sirens blaring. Then, as the police rushed to the barn, she climbed into her little Festiva and took off at a breakneck pace, following the flashing lights toward the county hospital, praying as she had never prayed before.

CHAPTER FIFTEEN

Cassie pulled up to the emergency room doors behind the ambulance. Everything happened in a whir as the back doors of the vehicle were whipped open and Jaimé's stretcher was whisked out. Cassie scurried along beside, trying to stay close without getting in the way. After checking Jaimé's vital signs, they transferred him to a hospital gurney and, with a medic at either end, wheeled the bed through swinging doors and out of sight. Cassie fought to go with him, but a nurse held her back.

"They're rushing your husband to the operating room, ma'm. The doctor will let us know as soon as they find out anything. Right now we need to have you answer a few questions, Mrs...."

"Alexander," Cassie answered automatically, "Cassandra Alexander."

The nurse eyed Cassie quizzically, "Aren't you the...."

"Yes, and that man isn't my husband...yet...." Cassie supplied, while fear vied with hope to add a quaver to her voice.

"Should we call his next of kin?"

"His parents, yes, oh yes! And the children, Oh my heavens, I didn't think about the children!" Not trusting herself to make the call, she gave the nurse the telephone number.

"You'll have to move your car, then we'll get the information we need." Cassie quickly shifted the Festiva to a legal parking space then returned to the ER where an admissions clerk gave her a clipboard with a form to be completed.

"I don't have any insurance information. It's probably in Jaimé's wallet."

The clerk spoke to a nurse, who soon returned with a large bag containing all of the clothing that Jaimé had been wearing. Cassie searched the pockets of his overcoat, avoiding looking at the blood-spattered hole in its shoulder, until she found a long thin black wallet. She knew she should wait until his parents arrived, but the need to be close to something so personal to him was overwhelming. She smelled the scent of fine leather as she opened the pouch that held an array of cards, each neatly housed in its own slot. Performing such an intimate task somewhat eased the terror that gripped her heart. She readily found Jaimé's medical card and handed it to the clerk, then flattened his wallet and pressed it close to her heart.

"Papa! Where are you?" Tina Alvarez barreled through the swinging doors to the emergency room clutching her babydoll, followed closely by Ben and Jaimé's parents.

A nurse hurried in after them. "Please, you may all go to a waiting room where you can talk undisturbed."

After they had settled into stiff upholstered wooden chairs in a small, sterile-looking room, Cassie relayed as much as she could recall about the events that had transpired in the barn at Aunt Nell's farm. She glossed over the details for the benefit of the children, but told them honestly what had happened to their father and how concerned she was about his condition.

"I am so sorry I caused all of this. I wanted to go into the barn. If it weren't for me Jaimé wouldn't have become embroiled in any of this. He's got to live, he just has to!" With that admission, Cassie sunk her forehead onto her hands and gave way to the tears that she had welled up inside since the morning's trial. Juanita Alvarez slipped into the chair beside Cassie and pulled the weeping woman against her shoulder.

"You are not to blame, Cassandra. My Jaimé, he has been in love with you since he was jes a boy. He would move heaven and eart to protect you. He is a good man. God will give him strengt." Cassie was too distraught to notice that Jaimé's mother spoke in nearly perfect, if heavily accented, English.

An hour passed. Juanita Alvarez pressed the beads to her rosary through her fingers, reciting the litany quietly to herself in her more familiar Spanish. Dr. Alvarez paced the tiny room, stopping often to pat Cassie reassuringly on her shoulder. Ben had turned away from the others, so that they would not see him cry, and had fallen asleep on two chairs that he had pushed together. Tina slouched on a chair across from Cassie, casting surreptitious glances at her over the doll's head when she thought Cassie wasn't looking.

A second hour passed, and a nurse opened the door to assure them that she would notify them as soon as she heard anything. Cassie made motions of looking at an outdated magazine then restlessly tossed it aside. Tina batted her eyes to keep them open. She tentatively looked at Cassie, and tried to snuggle against her *abuela*, who dozed in her chair with her rosary beads still clasped tightly in her hand.

Cassie waited a few more minutes before opening her arms to the girl. The child hesitated only briefly before succumbing to her need for comfort. She shifted herself from chair to chair around the room until she sat next to Cassie. Then, at Cassie's urging, Jaimé's daughter climbed upon the lap of the woman she had tried so hard to dislike, clutching the doll with features so like her own close to her small chest. Cassie wrapped her arms around the child, and each drew solace from the other.

Cassie must have nodded off, her head resting in the tangle of Tina's hair. She awoke abruptly at the sound of a doctor's voice. The young woman looked weary. Her turquoise operating smock was flecked with blood—Jaimé's blood. She drew the skullcap from her head and sat down in a vacant chair by the door.

"Mr. and Mrs. Alvarez, I'm Dr. Tracy, your son's surgeon."

She waited an eternal minute before speaking again. Five sets of eyes skewered her with equal doses of hope and dread.

"Your son has a remarkably strong constitution. It took us quite a while to extract the bullet from his chest. Fortunately it didn't puncture his lung, but he lost a massive amount of blood, requiring a transfusion."

"Is he…" Cassie interrupted with growing impatience.

The doctor nodded toward Cassie, "He should recover. We'll watch him carefully to make sure a fever or an infection doesn't set in. He'll be uncomfortable for a while and may require therapy to regain the full use of his arm."

Dr. Tracy then looked to the Alvarez family, "He should sleep until morning. Why don't you all go home and get a good night's rest."

Relief washed over Cassie as she clung to Jaimé's daughter. The girl looked up at her with teardrops streaming down her round cheeks. "Papa's going to be okay?"

Cassie nodded as she wiped the child's tears away with the edge of her finger then opened her arms wider to include Ben in her embrace as he snuggled in beside her. She kissed each of the children on the top of their heads before asking the doctor, "Would it be possible for me to just wait here until he wakes up?"

Dr. Tracy considered her request for a moment, looking to Jaimé's parents for guidance.

"It would make me *mas*…" Juanita Alvarez struggled to find the right word, "…more easy if someone my Jaimé knows be in the room wit' him when he wakes up. *¿Es posible?*"

"I think that would be more than possible. As a doctor, I would say that would be advisable. It's frightening, even for a grown man," this was directed to Tina and Ben, "to wake up in a hospital room alone. Especially when one has been as traumatized as your father was. What do you think, children, should we let Mrs. Alexander stay?"

Tina put her arm around the back of Cassie's neck and drew herself up to plant a wet little kiss on Cassie's cheek and Ben gave the doctor a very serious nod.

"I guess that's settled then. Mr. Alvarez will be in recovery for a while longer, but I'll have the nurse show you to his assigned room, Mrs. Alexander, and you can wait there." To the others, she said, "Mr. and Mrs. Alvarez, children, rest well. We'll take good care of your son and father."

Cassie spent another hour watching the streetlamps outside the window of Jaimé's room before two interns wheeled in a gurney with her beloved lying on it. She blanched when she saw him. An unnatural pallor hung just beneath his normally bronzed skin tone. His bare chest and right shoulder were wrapped in bandages, while a thin hospital sheet covered the lower half of his body. An IV dripped fluid into his veins with a pulsating regularity. When they had lifted him onto the bed, the interns attached wires from a monitor to Jaimé's chest with white circles of tape. They then inserted an oxygen tube into his nostrils, draping the loop of the hose over his ears.

It wasn't until a nurse came in that anyone acknowledged Cassie's presence, looking at her with thinly veiled curiosity. "Dr. Tracy said that you could stay the night with Mr. Alvarez, Mrs. Alexander," the grim-faced older woman stated in a starched tone that let Cassie know she didn't approve.

"Thank you. And please call me Cassie." The matronly nurse ignored Cassie's invitation, checked the patient's vital signs one last time, and instructed "Mrs. Alexander" to press the call button should Mr. Alvarez need attention. Then she and the interns left Cassie alone in the room with Jaimé looking still as death. Cassie pulled the straight-backed aqua blue vinyl-covered chair as close to Jaimé's bed as physically possible and clasped his hand loosely in hers, watching for any indication that he was cognizant of her presence.

Though she couldn't remember doing so, Cassie must have fallen asleep sometime toward early morning. When she awoke, sun was streaming through the hospital window.

"Mornin', sleepyhead!" Cassie became fully alert as she heard the familiar, if weak, voice from the bed at her side.

"Jaimé! Oh my dear God, you're awake!" She fairly leapt the few feet to the head of his bed where she stood motionless just staring at his beautiful face before bending to caress his pale lips with the gentlest of kisses. "I thought I had lost you. After all we had gone through, I thought Paul finally won."

"Nah, can't happen. We wrote the script for this flick—this cowboy's going to get his girl and ride off into the sunset." He closed his eyes and winced in pain as he lifted his left hand to touch her, "though it may be a few weeks until he can saddle his horse."

Cassie laughed with relief as she lowered her lips to him, reverently touching them to his brow and then to each cheek, before settling, again, on his mouth—this time letting the kiss deepen into the happily-ever-after that would surely come.

A slight cough brought her upright as a nurse hovered near the end of the bed. "I see Mr. Alvarez is awake and responding normally," the young man said with a smile. "This is a very good sign!" Cassie blushed as the man swished the IV bag attached to the pole that stood at the head of Jaimé's bed opposite of where she sat. The nurse checked the blood pressure and heart monitors, took Jaimé's temperature, and jotted some notes on a clipboard. He then winked at his patient and suggested he and Cassie "take up where they left off...."

Cassie stayed with Jaimé while he devoured a full breakfast, helping him open his milk carton and pouring just a touch into his mug of steaming black coffee. When he had settled back onto his pillow and the food tray had been retrieved by a volunteer dressed in a uniform that matched the vinyl-covered chair, Jaimé suggested that Cassie get herself something to eat at the hospital cafeteria. Though she protested that she wasn't hungry, the lure of a hot cup of tea proved irresistible—especially when the nurse returned to bathe Jaimé and assist with his personal needs.

Cassie stayed in the cafeteria a discreet half-hour, having succumbed to the smell of a raisin bagel toasting, and slathering one for herself with a layer of cream cheese to enjoy with her tea.

By the time she reappeared in Jaimé's room, it was crowded

with his family. Tina and Ben were talking at once, both in evident relief to see for themselves that their father had survived. Jaimé's mother extended her arm to Cassie and pulled the younger woman within its fold, as they stood together at the end of the hospital bed.

Jaimé smiled at Cassie in a greeting meant for her alone, before returning his attention to the children at his side. Dr. Alvarez leaned against the ledge by the window, watching his son, while occasionally lifting a finger to his eye and rubbing it along his lower lid. At one point, he turned away from the room, retrieved a handkerchief from his pocket, and quietly blew his nose. Jaimé's gaze shifted to his father, and when the older man again faced his son, they exchanged the briefest of glances filled with mutual admiration and love.

A middle-aged nurse Cassie hadn't seen before came into the room to check Jaimé's vital signs and suggested that he might need to rest for a while. Jaimé winced as Tina leaned on his shoulder to plant a kiss on his cheek, but regained his composure sufficiently to grin at her when she lifted her head. Ben stepped to his father's bedside and informed him not to worry, that he would take care of Tina while his father was recuperating. Amusement tinged the looks exchanged by Jaimé's parents, as they told their son that they would return with the children that evening. Cassie walked to the edge of Jaimé's bed and brushed his lips with hers, assuring him that she wouldn't leave the floor, come hell or high water! She then joined Jaimé's family in the hall and escorted them to the elevator.

Tina clung to her side, refusing to let go even after her *abuela* promised that they would return later in the day. Cassie smoothed her hand down the length of the child's silky black hair, caught her chin in the cup that Cassie formed with her palm, and tipped the girl's face up so that she could look Cassie in the eye.

"I'll take good care of your father, honey. I give you my word that nothing will happen to him while you are gone!" Cassie guaranteed the child.

Tina threw her arms around Cassie, then abruptly let go and

ran into the elevator with her grandparents. Ben hung back just long enough to also give Cassie a shy hug before dashing through the doors that his *abuelo* held open.

Cassie walked slowly back down the hall, hoping to allow enough time for Jaimé to fall asleep. She needn't have concerned herself, though, as he was snoring softly when she entered the room. Relieved, Cassie fell into the hard vinyl chair, letting her exhaustion overcome her.

When she awoke, a nurse was checking Jaimé's IV bag and a volunteer was attempting to maneuver around Cassie to remove the patient's lunch tray from the portable table that extended across the middle of his bed.

Jaimé flashed Cassie a heart-stopping grin, while allowing the volunteer to fuss over him. The woman was half-again his age and obviously smitten by her patient.

As the nurse shooed the elderly volunteer from the room, Windy and Anita walked through the door.

"Hey, man, is it ever good to see you!" Windy exclaimed as Anita rushed to the opposite side of the bed from Cassie to give Jaimé a hug, then stopped with her hands in midair to assess where she might do so without causing him further injury or pain. She settled for resting her palms on her hips and shaking her head, "Jaimé Alvarez, you are a sight for sore eyes! I nearly had a heart attack when I saw you lying on the barn floor last night!"

Jaimé laughed as he took Cassie's hand in his. "I'd be lying in the morgue if it weren't for you two, I understand. I don't know how you happened to be outside the barn door, but thank God you were!"

"It was just a hunch," Windy said as he joined his wife at Jaimé's bedside. "'Nita here just felt like she needed to be with Cassie. So, soon after you left *Tía* Juana's, we followed. When we saw the light on in the barn, and your car parked by it, we headed that direction. We heard the first shot crack through the air and 'Nita immediately hit 911 on her cell."

He wrapped his arm around Anita's shoulder, "I told her

to stay in the car while I headed to the barn to investigate what was up, but does she ever listen to me?" He gave her arm a gentle squeeze, "No!"

"And you're lucky I didn't. I was the one who grabbed the gun from *el bastardo's* hand, if you recall!"

"You were both magnificent!" Cassie declared from her perch on the other side of the bed.

"Talk about magnificent, that was one heck of a shove you gave Paul, Cas!" Windy complimented her. "It sure sent him flying on his a… butt!"

"I thought I would find you here!" Harvey Walton directed his comment to Cassie drawing everyone's attention to where he stood in the doorway, fedora in hand. "And you, Jaimé my friend, should definitely take better care of yourself!"

"I've had a very busy morning. In fact, thanks to the four of you, I've hardly slept a wink all night!"

"What's happened with the case?" Jaimé asked, tightening his grip on Cassie's hand as he attempted to lean forward.

"Well, all charges against this little lady have been dropped," he pointed the crease of his hat in Cassie's direction.

"*Yes!*" Anita exclaimed with her fist pumping the air.

Cassie sunk her forehead against the strong arm of the man on the bed beside her, her relief nearly palpable.

"What about Paul?" Windy asked.

The lawyer nodded to the couple from his position at the end of the bed. "The toad developed a sudden diarrhea of the mouth once the cops found his wife running out the door of their manse with a suitcase full of money and a ticket to Belize. She also had several passbooks to offshore accounts in her possession.

"Seems our Mr. Alexander had been skimming profits from O'Shay's for several years and had also set up his own little drug-running business. What he allowed the auditors to find was just the tip of the iceberg in order to indict Gracie here. He transferred the bulk of his offshore funds to his wife's maiden name, so that they couldn't be traced to him when he and the little woman 'disappeared' into the black hole of the Bermuda Triangle."

All eyes were on Harvey as he took a swig from Jaimé's water bottle and wiped his face with the back of his hand, obviously enjoying the drama of being the one to unravel Paul Alexander's carefully crafted scheme. He continued, "When the wife found out that Paul had been arrested, she panicked and decided to head out on her own. Only, as they say, timing is everything. A sheriff's car pulled up behind hers just as she was about to back out of her driveway."

"Not Billy Joe! I would have put money on his being involved in this right up to his scrawny neck," Anita said.

"Crenshaw? Oh heck yes, up to his nostrils and higher. It was his deputy, the redheaded Irishman. What's his name? Oh yeah, Moran. Anyway, it was Moran that made the arrest.

"Once Alexander's mouth got to running, it couldn't be stopped. Seems Sheriff Crenshaw was blackmailing old Paul to the tune of fifty-grand a year. Though it's still a mystery as to what Crenshaw had over your ex—he clammed up when he came to that point in the story."

Cassie took a deep breath before interjecting, "Paul caused his parents' accident and murdered my father, too. I suspect that Billy Joe Crenshaw covered for him at the time."

"Well, you were right about that one, Jaimé," the lawyer said, and at Cassie's questioning look, continued, "Our man here was convinced that Paul was responsible for both his parents' accident and the death of your father, but we had poured over the sheriff's records and couldn't find anything amiss. Most likely, we couldn't find anything because the sheriff skewed his reports to protect his friend then put a hefty price tag on his silence. I don't know which one is more of a scumbag—they deserve each other!"

"Poor Craig, I don't think he knew what Paul was capable of," Cassie lamented, remembering the shock behind the tall, gangly man's horn-rimmed glasses when Paul pointed his gun at his co-conspirator. "What I don't understand is why they were in the barn to begin with. I know Craig said something about getting his share of the money."

Harvey Walton rubbed his hand along the side of his cheek, momentarily distorting his features before resting his elbow on the portable hospital table across the end of Jaimé's bed. "Greed, pure and simple."

"Greed?" 'Nita asked.

"Yep, greed and hatred—dulls the senses. Seems Paul wasn't satisfied with framing Gracie, here, for embezzlement. He wanted her put away for good. So, he planned to kill Craig Herman in her barn with a gun he had purchased for her when they were still married and, if I could make out his ranting correctly, sneak into the house and shoot our colleague here," he pointed to Jaimé as Cassie let out an audible gasp, "and incriminate his ex-wife for the murders."

"When you interrupted Alexander and the Herman guy in the barn, ol' Paul thought you had played right into his hands. What he didn't figure on is our Gracie's strength, nor the strength of your friendship and loyalty to her," he picked his fedora up off of the table where he had dropped it, and pointed it at Anita and Windy. "You guys have something real good going here."

"I call this case officially closed. You'll be getting my bill, Alvarez, just as soon as that right hand is strong enough to sign such a whopping big check!" Harvey Walton's shrewd eyes twinkled and a smile twitched at the edge of his mouth as he tipped his hat and set it back on top of his close-cropped iron gray hair.

"Harvey, wait a minute!" The lawyer stopped in the doorway as Cassie quickly made her way to him. She grabbed the lapels of his wool greatcoat and kissed his cheek. "Thank you, Harvey Wallbanger," she said so that only he could hear, "You are truly the best damn lawyer in all of the Midwest!"

A grin split the lawyer's face, "You take care of yourself, kid, and if you ever get tired of that beat-up bum in the bed, look me up." With that he backed out the door and ducked down the hall.

"Amazing! You made the unflappable Harvey Walton blush!" Jaimé marveled as Cassie returned to his side, "And are you ever going to tell me the story behind this 'Gracie' thing?"

"Not in this lifetime," Cassie smiled as she stooped to steal another kiss from her intended, "not no way, not no how!"

EPILOGUE

may

"Cas, you have to stand still if you want me to tack this in place," 'Nita cajoled as she gave a last minute tuck to the shimmering gauze that draped loosely over the fitted ivory sateen sheath of Cassie's wedding dress. The transparent overlay was attached at the scooped neckline, its muted floral print flowing freely over the bride's bare arms and trailing into a "V" at each wrist, as well as in the front and back of the fitted street-length skirt.

Cassie stood in the dining room of the farmhouse, as she watched vehicles come and go through the windows on the sun-porch beyond. 'Nita positioned a garland of yellow-centered oxeye daisies, miniature sapphire blue irises, and early-blooming pastel pink tea roses on her friend's sassy new layered hairstyle.

Cassie toyed with the emerald pendant that dangled against her chest, then fidgeted with her left, then right earring, remembering the joy and the angst of December. She thought about the problems that she and Jaimé had yet to work through—problems that paled when the image of the tall, dark and handsome prince who awaited her in the back yard formed in her mind.

She could hear Aunt Nell humming from the room behind her. Her aunt had moved back home in April, taking over the downstairs bedroom, while Cassie had spent the spring redecorating the upstairs in preparation for Jaimé and the children's arrival after the wedding.

"Yoohoo! Cassie dear!" Her mother opened the front door and poked her head in, "Are you decent? May I come in?"

"Yes, Mother," Cassie called, "We're in the dining room!"

When Martha Mikhailov walked into the room, however, she was not alone.

"Mother! You didn't tell me you were bringing a man!" Upon closer scrutiny of her mother's companion, she exclaimed, "You're the fellow with the burgundy Cadillac!"

"The burgundy Cadillac?" Anita repeated. She peered at the tall, slightly-stooped man with thick wavy, white hair, who leaned lightly on a cane.

"Theo Andropoulus," he extended a gnarled hand first to Anita and then to Cassie, giving each a firm handshake.

Cassie withdrew her hand slowly, curiosity getting the best of her as the elderly gentleman laid his palm on her mother's shoulder. "Mo*ther*, I think you have some explaining to do!"

Martha Mikhailov reached up and patted the hand that gently massaged her collarbone. "Theo has been my companion, my secret, for more years than you need to know." She quickly added, "I was never unfaithful to Leopold, but Theo did help me through some very hard times."

"Theo Andropoulus—now I remember why you looked so familiar when I saw you coming out of mother's apartment! You owned the restaurant where mom worked that one summer."

Theo nodded, "We lost touch after that, until we ran into each other at a gas station several years ago. I was having trouble working one of those confounded credit card machines, and Martha offered to help me." He spoke with a slight Mediterranean accent, "We spent the afternoon talking. Seems we both needed a shoulder to lean on."

He went on, "My wife had been comatose from a brain aneurism for many years. She passed a year ago March, and your mother and I have, well, deepened our relationship since then. I have asked her to marry me, and she has, much to my delight, agreed." Martha's eyes lit up as Theo Andropoulos wrapped his arm around her shoulder.

They heard a thud from the bedroom beyond, and turned to see Nell standing in the door, one thick-soled shoe in her hand and one lying on the floor in front of her as she stared open-mouthed at her sister.

"I'm glad you're here, Penelope," Martha Mikhailov smiled at her sister before continuing, "We've already talked to Jaimé and to the pastor, and if it's alright with you, Cassie, since everyone's assembled, we were wondering if we might have a double wedding? Theo and I have the legal paperwork, as we were planning to elope. But, this morning, the craziest idea hit me...."

The other shoe hit the floor, and Cassie laughed, "My thoughts exactly, Aunt Nell...what my grandfather would call another 'hare-brained scheme'!

"And, my deepest hope is that this one works out as well as the last, when I ended up with my two Moms." Then, to her mother and Theo Andropoulus, she said, "I would be honored to share my wedding day with you both! Welcome to the family, Theo!"

They all walked to the backyard together, with Anita and Aunt Nell in the lead, followed by Theo, flanked by both brides.

Rows of white folding chairs faced an ornamental garden that Cassie had carved out of the lawn and planted with spring wildflowers and aromatic herbs. Antique galvanized tin oil and watering cans filled with skillfully arranged bouquets of golden coreopsis, "love me-love me not" Shasta daisies, stately bearded irises, and bold pink peonies added splashes of color at strategic locations throughout the yard, while the streamers from white satin bows fluttered in a light breeze.

Theo skirted the outside of the chairs to join Jaimé at the front of the aisle that divided the rows of seats. A string quartet played the first chords of Bob Dylan's "If Not for You" as Ben escorted his sister down the aisle to where their father stood, looking every bit the prince in a white tuxedo. Midway, a tawny yellow cat joined the processional, winding his way around the children's legs, and much to the amusement of the onlookers, plopping his plump body down between the two as they turned to watch their soon-to-be stepmother join their soon-to-be step-grandmother.

Cassie and her mother walked down the aisle together, each mesmerized by the man who waited for her at the end of the makeshift corridor. When, at last, they stepped to the front of the assemblage, Cassie and Jaimé moved to the left and Martha and Theo to the right. Tina and Ben stood between them, forming a semi-circle around the minister.

With an azure sky as backdrop and doves cooing their love song, Cassandra Grace Mikhailov Alexander placed her hand in that of the man with whom she had fallen in love so many years ago. She gazed into his deep brown eyes and found, here in the fertile farmlands of Northwest Ohio, the ending and the beginning—the happily ever after and opening credits for the rest of her life.

Cassie and Jaimé joined their guests for a catered buffet under a large white tent that had been erected near the herb garden. After the bridal bouquet had been tossed and the garters caught, the younger bride and groom, the Windmillers, and several other revelers adjourned to the old Tecumseh High School where they were greeted with much fanfare and applause by those gathered for the annual Alumni Banquet and Dance.

the end

ACKNOWLEDGEMENTS:

There are so many people to whom I owe a debt of thanks for their encouragement and assistance with *Only in the Movies*, I can only ask the forbearance of anyone I may have forgotten. First and foremost, I cannot thank my husband and editor-in-chief, Chris, enough for the unflagging support he has given me over the many years I have practiced my avocation.

A very special thank you to our daughter, Sascha Instone, for sharing her artistic talents to illustrate my book cover and to our favorite son-in-law, Chuck Instone. Love and gratitude to our Oregonians, Jude and Wendy Geist, not only for the addition of the Pacific Northwest to our traveling itinerary, but also for allowing us intensive grandparenting sessions when we visit the Willamette Valley.

Many thanks to Geena Wooten, writing partner extraordinaire, to my sister and close friend, Carol Erickson, and dear friends, Anne Tracy, Linda Babcock, and Vicki Steensma for lending their editing skills to my initial manuscript. A special thank you to Mardi Losoya Rush for her suggestions and sharing her Latina culture with me, and to Rosalinda Long for her assistance with a crucial dialogue translation. Thank you, Floyd Ramsier, for your legal expertise.

Many thanks to Penguin Dave Feldman, author of the *Imponderables* series for his inspiration and publishing advice and to Jack Estes of Pleasure Boat Studio for his patience answering my many questions.

I am indebted to Laura Tolkow for sharing her graphic design talents and to Ruth Josimovich for her professional editing skills—her suggestions strengthened the manuscript and encouraged the author. Thank you to Beth Hofer for her excellent proofreading.

I owe a huge debt of gratitude to the Doobie Social Club for all the years of friendship and support—the stories we could tell! Hugs to Sandy Rosselet and the PHS Slumber Party Gang for all of the bottles of wine we've emptied late into the night building on friendships rooted so long ago. Thank you to Rosemary Laurey and the Central Ohio Fiction Writers for sharing your love of writing with me.

In memory of Karl Erickson, a special brother-in-law who made a crucial suggestion to my manuscript before deciding romance wasn't his genre and of Susan Schaefer Waring, my friend and confidante since first grade. We deeply miss you both!

Last but not least, I am indebted to the love and loyalty shown to me by Buffy the Cat and my late computing buddy, Fuzz E. Dog—my very own Slack-Eyed Joes.

JAG

AUTHOR'S NOTE:

I wrote my first novel in junior high and haven't stopped putting pen to paper (fingers to keyboard) since.

During my many years on the staff of Bowling Green State University's internationally-renowned Browne Popular Culture Library, I handled hundreds of thousands of romance and other genre fiction books, dating back to the nickel weeklies and dime novels of the late 1800s, all feeding my avocation to write and publish a work of fiction.

Over the years, I joined writers' groups, attended conferences and workshops, read books on how to write, immersed myself in the Internet, and finally, submitted my manuscript to agents and publishers. But neither they nor I could find my niche.

That's when I discovered the world of self-publishing, and with a little seed money, a bit of work, good friends to lend a hand, connections to the right professionals, and a lot of determination, *Only in the Movies* is now a reality.

I hope you enjoy your journey through Cassie and Jaimè's world!

Jean Ann Geist

Jean Ann Geist is available to give presentations to area libraries and groups on her experience in the self-publishing world. She may be contacted through her website at www.JeanAnnGeist.com.